T0299557

Joanna Courtney's first literary accolade was a creative writing prize at primary school and from that point on she wanted to be a novelist. She was always reading as a child and often made up stories for her brother and sister on long car journeys, but it was when she took a degree in English literature at Cambridge, specialising in medieval literature, that she discovered a passion for ancient history that would define her writing.

Joanna began writing professionally in the sparse hours available between raising two stepchildren and two more of her own, primarily writing shorter fiction for the women's magazines. As the children grew, went to school and eventually left home, however, her time expanded and she started writing novels. Her first series, The Queens of the Conquest, is about the women married to the men fighting to be King of England in 1066. Her second traces the real stories behind three of Shakespeare's most compelling, but least realistic heroines – Lady Macbeth, Ofelia and Cordelia.

It was whilst researching Cordelia, a tribal leader in middle England c500 BC, that she realised Cleopatra, a famous 'ancient' queen, ruled far later than Cordelia, coming to her throne in 52 BC, and a new idea was born – to explore the stories of three vital women, living and ruling in the vibrant and heated world around the Eastern Mediterranean in the years either side of the birth of Christ. *Salome* is the second in this series, with *Cleopatra and Julius* out now and *Magdala* to come in 2025.

Get in touch with Joanna on
Facebook: /joannacourtneyauthor; Twitter: @joannacourtney1;
or via her website: www.joannacourtney.com.

ALSO BY JOANNA COURTNEY

Shakespeare's Queens series

Blood Queen
Fire Queen
Iron Queen

Cleopatra and Julius
Salome

SALOME

JOANNA COURTNEY

PIATKUS

PIATKUS

First published in Great Britain in 2024 by Piatkus

1 3 5 7 9 10 8 6 4 2

Copyright © 2024 by Joanna Barnden

A CIP catalogue record for this book is available from the British Library.

TPB ISBN: 978-0-349-43298-4

Typeset in Baskerville by M Rules

Printed and bound in Great Britain by Clays Ltd, Elcograf S.p.A.

Papers used by Piatkus are from well-managed forests
and other responsible sources.

Piatkus
An imprint of
Little, Brown Book Group
Carmelite House
50 Victoria Embankment
London EC4Y 0DZ

An Hachette UK Company
www.hachette.co.uk

www.littlebrown.co.uk

For Hannah – my smart, kind, caring, endlessly wonderful daughter. I love you.

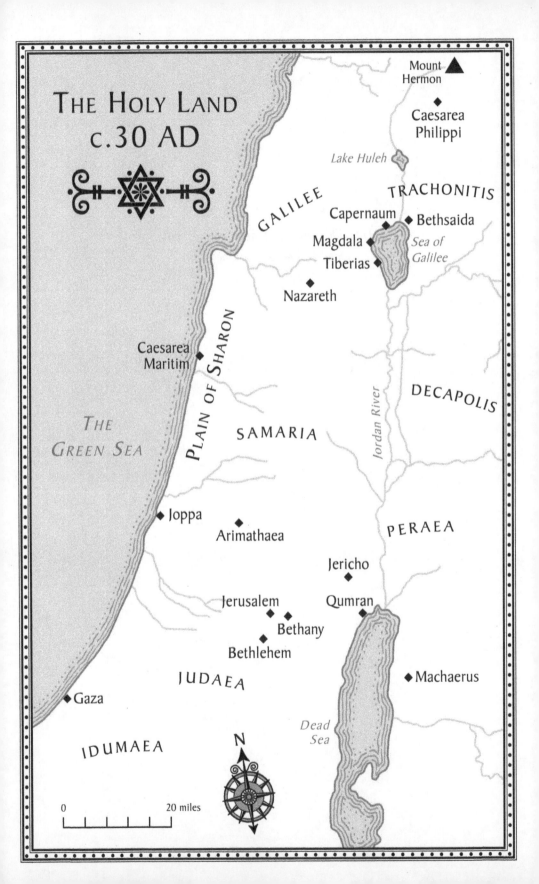

THE HOLY LAND c.30 AD

THE GREEN SEA

GALILEE

TRACHONITIS

Mount Hermon

Caesarea Philippi

Lake Huleh

Capernaum

Bethsaida

Magdala

Sea of Galilee

Tiberias

Nazareth

Caesarea Maritim

PLAIN OF SHARON

SAMARIA

DECAPOLIS

Jordan River

Joppa

Arimathaea

PERAEA

Jericho

Jerusalem

Qumran

Bethany

Bethlehem

JUDAEA

Machaerus

Gaza

Dead Sea

IDUMAEA

N

0   20 miles

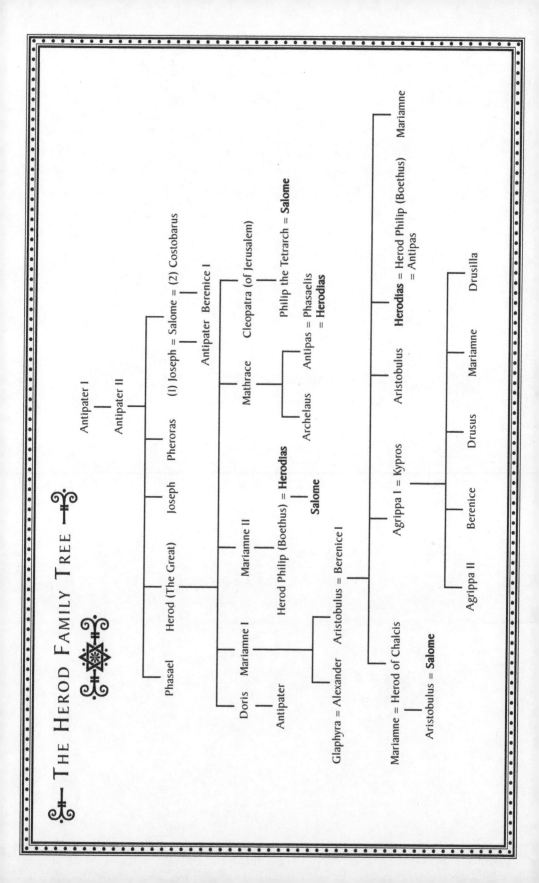

The Herod Family Tree

Prologue

Salome

The notes rise up from the flute, catching the last whispers of the day and tugging relentlessly at her limbs.

Come, they whisper, *dance*.

How can she resist?

She is up, pulled by the tune as if it is piping right into her heart, and there, on the hill above the Holy City, she dances. There is no shape to it, no arc, no well-crafted story or sense of meaning to the movements. Or none, at least, that any observer might see. But the music moves her limbs in its own way, delving into her gut and finding new pathways in the twists and tangles of her thoughts and feelings, in the confusions, delights and sorrows that have shaped her life so far. The meaning is not in the dance, but comes *from* the dance, and she gives herself up to her limbs, feeling the knots of life loosen with every unformed step and abandoned leap.

Others are dancing too, and the flute, encouraged, picks up its tune. From somewhere in the camp a lyre joins in and then a tambour and, as the sun drops behind the Holy City and its dark walls are absorbed into the softness of the night sky, it seems that all life in Jerusalem is up here, amongst the ordinary folk. The light is from their campfires, the music from their hand-carved instruments and the joy from their simple pleasure in being together. It infuses Salome and she abandons herself to something greater than her own concerns. Is this the soul? If so, it is, for now at least, at one with the rest of her and she lets it lead her where it will.

PART ONE

Part One

Chapter One

Salome

Salome flinched back against the padded bench seat as a sun-browned hand hooked through the carriage window, all bone, sinew and paper-thin skin. The fingers groped for her, each one seemingly an independent creature trying to burrow into her royal flesh.

'God bless you, Princess.'

The hoarse words were less exhortation, more bitter resentment, and Salome cringed away from the base need, and then hated herself for doing so. It was always the same when they came to Jerusalem – the city was a mixture of excitement, fascination and horror that swirled in her stomach and stuck to her skin.

Thankfully the carriage edged on, the driver cracking his whip to try and part the crowds cramming the narrow streets, and the hand was forced to withdraw. Salome looked to her father, Herod Boethus, sat on her far side, and he gave her a kindly grimace.

'We'll soon be there, Salome.'

'If we were in the Herodian palace, we could have gone round the edge,' Herodias, her mother, snapped from the opposite.

'But we would have to share it with the Roman Governor,' Boethus said mildly.

5

'Not if all was right in the world.'

'Is all ever right in the world?'

'Perhaps not, but if everyone took that attitude it would be a hell of a lot worse. Ah, the Temple!'

Their carriage had drawn up outside the vast Temple complex at the heart of the Holy City and Herodias, thankfully distracted, leaned out of the window to take it in. Salome watched her, astonished. Her mother seemed oblivious to the pawing of the poor as she gazed up at the monumental structure. It was beautiful, Salome could see that, but it was also teeming with life.

From here they could only catch a glimpse inside through the huge Shoshan Gate but Salome knew exactly what was within. At the heart of the complex was the sacred Court of the Priests, holding the High Altar and Holy of Holies within which God dwelled. Surrounding it was the Court of the Israelites, which was beautiful, but she had only ever seen it from the balustrade of the adjacent Court of the Women, beyond which no female could pass. Something that annoyed Herodias no end.

The inner courtyards, however, were only used for full worship and most of the time everyone swilled around in the vast Court of the Gentiles that surrounded the Temple proper on all sides. There they could meet friends, listen to preachers and buy Temple shekels, sacrifices and all manner of holy goods from the myriad stall holders set up below the central steps. The courtyard was open to all and large enough to take at least ten thousand people, and at Pesach it often had at least that many crammed into its colonnaded walls.

Through the wide-open gates, Salome could see that already people were fighting for the holy space and the air was rent with pitiful bleating as thousands of lambs were driven in from every direction, confused and disorientated. Every Jewish family was required by law to travel to Jerusalem for the Pesach festival and every one had to sacrifice a lamb or, if they were really poor, a dove, to give thanks for the great covenant made between Moses and God when He sent the prophet to lead the Jews out of slavery and into the Promised Land.

It was a fine tradition that, in times past, had kept the farming people in touch with one another at least once a year, but these days, with the Holy Land so populated, it turned Jerusalem into a charnel house. Already Salome was dreading the Sabbath when the Temple ran with the blood of all these young animals and people staggered through the streets carrying their bleeding carcasses home to eat. She hated seeing the high priests with their white robes drenched in blood and hearing the death cries fill the air from dawn till dusk. And she worried – though obviously she wouldn't ever say as much out loud – about the God that required this mass killing.

'Isn't it magnificent!'

Herodias had no such qualms. It fascinated Salome every year to see her mother, withdrawn and sullen on their quiet estates near coastal Joppa, come alive when they reached Jerusalem, and now that, newly turned fourteen, Salome was becoming a woman herself, it was even more intriguing. Her mother seemed to feed off the visceral energy of the crowds, to draw strength from the very stones of the city and to relish the parade of ceremonies and feasts that filled Holy Week. She was a beautiful woman, even past her fortieth year, but in Jerusalem that beauty radiated, as if she were physically taller and more vigorous just from drawing in the Temple air.

'Magnificent,' Boethus agreed.

Herodias tutted.

'Stop repeating me, husband. Be a man not an echo.'

'But you speak so well, wife, that you deserve echoing.'

Herodias' eyes narrowed.

'What I deserve is a man who can stand up and be counted, a man who can lead – who can rule.'

Salome bit her lip. It always got round to this sooner or later, as if Herodias stored up all her anger in the countryside and Jerusalem

7

ripped the lid off it. It was unusual, however, for her to burst before they'd even reached the palace.

'Is that the High Priest?' Salome cried hastily, pointing to where, high up on the parapets that ran around the Inner Courtyards, a man had emerged from the beautiful Gate of Susa in a jewel-encrusted gown that sparkled in the midday glare.

'Where?' Herodias was thankfully distracted again. 'Oh! It is, yes. Doesn't Caiaphas look fine? I'm so glad he's tall. The robes show to much better advantage on a larger man. Annas was very wise, but he didn't cut such an imposing figure.'

'That's important in a priest, is it?' Boethus asked.

'Of course it is. The people want to be able to look up to their leader, as you would know if you had even a shred of leadership quality in your feeble bones.'

Salome rolled her eyes. Sometimes her father really did bring it on himself. Herod Boethus had been sole heir to Herod the Great when he'd married Herodias twenty-three years ago. The once-imposing king had, however, descended into paranoia in his final years and had several of his many sons executed for supposedly plotting against him. In the killing spree, Boethus had only escaped with his life by agreeing to retire as a private citizen. It seemed to Salome that it was a deal that had suited Boethus perfectly, as he was never happier than when overseeing his farm, tending his gardens or playing music in his sprawling villa, but it had not suited his wife at all. Herodias was not a woman made for private living.

Salome shifted uncomfortably as more hands clawed their way into the royal carriage. The palace was barely fifty steps west, but it would take hours to get there at this rate. She would willingly get out and walk, save that she feared the press of people. Jerusalem at Pesach was rarely more than half a step from a riot and with so many stones set loose from the roads by the crowds, there were always weapons on hand if something set them off.

She clasped her fingers in her lap and prayed for patience but now Boethus was pulling a leather pouch from his travelling bag and drawing out a handful of coins. He winked at Salome as he drew back the curtain and, with surprising strength, flung them onto the long steps leading up to the Shoshan Gate. They hit the stones with loud chinks and the scramble was instant. The road emptied before them as people fell onto each other in the rush to grab at the silver and, with a crack of his whip, the driver was able to leap forward.

'Well done, Father,' Salome cried.

'About time,' Herodias said begrudgingly but Salome saw a small smile cross her lips as they turned the corner and, finally, drew up outside the Hasmonean Palace.

It was not as new or as large as the Herodian one, built along the west wall by Herod the Great at the same time as the Temple thirty years ago, and Herodias was always complaining about that, but Salome preferred it. It was deeper into the city, built in a more elegant style and far richer in history.

'How lovely to be back in the home of your ancestors, Mother,' she said, as the guards rushed to open the gates and let them in, beating back any peasants foolish enough to try and force their way through.

'True Jews,' Herodias purred. 'Brought up in the Holy Land and prepared to stand and defend it against outsiders instead of welcoming them in and handing them our finest palaces.'

'This *is* the finest palace, Mother.'

'No Roman should have *any* palace here. Ignorant boors. They don't deserve one inch of this land, let alone the best inches, and if we had decent rulers they'd be booted back to Italia where they belong.'

'It was Herod the Great, I believe, who did a deal with the Romans to keep control of Judea,' Boethus said.

'I know! Not so great if you ask me – though he, at least, was strong enough to keep the title of king, unlike any of you lot. Talking of which, there's Philip.'

A strange gleam came into Herodias' eyes as she spotted her

Uncle Philip, which surprised Salome as Herodias was usually railing against him for 'hiding' in his tetrarchy of Trachonitis, up in the North-Eastern corner of the Holy Land. The only one of Herod the Great's heirs that Herodias ever seemed to have time for was Herod Antipas, the eldest. Antipas was ruler of Galilee and Perea and apparently building shining cities on the lush sea, but he was still only a tetrarch. Ever since Archelaus, the eldest brother, had blown his inheritance of Judea with terrible management, all-but inviting the Romans to turn it into a full Roman province, they had all been robbed of the title of king.

Tetrarch was a shadow of a title in comparison – at least in Herodias' book. Now, though, she was rushing over to Philip, clasping his hands and kissing his cheeks with the sort of eagerness she usually saved only for foreign visitors who might be able to do her a favour. Salome watched curiously. Uncle Philip did not seem especially surprised by this exuberance from his dour niece and she wondered what on earth her mother was plotting. But now a fine horse was galloping into the palace courtyard and Salome felt her blood rush to her face as she recognised the rider.

Aristobulus, her cousin and just about the only other family member under twenty, was riding high on a fine chestnut stallion. It was frothing at the mouth, as if it had been ridden hard and Ari himself was flushed from exertion, his dark curls shining with sweat and his hose clinging to his thighs. He looked, quite simply, magnificent. Her mother might rave over the architecture of the Temple and the Hasmonean palace, but Salome could gaze on Ari all day long. Not that she would of course. That would be indecorous. And embarrassing. And . . .

'Salome! Are you going to lurk in that carriage all afternoon?'

'Ari! Of course not. I was just, er . . .'

'Helping her old father down,' Boethus supplied, giving her arm a little squeeze and making a show of clambering down with her assistance.

'Always kind,' Ari said.

Salome smiled up at him.

'I know my duty.'

'You are an excellent daughter.'

'And will make an excellent wife,' Boethus said, then wandered off leaving Salome spluttering for something cogent to say.

She might, at fourteen, be allowed to marry, but her mother had always said she did not want to see her wed too early, so this sudden comment threw her and she wasn't quite sure what to do with herself.

'You look well, Salome,' Ari said. 'You've grown.'

Salome looked down, increasingly flustered. She *had* grown in the last year, and not just upwards. Her body had curved at both hips and breast and she was having to adjust to this new fleshliness to her previously lithe form. Nothing fitted her any more and she'd found herself cooped up with dressmakers for ages. Herodias was delighted and had ordered adult-length gowns with figure-hugging bodices that made her feel very uncomfortable, though, looking at Ari's eyes as he took her in now, she could see perhaps her mother had, for once, been right.

The main issue was that this new form had changed the way her body moved. Dancing was her favourite pastime but with her new figure she was forever losing her balance when she tried her previous moves. Not that she could say that to her gorgeous cousin.

'I do feel older,' she managed eventually.

'You *look* older. And more beautiful.'

'I do?' she squeaked.

Now it was Ari's turn to look flustered.

'Jerusalem seems busier than ever this year,' he said, scuffing the heel of his riding boot against the cobbles.

'Doesn't it?' Salome agreed, snatching at this safer topic. 'It feels unsettled too.'

'It always does but, yes, this year feels close. The new governor arrived yesterday and people never like to be reminded we're under a foreign heel.'

'Have you met him?'

'Pontius Pilate? Not yet, but I hear we're all invited to dine with him tonight.'

Salome groaned.

'In the Herodian palace? Mother will love that.'

Ari rubbed his hands.

'Sparks always fly with your mother around.'

'I know. It's awful.'

'It's fantastic. At least she's prepared to say what everyone else is thinking.'

'And are too diplomatic to speak out loud.'

'Cowardice.'

'Or wisdom. The Romans have all the power, Ari.'

'For now. Oh, but look, your mother wants you.'

'She does?' Salome looked around, surprised. Her mother was usually glad to be shot of her in the city, where there were so many more interesting people to talk to but, sure enough, Herodias was beckoning her over. 'I'd better go.'

'You better had. But, hey, sit with me at dinner, Lola?'

Salome flushed. Only her father and Ari ever called her that. She liked it.

'If I can,' she agreed, shooting him another smile and heading across to her mother, remembering just in time to pick up her newly-long skirts and avoid sprawling at his feet.

'Can I help you, Mother?' she asked.

Herodias took her arm – another surprise.

'You can, daughter. We need to go and unpack your gowns and summon the maids. I want you looking at your finest this evening.'

'To meet the new governor?'

Herodias sniffed grandly.

'To hell with the governor. No, for your husband.'

'What?!'

Herodias hustled her up the west staircase towards their rooms.

'Decorum, Salome! You're a woman now – and soon to be a married one.'

'To whom, Mother?'

'We won't rush it of course, just like I always promised you. We'll have a decent betrothal period. We don't want any unwarranted gossip. Not that there will be, I'm sure, with such a fine man.'

'Who is he?'

'And with such good prospects.' She hustled Salome into her own room and, closing the door, clasped her shoulders with a rare smile. 'You've done well to grow so pretty, Salome. It's got you noticed.'

Salome remembered Ari's eyes on her new curves and felt her heart beat a little faster.

Sit with me at dinner, Lola. Oh, what a husband!

'Not that you wouldn't have been noticed anyway, with my pedigree,' Herodias was going on.

'And father's,' she reminded her.

Herodias waved this away.

'*I* am the Hasmonean. *I* am the granddaughter of Mariamne. *I* am the true Jew in this family – and you, of course. That's highly desirable, Salome, but, even so, it helps to have other charms. Men are very shallow, as you'll find out all too soon.'

'With *whom*, Mother?!'

Herodias blinked.

'Why with your new husband, of course. With Philip.'

'Philip? Your Uncle Philip?!'

Herodias clapped.

'That's the one. My rich Uncle Philip, with his lovely tetrarchy of Trachonitis.'

'That you despise because it's miles away from Jerusalem? And full of pagans?'

'That I admire greatly for its fertility, riches and stability. Philip is a good man, Salome.'

That much was true. Philip was a good, kind, honest man. But . . .

'He's fifty-two, Mother.'

'I know,' Herodias said robustly. 'Perfect. Take it from me, daughter, you can't beat a husband who's close to the grave. It gives you options.'

Salome gaped at her.

'But, Mother, that's so old. How can I ever love him?'

'Love?!' Herodias shrieked. 'This isn't about love, child. Love is for people who have no land. You are a Princess, a member of the royal household. Your marriage will be about respect, ambition, authority. It will be about shared achievements and power and that, believe me, is worth far more than love.'

'But . . .'

'No buts. Listen to me, Salome. As you know, Herod the Great's kingdom was badly splintered when he died, but there is scope to bring it together again. One man should rule the whole Holy Land, from Galilee and Trachonitis in the north, down to Judea and Perea in the south.'

'Or one woman . . .?' Salome teased.

'If only,' Herodias snapped. 'But that perfect solution is sadly far out of reach so we must be practical. Herod's only grandsons – my brothers – are from Mariamne's line.'

'Of which you are very proud . . .?'

Herodias' eyes narrowed.

'Of which I am, *rightly*, very proud. However, as you know, Herod fell out with Mariamne.'

Salome gave a low laugh at her mother's understatement. Herod the Great had had the beautiful Mariamne – his wife and supposed true love – executed on an uhinged suspicion of both adultery and plotting to kill him.

'Concentrate, Salome,' Herodias urged, 'for I have thought about this most carefully. Were you to marry one of Herod's grandsons, say . . . Aristobulus,' Salome's breath caught but Herodias was already shaking her head, 'any claim by your son would come second to all three of my own brothers – of Mariamne's line. Were you, however, to bring forth a son born of one of Herod the Great's own sons – like Philip – he would have the highest possible claim.'

'But, Mother,' Salome protested, trying to think this through. It seemed that in order to produce an heir to a splintered throne, she had to marry a wrinkled old man instead of a strong, fit, funny, young one. 'I don't think I want—'

'It is done,' Herodias snapped. 'And you will be glad of it.'

Salome sank onto her stool, defeated. She had long known that her marriage would be for dynastic reasons but had harboured hopes that Ari, by far the finest formed of the Herodians, might fulfil those. Her mother had calculated more precisely, however, and she would not, it seemed, be sitting next to Ari at dinner tonight. Jerusalem pressed hard upon her once more.

Chapter Two

Herodias

Herodias watched all eyes turn as Salome stepped up to the top of the central staircase, and smiled in satisfaction. She looked magnificent. The hair had taken forever, of course, and goodness the girl had complained about the uplift on that bodice, but it had been worth it. She looked every inch the princess. She wasn't happy, Herodias knew, and she understood that, really she did. She'd seen the way her daughter chatted with her cousin and, God bless her, any woman would rather have that fine-looking specimen than Philip, who'd been handsome enough in his time but was now, even she had to admit, rather wrinkled and worn. It was tough, but that was life as a royal. She should know. She'd married Boethus when he was both handsome and with prospects, and look where that had got her – life on a bloody farm.

Herod Philip was their best chance of producing a direct heir to Herod the Great. Besides, he had a fine tetrarchy, even if it was in the north, whereas Ari had little more than a commission in the Jewish army. The last thing Salome needed was to trek around after a garrison, even if it did mean getting that young man in her bed at night. At least she wouldn't know what she was missing, Herodias reminded herself, and there was no way Philip would last more than ten years, especially if Salome got his pulse racing. All the girl needed was long enough to produce a son and then she'd be able to move on to something more suited to her personal tastes.

Options, that's what this match offered her daughter – money, power and options. She should be grateful.

She avoided Boethus' eye as she took his arm to walk down the stairs behind their daughter. He doted on Salome and wasn't convinced about this match with his half-brother. He'd drivelled on about her 'happiness' but as usual, in the end, he'd gone with her wishes. He was such a sap. Still, Philip was waiting at the bottom of the stairs and if his legs were a little bandy and his hair rather thin, at least his clothes were fine and his bearing proud. Salome, to her credit, accepted his arm graciously and managed to avoid looking left to her young cousin, who was simmering in a most becoming manner. It was hard but it was life, and the sooner Salome learned that the better.

Take tonight, for example. They ought to be able to celebrate this happy betrothal in the comfort of their own palace but, oh no, they'd been summoned by the pompous Roman governor. 'Invited' Boethus had called it but she knew the Romans and this was definitely a summons. No doubt the blasted man would be lording it over them, parking his bony Roman arse on their ancestral throne and trying to impose his boorish Roman rules on their far more nuanced, cultured society. It was nonsense. Moses had brought the Jews to the Promised Land several thousand years before the first Romans were being suckled by wolves, or however the ridiculous story went, and now just because they had bigger boots and more swords, they were lording it over them. Well, it wouldn't last. It never did. And if she had anything to do with it, they'd be out of here sooner rather than later.

It was time Boethus came out of 'private life' and stepped up to rule. Judea was the heart of the Jewish nation and it would surely not take much to oust this new governor and get the kingdom reinstalled. Caiaphas would help and the whole of the Sanhedrin – the Jewish council. It might take a little time, but they could make it happen if they focused. This betrothal was just the start. Draw the tetrarchies under one tightly linked family, wait for this new governor to trip up and strike!

Of course, there was the small issue that Boethus didn't actually want to come out of the countryside . . .

Herodias shook it away. He was a Herod and couldn't choose his destiny any more than Salome could. She looked around as the carriages drew up to take them to the governor. Herod Antipas and his wife weren't here yet – something about preachers blocking the road from Galilee – and she'd hoped that would get them all out of this dinner. Yet word had come that he was close and would join them at the Herodian palace shortly, so it seemed there was little for it but to step into the carriage and go.

At least it would be quieter in the city now, with the peasants up on the Mount of Olives, erecting their rough little tents for the week. She could hear them hammering pegs into the hard ground and calling to each other in their coarse accents, could smell the smoke of their fires and the grease of their cooking pots. It must be a curious life, all bundled in together, but they seemed to like it. They certainly had enough children, so the lack of privacy clearly didn't bother them.

Herodias clutched briefly at her own belly as the carriages set off. It seemed unfair, really, that Perean peasants could churn out endless kids they could barely afford to feed, whilst Herodias' royal belly had allowed three boys to wither within before finally producing Salome. She felt a stab of pain, as deep and real as those three dark losses, and for a moment longed to curl up in bed and miss this hard night ahead. But where would that get her? Perhaps losing those three princes had been God's way of telling her that she was strong enough to do the job alone? Perhaps it was His way of telling her not to rely on men? Certainly, there was no point in thinking it anything else or she might as well just give up now, get down on her knees before this Roman governor and suck his . . .

'Herodias!'

She jumped and looked to her husband.

'What?'

'Everyone is waiting for us.'

She blinked and looked around. They'd arrived at the Herodian palace and the rest of the family was hovering uncertainly in the courtyard. Three red and gold guards stood outside the door, showing no sign of offering a welcome, and clearly someone was going to have to actually knock on the damned door. Typical Roman politeness.

Gathering her skirts, she swept out of the carriage and straight up the steps. The guards stood to attention and she looked down on them, thankful for the large wooden soles she always wore on her shoes – a little height gave a woman so much more authority and no one should be looking beneath her skirts to see from whence it came.

'I am Herodias, Hasmonean Princess and Lady of Judea.' It wasn't strictly speaking her title but she'd found that if she said it with enough authority people rarely questioned her. And, of course, she *should* be Queen of Judea, as promised at her betrothal. She stared down the guards. 'My family and I are, I believe, summon ... invited for dinner with the governor.'

The guards looked to one another.

'That's correct,' the eldest of them said eventually. 'But you are early.'

'Early?!'

'Pontius Pilate has not yet finished the business of the day.'

Herodias gaped at him, astounded at the insolence.

'He issued the invitation. We would have been quite happy not to come but if he is so tardy in running his affairs, the least you can do is show us in to wait in comfort.'

They looked to one another again.

'We've had no such orders, my lady.'

Herodias stamped her foot.

'Then go and get them.'

The guards shifted, the rest of the Herods, below, did the same. Herodias groaned but then, praise God, a new voice barked: 'You heard the lady – jump to it!'

The imposing figure of Herod Antipas was striding into the courtyard and the guards bowed low. One of them shuffled through the door whilst the others tried desperately to look anywhere but at the new arrival. Antipas took the steps two at a time to grasp Herodias' hand, bow low over it and drop a kiss onto the back. Her skin tingled.

'Antipas! Thank the Lord someone with a few guts has turned up.'

He laughed.

'I know Romans, Herodias. They need plain speaking and simple instruction. Now, here, please, take a seat.' He swept off his cloak and placed it across a low wall for her to sit upon. 'Are you well? You look well.'

He stood solicitously over her, chatting as if they were at the finest drinks party, and, despite the ridiculousness of the situation, she felt herself swell with his attentions. Antipas, son of Herod's fourth wife, was half-brother to both Boethus, son of his third, and Philip, son of his fifth. Boethus was older but, when retiring from public life, had also ceded the position as head of the family to Antipas. Herodias had to say that it suited him far better.

He wasn't especially tall – in fact, in her wooden soles he was only just level with her – but he was broad and fit and carried himself with a zest missing from her own husband, who only truly came to life when playing his damned lyre or cutting a bunch of roses. Antipas, in contrast, spoke with ease and grace and looked deep into her eyes when he did so. Very deep actually. She felt something pulse in parts of herself that had only offered pain in recent years, and fought to keep her chin high and back straight.

'You've had a tough journey, my lord?'

'As always. Galilee prospers, you know, which is excellent save for the fact that prosperity brings people and people clog the roads. They like to see me and I don't want to deny them that privilege, so it necessarily takes time to get anywhere.'

'You have come on horseback.'

'As you see. I find a carriage so confining.'

'Me too! But Boethus says it is undignified for a lady to enter the city on horseback.'

'Surely that depends on the lady.'

Herodias prayed she wasn't blushing too deeply; it was very hot in this stuffy courtyard. When would the damned Roman let them in?

'Does your wife ride?'

He shook his head.

'She is, sadly, too ill to travel at the moment. And, besides, she does not like horses. Do you?'

'I love them. Such noble creatures.'

'Powerful too,' he said, low-voiced.

'And fast.'

'You like it fast?'

This conversation was getting away with her but, oh, it was fun. All Boethus ever wanted to talk about was his boring old plants and she couldn't remember the last time he'd come to her bed. Not that Antipas would come to her bed, obviously. Not that she'd let him.

'I like it fast,' she heard herself confirm and was thankfully stopped from adding 'and hard' by the return of the guard.

'Enter.'

'Enter, *please*,' Antipas thundered. 'You are not in Rome now, ignoramus.'

'Enter, please,' the guard muttered, throwing back the door and pressing himself against it to let Antipas through. Antipas took his time, offering Herodias his arm to escort her inside. Herodias glanced back to Boethus but he was hovering uselessly behind Salome and Philip and, really, what did it matter? They were all family and it was important that she made an impression on this wretched new governor, which was far more likely to happen on Antipas' strong arm than Boethus' feeble one.

'Herod Antipas, welcome to my home.'

Pontius Pilate was a man nearly as ridiculous looking as his name. Tall and thin with a hooked nose and watery eyes, he was wearing a toga that seemed made for a man twice his girth and fidgeted at its many folds.

'Governor.' Antipas gave him the tiniest of bows. 'Welcome to our lands.'

'Granted at the behest of the emperor,' Pilate said pompously.

'The emperor, my dear friend,' Antipas said. Pilate blinked. 'Did you not know?' he went on smoothly. 'Tiberius and I were raised together in Rome. We learned Latin and Greek side by side. We studied the stars with each other. He is very keen on the stars, is he not?'

'I believe so,' Pilate stuttered.

'You've not met him?'

'Of course, of course. That is, I've, er, been in the same room as him.'

'I see.' Antipas let this hang for a deliciously long time before adding, 'He's a cultured man, of course. Well-travelled and open-minded. He's very respectful of the Jews. He sent you a letter, I believe?'

'A letter?' Pilate's bony cheeks were scarlet. Clearly, he had hoped to keep this particular missive from the local leaders.

'He sent me a copy. We converse. Regularly. He asked you, I believe, to treat the Jewish people under your charge with all due respect.'

Pilate coughed awkwardly.

'As I, of course, would do anyway.'

'Of course. Still, good to have it official. The Jewish religion is a fine one and most specific in its laws. It's good that you understand that and do not wish to impose your own.'

Pilate's cough worsened.

'Order must be kept.'

'Naturally. And it will more easily be done so, if you respect our customs. I will look forward to being able to write to Tiberius and assure him that you are doing so. Now, what's for dinner? I've been on the road all day and cannot wait to sample your kind hospitality.'

And with that, he swept a still sputtering Pilate forward, leaving Herodias to stand and watch in admiration. Her whole body felt alive in a way it hadn't for far too long and she looked guiltily across to her daughter, standing stiffly next to the man she had betrothed her to this very day. Was it a mistake? Should she have given her Aristobulus instead? But no. Love was an illusion and lust merely a passing shiver across the skin. It was land that counted. Land was power and a woman needed every bit of that she could get.

Head high, Herodias marched into dinner with the wretched governor, secure in the knowledge that Pontius Pilate was a weak man. She just had to be patient and stay firm to her purpose and one day she would be Queen of Judea, as God had surely intended all along.

Chapter Three

Salome

Salome gave a sigh of relief as the carriage passed out of Jerusalem's walls and the horizon opened up before her. It had been a hectic Pesach and she would be glad to get home to the quiet of her father's estates to think about all that had happened. She was betrothed, and to a man barely two years younger than her father. She had not realised until the very moment her mother had announced it, but she'd always harboured hopes – assumptions even – that she would marry Ari. It had seemed a much more obvious match to her, but she'd been thinking, not in terms of property and connections, but age and interest and, well, attraction. She remembered the way Ari had spoken to her those first moments before the damned announcement and swallowed a sigh.

'What's wrong with you, girl?'

Clearly, she hadn't swallowed quietly enough.

'Just sad to be going home, Mother.'

Herodias looked askance at her but chose not to pick this particular fight. She looked pretty sad to be going home too. It had been a very lively Pesach. The Holy City, always a melting pot at festival time, had felt even busier than usual. The new governor's soldiers had prowled out of the Fortress of Antonia in the Northern corner of the Temple every day and patrolled along the balustrades that ran around all four sides of the Court of the Gentiles in huge numbers – inevitably creating greater unrest as people played up to their dark expectations. There had been pockets of rebellion everywhere, ready to leap into violence at any moment, and the prison cells must have been crammed with all the poor people Salome had seen dragged off for something as simple as tripping up a neighbour in the queue for the sacrifice.

Caiaphas and the other Sadducees – the priestly caste who ran the Inner Temple – had seemed more insufferably grandiose than usual and, in response, the Pharisees had upped their ostentatious attempts to 'move amongst the people'. A self-generating group, the Pharisees prided themselves on their minute observation of even the remotest of Jewish laws and saw it as their duty to spread their knowledge amongst the normal folk. It was not a duty that was always appreciated and Salome had been distressed to see many ordinary people 'supervised' in the Mitzvah baths by self-righteous Pharisees, their phylacteries – ostentatious boxes containing scripture – strapped to their foreheads like a slap. Their cleansing ritual outside the Temple should have been a treasured annual time of purity, but they had been hassled and harangued about the 'right way' of doing it to such an extent that most had hurried through the ritual, flustered and upset. It had not felt fair and Salome had thanked God that they had their own baths in the palace, so she'd been spared the scrutiny of these self-appointed guardians of the law.

Then there had been the Essenes. This sect lived in seclusion in various communities around the Holy Land, the largest being at Qumran in the hills above the Salt Sea. They came to Jerusalem, like everyone else, for Pesach and usually kept to themselves. Marked out by their simple white tunics, bare feet and lack of family, these groups of men were usually to be found gathered together, praying in the hours before dawn and discussing the finer points of philosophy in the shade of the colonnades around the Court of the Gentiles. This year, however, more of them had been preaching, joining the other men – and the occasional woman – who chose to mount a box, stone or step to share their thoughts with the faithful. The Essenes spoke of the blessings of poverty, so were very popular with the normal people – and very unpopular with the Sadducees and Pharisees who saw wealth as a sign of God's blessing and looked down on those without it. It had all created a very tense atmosphere and Salome had been on edge almost the entire time.

Herodias, in contrast, had thrived in the melting pot and was looking back at the city walls with clear longing as they drove away. She always hated leaving Jerusalem, but Salome had an uncomfortable feeling that this year it was as much to do with her Uncle Antipas as the city itself. With his wife, Phasaelis, missing from the palace, Herodias had stepped up as senior lady for the various feasts and ceremonies, and it had suited her more than Salome had found comfortable. Herodias had laughed and chatted and, frankly, shone in a way Salome had not seen before. It had been nice, if she was honest, to see her mother glowing, but awkward too. Her father had sunk further and further back into the shadows as the week had gone on and she knew he was twitching to get into his gardens and just prayed Herodias didn't turn her unhappiness his way.

'The roads are so slow. What's going on?' Herodias leaned impatiently out. 'Perhaps we should go back, wait another day or two.'

'No!' Boethus rapped.

She glared at him.

'You'd rather bake here all day than return to the beauty of the Hasmonean palace?'

'Yes.'

'Ah well, at least we'll be able to enjoy some riveting conversation.'

Salome looked to the ceiling for patience. It seemed Herodias *was* going to take her unhappiness out on him. She leaned out herself.

'There's someone in the river, look.'

'In the river? Why would that hold us up?'

'He's attracting quite a crowd.'

Salome pointed to where a strange figure of a man was standing knee deep in the River Jordan, arms thrown wide as he addressed a crowd that was spilling across the road and growing rapidly.

'I knew we should have gone the other way,' Herodias groaned.

'Through Samaria?' Boethus asked. 'You would find bandits and revolutionaries less of an inconvenience than a lone preacher?'

His tone was unusually sharp and it was clear that the delay was getting to him too. It would be a horribly long journey home unless they could get past this man, but Salome had to admit that she was fascinated. She was used to people preaching in the Temple and around the synagogues in other towns and cities, but from the middle of a river was a new one.

'What's he doing?' she asked, leaning further out to try and see.

'He seems to be bathing people,' Herodias said, squinting down the road. 'Though, goodness knows, he's the one who needs it.'

The figure did indeed look filthy, though as the carriage edged closer Salome could see that it was not dirt across his skin but simply that he was nut-brown from continued exposure to the sun. His hair was long and matted, pulled back with a piece of string, and his white tunic clung to his sinewy body. A camel-hair coat and staff, lying on the river bank, seemed his only other accoutrements.

'I think he might be an Essene,' Salome said, pointing to his tunic.

'Nonsense,' Herodias rapped. 'Essenes travel in groups, like sheep. This one's all on his own.'

Boethus leaned forward, suddenly interested.

'It could be the one they call John.'

'John?' Herodias sneered. 'Inspiring!'

Salome turned.

'You know who he is, Father?'

'I heard talk in Jerusalem of an Essene who has left the community. He was, so I'm told, too extreme for them.'

'For the Essenes?!' Herodias scoffed. 'Good God! He must be a madman.'

27

'That's not what I heard. He's preaching the coming of the Messiah. He says the time is now.'

'Now?' Salome gasped. 'Really?'

'So he says.'

'So the madman in the camel coat says!' Herodias scoffed. 'That doesn't make it true, Salome.'

'*They* seem to think so,' she said, indicating the still growing crowd. 'They're all wading into the water to be with him. Oh!' She gasped as the man – John – took a young woman by the head and dunked her, with some firmness, beneath the water. 'He's killing her!'

'Mad,' Herodias said smugly.

'He's baptising her,' Boethus corrected as John pulled the woman back out.

She sucked the air in as if it was the first breath she'd ever taken on this earth. Her face was shining with the sort of joy the people in the Mitzvahs had been denied by the Pharisees, and Salome watched in fascination.

'Baptising?' she questioned her father.

'It's an Essene tradition, like cleansing, I suppose, but more than that. This man is offering people baptism as a way of acknowledging their desire to turn from their sins and open their hearts to God in order to be ready for his coming. It is not so much a cleansing of the body as a cleansing of the soul.'

'The soul?!' Herodias wrinkled up her nose. 'How very indulgent.'

'Hardly.' Boethus was unusually robust in his opposition to his wife. 'Listen to him.'

Herodias rolled her eyes but did quiet enough for Salome to catch some of the man's words over the rumble of the crowd.

'The time of the Lord is coming,' John assured them. 'It has been written in the stars and sung out by the archangels – by Gabriel and Michael and Raphael.'

'Since when did the angels have names?' Herodias scoffed.

'I believe the Persians named them,' Boethus said.

'The Persians? Easterners?! And this makes this madman, this John, more credible?'

'The Persians are very deep thinkers,' Boethus said calmly. 'Many of them follow Zoro, who taught the existence of one God nearly as far back as our own people.'

Herodias stared at him, stunned into silence.

'Zoro?' she stuttered eventually.

'Correct. There are many Zoroastrians in the East – learned Magi who study the stars and can predict the future.'

'And these are the stars that tell us the Messiah – the *Jewish* Messiah – is coming?'

'So they believe.'

'How do you know all this, Father?' Salome asked.

Boethus spread his hands wide.

'Because I listen more than I talk.'

She stared at him, thinking this over, opened her mouth to ask more, and then thought better of it and turned back to John.

'Now is the time!' he was crying. 'Not tomorrow. Not next week. Not once you've got home and tidied the house. Now! The Messiah is coming and you do not wish Him to find you wanting. You must cast off sinful thoughts, you must cast off sinful deeds. It is simple. God asks nothing more of you than to look at yourself until you like what you see – not the mean thoughts about your neighbour, not the petty arguments with your brother or sister, not the money you have hidden away so no one else can get at it.

'God does not like those parts of you. He likes the parts that give to others, that share all you have, that look for the good features in those around you and for the good features in yourself. We all have goodness in us but for many it is masked by petty sins. Why be dragged down by those? Turn from the darkness; embrace the light. You will walk in righteousness and when He comes, you will be ready. People of God, step into the water with me. Ask for forgiveness, pledge yourself to kindness and charity, and take the water as a symbol of your step onto the New way!'

A cheer ran around the crowd and many poured forward, eager to do just as the curious figure asked of them. Two men standing next to his coat, held out boxes, and they tossed coins and jewels and even pieces of crockery and knives into them. Herodias laughed.

'Oh, very clever. Very clever indeed. Turn away from your nasty, encumbering riches – and give them to us instead. The man's got a fabulous racket going.'

'I'm told he uses the money to keep himself and his followers on the road,' Boethus said.

'And in the taverns!'

'He does not drink intoxicating liquor, nor eat anything more than he can find in the hills and by the roadside.'

'So he says. Look – that man just gave him a band of gold. What's he going to buy with that?'

'Some sandals?' Salome suggested. 'His poor feet must be torn up if he's travelling all day long.'

Herodias squinted at her.

'He could buy a hundred pairs of sandals with that gold, girl. Look at this man. Listen to him, as your father urges. What is he asking of people?'

'That they live a good life.'

'And that they give him all their riches in order to facilitate that. Since when did being poor become so fashionable? This is a scam, girl. This man has supposedly left the Essenes – nice hook, should intrigue people – to preach on the road, which he will doubtless do for the summer months, and then he'll take his haul of gold back to Qumran and they'll all have a lovely warm, rich winter off the back of it.'

'That's a bit cynical,' Boethus told her.

'Realistic, husband. Oh, I don't doubt he's in earnest about the good-life stuff. He's very convincing and I'm sure he means well. But that doesn't stop him profiting from people's gullibility. It won't be him that suffers when the cold comes, will it? It will be those people there who've given him their money. They won't be able to afford to feed their children, or buy them new clothes as they grow. Will their souls be the better for that suffering? I don't think so.'

Salome looked at her mother, thinking this through. It was all very puzzling but she had to admit that Herodias had a point.

'It must be possible to feed your family and live a good life, surely?'

'Of course!' Herodias seized her hands. 'Of course it is. Are you a bad person, Salome?'

Salome swallowed.

'I don't think so.'

'Good, because you are not, and you must stay firm to that. It's very easy to tell people that they are sinful – and very effective. But retiring from the normal responsibilities of life to contemplate your soul doesn't help anyone. That's to say, of course you need some time to do that, which is why our blessed faith has festivals, to allow the people time from work to attend to the needs of their souls, if we must call them that. But the world must turn too. The corn must be sowed and harvested, the fish must be caught, the fences must be built and the houses sealed. What does this John know of normal life? He is a single man, living in a remote community with little responsibility for anyone bar himself. It's easy to change the world that way. He should try it with five hungry children around his skirts and an ill mother in the back bedroom.'

'As you have, wife?'

Herodias sucked in a breath.

'I lost three babies, as well you know.'

Boethus nodded.

'I do know. I'm sorry. That was mean.' He reached out a hand for Herodias and, to Salome's surprise, she took it and clasped it so tight that she saw her knuckles whiten. Herodias' eyes were closed and Salome saw her physically fight a pain she had not truly realised was there before.

Herodias won.

'My own privileges do not stop me seeing the suffering of my people. That is what a good ruler does. That, and then act to try and alleviate them. Yes, we too take money from the people in the form of taxes, but we spend them for their benefit. We spend them on roads and river drainage. We spend them on sanitation and storing up reserves in case of drought or famine. It's all very well for the little people to worry about their souls; a ruler has to worry about their safety and prosperity to enable them the luxury of doing so.'

'That's true,' Boethus agreed, still awkward. 'I didn't mean . . .'

But Herodias was not done. She drew herself up tall in the carriage.

'I may not be a biological mother to more than this one dear child . . .' Salome blinked. 'But I am mother to all our people – or I would be, if you, Boethus, did not live in as much obscurity as the damned Essenes.'

She blinked back angry tears and Salome watched her uncertainly. It had been a hard Pesach for them all and now, more than ever, she wanted to get home to think these ideas over. Ahead of them, however, John was baptising more and more people and, even for a royal, it would be a long wait yet before the road was clear and their carriage could move.

Chapter Four

Herodias

Herodias strode the corridors of the Hasmonean palace, relishing having it almost entirely to herself. Boethus had been meant to travel to Jerusalem with her for Sukkot but he'd been in bed with a nasty cough for several days and she'd cautioned him against the trip for his health. He had not, she feared, been fooled by her concern.

There'd been a time when they'd been good together, back at the start of their marriage. Not loving, as such, but certainly passionate. He was an intelligent man, with a very real interest in the world, and he'd been able to challenge her in ways that she'd enjoyed. She'd been excited by their union and thrilled by their future as King and Queen of Judea.

She'd not been stupid. Everyone had been able to see that Herod the Great's kingdom was likely to get broken up at his death. Even if the stubborn old man had stuck with a single heir, the will would most likely have been contested and some sort of settlement made between the brothers. Boethus was the eldest though and Judea would have been theirs, *should* have been theirs. They should have led the family, and they should have been based in Jerusalem and Jericho, at the heart of the Jewish

33

nation. She'd been ready for that, eager for it. And she'd have been good at it.

Instead, King Herod had become paranoid and anyone who could get close to his sick bed had played on that. Boethus should have stood up and fought for his rights with the rest, but the thinker in him had come to the fore and instead he had taken the offer of private estates near the Green Sea, turning his back on politics just like that. And turning *her* back on it too. God, she missed it.

For years, battling to bring a son into the world had distracted her and then, of course, having Salome had kept her busy – not to mention hopeful once more of producing a boy. But now her poor body was drying up so there was very little chance of another child, not the least because she and Boethus rarely shared a bed. He preferred playing his lyre to playing his wife and that was fine with her. He didn't have the fire to ignite her these days anyway.

Herodias paused on the balcony, looking down into the great central courtyard where so many of her ancestors must have walked in years past. She could almost trace their footsteps across the marble tiles, marking out a line of rule she must follow. That was a sacred duty and one that could not be obeyed from a private estate, however large and profitable. Rulers were never traced across flowerbeds.

Turning, Herodias snatched up her skirts and took the stairs in the Eastern corner, up to the tower that looked out across the whole of Jerusalem. God, it was beautiful. Could there be any other city in the world quite like it? It had grown, as the Jewish nation had grown, fanning out from the original City of David, running down from the Temple on the eastern side, with the royal Upper City of Zion fanning west in a profusion of elegant buildings, before the more quietly elegant Mishneh area heading north. These days the new suburb of Bezetha was rising up the hill above, straining at the third wall as more and more merchants and workers moved into the Holy City, but Herodias preferred to keep her eyes trained on the profusion of ancient buildings in the centre.

34

She looked west to the Herodian palace on the edge of Zion and shivered. How had they let the Romans get their grubby hands on this sacred place? It was Archelaus, Antipas' brother, who had done it. He'd taken Judea on Herod's death and fought to keep it. She'd admired him for that, almost as much as she'd hated Boethus for not doing so, but the damned man had been useless. Far too eager to please the people, he'd promised endless concessions and then, unsurprisingly, been unable to deliver them. Riots had ensued. They always did. These ones, though, had been so bad that word of them had reached even the emperor. He'd lost no time in sending Archelaus into exile and seizing Judea as a province.

Antipas had tried to fight the ruling, but he'd already held Galilee and Perea, and the Romans didn't want anyone having as much power as Herod. The first governor had arrived weeks later and now they were onto their fourth, and the wretched man was as useless as the rest. Pilate didn't even live permanently in Jerusalem, preferring the fancy new port at Caesarea Maritima, with its Hellenistic layout and its polyglot population. He was afraid of the Jews, she was sure of it. And he was probably right to be.

She stared at the Roman-stolen palace, noting big flags flying from all four corners. She was sure they hadn't been there before and assumed they were meant to indicate that Pontius Pilate was in residence, as if anyone cared. They were in Rome's usual, arrogant red and gold, and the wind was flapping them imperiously over the pilgrims below. By the sound of it plenty were gathering to see them and, for a moment, she despised her people – better just to ignore the damned Romans and not grant them the satisfaction of caring one jot what they did.

Herodias pulled her eyes away from the Palace to drink in the magnificence of the Temple. There were plenty of people there too but not to the extent of the Pesach crowds and the city was just pleasingly bustling. It was cooler, too, at this time of year, so tempers did not fray as easily and the Holy City had a buzz of excitement rather than violence.

She glanced up the road from Galilee. Antipas would be on his way. He had told her at Pesach that Sukkot was his favourite festival and that he always made the effort to be in the Holy City for it. The week-long harvest festival commemorated the dwelling of the Israelites in sukkot – temporary shelters – during their forty-year sojourn in the Sinai desert with Moses. Herodias loved all that it said about the fight and determination of the Jewish people.

'It's my favourite festival too,' she'd told him. 'From the time when I lived with my grandmother.'

'The Lady Salome?'

Herodias had nodded and smiled at his comic grimace. Her grandmother had been the sister of Herod the Great and a formidable lady with a reputation for ferocity. It had been well deserved, for she'd had a fearsome temper, but she'd also been intelligent, sharp and, if you caught her on the right day, very good fun. She'd been one of the few of King Herod's fawning crowd of relatives with the sense to play him with care, and had come out of his death with vast estates in the rich Jordan valley and, as a result, the sort of influence that had been Herodias' model ever since. Herodias had lived with her whilst her brothers were sent to Rome and, though she had often resented the chance the boys had had to see the world, she'd learned much from the woman after whom she had named her only daughter and had fond memories of her, particularly at Sukkot.

'We used to build a shelter in the garden and sleep in it all week,' she'd told Antipas, the memory flooding across her mind in vivid colour. 'It was wonderful. Grandmother would laugh at me for preferring the simple tent to my luxurious bedroom but I loved the adventure. I loved how the walls moved in the breeze and the way we slept in it together.'

It had felt too intimate a memory, suddenly, and she'd turned away, but he had quietly taken her hand.

'I think that's lovely, Herodias. Even as royals we can appreciate the simple things in life.'

She thought of that now and frowned. This Essene, John, was still out baptising people, encouraging them to strip life back to bare necessities and a tiny part of her – the part that had loved her childhood sukkot – understood that. But even tents had to be paid for and erected and filled with bedding and food. God might provide for an eloquent preacher but everyone else had to work for a living, and rulers were no exceptions.

She shook herself and made a note to issue some dinner invitations. Caiaphas would always come to the palace with his wife and, no doubt, his father-in-law, Annas, who was no longer high priest but was still highly influential in the Sanhedrin. It always helped to keep them sweet and, besides, she was better with company. It was nice to be alone for a little time, but it left far too much space to think. She was more a woman of action.

She looked again to the Galilee Road and, there, unmistakably, was the churn of dust that marked out a carriage. Antipas! Would he come straight to the palace? Was he alone, or with his wife? What would he say when he found her here? Herodias considered going back to her room to check her toilette but she knew it was immaculate and it was more fun standing here, high above everyone else, and watching him arrive.

Once she knew he'd seen her, she headed down, forcing herself to go slowly so that she stepped into the courtyard just as he was dismounting.

'Herodias. What a pleasure.' Antipas bowed low over her hand and looked surreptitiously around. 'You are alone?'

'Alone,' she agreed. 'Alas, my husband was not in good health so it seemed unwise for him to travel.'

'My wife also.'

'A shame.'

'Yes. And your daughter?'

Herodias shook her head.

'Salome preferred to stay and tend her father. She is very dutiful.'

'A well brought-up child.' He offered her his arm to escort her through to the main hall. 'And an attractive one too. My half-brother is a lucky man. When will they marry?'

'Oh soon, soon. Next year perhaps? There is no rush. The girl is only just fourteen.'

'And a betrothed has as much right to her intended's goods on his death as a wife ... ?'

'Antipas! That is not a consideration.' She shot him a sideways look. 'I merely think of her tender years. Her body is still maturing into childbearing and it is best not to rush it.'

'You are a caring mother.'

She grimaced. 'I am not as caring as she would like, I fear, but I am fierce in my protection of her.'

Antipas smiled.

'Like a mountain lioness.'

She had to admit it wasn't a comparison that displeased her.

'I have claws, yes.'

He smiled again and stepped a little closer.

'I would not want to fight you.'

Herodias felt her breathing quicken.

'I trust I would not give you cause.'

'We shall have to see.'

He glanced around but, as always, there were many servants standing ready to meet their needs.

'We are not, it seems, so alone,' he murmured and Herodias heard need run through his words and felt her whole body thrill to it. This was not right, she knew, but it had been so long since she'd been with a man who made her feel alive.

'Not yet,' she told him, and felt the charge grow between them.

For now, though, shouting in the courtyard indicated that, as usual, business was interrupting pleasure and, sure enough, Caiaphas strode into the hall, radiating fury.

'Graven images!' he all-but shouted. He was a man who stood on his dignity, but rage had taken that from him. 'Pontius Pilate is flying graven images on his damned flags.'

38

Herodias thought of the flags she'd seen snapping in the wind above the Herodian palace and groaned. Were Romans really this stupid? Jewish law, as passed to Moses from the Lord God himself, expressly forbade the parading of graven images and it was a rule strictly followed in the Holy City. The only exception were the many coins now in circulation bearing the heads of rulers, but even they were not allowed in the Inner Temple, which had its own image-free shekels that pilgrims had to buy from the stalls around the Court of the Gentiles. It was good business for the money-changers, for sure, but an important principle too. Heathens worshipped images, Jews worshipped the almighty, unseen God. Now there were eagle standards flying high over the very heart of the city. No wonder all the previously peaceful pilgrims, camped in their sukkots around the city, were crowding around the palace walls.

'They can collect our taxes,' Caiaphas raged, pacing again. 'They can take our palace, they can put guards on our Temple, but this! This is just, just ...'

'Insolence, disrespect and unnecessary imposition of boorish Roman ideas on our ancient culture,' Herodias suggested.

'Exactly!' Caiaphas stopped and dropped to his knees before them. 'He must be stopped. The people are going wild and they are quite right to do so.'

'Perhaps we should just leave them in the hope they rip him to pieces,' Herodias suggested. Antipas looked sideways at her and she shrugged. 'It would be quick.'

'It would be barbaric.'

'As is taking someone else's lands and imposing your idiot images upon them.'

'True.' He grinned at her. 'But they'd only send another governor. They've got thousands of ex-senators gasping for office, especially somewhere as rich as Judea.'

'So we have to be clever?'

'I'd say we can manage that. I'm on my way to visit Rome and report to the emperor about business in the Holy Land and it seems I will have a lot to report. Let's go and have a word with Pompous Pilate.'

Herodias giggled then heard herself, silly as any girl, and clapped her hand over her mouth.

'When?' she asked.

'Now.'

God, she liked decisiveness in a man.

❖

That night, guests finally gone, they toasted each other with sweet wine.

'Pilate crumpled before you, Antipas.'

'Because he knew I was right. Caiaphas was right, too, but I don't blame that Pilate man for ignoring him because he's a prig and a bore.'

'Antipas!'

'Well he is, but that's no excuse for the fool governor. What the hell he thought he was doing I have no idea. Either he's so stupid that he doesn't know about the Jewish prohibition on graven images – which would be a crime in itself given he is meant to be ruling us – or he was deliberately provoking violence, which is even worse. He's the fourth Roman governor of Judea and none of the others have seen fit to fly the Eagles. He can have them on his own dammed bedcovers if it turns him on, but not over the Holy City. If you're a guest in someone else's house then you obey their rules. It's simple courtesy.'

Herodias sighed.

'I'm not sure he sees himself as a guest.'

Antipas' eyes narrowed.

'No. You're right, Herodias. And therein lies our problem.'

'Ours?'

He leaned closer. They were sitting at the end of the long table, nothing but its corner separating them. The light from the guttering candles was low and the servants, gathered at the far end, were yawning and inattentive.

'Our family's as a whole but, you and I, Herodias, seem to be the only ones who care.'

Her insides turned over.

'We do,' she agreed.

'We should be together.'

'On this matter?'

'On everything.'

Beneath the table she felt his hand lie gently on her thigh and involuntarily parted her legs. Antipas gave a low moan.

'I want you, Herodias. I want you in my bed and I want you at my side. Marry me.' She gasped and the servants leapt to attention. Antipas smiled. 'I've shocked you?'

'Of course.'

'It shocks you more that I want to marry you than that I want to bed you.'

'It does. I'm no shy virgin, Antipas, though Lord knows it has been far too long. But I am no fool either. I am married already, as are you.'

He shrugged and his hand crept upwards, making the blood pulse deep inside her.

'The Romans, on the whole, are fools, but one thing they may have right – divorce.'

'Divorce?!'

'Sssh! They do it all the time. If a partnership no longer suits, it can be dissolved by decree of the emperor.'

'The emperor? Your friend the emperor?'

'My friend the emperor, yes. I am on my way to visit Rome, Herodias. I will be requesting an audience with Tiberius to discuss his insolent governor. It would be a matter of moments to add a further request.'

'To … to …'

'Divorce my wife and marry you, yes. Both our marriages are barren.'

'I have Salome,' she protested.

'I apologise. You are right. But since her . . .'

'Since her, nothing but loss.'

'Exactly. Our unions cannot be blessed by God. We were made for greatness, you and I – we should be together.' He leaned in urgently. 'I want you, Herodias, and not just for a night of passion. I want your body with every inch of mine but I want your mind too. I want your will, your drive, your power.' Herodias could feel herself melting and sunk down in her seat, pushing against his hand. His eyes darkened. 'We should be together. Not just for each other but for the Jewish nation. Say you'll do it, Herodias, say that if the emperor permits it, you will divorce Boethus and marry me.'

Herodias' heart pounded against her bodice.

'And if he doesn't?'

Antipas gave her a sideways grin.

'Then we shall have to make do with the night of passion.' She fought to breathe and glanced nervously to the servants, but now Antipas was rising. 'Come, I have something to show you.'

'Do you indeed!'

He grinned and offered his arm and she took it, giddy with expectation. She was surprised again, however, when he led her, not to the stairs up to the bedchambers on the first floor, but towards the garden.

'Outside?'

'It's a surprise. This way.'

He led her across the scented herb gardens, through the archway at the bottom and down towards the orchard. As they turned in through the pomegranate trees, she gasped in pleasure. There, pitched at the very centre of the grove, was a simple sukkot.

'After you, my lady.'

Antipas lifted the door flap and ushered her inside. There was nothing within bar a bed, furnished with silken sheets and a rich coverlet. Faintly, beyond the palace walls, she could hear the people in the streets of Jerusalem and up on the Mount of Olives, but it was as nothing over the rustle of the night breezes in the fabric of the plain walls.

'It's beautiful!'

'As, Herodias, are you. Say you will marry me.'

Herodias looked around at the tent, at the promise of the bed and back into the eyes of the man she'd come here to meet but had never expected to offer her so much.

'I will,' she said, standing tall before him. 'I will marry you.'

And then his lips were on hers and they were falling onto the bed and she heard nothing bar the rustle of the walls and the pounding of her own blood against his.

Chapter Five

Salome

'Can you play that section again?' Salome asked.

Boethus took his fingers from the lyre and looked at her, head to one side.

'Again, Lola?'

She nodded.

'I can't get this bit of the dance right. It's close, I know it is, but I just can't work out what to do with my arms.'

Boethus shook his grizzled head fondly and stretched out his back. He often played for her when she wanted to create a new dance but his cough last autumn had weakened him and he still looked worryingly frail. For a time over the winter, with the temperatures out here on the coast dropping dramatically, Salome had even feared for his life, but he had pulled through and the new warmth of spring seemed to be helping him. Even so, it wasn't worth taking the risk. She dropped her scarf and ran over to him.

'Is it too much, Father? We can do it again later if you want to rest.'

He reached for her hand.

'Why would I want to rest when I can watch you dance, sweet one? It is the finest relaxation of all.'

44

She laughed.

'Not at the moment it isn't but I'll get it right, I swear I will.'

'I *know* you will. You always do.'

Boethus lifted his lyre and picked out the same section of the tune that was baffling her and suddenly, watching his fingers flicker over the strings, she knew the shape she wanted in the air. Leaping up, she grabbed her scarf again and danced.

'Again!'

It was so close. The music sounded like water on the roof before a storm and she closed her eyes to better capture the build of pressure within. She thought of Ari and remembered the way emotion had risen within her when she'd spoken to him just before the storm of her betrothal. Her father played on, the tune gaining momentum, and she let herself go. Everything felt better when she danced. All the troubling thoughts and feelings battering around inside her seemed to find more natural shape in her body than in her head and she let them flow out of her unimpeded.

Eventually the music ran down and she stopped, panting but happy.

'I'd say you've got it right, Salome.'

She blinked, focusing back in on her father.

'I don't know about that. It's a little raw yet but it's a start.'

'Are you preparing for something particular?'

She shook her head. She'd performed for her parents' guests in the past, but not since her body had taken on its womanly shape and she wasn't keen to do so until she had got it under better control.

'This is just for me.'

'And why not?' He held out a hand and she went over to take it, sinking down onto the grass at his feet. The first of the spring flowers were starting to bloom and she caught the sweetness of them on the breeze and drank it in. 'It looked cathartic.'

She considered the word.

'It was. Sometimes, after I've danced, I feel . . .' She battled for the word, but as usual it was more troublesome to find than the

45

movement. '"Cleansed" is perhaps the closest I can get. Does that sound silly?'

'Not at all,' he said but she was already shaking her head at herself.

She remembered all those pilgrims piling into the Jordan to be baptised by the man called John back at Pesach and knew that the frivolous act of throwing herself around the orchard carried nothing like the weight of that great act.

'Do think all those people John baptised are still living in the new way now, Father?'

He squeezed her hand.

'I don't know, sweet one. Some of them may be but most are probably just lost in the daily grind of feeding their families.'

She grimaced.

'We should do more.'

'You would give them your jewels?'

'Maybe.'

'But then what would they have to aspire to?'

She squinted up at him. With the sun shining through his white hair, he looked almost angelic, like Gabriel or Michael or whatever it was the baptiser had called them. The point, however, was far from celestial.

'I don't think many of those people aspire to be a princess, Father.'

'On the contrary, I think they all do, at least when they are young.'

'But they must know it to be impossible, so it is surely just a tease?'

He conceded this with a tip of his head.

'Perhaps so, but it must help to know that not all life is drudgery.'

'Not if yours is!'

'Also fair. Would it help, do you think, if yours was drudgery too?'

She squirmed.

'I don't know, Father, but it might feel less unfair.'

'What might?' a sharp voice demanded and they both looked over to see Herodias standing before them, hands on hips.

Salome swallowed. Her mother had been in a strange mood all winter, alternating between picking fights with her and smothering her in affection. Neither felt comfortable and it had been getting worse in the last two weeks. Herod Antipas was coming to stay on his way back from some trip to Rome and Herodias had been in a frenzy of preparation.

'Is he bringing the damned emperor with him?' Boethus had asked yesterday as yet more food had arrived.

'Of course not,' Herodias had snapped. 'It's just that we hardly ever get guests here these days so I want to make the most of it.'

'I see. Will his wife be with him?'

'No. She's too frail to travel.'

'Like me.'

'Yes.'

'A good job then, Herodias – wife – that you are so able to march forwards without me.'

Herodias had offered no reply but simply swept from the room, leaving Salome with the usual uncomfortable feeling that there was more to the words than she could understand.

'What might be less unfair?' Herodias demanded again now, as if she had a right to know every bit of Salome. Well fine. She stuck her chin up and answered.

'If I didn't have so much more wealth than others.'

Herodias reacted with predictable horror, throwing her hands in the air as if Salome had uttered the greatest of blasphemies.

'You are a royal princess, Salome. You have more wealth than others in the same way that a horse has more legs than a human. It is an inherent part of your role.'

'That's not true,' Salome protested, pushing herself up off the grass to face her mother. 'I can give up my wealth in a way that a horse cannot give up his legs.'

'He can with the right blade.'

'Mother! He would die.'

'But he would still be a horse.'

'As I would be a princess without jewels and palaces.'

'A very poor one. And more to the point, a very ineffective one. Without wealth you would be able to do nothing for your people.'

'I do nothing for them now.'

'But that will change once you are fully grown and running a house – and a region.'

'Trachonitis?' Salome said dully.

'Exactly. If you wish to be so useful, daughter, then I can arrange your wedding within weeks. Is that what you would like?'

'No! That is, I don't know. Maybe. If it has to be, then perhaps I should just get on with it.'

'Perhaps you should,' Boethus agreed.

Salome swung round to him, amazed.

'You would have rid of me, Father?'

'No! Oh, sweet one, no. I would keep you here as my little girl forever more but that is not the way the world works. Women marry.' He pushed himself up from his chair, grabbing for the stick that he used everywhere he went now. 'And remarry,' he added darkly, making off across the grass.

'What?' Salome ran after him. 'Father, what do you mean?'

He sighed.

'Ask your mother, Salome.' He looked back to Herodias. 'She is looking very well these days, do you not think? Very attractive.'

Salome looked back to Herodias, confused.

'She is a beautiful woman.'

Herodias flushed and her hand went to her hair with a most unusual flutter.

'Thank you, Salome,' she said and, if Salome had not known her better, she would have sworn there were tears in the words.

'A beautiful woman,' Boethus agreed sadly. 'And one I have wasted.'

'Father?'

Salome turned to him again but her parents were looking at each other in a most unfathomable manner. If they had been dancing it would have been something ripped through with longing and regret and a deep sense of separation.

'What's going on?' she demanded.

'Ask your mother, Salome,' Boethus said again, tearing his eyes away and making for the villa with the slow tap tap of his stick on the path. Then he was gone and Herodias was looking to her feet and Salome had no idea what on earth to make of any of it.

◈

Two days later horses clattered up to the front of the villa. Salome, reading in her room, only half heard, but could not miss the sight of her mother whirling past the door at almost unseemly speed. She crept to the top of the stairs in time to see Herodias stop herself at the doors, adjust her hair and, with a deep breath, step grandly outside. Her father was in the garden and made no effort to join his wife, so Salome darted along the top landing to the front windows in time to see Antipas leaping from his horse – or trying to. He was not as young as he clearly thought himself and his legs crumpled a little from so much time in the saddle so that he had to adjust himself awkwardly in order to kiss Herodias' hand. Not that she seemed to notice.

'Herod Antipas. Welcome to our humble home.'

Why did people do that, Salome wondered. There was nothing humble about their home, as both knew all too well, but these word-games must be played.

'I am most glad to be here.'

He was looking at Herodias with a notable intensity that made Salome squirm and all at once she knew what was going on here. Indeed, she had known all along and had just been hiding from it. She might be an innocent herself but even a princess did not live in seclusion, and she had seen enough of the relations between men and women in the bushes and back alleyways at night to understand. It was all in the way their bodies leaned towards each other and their eyes locked in an ancient dance. What – if anything – it meant for herself, however, she was not sure. Nor why her father was doing nothing to stop it.

'Was your visit successful, my lord?' Herodias was asking with loud cheer that fooled no one.

'Most successful,' he agreed.

'You, er, concluded all your business.'

'All of it, yes.'

Again, Herodias' hands did that fluttering thing Salome had noticed the other day and she realised that she was nervous. Her sharp, certain, commanding mother was nervous.

'You must be hungry after your journey.'

'Oh, I am.'

Salome sighed at the wealth of meaning the man injected into the simple words. This was mortifying. Where on earth was her father? Someone, surely, had to stop this nonsense going on in his own house? Pushing herself away from the window, she drew in breath and headed for the stairs.

'Great-Uncle Antipas,' she greeted their guest loudly.

He flinched at the title but recovered.

'Salome. How lovely to see you. Are you well?'

'Very well, thank you. And you? You look a little saddle-sore.'

He bristled.

'No, no. Not at all. Fit as my horse, I am.'

'Just with two less legs.'

He frowned in confusion and Herodias glared at her.

'Let us order refreshments for our guest, daughter.'

'Of course, Mother. And I'll fetch Father, shall I?'

'Oh, don't bother him if he's happy in his garden.'

'Not at all. I'm sure he will be keen to greet his half-brother.'

'Don't bother him.'

Herodias' voice was sharp and Salome stopped, stung.

'Why not?' In reply Herodias looked to Antipas and that, above all else, held Salome. Her mother never deferred to anyone. Nervously, Herodias turned to the man at her side. 'Why not, my lord?'

Antipas looked around the hall, shifting uncomfortably in his riding breeches. It was clear he had not expected things to come to a head so fast but with a nod to Herodias, he squared his shoulders and stepped forward.

'Emperor Tiberius has granted me a divorce from my wife, Phasaelis.' Salome stared at his lips, willing herself to take in every single one of these troubling words. 'And he has granted Herodias . . .'

'My mother.'

'Your mother, yes, a divorce from Boethus.'

'My father.'

'Correct.'

'In order that you and she can, then, marry?'

He allowed himself a small, relieved smile.

'Exactly.'

'Because?'

He looked awkwardly down at her.

'Sorry?'

'Why is this to happen?'

'Erm. I'm not . . . That is, perhaps something you should ask your mother.'

'Very well.' Salome looked to Herodias. 'Mother?'

'Salome! Surely we can talk about this in private?'

Salome put her hands on her hips.

'I would have thought so, Mother, but we have been here together all winter and you have not thought to bring it up.'

'Because I did not know if it would be granted.'

'But you knew of the request.'

'I . . . Yes.'

'And you did not think that I, a betrothed woman, deserved to know of it?'

'I did not wish to trouble you, daughter.'

Salome ground her teeth.

'Well, in that you have failed, I'm afraid. I am very troubled.'

Herodias was shooting her dark looks, but so what? This was a mean, low trick and Salome saw no reason why she should make it easier for her. An affair was embarrassing enough, but this!

'Divorce,' she said, feeling her way around the word. 'You are going to divorce. Is that legal within Jewish law?'

'We are a Roman state, daughter.'

'A fact that you hate, that you rail against, that you fight with every inch of your breath – usually.'

'And still do, truly. But the law is the law.'

'And Jewish law, I believe, states that you cannot marry your brother's wife.'

'Jewish law states that you cannot marry your brother's *widow*.'

'Right. But his divorced wife . . .'

'Is not mentioned in scripture.'

'How convenient.'

Herodias' eyes narrowed and she drew herself up.

'You are being insolent, girl. It is not your place to question the judgement of your elders.'

'But it is my place to accept the impact of that judgement upon my own life?'

'Yes. It will be good for you. You can come and live with us in Galilee. It is in the north, you know, towards Trachonitis, and will allow you to escape the confines of this hidden-away estate and learn a little more of the world. Then, perhaps, you will understand.'

'And my father? He will understand too, will he?'

Herodias shivered, but Antipas stepped up and placed a strong hand around her waist and she calmed. Salome looked at them, linked together, and felt helpless before their combined strength. The situation plucked at her very skin and she tugged on her dress, suddenly too tight against it.

'He will understand,' Herodias confirmed, her certainty returned.

'Well, we'll see about that,' Salome shot back, then turned and made for the garden.

◆

Boethus was amongst his roses, choosing blooms for the table. She hated herself for bringing him this news but what more could she do?

'Father, Antipas is here.'

'Is he?' Boethus looked up from the rose he was plucking and gave a long sigh. 'Oh, good.'

'He says ... he says he has an imperial decree for your divorce from Mother. And his own from Phasaelis.'

'Does he indeed.'

'And that they will marry.'

'Marry!'

He stroked his finger down the rose stem, apparently not noticing as the thorns drew blood.

'Father, please.' Salome reached out to take it from him. 'Will you come in?'

'Is it worth it?'

She looked at him sideways.

'Of course. Are you not going to fight for her?'

'I have not the weaponry, my dear.'

'You do! All she wants is for you to stand up and be a ... a ...'

'A man? Your mother, Salome, is more man than I.'

'And that does not bother you?'

'It is a fact, that is all. She has the ambition and desire to rule and it is unfortunate for her that she has it trapped within a woman's body and must find a man to wield it for her.'

'Why can you not be that man?'

He spread his arms wide, indicating his green-stained gown, his bony fingers and the pretty flowers in the basket on his arm.

'I am not up to the job. I have tried. I promise you that I have tried but I am old, Salome, and weary.'

53

'So you will let her go, just like that?'

'If she wishes it.'

Salome stared at him – so worryingly wizened, so infuriatingly accepting, so heartbreakingly disappointing.

'It is hard,' she threw at him, 'to know which of you to hate more.'

He flinched but swiftly recovered.

'Do not hate, daughter.'

'Why not?'

'It is not good for the soul.'

'Neither is having riches, or power or privilege, but apparently that is part of who I am, so why should hate not be so too?'

'Salome, please. This is political, not personal.'

'Really? Because it feels very damn personal to me. You will just let her go?'

'If that is what she wants.'

'And me, too? You will just let me go?'

'Ah, Salome, my dear, sweet Salome. You are the light of my life and I will never let you go.'

'I can stay here then, with you?'

He shifted.

'What does your mother say?'

She let out a scream.

'What does it matter what my mother says? What do *you* say?'

'I say that I love you and I want the best for you.'

'Which is here.'

'With an old man and his flowers? You are young, Salome. You will marry. You need your mother.'

'I do not!' Salome said, hot tears falling irritatingly from her eyes. Everything she had known was falling apart underneath her and no one cared. 'I do not need her and I do not need you. I hate you all.'

She turned back to the villa, running for the room that would not, it seemed, be hers for much longer, and flung herself onto her bed. She longed for her mother to come and hold her, as she'd done

54

when she'd had nightmares as a child, but knew that if she did, she would push her away. It was all too dark and confusing and she sprang up again, filled with dark energy. She could hear Herodias calling her name, but would not step to her mother's tune, not yet. Ramming a chest against the door to keep the rest of the world out, she kicked off her shoes and danced until she could dance no more.

Chapter Six

Herodias

Herodias shifted in the saddle, every trot of her fine horse sending ridiculously pleasant reminders of last night through her body. This second marriage had been a revelation. She'd thought herself dried out, finished as a woman, but Antipas had brought her to life again and it felt like a miracle. Surely this much pleasure had to bear fruit?

She clasped tighter at the reins, refusing to allow herself to think of such things. The hurt of the three boys she had lost before Salome sat like scars across her womb and she feared they had sealed it against any future babes. Besides, she was into her forty-third year and her bleeds were becoming irregular, which meant there would be no way of telling if God had blessed her at last or simply taken away all capacity.

'Don't think about it,' she muttered to herself.

This was enough – this pleasure, this happiness. For now, it was enough. Antipas was an attentive and vigorous husband and she was, finally, arriving in what would be her new home. She forced herself to look at the road ahead, rather than back down the dark paths in her mind, and caught her first glimpse of the gleaming rooves of Tiberias. Her stomach squeezed. She'd heard wonderful things of this new Galilean city, but mainly from Antipas, its creator, and she prayed he had not exaggerated. After far too many years stuck out on a country estate, she was so very ready for city life and the precious potential of her new home felt fragile.

It had been a long road to get here. She'd had to be patient – not, she knew, her finest quality. Antipas had been most apologetic but the demands of rule were great and she had asked to be subject to public life, so she could hardly complain. Even so, to wait four months from her wedding day – and that a very quiet, behind closed-doors wedding too – to enter her marital palace had felt hard.

The first problem had been that Antipas' previous wife, Phasaelis, had not taken the news of the Imperial decree of divorce quite as calmly as Boethus. The second had been that Phasaelis was the daughter of King Aretas of Nabatea, the wild hill-country bordering Antipas' second tetrarchy of Perea, south of Jerusalem. King Aretas had not taken it calmly either. Herodias and Antipas had been forced to ride, not for pretty new Tiberias on the shores of Lake Galilee, but for the ancient and forbidding fortress of Machaerus, overlooking the mountainous borders with Nabatea. Herodias had to admit that her heart had squeezed unpleasantly when she'd stared up the almost-sheer mountain to the grey-walled fortress perched atop. It had looked more prison than palace and it had only been Salome's pathetic little gasps of horror that had stoppered her own.

To be fair to the place, the views from the top had been magnificent. On a fine day you could see right up the Jordan valley, almost as far as Galilee. It had felt like too much of a tease to gaze on what should be her new home, however, so she had confined herself to the equally fine views of Jerusalem, just a few miles away. Every morning she'd strode the battlements, looking across to the Temple, and reassured herself that this marriage had been the right move. The law was important, of course, but sometimes you had to be bold enough to interpret it flexibly for the greatest benefit of all; this was not so much for Herodias herself as for the Jewish nation. She had to admit though, as her horse picked up pace and another increasingly familiar sensation shot between her legs, that she wasn't exactly suffering.

'Tiberias!' Antipas exclaimed just ahead of her and she smiled to hear the joy in his voice.

He had seen Aretas off eventually and all that unpleasantness was, pray God, behind them.

'I am excited to see it,' she told him eagerly.

'You should be. It has taken five whole years to build and it is a jewel of a city, though I say so myself.' He reached for her hand. 'I am grateful that, finally, it has a jewel of a woman to grace it as it deserves.'

Herodias squirmed. He was always saying things like this. At first, she'd thought it simply part of his political charm but, when he looked deep into her eyes in bed and told her how happy she made him, it felt alarmingly real. And rather uncomfortable. She was glad she made him happy, of course, and he made her happy too, but these outpourings didn't feel very dignified.

'I hope I will do it justice,' she said primly and he smiled.

'I know you will.' He turned back. 'Salome, come and see. We are nearly at Tiberias!' Salome, trotting sullenly behind them as if she were stuck on a donkey and not a fine grey mare, came reluctantly forward. 'Can you see the palace down on the lakefront there?' Antipas asked her, pointing to a long, white villa, sparkling with gold trim.

Herodias stood up in her stirrups to see it more clearly but Salome just gave a moody little shrug.

'It's very shiny.'

'It's brand new.'

'So it has no history?'

Herodias cringed but Antipas fielded her easily.

'Do you think history is only contained in bricks, Salome? Or is it, perhaps, in people, in lines of blood. This palace stands as testament to the Herods, just as the Temple does in Jerusalem.'

'The Temple surely stands as testament to God.'

'It stands in worship and honour of God, but also as testament to the Herods who raised it in His glory.'

Salome merely grunted and Herodias took this as concession of the cleverly made point and was proud of Antipas. He had been so good to her daughter, showering her with gowns and jewels and the fine mount she rode now. He had also paid her much attention, pointing things out to her and asking for her opinion, which had rarely been given and even more rarely been positive. Salome was cross, she understood that, but four months was a long time to carry a grudge. Surely any young girl should be delighted with the chance for riches and adventure and the opportunity to see more of the world than a few acres of her father's orchard.

'You shall have fine rooms of your own in the palace,' he told her now.

'Until I am married,' she shot back.

'Until then, yes. You may decorate them as you wish.'

'I'm not sure it will be worth it for so short a time.'

Herodias ground her teeth. The girl was impossible. One minute she was all complaints about being betrothed to Philip and the next she was rushing to his bed. She had sworn that she would not send the girl under the Chuppah until she was sixteen. Her own marriage had been too young, her body too frail to cope with the princes who had taken fruit in her womb. No wonder they had shrivelled within her. The three dark losses still crept through her nightmares in wisps of pain and fear and she did not want that for her daughter. At this rate, however, she might change her mind. Salome seemed robust. Her hips had rounded nicely and she had fine breasts. Physically she looked ready for childbearing but emotionally she was still a child, as she was proving most tiresomely right now.

Antipas dropped back to find messengers to ride ahead with news of their arrival in the city, and she seized the chance to talk to her recalcitrant daughter.

'I know it has been hard these last few months, Salome. I have not enjoyed it much either.'

'You chose it; I did not.'

Herodias laughed.

'You are right. I was lucky for once. We do not often get to choose our fate, especially as women. But we can make the most of it.'

'I miss my father.'

'Your father who let you go without a second glance.'

Salome's little cry of distress was heartfelt and Herodias felt mean but, really, when would the girl learn?

'Look, daughter, I'm sorry this isn't what you planned but we're here now and it's beautiful. Can you not enjoy it?'

'We'll see,' was all Herodias got in response and she was grateful when Antipas returned and began talking her eagerly through the various buildings gracing Tiberias.

'The main synagogue is modelled upon the one at Jericho, only with additional courtyard space for teachers. It is very important, is it not, that the young have a chance to learn?'

'Very,' Herodias agreed, throwing Salome a dark look, but the girl had her head down and her face hidden by a curtain of hair. Fine, let her stew; Herodias was going to enjoy her new home.

The city was beautiful. Laid out in a Hellenistic grid pattern, the streets were graciously wide, with smart walkways either side to keep the people safe from wagons and carriages. At every junction were squares, some small with just a few benches that would, in a year or two, be shaded by the rapidly growing trees, some far larger, leading up to synagogues or law courts with space for speakers and the crowds they always attracted. There were several wells to cut water queues, plus shops and market stalls selling every conceivable item, and a number of gymnasiums and sports grounds, packed with young men. Then there was the lakefront – a shining parade of beautiful homes, kissed by the fresh breezes off the water, with the palace at its centre.

'Oh, Antipas – I love it!'

He beamed and right there, in front of the crowds rapidly gathering around them, he leaned over in his stirrups and kissed her full on the lips.

'Must you,' Salome groaned behind them, but she was thankfully drowned out by the delighted people.

They pulled up outside the palace gates to a curve of smartly uniformed staff waiting to greet them. At the centre was a broad-chested man with an impressive shock of white hair who came striding forward and kissed Herodias' hand flamboyantly.

'This is Chuza,' Antipas told her. 'My steward of many years standing and as fine an organiser as any you will meet.'

'A pleasure to meet you, Chuza.'

'The pleasure is all mine, my lady. It is an honour to serve.'

Herodias flushed. The words were clearly designed for show but she appreciated them all the more for that. The crowd was now ranged all along the waterfront, watching her arrival keenly, and it was good to be welcomed in style.

'This is my wife, Johanna.'

Chuza put a hand back and a sprite of a young woman, petite and slender with an annoyingly attractive face, bound forward and dropped into a graceful curtsey.

'Welcome, my lady Herodias. I trust all is to your liking.'

'It is beautiful,' she agreed, wishing this particular part of her new home were a little less so.

'Isn't it?' Johanna agreed eagerly. 'I only arrived myself six months ago when my dear Chuza was kind enough to choose me as his wife but I love it. It's so bright and spacious.'

'It is,' Herodias agreed.

'And no one cares about the graveyard thing any more.'

Herodias saw Chuza draw in a horrified breath and the girl clapped a hand to her mouth. Herodias tensed as Salome stepped forward, a new spring in her step at this hint of trouble.

'What graveyard thing?' she demanded.

'A small building issue,' Antipas said quickly, 'that is all.'

'Are these Jews?' Salome asked, indicating the crowd.

Antipas clearly did not like the question and Herodias looked around her. There were plenty of unmistakably Jewish features but a significant mix of others amongst them. She turned uneasily to her husband.

'We welcome all here in Tiberias,' he blustered. 'And we have many visitors and traders. It is what makes the city thrive.'

'Of course,' Herodias agreed hastily. 'Though it does seem unusually . . . diverse.'

'Oh, that's not unusual these days. People travel. They move to where they think they are most likely to prosper and a fine new city like this . . .'

'The graveyard thing?' Salome said more loudly.

'It's nothing, my lady,' the steward, Chuza, assured her. 'It is simply that towards the end of construction of this beautiful city of Tiberias the builders uncovered the remains of an ancient burial ground.'

'Really ancient,' Johanna said, tripping over herself to explain. 'And right on the outskirts, barely in the city at all.'

'But within the walls?' Herodias asked, her stomach churning. No true Jew could live on top of a graveyard, or even close to it. It broke all the most basic purity laws.

'We have diverted the walls.'

'But you do not know how far the graveyard extended?' Salome asked, a nasty edge to her voice.

'No,' Antipas admitted. There was an uncomfortable pause. Then he shrugged. 'It is unfortunate but I do not see it as a major problem. The priests have performed purification rituals and the people have been informed. I have offered generous terms to householders and many, as you can see, have taken them up. Those who do not like it, do not have to live here.'

'I do not like it,' Salome said, loud and clear.

Antipas looked at her and then at Herodias. He was doing a good job of seeming calm and in control but Herodias could see the panic in the back of his eyes and hated it. She looked around the shifting crowd. The people of Tiberias seemed to be holding their breath, as if what she had to say on the matter was important. It was a heady feeling but a tricky one too. She had been brought up in horror of corpses and could almost feel the ground pulsing through her sandals, as if the dead were pushing up from their dark, dirty graves beneath her. But, then, she had been brought up in horror of divorce too ... She had chosen her path and must tread it firmly, even when it was thorny.

'It seems to me,' she said clearly, 'that a place so blessed in its location, bearing and people cannot be cursed by God. If the priests have performed the purification, then we must trust in their holy authority and embrace this gift of a city in all good grace.'

Antipas clasped her hand, his grip gratefully tight as the crowd cheered.

'I still don't like it,' Salome chuntered behind them.

Herodias groaned but Johanna bounded forward and clasped her daughter's hands.

'You must be Salome. Welcome, welcome. It will be so wonderful to have someone else young about the palace.'

'Oi!' Chuza protested, but good-naturedly. Johanna threw him a seductive smile and pulled Salome forward.

'Do you dance?' Herodias heard her ask her sulky daughter and saw Salome's tight shoulders loosen for perhaps the first time since she had told her of the divorce.

'I love to dance,' she heard her reply and, as the two young women disappeared arm in arm, Herodias thought that perhaps Johanna, despite her infuriating beauty, would turn out to be the greatest blessing of this elegant but troubling new home.

Chapter Seven

Salome

Salome sat as still as she possibly could, watching two butterflies weave around each other in the still morning air before finally dipping off over the balustrade and across the wide blue sky over Lake Galilee. She sighed. She had to admit it was lovely here, despite the fact the whole damned city was built over the dead and would surely sink into the water at any moment.

Herodias hated the graveyard issue. Salome had seen her mother's face when Antipas had admitted to the contamination and knew that it revolted her, but she'd stood at her husband's side all the same and Salome had to admit to being impressed. Not that she'd tell Herodias that. She didn't deserve any praise at all. She'd uprooted Salome without a moment's thought to satisfy her own lusts and ambitions, and she had to take the consequences.

Even so, Tiberias was pretty nice. Until coming here, Salome had thought all cities as cramped and dirty as Jerusalem, so this spacious, gracious one was a pleasant contrast. And as for the lake ... She pushed herself up to lean on the balustrade and look out across the water. She was used to the Green Sea, not a mile from her father's estates, but there was something about this contained, complete water, that appealed to her.

Lake Galilee was about half a day's boat ride across and a full day's along, and Tiberias sat halfway down the west bank. On a day as clear as this one, she could just make out the roofs of Capernaum and Bethsaida at the top end and she enjoyed watching the boats make their way down to the rich fishing grounds in the centre from those bustling ports. Usually, the fishermen were hauling in their nets just as Salome rose to break her fast and she admired their industry.

Opposite Tiberias, across the lake, was the top end of the Decapolis, the free state of ten Greek towns that held the rich lands along the east bank of the Jordan. It ran all the way down to Antipas' second province of Perea, which nudged up to the north shores of the Salt Sea. On the other side of the river, between here and Jerusalem, was Samaria – a place of bandits and criminals, who worshipped strange, corrupt gods and were hostile to Jews. Salome had worried that Galilee would be similar but, in fact, it seemed a temperate oasis of thriving industry and agriculture. The waters kept the lands around rich in corn and barley, and olives grew all the way up the higher slopes.

The people seemed largely content, with the only dark blotch the omnipresent Roman tax collectors, bleeding them of their hard-earned profits and reminding them constantly that they were under foreign control. Salome's mother hated that even more than she hated sleeping above the dead. Herodias dreamed of freeing the Holy Land of their hated interference and Salome admired her for that. Salome could see that Antipas was a sharper tool for the job than her own dear father but how many laws would her mother have to break to put Jews back on a throne. And at what cost?

Salome shivered, despite the warmth of the day, and was grateful when she heard a piping voice calling her name.

'I'm on the roof, Johanna!'

Johanna's pretty face appeared out of the stairwell and she clapped at seeing Salome.

'Found you at last. Why are you hiding up here?'

'The view is good.'

'It is.' Johanna came to her side and pointed up the lake. 'Somewhere up there in Capernaum is my family.'

'What do they do?'

'They're fishermen, of course. Everyone around here is a fisherman, or a chandler or a boat-builder. Sometimes I wonder why the lake doesn't run out of fish, we drag so many of them out of it every day but it seems fish multiply faster than people.'

She patted her stomach which was slowly swelling with Chuza's child and Salome put a curious hand to it. Her friend was about five months gone by the royal doctor's reckoning.

'Five months gone but four still to go,' Johanna had told her with a dramatic eye-roll. 'It takes forever.'

'A baby is a complicated thing.'

'I hope not. I can barely take care of myself and Chuza, so I need the baby to be easy.'

From all Salome had heard, babies were not easy. She in particular, so her mother had told her endlessly, had been impossible to please. Obviously, Herodias had had a raft of staff to help but it still seemed to have pained her.

'You just used to cry and cry,' she'd told her more times than Salome could count.

'Maybe I was unhappy,' she'd suggested once.

'Maybe you were just demanding.'

'As you've taught me.'

Herodias had had no answer for that.

'I'm sure Baby will be just lovely,' Johanna said now and Salome thought that perhaps, with such an attitude, it would. Certainly, if it was anywhere near as bright and sunny as its mother, it was unlikely to cry in the way Salome apparently had.

'Do you like being married?' she asked Johanna.

'Oh yes! Chuza is lovely. I was so excited when he knocked on our door one day and asked for my hand.'

'Just like that?'

66

'More or less. The poor man was widowed last year and looking for a new wife. He'd seen me in the market and asked where I lived and then he just strode up to the door. Father was astonished. And delighted. Well, Chuza is an imposing man, right? And a royal steward doesn't come knocking every day. Father said yes there and then, until mother pulled him up and reminded him to talk dowries. That was embarrassing! Luckily Chuza's got plenty of money, at least compared to the likes of my family, so next thing I knew I was under the Chuppah with my groom!'

'He's very big.'

'He is. It makes me feel very safe. It can get a bit squashy, mind you, when, you know ... but it's worth it. He can pick me up with just one arm and lift me right over his head.'

'Do you like that?'

Johanna considered.

'It makes me a bit giddy, but it's fun. And he doesn't do it all the time or anything. It's not, like, our favourite thing to do. He just, you know, can. He's very kind to me and very generous. I get lots of nice dresses and I love living in the palace. Back at home, I had to share a bed with my two sisters and they didn't half squirm. Chuza and I have an enormous bed and I sleep so much better. Plus, I don't have to help with the laundry or cook any meals. Isn't that wonderful?'

Salome couldn't help smiling. Her new friend was a little manic at times but her enthusiasm for life was impossible to resist.

'What do you do?'

'As little as possible! I find just going around praising other people for doing a good job makes them all very content. Then they get on with it and I don't have to.'

Salome shook her head in admiration.

'You're smart.'

'Smarter than I look,' Johanna agreed easily, 'and I like to keep it that way. I find it's always best if people underestimate you.'

'It doesn't matter if they have a low opinion of you?'

'Why should it? It's my own opinion that counts, surely? And that of the people I actually care about. Chuza doesn't think I'm stupid.'

'Neither do I.'

'There you go then! Oh, but . . .' She clapped a hand dramatically to her forehead. 'I must be a bit stupid because I came up here to tell you that the most divine pair of musicians are in the palace. I found them in the marketplace and brought them back to entertain your parents . . .'

'My mother and stepfather.'

'Right. Well, to entertain them at dinner later but they need to practise so I thought, whilst they did, we could dance.'

'Dance?!'

Salome felt the day light up further. She glanced westwards, towards her father's estates, guilty for enjoying herself in this stolen new life, but all she could see were barren hills. Besides, he had let her go without a fight so why should she feel guilty?

'You need your mother,' he'd said, which was nonsense.

She was fifteen now and didn't need to be cared for as she had when she'd been an endlessly crying baby. It was more Boethus that she needed. He was the one who had talked to her about history and philosophy and all the troubles of life. Herodias hated discussion. She had a set of ideas and did not want them challenged, even when the challenges – like a graveyard beneath the city – were staring her in the face. Still, she had to admit that Tiberias had brought new pleasures and she looked eagerly round as Johanna bellowed down the stairs and two men bobbed up onto the roof, one with a lyre and one with a flute.

'Here?' Salome asked.

'Why not? You dance beautifully, Salome, so do it before God.'

'God can see us everywhere.'

'True, but why make Him squint.' Salome burst out laughing. Johanna had such a refreshing outlook on life and she was so glad she'd met her. 'Come on – let's dance!'

There seemed little point in arguing with her friend in this mood and the musicians she'd found were good, playing fast, lilting tunes that caught at Salome's feet and arms in a delicious way. She let herself lean into them, casting off all the melancholy of the last few months. It had annoyed her to screaming-point when her mother had blithely suggested she should 'make the most' of her new situation, but today, with the sun shining and the breeze caressing her skin and the music rippling through her entire body, it felt impossible to do anything else.

It was only when the musicians ground to a halt and she stopped, hearing her own breathing come hard and fast from her chest, that she realised Johanna had long since sat down and she was the only one dancing.

'Johanna, you should have—'

Her words were cut off by a round of applause, drifting up from the seashore. Horrified, she spun round to see a large group watching. She put her head in her hands.

'Johanna! Why didn't you say?'

'And rob them of such beauty?'

Salome's stomach squirmed.

'It was not beauty. There was no craft to my movements, no meaning to the dance.'

'Which is what was so joyous about it. They loved it, Salome.'

'How do you know?'

'Because, silly girl, they would not clap otherwise. Look.'

She jumped up and peeled Salome's hands from her face, forcing her to look out. The crowd clapped again.

'This is so embarrassing,' Salome groaned. 'I'm a princess, not a performer. Mother will be horrified.'

'Your mother is not here and, besides, I think she can perform as well as anyone. How she handled the graveyard issue was majestic.'

'You noticed she was not happy.'

'Of course, but the men did not.'

Salome nodded. Men, it seemed, did not notice much. Save

perhaps the one standing below them, still looking up at her. He was tall and good-looking with a commanding bearing and it was clear that the crowd were here for him as they were looking back to him now, Salome already forgotten. That was a relief and she wished he would look away too. She peered down to see what he was selling but he had no stall, or cart. A preacher then, perhaps, save that it was not the Sabbath and he wore the clothes of a regular workman. As she stared, he lifted a hand in a wave. His eyes met hers and the first thing she saw in them was kindness.

'Who's that man?' she asked Johanna.

Her friend leaned over the balustrade.

'Him? He's called Jesus, I believe, son of a carpenter from Nazareth, up in the hills.'

'What's he doing here then?'

'He and his father are part of the team of constructors in Tiberias. I've seen him around, how can you not?' She nudged Salome. 'Handsome, isn't he?'

Salome flushed.

'I didn't notice.' The man had turned back to his group and was talking earnestly to them. 'Why isn't he working now?'

'Break time?' Johanna suggested. 'He has ideas apparently.'

'Ideas?'

'Essene ideas. I think he might have worked in the community at Qumran at one point, with his cousin, John.'

'John? John the Essene?'

Johanna laughed.

'That would be logical, yes.'

'The one who has been baptising people in the Jordan?'

'I believe so. Quite the family, aren't they? I heard Jesus talking the other day when I was out shopping. He's nearly as easy to listen to as he is to watch. He has this lovely low voice, one of those ones that you can't help but concentrate on. And he has such a way with words. He talks in stories.'

'Stories?'

'Little slices of ordinary life to explain teachings to you. It's an Essene thing apparently, meant to make it easier for us uneducated lot. And it does too. He had this brilliant thing the other day about lighting a lamp and then putting it under a bushel basket.'

Salome squinted at her.

'Surely that would be a foolish thing to do?'

'Exactly his point. You should set your lamp on your lampstand where it can give light to all in the house, and it's the same with us – we have to do good deeds so that everyone can see the light inside us that comes from turning to God.'

'Right. That makes sense, I suppose.'

'It does!' Johanna agreed happily, then her face fell and she added, 'He must be a bit mad though; he says that it's good to be poor.'

Salome sighed. 'So does John the Baptiser.'

'That can't be right, can it? Everyone knows it's rubbish being poor. But that Jesus, he says we shouldn't measure riches in gold, but in what is in our heart.'

'It's a nice idea.'

'It's a weird idea. You can't eat what's in your heart. Well, you can, I suppose, but then you'd be dead.'

Salome laughed.

'Are you sure you're cleverer than you look, Johanna?'

Johanna pulled a stupid face. 'That depends on how clever you think I look. Anyway, that Jesus is either very clever, or very mad. But my sister visited me the other day and she says some of the main fishermen at Capernaum follow him when they can, so there must be something in him.'

Salome looked at the man again. Thankfully he now had his back to her, so she had time to take him in. He was nothing like his cousin. His clothes were simple but clean and neat, his hair was brushed and his hands expressive. He had workman's fingers, strong and calloused, but they moved like water and made her want to dance again.

She shook her head. She'd made enough of a fool of herself already and she could only hope news of Antipas' new stepdaughter performing for the masses on the palace roof wouldn't get to Antipas or Herodias. It was hardly becoming.

'Let's go inside,' she said, grabbing Johanna's arm. 'It's hot up here.'

'It is,' her friend agreed easily. 'Cook was making lemonade when I came up. It must be ready by now.'

'Perfect.'

Salome edged Johanna down the steps, but, as she went to follow, she paused and turned back. The man, Jesus, was heading into the town, presumably to wherever he was working and the crowd were reluctantly dispersing. Someone asked him something and he paused to answer them, then looked back up at the palace. His eyes met Salome's and she was caught. There was nothing of a madman in them. She'd seen madness. The poor lepers and the unfortunates who'd lost their minds were always at the palace gates and their eyes were clouded and unfocused, as if they were looking back in on their own spiralling minds rather than out at the world before them. This man, though, this man understood the world. If he believed it was good to be poor, she thought uncomfortably, then what did he make of her?

Suddenly she longed to speak to her father. He would be interested in this Galilean carpenter with his ideas about poverty and hearts and bushel baskets. He would be happy to discuss him and his fellows. He would be happy to sit back and let Salome form her own thoughts, pulling words together in the same way she pulled movements in a dance – slowly, a jumble at first, but finally forming into something that made sense, at least to her.

She would ask her mother if she could visit Boethus, perhaps on the way to Jerusalem for Sukkot. It was her mother's favourite festival, so it might make her disposed to be obliging, especially if Salome was nice to her beforehand. She sighed. It stuck in her throat, but needs must. Galilee, it seemed, was an interesting place to be right now and perhaps it was time she admitted that to Herodias.

Chapter Eight

Herodias

Herodias stretched out in bed as Antipas threw back the curtains, letting the early sun play across her body. The light was amazing here. It had a translucency that was new to her and it seemed playful, sparkling up from the water and bouncing off any available surface with exuberant joy.

She tutted at herself. Listen to her, talking like a damned poet. It was ridiculous.

Still, there was plenty to be joyful about. Her new home was wonderful and did not appear to be cursed. Perhaps this graveyard had just been one little clutch of burials, now safely beyond the sturdy walls of Tiberias. More and more Jews were moving in all the time, enticed by the attractive rates Antipas had set for both housing and trade, and on the Sabbath the whole place rang to the sound of bells calling the faithful. There were many fine synagogues here but the other day Antipas had given her permission to erect a new one, all of her own, and this morning she had the finest architects and craftsmen calling on her to discuss designs.

Her marriage continued to blossom, especially at night, and she was even starting to relax into Antipas' exuberant expressions of affection. She had not yet bled and, although she did not really feel

74

pregnant, perhaps that was because this one was as firmly lodged as Salome had been, and not clinging to mere threads of her womb like her lost princes. Even Salome seemed to have cheered up. She was dancing again and taking an interest in the world, and the other day she had told Herodias that Tiberias 'isn't too bad a city', which was high praise indeed considering her attitude when they'd first arrived.

She'd made no mention of her marriage, which was a relief. Philip wrote to Herodias regularly asking if his bride was ready but Herodias put him off, claiming Salome was not yet ripe for childbearing. She was of course, and had been for several years, but he was not to know that. When he'd expressed surprise in his latest letter, she'd told him that noble blood bloomed later. Nonsense, as far as she knew, but he'd taken it like a lamb. She would not be able to get Salome past sixteen unwed, but she might have her here for a few more months and it was a relief that the girl was not trying to murder her with dark looks every time she passed.

Then yesterday Antipas had brought the best news of all.

'Might you, my dear, be up to a little travel?' he'd asked her, as they'd sat on their private terrace enjoying a final glass of a delicious local wine before bed.

'Travel?' She'd been on alert instantly. 'To where?'

The answer had thrilled through her: 'To Rome.'

He wanted to take her to meet the emperor, he'd said. He thought Tiberius would be very taken with her and that he would see that, with her at his side, Antipas could be trusted to rule more of the Holy Land.

'Judea?' Herodias had breathed.

'Perhaps, eventually. Your brother, Agrippa, is still in Rome, is he not?'

'He is,' she'd confirmed. 'I haven't seen him for years but ...'

'Family is family. I hear he moves in all the right circles, so perhaps he can put in a good word for us. The emperor simply needs to be helped to see that Judea could be so much more expertly run by someone who understands it. It shouldn't be hard, especially

75

if that idiot Pilate keeps rubbing everyone the wrong way. King Herod was a great friend to Rome, you know, and Rome to him. Personal connections – they work every time.'

'And you want me to come and make a, er, personal connection with Tiberius.'

He'd grinned. 'Not *too* personal, my dear. I'm not sharing you with anyone else.'

'Antipas!'

He'd leaned in and kissed her.

'Don't worry. The emperor is more interested in celestial bodies than human ones, of either variety. He has set up a great astrology laboratory on the island of Capri and has many learned men studying the stars.'

'What do they predict?'

'Greatness for a ruler of Judea, I am told.'

'You?'

'*Us*, sweet one. We are far greater together, just as I knew we would be.'

And then he had proceeded to show her just how great they were together in ways that made her body flame in recollection. She let out a small moan and Antipas turned from the window and looked down at her.

'How is a man meant to get out of his bedroom and on with the business of the day with such a temptation within it?'

She smiled lazily and nearly tugged him back down but then she remembered Rome and rose to join him instead.

'When will we leave, Antipas?'

'For Rome? After Sukkot? We would not want to miss the anniversary of . . .'

He let the word dangle but she needed no further reminder of that first marvellous night in the simple sukkot in the gardens of the Hasmonean palace. That was the night he had asked her to marry him, the night he had shown her that she was not dried out yet, either as a woman or a political force.

'We would not,' she agreed. 'But will the seas still be open that late in the year?'

'Just. It will be good timing. We can impose ourselves upon Jerusalem then sail from Caesarea Maritima. If we are lucky, we will be able to travel to the port with the Governor.'

'Lucky?!'

'Lucky, in that news of our impending visit to the emperor will surely cow Pilate into good behaviour.'

Herodias frowned.

'I would rather lure him into bad; it is a surer way of getting rid of him.'

'You, my wife, are a wicked woman.'

Antipas reached out and grabbed her, pulling her close so that she felt his arousal hard against her. She licked her lips. Maybe the packing could wait a little longer . . .

❖

Herodias looked down the dinner table, noting the empty plates with satisfaction. The new chef she'd recruited was excellent. The lake-fish with olives and garlic had been delicate, the wild boar rich and succulent, and the figs in honey the perfect way to round off the palate. Their guests, two foreign ambassadors from Persia, were sitting back with sleepy contentment and all they would require now was a little goat's cheese and sweet wine to send them home ready to tell all they met of their sumptuous hospitality. If she and Antipas could gain a reputation as fine hosts, it would surely help their bid for Judea.

Antipas was looking at her with pride and even Salome had been on her best behaviour. She was getting more beautiful with every day. Truly, sometimes, it was like looking in a mirror of her own younger self, save that Salome was nowhere near as biddable. She'd asked to visit her father again just before dinner, which was awkward, given that she hadn't had a chance to show her the letter yet. Well, maybe she'd had the chance but, if she was honest with herself, she'd avoided it. The girl had been so much nicer this last week and she didn't want to ruin it all with the news. It wasn't as if Boethus was going to be any less dead in a few days, and there wouldn't have been time to get there for the funeral anyway.

Herodias looked nervously to Salome, who'd been very graciously asking their guests all sorts of questions about their homeland. In fact, she was still at it. Herodias really must explain to her the difference between showing an interest and becoming intrusive.

'Do you know any Zoroastrians?' she was asking the elder of the two.

Herodias squinted at her daughter. Zoro – what? She vaguely remembered Boethus muttering something about them at one point but had paid little attention.

'Of course,' he agreed easily. 'I am a practitioner myself.'

'Truly?' Salome looked as if he'd said he was made of gold. Herodias glanced to Antipas but he seemed as confused as she. 'You believe in one God, as we do?'

'We do, Princess – one God who will come to earth to save us all. It is written in the stars.'

'In the stars?' Herodias questioned, confused. She really should have refused that last glass of wine, but it had all been going so well.

'The Star of David will herald the coming of the Messiah and the angels will sing of his glory.'

'I see,' Herodias said. 'And how will we know this star?'

'It will be low and bright and steadfast in its travel across the skies.' He leaned in. 'Some say it has already been seen.'

'When?' Salome gasped.

'Thirty-two years ago. Our most learned priests tracked it in the Eastern skies.'

Herodias looked sideways at the man. He had a piece of fish in his long beard and his eyes were hazed with wine.

'So where is this Messiah then?' she asked, as gently as she could manage, though clearly this was all nonsense.

'He has not yet shown himself.'

'In thirty-two years?!'

The man shifted.

'It is possible. He could have been a child.'

'The Messiah? A child?'

'Well, not any more, obviously. We shall just have to keep watch.'

Antipas leaned forward.

'You think it likely?'

The ambassador shrugged.

'I think it possible. There is a man preaching much the same thing around Jerusalem, I believe? An Essene? I think he's called John?'

Herodias prayed for patience. This was all she needed.

'Have you seen him?' she asked.

'I have not, gracious lady.'

'Well, if you did you would not be so credulous. He is a wild man, who tells everyone they should live in poverty. He was thrown out of the Essene community for being too extreme.'

'Many prophets have been persecuted,' the Persian said, nodding his head sagely.

'And many fools have tried to pass as prophets.'

'True, true. Crowds follow this John though, do they not?'

'They do,' Salome agreed. 'And his cousin.'

'His cousin?' Herodias sat up straighter. 'There's another of them?'

'Jesus,' Salome told her. 'He's a carpenter working here in Tiberias.'

Herodias looked to the richly decorated ceiling and counted to ten.

'You're telling me that the Messiah, the Saviour of the Jewish race, is being heralded by a wild man in the desert and a carpenter from Galilee?'

'It does sound a little unlikely,' the second of the ambassadors said. 'Ooh, cheese lovely!'

Salome, however, the little brat, was not to be deflected.

'Many people follow them. They say John is most eloquent.'

'For a wild man,' Herodias qualified.

'For any man. And Johanna says Jesus tells wonderful stories.'

'Stories?!' Herodias threw her hands in the air. 'Enough of this. Please, gentlemen, help yourselves to cheese. And some sweet wine, perhaps?'

She waved the head server over and the conversation was thankfully ushered out on the deep gurgle of wine in glass. Or so she thought. The elder man drank deeply and then looked at her over the rim of his drink.

'I hear this John is very critical of divorce.'

Herodias jumped and a piece of gooey cheese fell from her knife and onto her best dress. She bit back a curse.

'Many are,' Antipas said lightly.

His own wine, she noticed, was going down fast.

'Especially those, like this man, who have never married themselves,' Herodias snapped. 'The Essenes advocate celibacy you know. Where, I ask you, would we all be if everyone followed that teaching?'

'Heading for oblivion,' the second ambassador supplied obligingly. 'And even quicker if we all gave up work to preach.'

'Exactly!' Herodias beamed at him. 'It is good, of course, to have thinkers and teachers amongst us. It is, indeed, essential for a civilised society. That is why we have priests, learned men who study for many years to understand the law and scripture so they can guide us appropriately. These men, these peasants, are simply standing up and spouting their own ideas and we are meant to take them as law.'

'I'm told they know the scripture very well,' Salome put in. When would the wretched child go to bed?

'As they should – as all good Jews should. It is why we are taught it as children, why we attend synagogue, why we travel to Jerusalem every Pesach. The scripture is the bedrock of our faith, granted to Moses on Mount Sinai and expounded throughout the years by those who devote their lives to its understanding.'

Salome shifted.

'That is true, Mother.'

'Thank you, Salome.'

'But surely it does not mean that no one else can have an opinion?'

'Of course not,' Antipas rushed to assure her. 'Debate is healthy.'

'It is,' Salome agreed. She looked to Herodias. 'Talking of which, when can I go and visit my father?'

Herodias swallowed. She crossed her fingers in her lap.

'Maybe next week?' she suggested. 'If you're not too tired?'

'Really?' Salome leapt up and threw her arms around her neck. 'Thank you. Thank you so much. I won't be too tired, really I won't. In fact, I'll go to bed now.'

'Oh, what a shame.'

'Well, if you really want . . .'

'No, no, no. It would be selfish of us to hog you, sweet one. Off you go and I'll see you tomorrow.'

Salome nodded and bestowed a kiss on both her cheeks and, to his barely hidden astonishment, on Antipas', then was gone. Herodias thought of the bad news she had yet to deliver and swallowed again. The cheese was as stuck in her throat as it was on her dress, but at least the conversation could be turned now.

'So, gentlemen,' she said, smiling on the Persians. 'How is the harvest back home?'

Chapter Nine

Salome

'Ah Salome. Come in, girl, come in. Take a seat. I have good news.'

Salome edged into her mother's rooms and eyed the low couch suspiciously. Herodias did not look like she had good news and Salome preferred to stand. Her restless legs were more easily controlled that way.

'Sit!' Herodias said.

Salome did.

'What news, Mother?'

Herodias clasped her fingers in her lap, rarely a good sign.

'You are a woman of property, daughter.'

'Property?' Now that Salome hadn't been expecting. 'Has my stepfather . . . ?'

'Not Antipas, no, although he has been very generous with you, has he not?'

'Yes, Mother. But then . . . ?'

'Your father has, er, gifted you land.'

'Why?'

'As a sign of his loving care. There's a letter.' She lifted a parchment and Salome reached eagerly for it but Herodias kept it back. 'This is excellent news for you as a woman, you understand that? It gives you independent means.'

'So I don't have to marry Philip?'

'No, no. That is, yes, you do. It is right for the family.'

'Of course. And if it's right for the family . . .'

'It is right for you. Exactly. Besides, you swore a betrothal oath to one another, remember? The union has been blessed by the High Priest himself. There is no getting out of it now.'

'I could divorce him.'

'Salome! Divorce is only for extreme circumstances.'

'Of abandonment or cruelty, I know . . .'

Salome saw her mother flinch, but it was true. She'd checked. Nowhere in scripture did it state that you could divorce your husband – or wife – for political gain.

'Mine was a very particular situation,' Herodias said tightly.

'If you say so.' Salome shook herself. They could argue about this for hours – already had on a number of occasions – but today was not about Herodias. 'Where is this land Father has gifted me? And why did he not wait to tell me himself? I am travelling tomorrow.'

'Hmmm. This letter is two weeks old. It must have been delayed on the road.'

'Do you think, then, that he doesn't know I am coming?'

'I think that very likely, yes.'

Herodias was fidgeting in a way most unlike her usual self. Salome felt unease rise in her stomach.

'Where are these lands, Mother?'

She gave a little cough.

'He has gifted you his estates near Joppa.'

'All of them?'

'Yes.'

'But where will he live?'

Herodias looked a little green. Salome's stomach churned harder.

'I say gifted, my sweet one. I mean more . . . bequeathed.'

'Bequ . . . ?' Salome's fears solidified in her stomach and she had to dash to the window to throw them up into the flowerbeds. She stared down at the bile coating the poor plants and saw her own life swimming there. She swung back round. 'How dare you, Mother. How dare you tell me like this? Father is dead? He has died, alone and abandoned, without the care of those who most owed him it, and you choose to present this as "good news"?'

Herodias stared at her bullishly.

'The property is good news.'

'But drowned in the sorrow of his passing.'

'Land, thankfully, never drowns.'

'Mother! This is harsh, even for you.'

'We cannot shirk reality, daughter.'

Salome's legs buckled as the truth of the news overwhelmed the callousness of its telling. Boethus was dead. She would never hug him again, never sit at his feet and debate with him, never dance to the tune of his lyre.

'His funeral . . .' she cried.

'Is gone.'

'Without me there to mourn him as he deserved?'

'I'm sorry, Salome, but you know the dead must be buried before sundown on the day they die, especially in the summer. And he died just before the Sabbath. They could not have him defiling the land.'

'As the graveyard defiles Tiberias?' Salome threw at her.

'Boethus has a tomb. You can pay your respects there. You can still travel tomorrow.'

'Oh, I will.' Salome was awash with emotion. Sorrow swirled all through her, anger riding high on its back. She seized at the anger. 'I will travel and I will mourn him and I will live there, on *my* lands, until such time as I must marry. You are right, Mother, this "gift" is indeed good news, for it will get me away from you.'

'Salome! You do not mean that. You are upset, sad . . .'

'Furious! You tore me from Father with barely a moment's notice. You deemed me woman enough to be betrothed but not woman enough to be taken into your confidence about your own marital plans. You dragged me to a fortress in the mountains in case King Aretas – rightly – attacked your new husband for his disrespect and cruelty to his daughter, and then you brought me

84

here, to a defiled city and, as a final indignity, hid the news of my father's death from me.'

'The letter was delayed on the road.'

'It was delayed in your bosom, Mother. That was cowardice. You are all cowardice and I have had enough.'

Salome ran out of her mother's elegant rooms and across the central courtyard to the main doors. The sleepy guards leapt to attention.

'Open them please.' They looked nervously to one another and then to Herodias, who had followed her out. 'Open them!' Salome shouted.

They jumped to it and she stepped through.

'Where are you going?' Herodias demanded.

She had no idea, just knew that she had to get away from the clagging beauty of this stolen palace.

'Out.'

'Salome, no. Not into the city.'

'Why not? I am safe surely, as daughter of the respected ruler? And as a woman of property?'

'Salome, you are being foolish.'

Salome stopped and glared back at her mother, framed in the doorway.

'At least I am not being cruel. Thank you so much for the good news. Goodbye.'

It was only once she was out and marching down the street that she realised she had not asked for the letter. Her heart ached to read her father's words but she was not going back now. Boethus was dead. It must have been his cough. She'd known it was more serious than he was letting on, known it had weakened him. That was, most likely, why he had not fought her leaving. He had wanted to spare her his decline.

'Why Father?' she threw at the relentlessly blue skies. 'I would have nursed you. I would have cared for you.'

Why drag it out? she could almost hear him reply. He had never been one for fuss. He'd hated crowds, despised doctors, been happiest when at one with his plants. He would have died like a wounded cat, she knew, curled up alone and surrendering to his fate. The thought of it cracked her heart and she walked faster and faster, with no idea where she was going save that it was as far away from the palace as possible. What use was being a princess if you could not even be with your father on his deathbed? What use were riches if they could not buy you cures? What use were lands if you could only pass them on to someone else?

She thought of the Essene, John, urging people to live in poverty. Was loss easier if you had little to lose? She was not fool enough to believe that to be true. Poverty, as far as she could tell from her privileged position, was a curse that brought little but ill health and suffering, and it seemed to her that only those who could step out of it again if they chose might actively embrace its charms. This John was from a good family. Johanna had been looking into him and had told her the other day that he was the son of Zechariah, a priest in Judah, who had served in the Inner Temple. He was cousin to a prosperous carpenter and an educated man who had lived with the Essenes. If he tired of life on the road, he had places to go – unlike those he was exhorting to hand over what little they had.

If John's father dies, I bet he'll get to his funeral, she thought miserably. And then hated herself for it. This was hardly the Essene's fault, but her own. Why had she not refused to leave with her mother and Antipas? Why had she been so passive, so meek? Yes, Boethus had told her to go but he had not meant it. He had been trying to leave her free to choose and, like a fool, she had simply let Herodias carry her along. Well, never again.

Salome turned down another street, noticing as the shade closed in on her, that she had made it out of the bright main streets and into the tighter districts at the outer edges of Tiberias. Here the roads were narrow, the doorways so close that one man could spit onto another's doorstep. There was no marble, no cobbles, no gracious walkways. People huddled in alcoves and squatted on the street. From within the packed buildings, the chatter of voices mingled with the ring of hammer on steel, the grind of hand mills and the cries of children. Salome shrunk back and turned to try and retrace her steps, but this area was a maze and she'd paid too little attention to be sure which way was home.

'It's not home,' she said fiercely, then picked a road and followed it.

Before long she came out in a small square. Children were playing in the dirt, mothers keeping half an eye on them as they queued for a small clutch of market stalls in one corner. It must be break time in some workshop or other for men were lounging against the walls at the shady side, chewing on tough slices of bread and wizened meat. Everyone's tunics were dark and worn, laundered many times, and Salome felt desperately self-conscious in her fine palace gown and skirted around the edge, looking for another way out.

'It's alright for the likes of them,' she heard one man say to his companions. 'My wife'd kill me if I divorced her to shack up with something better.'

Salome froze.

'And God would strike you down if your wife didn't. That's what John says, the one who's preaching in the Jordan. Heard him myself, on the way back from Jerusalem. It's against scripture to put your wife aside.'

'Or your husband.'

'And quite right too or what sort of a mess would we all be in? It's a Roman thing, John says.'

Salome startled as spittle hit the dust from every quarter.

'No morals, the Romans.'

'No manners.'

'No sense of decency.'

Salome supressed a smile at the sight of these lowly men denouncing the decency of the prim Romans but the man's next words were darker.

'No shame, coming here, taking our money to fund their precious empire. And them lot at the top are no use. Do they stand up for us? No! Do they fight to keep the Holy Land for the Jews? Oh no! Just roll over and suck their damned dicks.'

'Moshe, hush! The children.'

Moshe tutted loudly.

'The children need to learn to stand up and not let themselves be shafted for the sake of a bit of marble and some fancy piping. That lot aren't even kings any more and still they kowtow to Tiberius, jumped up little Italian. That divorce was "decreed" by the emperor. The emperor! What does he know of Jewish law, or custom? What right does he have to interfere in Jewish affairs?'

Salome pressed herself against the wall and looked around, both fascinated and repulsed. What the man said was true, she supposed, but it was also dangerous. There were far less Roman soldiers in Tiberias than Jerusalem but there was still a garrison stationed here – a condition of the building of the city – and they could surely appear if there was trouble.

The men were greeting Moshe's pronouncements with rough acclaim, banging their eating knives against the wall and shouting agreement. Salome noticed the women abandoning their purchases to whip their children home and looked around again for escape but there were only two roads out of the square and they were both blocked. She should perhaps step into the gaggle of mothers and let them carry her away from the bubbling rage of the menfolk, but several of them had shot her dark looks and she could not trust them not to point her out.

'Salome!'

She spun round and, to her huge relief, saw a familiar figure running over.

'Johanna! What are you doing here?'

'Following you, idiot. What are you doing in this part of the city?'

'Hearing some truths.'

'Hearing some *opinions*. Come on, let's go.'

'Gladly,' Salome agreed, but their way out was still blocked and now people were looking curiously at them.

'Hey, you girl – who are you?'

'Just maids,' Johanna said, her voice rougher than Salome had heard it before.

'Fancy maids in those clothes.'

'Palace maids,' one suggested.

'That one's called Salome,' another cried. 'I heard it.'

Johanna grabbed at Salome's hand and Salome felt her fingers hot and clammy in her own. She clutched at her.

'Isn't the fancy new princess called Salome? Daughter of the whore.'

Salome prickled.

'She's not a whore,' she shouted.

'Oooh!' The man called Moshe came striding across, one hand in his belt, the other holding his eating knife aloft. 'So, seducing another woman's husband doesn't make you a whore then?'

'No more than seducing another man's wife!'

'Salome,' Johanna hissed. 'You're not helping.'

'What would you know, Princess? Bet you're a virgin.'

'For now,' someone added menacingly.

The men were drawing close, bringing the heat of their bodies, the musk of their sweat, the pulse of their communal menace.

'You wouldn't dare,' Salome said, as fiercely as she could manage.

'Oh, wouldn't I?' Moshe thrust his hips at her and the men at his back cheered. 'John the Baptiser says that we shouldn't keep our wealth to ourselves. He says that we should share what we have – *all* of it.'

Salome was shaking all over but she'd got herself into this, Johanna with her, and she had to stand strong.

'He also says that we should be celibate.'

Moshe frowned.

'Does he?'

89

'That our bodies are God's Temple on this earth and must be revered.'

'That can't be true.' He looked back to his men. 'How could that be true?'

Salome had no idea if John had said anything like that, but this was her chance and she seized it. Dragging Johanna with her, she ducked through the slim gap between Moshe and his backers and made for the now thankfully clear side street. Several of the men cried out, but she and Johanna had a head start on them and ran with all speed, ducking and twisting through streets that were, thankfully, widening with every turn, and praying that, somehow, they came into a more orderly part of the city before the men baying behind them caught at their skirts and brought them to the ground to do God knows what to them. Salome heard Johanna panting and glanced back to her rounded belly in fear. She could not lose the baby, not on her account.

'Here!'

To her huge relief, she caught a glimpse of translucent blue that could only mean the water and pulled her friend towards it. They stumbled out onto the lakeside to see they were at the north end, where the fishing and trading boats docked. The palace was within sight along the curve of the water but it was a way off yet and there were many rough men working the docks who looked up curiously as their pursuers crowded after them.

'Grab them!' Moshe called. 'They're traitors and whores.'

'We are not,' Salome shouted back. 'We're just women, carried on the tide of men's affairs.'

'I'll carry you into my bed, you insolent whore!'

'In there!' Johanna gasped.

She could barely speak but she pointed desperately to the law courts, just a few buildings further down the lakeside. The men were closing in fast and they wouldn't make it on time but Roman soldiers were guarding the steps and looked over at the fuss.

'Help!' Salome screamed. 'Please, help!'

The guards stood to attention and two, at command from their superior, moved towards them. The workmen hesitated. Salome tried to pull Johanna on but she was doubled up over her taut belly, gasping in breath.

'Help!' she cried again. 'These men are trying to assault me.'

Her voice sounded cultured, even to herself, and as the Romans got closer she saw them note her fine clothing and cream-smooth skin and move faster. Within moments they were either side of her and Johanna, swords drawn. Salome felt relief course through her, though run through with shame.

'Them lot at the top are no use. Do they stand up for us? No! Do they fight to keep the Holy Land for the Jews? Oh no! Just roll over and suck their damned dicks.'

Is that what she was doing here?

'I haven't run to these men because they're Romans,' she called to the crowd, not that they heard her.

Her pursuers were prowling still but the first two soldiers were joined by more and the locals paused, milling around furiously.

'Whore!' they shouted. 'Daughter of a whore.'

Anger bubbled deep inside Salome. Her mother was a calculating, ruthlessly ambitious, fiercely determined woman. But she was not a whore.

'Divorce is not the worst of crimes,' she shouted back.

'Salome!' Johanna panted desperately. 'Shut up!'

'John the Baptiser says it is.'

'John the Baptiser is but one man.'

'And you but one woman – and a worthless one besides.'

Salome bit back tears. They were just words, stupid, tangled, ignorant words. She should close her ears and walk away, but it was hard with the men ahead and Roman soldiers behind.

'I ...' she started, but at that moment Moshe bent, picked up a stone from the road and, jeered on by his impromptu followers, flung it hard in her direction.

Salome caught the movement and ducked, but not in time. She

felt the stone connect with the side of her head, felt the bite of pain and the bloom of blood, hot across her face. The blue skies swirled into the marble pavements and she staggered. A roar of triumph filled the air, followed by more of fury and fear. Salome blinked sticky redness from her eyes and sunk to her knees, Johanna's arms going around her as the soldiers closed ranks.

'Get them out of here, fast!' she heard one soldier hiss.

She felt people tug on her arms but the noise and the smells and the nauseous taste of iron filled her being and she could not make her legs work. And then, over the melee, came another voice – loud and clear and ferocious.

'How dare you! Get back. All of you. Get back before I have each and every one arrested, thrown into the cells and tortured until you cannot walk, or eat or hug your children goodbye as you are ripped from this miserable world.'

'Mother?' Salome croaked.

How could it be? Was she dead? Was she dreaming? She fought to listen but her head was spinning so.

'Carry her,' the voice was ordering. 'Gently. And bind that wound, now. I don't care what with. Here.'

Salome heard a rip of fabric and felt hair brush, soft and scented, across her face before a silken fabric was wound around it.

'Tighter, man! It's a bandage not a fashion accessory. Oh, here!'

The fabric tightened so that Salome gasped at the constriction, but it did, at least, seem to be holding her head together so that a handful of thoughts found some purchase in her befuddled mind. She forced her eyes open to see that she was being carried up the steps into the blissful peace and cool of the law courts. Someone laid her on a marble bench, cold and hard beneath her, but the next moment someone else was sliding their own body beneath her head and cradling it tight against a bulging bosom. Salome heard the fierce beat of an angry heart and let it thud through her.

'Don't die, Salome,' Herodias whispered. 'Please, please don't die.'

'I won't,' she promised. 'I won't, Mother.'

'Oh, thank God.' Herodias let out a small sob, swiftly contained, and the last thing Salome heard as she slid into blissful rest against her, was her tight command: 'Arrest the stone thrower, now! And arrest John the Essene. What for? Inciting riot of course. And ordering harm on the royal princess. He will pay for this. I swear to God Almighty, he will pay.'

Chapter Ten

Herodias

Rome! Herodias peered out at the streets as they unfolded before her and thought there was something of Jerusalem about this mysterious city at the heart of the known world. Certainly, she felt she knew it already. Perhaps it was because as a child she had plied traders for details of the place, jealous that her brothers had been sent there for schooling whilst she had been left in Judea with her grandmother. Perhaps it was because she and Antipas had passed the time on the long journey around the Green Sea with him sharing his memories of his ten years there as a young man. Perhaps any capital city had this bustle, this noise, this mix of the very rich and the very poor, but she certainly felt strangely at home here.

'It's not as pretty as Tiberias,' she said to Antipas.

He beamed.

'Nowhere is as pretty as Tiberias, though there are improvements to be made yet.'

He reached for her hand and she let him take it, because it felt rude not to, but the reminder of the way trouble had boiled up in the lakeside city still made her want to storm and rage and throw things. Seeing her Salome stood there, flanked by just two spotty young soldiers, facing down a whole gang of ruffians to tell them

94

her mother was not a whore had affected Herodias more than she cared to admit. It crept into her mind at all times of the day and night, making her tingle with pride in her daughter and horror at the danger she had put her into. Thank God, she and Johanna had made it to the law courts and thank Him too that she'd been there that day, meeting the new judges. If Salome had died . . .

She shuddered.

'They are all locked up,' Antipas assured her.

'Including the bastard baptiser?'

'Including him, as well you know.'

'I know he should be dead. Those men threatened to rape my poor daughter because of his so-called preaching.'

'He did not actually tell them to do it though, Herodias.'

'He might as well have done. If you're going to put yourself in a position of authority then you have a duty to explain your teachings fully, not just throw them out as crunchy little morsels to be chewed up and spat out however the hearers wish. Those men were workers, simple folk whose only scriptural learning comes from the teachers in the synagogue and the preachers on the road. Who gave this Essene the right to tell them what to do? Has he any training? Does he answer to anyone? No!'

'You are right, of course,' Antipas agreed, 'and I will tell him as much when I interrogate him on our return.'

'You think he will listen?'

'I think he has the right to be given the chance. The people are easily riled. We know this from long experience; perhaps he does not.'

She gave a bitter laugh.

'You are too kind, Antipas.'

'Merciful, my love. It is a good quality in a leader.'

Herodias wasn't so sure about that. How heavily did mercy to one individual weigh against the security of the rest? Was it not a mercy to Salome, and to other women like her, to cut off the sort of evil men who thought it was their place to pound their own vicious, self-gratifying punishment into them? This Essene to be fair – if she must be – had not called for vigilante justice and the men, however simple, must stand up for their own boorish crimes, but still … She would be carrying out her own interrogation of this self-styled baptiser when they returned to the Holy Land.

For now, though, he was locked away in the impenetrable fortress of Machaerus, where he could do little harm and they just had to pray that the other one, his cousin, didn't take up his banner. She'd heard rumours that just before her men could get to John, he'd baptised this other man, this Jesus, and told everyone to listen to him. And that they were doing so – ignorant sheep. The Sadducees and Pharisees were getting hot under the collar about it and even the Essenes had dissociated themselves from these renegades. Antipas needed to kill John and cut the poison from the wound before it spread. Why could no one see that the Jews had enough enemies without stirring up trouble amongst themselves?

Herodias ground her teeth in frustration, then closed her eyes and told herself to calm down. It would wait. For now, she was in Rome and she had important business here. She wished Salome could be with them, but the girl had still been fragile and the doctors had advised against the rigours of travel. Johanna and Chuza had gladly offered to care for her and, in truth, they would do a better job than Herodias for she was not a woman made for bedsides. Her only concern was that Johanna's baby was due this winter, which might distract them from the princess. Still, the palace was full of staff, Salome was a big girl, and the whole episode had dampened some of her rebellious spirit, so it should be well.

Herodias' job, now, was to work her charms on the emperor and secure control of the Holy Land once more. Then they could stamp out the rebels and bring the people together as one strong, united group. King Herod had functioned perfectly well as King of the Jews beneath Roman tenure and Herodias was determined to convince Tiberius that she and Antipas could do the same. She had to focus.

'Will we see my brother tonight?' she asked Antipas.

'I am assured he will be there.'

'About time.'

They'd been in Rome for three days but Agrippa had apparently been too caught up in business to see them until now, and that only because they'd all been invited to a soiree hosted by some senator called Sejanus. Herodias had never heard of him but apparently the emperor was off stargazing on his island at the moment and this man was in charge of Rome. It seemed very peculiar to Herodias. Did the man not have family to deputise, rather than leave the whole empire in the command of some ex-soldier? And when was Tiberius coming back? These did not seem to be questions that anyone in the city could answer and she was very much hoping Agrippa would be more forthcoming.

The carriage climbed up the Palatine hill, where the wealthiest of Rome's citizens had their homes. There had been a prohibition on royalty within Rome's boundaries some years back that had created a rumpus when the city had feared Julius Caesar was trying to make himself king. Ironically, it seemed, his murder had ushered in the era of the emperor – a title more royal than royalty – and the stupid rule had been quietly forgotten. Not that she and Antipas were king and queen anyway. Not yet.

Herodias smoothed out her dress, hoping that it would be sufficiently imposing. Rome's females seemed to dress in a surprisingly dowdy style, especially given the way they romped in and out of each other's husband's beds. No one here had blinked an eye when Herodias had admitted to her divorce. She might just as well have said that she'd had a knee bandaged, or a gloss-treatment on her hair.

'Oh, me too,' so many women had told her. 'How do you find the second one?'

It had been most refreshing.

Even the emperor, it had emerged, had divorced his first wife, although that seemed to have been at the command of the previous emperor, Augustus, in order to marry Augustus' sister and secure the succession. It had not gone well. The second wife, Julia, had been so notorious a bed-hopper that eventually Augustus had been forced to banish her for bringing disrepute on the royal house. To add to the chaos, Tiberius had apparently wept in the street whenever he'd seen his rejected spouse so that she too – through no fault of her own – had been sent away.

These days, it seemed, Tiberius preferred the company of scholars and stars and came rarely to Rome. He preferred to be with a shipload of astrologers, who spent half their days on his island, indulging the emperor's interest, and the other half teaching promising young nobles such as his two young heirs, Caligula and Tiberius-the-Younger. That was an annoyance but Herodias had enquired about the location of this Capri and it was not so far down the coast of Italia. They could easily go there on their way home if that was what it took to see the man. Her brother would know the best thing to do.

They had arrived at a very fine villa and were shown inside by the light of a hundred torches. A number of guests were milling around in the beautiful gardens at the rear and Herodias felt a tingle of excitement. She hadn't been to a party for ages. Musicians were playing softly under a marble pergola at the centre, dancers and acrobats were performing at every turn, and myriad servers, in very scanty costumes, were carrying around wine in large jars.

'Salome would love this,' she said, watching as a small group of young women performed a pretty dance.

'We'll bring her next time, my love.'

'She'll be a married woman.'

'So we'll bring them both.'

He had an answer for everything and she reached up to plant a spontaneous kiss on his lips. He looked surprised.

'What was that for?'

She shrugged.

'For being here, for bringing me to Rome, for always seeing the best in situations.'

He raised an eyebrow.

'Have you been at the wine without me, wife?'

She batted at his arm.

'I can say nice things to my husband, can I not?'

'Apparently so. It's a revelation.'

'Fool. Ah, look – is that Agrippa?' Antipas squinted into the bushes, where an athletic man was emerging with a flagon of wine, two young women in tow. 'Perhaps not,' Herodias said hastily. 'It has been a long time since I was with him; I must be mistaken.'

'I fear not, my love. I have heard tell that he enjoys the, er, charms of Rome a great deal. Agrippa!'

The man looked around and, spotting them, came bounding over.

'Antipas, good to see you man. And this must be my little sister. Herodias, welcome, you look marvellous. Wine? Goodness, where are your glasses?'

'We've just arrived,' Herodias told him.

'Even so. First rule of any party – secure a glass at the door.' He clicked his fingers and a serving girl hurried over. 'Glasses for my fine guests here, and fast. They are gasping.'

He gave the girl a loud slap on her behind to propel her forward and Herodias looked around, aghast.

'No rush,' she assured the girl, but she was already gone and was soon back with two pretty goblets.

'Perfect,' Agrippa told her, leaning down to run a tongue along the back of her lithe neck. 'If you're lucky, I'll reward you later.'

She gave a forced little giggle and escaped. Herodias looked at her brother as he sloshed wine into their glasses.

'Do you bed all the servers, Agrippa?'

'Only the pretty ones.' He winked blithely at her. 'Mind you, Sejanus, bless him, only employs pretty ones. It can be exhausting.' He clapped Antipas on the back. 'Plenty to go round, if you know what I mean.'

'I am quite happy with my wife, thank you.'

Agrippa laughed.

'Of course you are, of course you are. Still, if she chooses to retire early . . .'

Herodias stamped her foot.

'I'm right here, Agrippa.'

'Apologies, sister. There are plenty of young men here too. Mind you, they're usually grabbed by the senators, so you'll have to be quick.'

Herodias frowned.

'Is all Rome bedding each other, brother?'

'Not all Rome, no.' He nudged her. 'You have to know the right places to look. Ooh, Vespasia darling, over here. You have to meet this one. She likes two at once, if you know what I mean.'

Herodias had had enough of this.

'Agrippa!'

'What? Never tried it, sister? You should.'

'I am not here for sex, thank you very much.'

'Really? Shame. There's loads of it about.'

'So I see. I have plenty at home, thank you, so am here to meet the emperor.'

'Meet the . . . ?' Agrippa burst out laughing. 'Did you hear that, Vespasia?' The young woman had reached them and was smiling vacuously at Herodias as Agrippa slid a hand down her handily loose gown. 'My sister here wants to meet the emperor.'

'Don't we all,' Vespasia said, simpering.

'Don't we all,' he agreed. 'Actually, no, I don't. I hear he's boring as hell. Likes to spend his nights looking at stars.'

'I hear there is much to be read in the stars,' Herodias said.

'Not as much as in the body of a beautiful woman.'

Herodias looked to Antipas, infuriated; they were getting nowhere.

'When is the emperor coming back to Rome, brother?'

'Never.'

'Sorry?'

'Last thing I heard from Sejanus, Tiberius had announced his intention of staying on Capri forever. He never really wanted to be emperor anyway, but all the other heirs kept dying until he was the only one left. Now he's bringing up his own heirs in safety and letting Sejanus run the Empire.'

'And where is this Sejanus?'

'Your gracious host? He's over there.'

He pointed out a small, squat man holding court in the centre of the lawn.

'Heavens,' Herodias said caustically, 'he's not fondling anyone.'

'No,' Agrippa agreed. 'He's not really into sex. Power is what turns him on.'

Herodias looked to Antipas.

'Sounds like my sort of man. Shall we go and introduce ourselves, husband?'

It was with some relief that she left her brother, who was far too busy down Vespasia's front to even notice. Sejanus, however, was more interested in the minutiae of some land law he was discussing with two earnest old men, than in meeting Jewish royalty, and after several awkward minutes they were forced to withdraw.

'This is a most strange party,' Herodias said to Antipas.

He shook his head.

'Rome is a most strange place. Sometimes I wonder how they rule the world. All I can say is that their armies are far more effective than their politicians.'

Herodias looked around in despair.

'How are we ever going to make an impact?'

Antipas kissed her.

'Patience, my dear wife, patience. Something will turn up.'

❖

And something did, a little later in the evening, when a stately woman approached Herodias where she was resting on a bench and trying to take in the decadence of the evening. She was no prude – she was a divorced woman for heaven's sake – but this was something else.

'Herodias of Galilee?' the woman asked and Herodias jumped at the respectful title.

'That is I. And you are?'

'Kypros, your sister-in-law.'

Herodias seized the woman's hand.

'You're Agrippa's wife?'

Kypros gave a rueful smile and sat down next to her.

'I am.'

'You poor, poor woman.'

She laughed.

'He's not all bad. These parties bring out the worst in him.'

'How do you bear it?'

She shrugged.

'The man has a great deal of energy. I am pregnant with my fifth child.' She put a hand over a slightly swelling belly and Herodias fought back envy. 'So I'm, frankly, glad when he can run off a little of it on someone else.'

'But everyone . . .'

'Knows our business? Of course, this is Rome. But they know, too, that he would be nothing without me at his back. As does he. That puts me in a position to . . . command.'

Herodias smiled, liking this woman instantly.

'And do you have any influence with the emperor?'

Kypros rolled her eyes.

'I used to. Tiberius and I got on very well at one time but he's weary of Rome now and talks only to Sejanus.'

Herodias sighed.

'Sejanus barely even spoke to me.'

'He will. You just have to choose your moment. Leave it with me, Herodias. How long will you be here?'

'Until the seas open again,' she said. 'It feels a long time. I fear maybe *I* am weary of Rome and I have only been here three days.'

Kypros patted her hand.

'You are not in the right parts, that is all. Tomorrow I will take you into the Jewish quarter.'

Herodias felt a light flicker within her.

'There is a Jewish quarter?'

'Of course.' Kypros winked at her. 'Where is there not? If you are here all winter you can join us for Hanukkah.'

Herodias smiled her first genuine smile of the wretched party. Hanukkah! The festival of light, celebrating the rededication of the temple after her own Hasmonean ancestors had liberated the Holy Land two hundred years ago, was precious to her. She'd been willing to forgo it for this trip but already it felt like it might be a highlight. She'd been so looking forward to seeing Rome, to joining high society, to wielding her influence in the heart of the Empire, but so far it had been nothing but disappointment. No one here cared about Judea.

She shook her head at herself. Of course they did not. Why should they? As a child she had been jealous of her brothers coming to Rome for their education but with startling clarity she now saw that *she* had been the lucky one. She'd never been corrupted by this strange city, never had her Judaism watered down by warped Roman ways, never lost her roots. No wonder she was the only one in the family who truly cared about reclaiming the Holy Land, for she was the only one whose feet had trodden its earth all her life. Oh, Antipas said he did and she knew he was her best chance, but left to his own devices, he would be happy ruling pleasant little Galilee from his pretty new city.

No, if there was one thing this trip was proving to her it was that the security of the Jewish nation rested on her shoulders and hers alone. Already she couldn't wait to get back.

Chapter Eleven

Salome

Salome reined in her horse and stared up the sheer cliff to the dark fortress of Machaerus perched on top. It had been built by some Hasmonean king, Antipas had told her the first time they'd come here, just after he'd snatched her mother as his wife. Herodias, obsessed with her Hasmonean lineage, had been very excited but Salome, still furious at them both, hadn't been listening. Now she wished she had as she'd love to know a little more about the people who'd lived here before her. There'd been something about it being destroyed by some Roman general, like so many things around here, and then being rebuilt by Herod the Great – also like so many things around here. That king had loved builders.

'Are you ready to ride up the mountain, Princess?' Chuza asked.

She pulled herself from her thoughts to look at the steward.

'Have my mother and stepfather arrived?'

'Not yet, I believe, but they will be here within a day or two and the staff have made everything ready for you. Shall we go?'

'In a moment.'

'Of course, of course. Whenever you are ready. Though the sun is dropping, Princess, and the road can be perilous in the dark.'

Salome glanced to the sun that was, indeed, heading for the

cypress-topped horizon beyond the distant roofs of Jerusalem to the west.

'I'm sorry, Chuza. You're right – let's go.'

'If you're ready, Princess?'

'I am,' she agreed.

It wasn't true but she wasn't sure it ever would be and there was no point getting herself thrown off those craggy cliffs just because she was nervous of some man held prisoner within the fortress' thick walls. *Prisoner*, she reminded herself. John the Baptiser wasn't roaming free around Machaerus. He would be in some cell, most likely chained and under constant watch by armed guards.

How come then, a voice nagged in her head, as their little caravan of horses and wagons began the steady climb upwards, *he has people coming to Galilee to talk to Jesus*. What sort of prisoner sends envoys? And receives them in return?

It was Johanna who'd reported the rumours. A few weeks ago, Jesus the carpenter had left his labours in Tiberias to base himself in Capernaum, working out of the house of a fisherman, Simon Peter. The man was well-respected in the town, so Johanna had told her, and his wife, Perpetua was a good woman. Peter and his brother Andrew were hailing the carpenter as a great teacher and it seemed the people agreed.

Not only that, but he was getting a reputation as a healer and every evening at sunset, when the heat of the day had cooled enough to bring the sick from their beds, people gathered around him for help. Sometimes the fishermen took him out to the other lakeside towns in their boat and one night he had come to the dock-side at Tiberias, horribly near to where Salome had been hit by the stone. Salome had wanted to stay well clear but Johanna had been desperate to see him. Since Chuza had said he would accompany them and, remembering Jesus' kind eyes, Salome had gone, praying he was not attracting the sort of violent crowds she now feared.

Sure enough, it had been a peaceful gathering. Jesus had spoken in a low, firm voice that demanded attention and Peter and Simon, aided by two other burly fishermen, James and John, had kept order amongst those desperate for healing. Salome had not dared get close enough to see if he was successful but the oohs of the crowd had suggested they were content. That's when Johanna had pointed out a man, dusty from the road, who was being ushered through the crowd and right up to Jesus.

'You see that man,' she'd said. 'That's Peter's brother Andrew, come from John the Baptiser with messages for the carpenter.'

'He can't have,' she'd scoffed. 'John's locked away. Antipas would never allow it.'

'*Herodias* would never allow it,' Johanna had corrected her. 'But she was too busy tending you at the arrest and it was Antipas who gave the orders.'

Salome had blinked at her in surprise. Her father would never have dared go against her mother's wishes but, then, that's maybe why Herodias had left him for Antipas. And her mother had been disorientatingly concerned about her at that point. She could still remember her distraught cry: 'Don't die, Salome. Please, please, don't die.' Dizzy and in pain, she'd been unsure she was going to be able to obey but the scarf had stemmed the bleeding, her skin had thankfully knitted together fast and the stone did not seem to have penetrated her brain. Certainly, she felt no different than she had before; save, perhaps, a little more kindly disposed towards her prickly mother.

The climb had steepened now and she had to focus on the road ahead. Her horse was beautiful but made more for the open road than this mountain track and it was struggling behind the squat pack donkeys leading the way.

'Steady does it, Princess. No rush.'

She could hear Chuza's nerves in his voice and glanced back to give him a reassuring smile. The poor man should not have to be here with her. Johanna had given birth a month ago to a bonny boy and Chuza had been the very picture of pride. He'd had a sling made, big enough to fit his broad frame, and often carried his son, Chuza-Amos, around the palace to give his wife time to rest. Anyone who said carrying babies was not man's work, had been roundly told that he didn't see why women should get all the joy and, besides, it was never too early to learn the job of steward.

The rest had certainly done Johanna good for she had bounced back from the birth within a week and been out of bed and about the palace doing her usual clever work of praising others in theirs. The two of them were such happy parents and Salome had felt awful when the orders had arrived from Antipas that she was to meet him and Herodias at Machaerus on their return from Rome, and that Chuza was to escort her. The baby was far too young to travel so that meant Chuza would have to be separated from the baby and she'd known that would be painful.

'I can travel with a guard,' she'd assured him. 'I will be perfectly fine.'

'I don't doubt it, Princess,' he'd said easily, 'but I would be disobeying my orders if I allowed it. The Lady Herodias has specifically requested my presence at Machaerus. She is planning a fine event for the Lord Antipas' accession feast and requires my organisational skills to ensure it goes well.'

He'd looked proud at that and Salome had seen his love for his son warring with his duty and felt sorry for him. She'd leaned in.

'I don't want to go either, but we will not, I suppose, be away for too long.'

'Just enough time to dazzle your mother's guests.'

'And see the Baptiser,' Johanna had put in.

'He will be locked away,' Chuza had said hastily. That's when Johanna had reported the rumours of exchanges between John and Jesus and then taken Salome to see it for herself.

'But what are they doing?' Salome had asked, watching the earnest conversation from afar.

Johanna had shrugged.

'Organising their mission, I assume.'

'Mission?'

'Jesus preaches the New Way too, though a gentler version than John. It's all about love.'

'Love?' Salome had questioned. It wasn't something preachers usually mentioned, let alone focused on.

'Love,' Johanna had confirmed happily, snuggling up to Chuza and their son. 'Jesus says that all the laws and commandments boil down to two things – love God and love your neighbour as you do yourself. Jesus says that if we hold those two principles in our hearts and do our best to behave in accordance with them, then God will be pleased with us.' She'd flushed. 'I mean, there's more to it than that, obviously. I heard him speak up on Mount Eremos the other day and he was very eloquent, but that was the gist of it. Simple, right?'

'Simple,' Salome had agreed, though simple was, in itself, confusing. She'd been brought up, like all good Jews, to believe that the law was a complex and multi-faceted thing that could only be understood by those with years of training. 'Though if it's that simple, why do we need priests?' she'd asked Johanna.

'Maybe we don't,' she'd said happily. But at that Chuza had clapped a hand over her mouth, looking nervously around. She might just as well have said that they didn't need rulers and they'd all, bar Johanna, been grateful when little Chuza-Amos had decided he was hungry and wailed his way into the tricky conversation, bringing it to an abrupt end.

Now, though, as Salome guided her horse up onto the stark plain at the top of the cliff and faced the fortress of Machaerus, she thought about it again. Somewhere in here was the man who had started all this fuss – the man who had stood in the Jordan and told people that they had to turn away from their sins and live a good life before it was too late and the Messiah was upon them. Somewhere in here was the man who had baptised Jesus the Carpenter, hailed him as the 'Lamb of God' – the Pesach sacrifice at the very heart of the Jewish faith – and told everyone to listen to him. And they *were* listening. Jesus was no longer working with wood but with people, and Galilee was alive with his teaching. Salome had a lot of questions for John the Baptiser – if she dared ask them.

❖

It was the middle of the next day before she plucked up the courage to approach the cells where John was being held. Chuza was very unhappy about her going to see the prisoner but, with Herodias and Antipas not yet arrived, Salome was mistress of the fortress and put her foot down.

'It is not a . . . conventional imprisonment, Princess,' Chuza told her, scarlet in the face.

'I had gathered as much, Chuza. Do not worry. The Baptiser is not a conventional man.'

'You can say that again,' he muttered and escorted her to the archway leading down into the cells. 'I will stay with you at all times and there will be four guards.'

'Is he violent?'

'Not with his hands.'

'Then . . . ?'

'I am told his words can be sharp.'

She smiled at him.

'We can surely parry a few words, Chuza?'

He looked uncertain but he was, for all his many skills, not an educated man and it did not surprise Salome that the eloquent speaker she had last heard from the river Jordan intimidated him. The steps down to the cellars were steep and seemed to go on for ever. With every one, a little more of the spring heat of the mountains leached out of the air until they were right in the bowels of the castle. Salome thought of Boethus with a spike of longing. Her father had loved a debate. He would have been here with her, for sure, stamping into the cell to probe this strange man about his ideas.

The thought gave her strength and she picked up speed as the steps finally levelled out. They were in a long corridor with several barred cells on either side. The bars to the closest one, however, stood wide open and Salome could see the Baptiser on a padded stool, apparently deep in contemplation. Three younger men sat cross-legged at his feet, and against the wall a sturdy table was covered in parchment and ink. A sharpened quill sat in a smart holder and the whole place had more of the look of a hermit's dwelling than a prison cell.

Chuza coughed loudly.

'Visitor for the prisoner.'

The guards snapped to attention but John did not even seem to hear, so deep was he in thought.

'You!' the nearest guard shook his shoulder. 'Stand up for the Princess Salome.'

John lifted his head slowly. His blue eyes, when they fixed on her, were hazy but still full of understanding, and his nut-dark skin was unblemished by cuts or bruises. He had been treated well. He pushed himself to his feet and gave a small bow.

'To what do I owe the honour?'

Salome moved closer.

'Surely you do not deem it an honour, John the Baptiser, for you see all men as equal.'

'And all women besides, but any visitor is an honour if they come with an open mind.'

'I try,' Salome said, 'though I find my mind already filled with many teachings.'

He inclined his head.

'A wise observation. We teach our Jewish youth so much, these days, that we leave little space for them to find their own thoughts. Will you sit?'

He indicated a spare stool opposite his own, as if this were his house to host. Chuza gave a low growl of indignation but Salome slid quickly onto the stool and waved John to sit as well.

'You have come from Galilee, Salome?'

'*Princess* Salome,' Chuza snapped.

John inclined his head again, though he did not even glance the steward's way.

'You have come from Galilee, Princess Salome?'

'I have. We arrived yesterday.'

'Have you seen my cousin?'

'Jesus? I have.'

'He talks well, does he not.'

'People seem to think so. He gathers great crowds.'

'Good, good.' He leaned forward suddenly, reaching a bony hand towards her leg before another growl from Chuza gave him pause. 'This is a vital time, Princess. Vital! The second coming is upon us, I swear it.'

'On whose authority do you swear?' Chuza demanded, on high alert for blasphemy.

'My own alone, but others will see the truth of it soon enough. We must all look into our hearts and examine what we find there.'

'The Princess' heart is pure and good,' Chuza said.

Salome wasn't so sure about that. Some of the thoughts she'd harboured about her mother, for example, were far from pure or good.

'It is very kind of you to say so, Chuza,' she told him, 'but I am in no way perfect.'

'You are not!' John agreed, his voice rising suddenly. 'You are a sinner, Princess.'

'Here, now—'

'A sinner, as we are all sinners. God knows your heart. He knows its every crevice, its every secret. It is up to you to know it too. It is up to you to acknowledge your faults and commit to a better life.'

His voice cracked with passion and the sound of it battered around the low-ceilinged cell. Salome flinched but kept to her stool.

'And how do you propose I do this, John?'

He leapt up.

'You must give up your worldly wealth.'

'All of it?'

'All!'

'And what, then, will I live on?'

'God's grace.'

'God will keep me in food? And clothes? Are you sure?'

'If you turn fully to him, yes.'

'So why, then, are there so many in poverty and suffering? Why does God not keep them?'

'Because they are wicked. Because they do not submit to his will. They lie and steal.'

'Because they are hungry, surely?'

'Because their hearts are impure. I have lived in poverty this last year and here I am . . .'

'In prison.'

'Alive and well and preaching. God will release me when He sees fit.'

'You foraged for food?'

'I foraged in God's fine fields, yes. And lived on the charity of others.'

Salome thought about this.

'But if everyone lived that way, no one would grow any grain or mill any flour or catch any fish and there would be nothing to offer in charity.'

Chuza gave a low laugh.

'She makes a good point, Baptiser.'

'She makes a narrow, ignorant point, Steward.'

'How dare you . . . ?'

Chuza rose, one hand on the dagger at his belt, but Salome put out a hand to stop him.

'It is just debate, Chuza. Just words.' Chuza did not look so sure, but he stayed his hand. 'Why is it ignorant?' Salome asked.

'Because it assumes a view of the world as it is now, not as it could be. If no one owned any land, the crops could grow freely and all could eat the same.'

'True, but someone would still need to sow the seed and till the soil and chase away the birds.'

'All could work together, in harmony.'

Salome frowned.

'Have you been on a farm, John?'

He waved this away.

'If all are pure of heart, it will work.'

That much, Salome supposed, was true.

'If the Messiah can affect such harmony, then it will be a miracle indeed.'

'The Essenes manage it.'

'The Essenes who threw you out?'

He flinched.

'They are ignorant too.'

Salome glanced to Chuza. The conversation seemed to be going in circles.

'So in the meantime,' she said, 'you would have me sell all my worldly wealth.'

'Not sell it, give it away to the poor.'

'Of course. And, what – follow you?'

'Not me. I am but a voice in the wilderness, sent to hail the coming of the great one.'

'Your cousin?'

'Perhaps. Many are giving up their old, sinful ways of life to follow him.'

'You would have me leave my palace and take to the open road.'

'If you truly wish to find God's light, yes.'

She shook her head.

'That is not easy as a woman. I would be vulnerable.'

'Not if you walked in God's light.'

Salome thought of the workmen in the crowded little square – how quick they had been to single her out, how violent in their intentions. She had never been more scared in her whole life.

'It would not be how *I* walked that would be the problem, but how others did.'

'Pah!' John spat on the ground at her feet and she flinched back so that her stool rocked. Chuza sprang up again.

'These are excuses, Princess,' John growled, 'weak, lazy, fearful excuses.'

'We cannot shirk reality. My reasons are not weak, but cautious. Not lazy, but wary. And, yes, fearful. With good reason. Have you ever been raped, John the Baptiser?'

It was his turn to flinch.

'Of course not.'

'Because you are a man? You are lucky. It happens to women all the time, especially those out on the road alone.'

'God will protect you.'

'God protects those who protect themselves.'

'No!' It came out on a scream. 'You are not listening. God protects those who give themselves fully to him. You are too bound in convention, Princess Salome. You think too much of the earth and not enough of the skies. What of your afterlife?'

'My . . . ?'

Salome looked to Chuza confused. The man truly was mad.

'Those who turn to God will, when they die, be lifted into eternal bliss.'

'Where?'

'In the heavens with the angels.'

'You know this?'

'I am sure of it. I have studied the stars, I have conversed with wise men, I have communed with God.'

'You have? Directly?'

'As you can too, if you open your heart.'

'And my purse?'

'Yes! See how it ties you, see how it binds up all you do. Cast off those ties, Princess, embrace the freedom of poverty.'

She shifted. He was looking at her so intently and some of what he said made sense, but only some. What was the afterlife he spoke of? She had read nothing of it in scripture, heard no priest talk of it before.

'It is not easy for me.'

'It is not easy for anyone. Just because you have more to lose does not make the end result any different. Do you fear for your poor soft feet without fancy sandals? Do you worry about your fine white skin without baths and unguents? Do you fret for your beauty without a feather bed on which to rest your pretty head?'

'Of course not,' Salome snapped. 'I fret for my basic safety.'

'You think it was easy for me?' He jabbed a finger at her. 'You think I walked into this life without a second thought? My father is a priest, Princess. He trained me to follow him. He was disappointed when I left to join the Essenes and even more so when I split with them to carve out the New Way.'

'And that pleases you?'

'No! But some things are more important than family.'

She shook her head ruefully.

'You clearly haven't met my mother.'

At that, however, John went wild. He picked up his stool and cast it with surprising strength at the stone wall. The young men scrambled back, eyes wide, and at Chuza's signal, the guards leapt forward to grab him. He fought in their grasp, twisting and turning his sinewy body in fury.

'Your mother is a whore, Princess, a jezebel.'

'How dare you!'

'She is the symbol of all that is ill in this world, casting off duty and propriety to satisfy her carnal lusts and ambitions.'

'You know nothing of my mother, or her divorce. She is a strong woman, with the welfare of the Jewish people at the very core of her being.'

'She is a weak woman, driven by the base needs of the flesh and she should be wiped from the earth as the plague she is.'

Salome gaped at him, writhing and almost frothing at the mouth like the madman he must surely be. She drew herself up tall.

'I came to see you today, John the Baptiser, because I had been told you were a man of intellect and thought. It seems, in fact, you are as driven by easy assumptions of the way the world is as you have accused me of being.'

'I see clearly—'

'You see what you want to see. There are nuances to every situation and you might do well to consider things from others' points of view before you propound your "New Way" with such blinkered absoluteness.' She pushed back her stool and strode into the corridor. 'Steward, see this cell barred please. And escort the unauthorised visitors from the fortress.'

'With pleasure, Princess,' Chuza said, gesturing the guards to push the Baptiser's protesting acolytes from the cell and secure the gate.

'You'll regret this,' John screamed, still twisting wildly in the guards' grasp.

Salome turned her back on him and made for the steps, craving sunlight. She had come hoping for answers about the great events that seemed to be sweeping the Holy Land, but had been given only judgements and impossible instructions. It was most disappointing.

Chapter Twelve

Herodias

MACHAERUS
ADAR (MARCH) 29 AD

'Salome! You are well? You look well!'

In truth, the girl looked surly and withdrawn, but she hugged Herodias with surprising enthusiasm and Herodias hugged her back, glad of the warmth. It had been a long, hard trip from Rome. The seas had been high and they'd had to take the long way around the coast instead of cutting across via Cyprus. The food had been dire, water scarce and she'd felt caked in salt from dawn till dusk. Never had she thought that forbidding Machaerus would look so palatial.

'And you, Mother, are you well?'

'Well as I can be, considering.'

'Was Rome good?'

'Rome was ...' She thought about it, 'not as nice as here,' she concluded eventually. 'It is a funny place, Salome, filled with funny people. It is only eight hundred years old, you know, so they have no roots, no sense of history or legacy. Oh, they think they do, but to hear them speak you'd think Augustus a god from times past, not a man who died just twenty years ago. They revere Romulus and Remus, who supposedly founded the city, but these are a pair of orphans who were suckled by wolves. Funny basis for an empire, if you ask me.'

'Very funny. Did you meet the emperor?'

Herodias bit at her lip. All the way home, in the various ports and stopping places, she had sung the praises of her visit, told everyone how well received they'd been and how many influential people they had met. She talked of the emperor as if she had dined with him and slid over any direct questions with her silkiest diplomacy and she was worn out of it. Surely here, with her own daughter, she could tell the truth.

'We did not – though tell no one. The man's a recluse. He lives on this island called Capri, where he's built twelve houses to mirror the Zodiac and where he spends his time gazing at the stars and talking with scholars. He invites promising youngsters out there to study with him and believes that we can better understand the world if we understand the skies.'

'There are people here who think that too,' Salome said.

'What people? Not the bloody Baptiser?'

'No, not him. He's mad.'

Herodias looked at Salome sharply.

'You have talked to him?'

'Yes.'

'What about?'

'Everything and nothing.' She looked uncomfortable. 'I told you, he's mad. He wants everyone to live in shared fields and trust God to deliver prosperity.' She peered up at Herodias. 'Do you think that's possible, Mother?'

'Of course not. How could it be?'

'But is it not what the Israelites did in the desert for forty years?'

It was clear she had been thinking about this a great deal and Herodias took time to consider.

'That is true, I suppose, but they had Moses to lead them. Moses was a prophet, Salome, but he was also a leader and a law-giver. Their community had rules and boundaries to ensure fair living.'

'True, but what about everyone else, were they all equal?'

Herodias had no idea. She strained her weary brain trying to come up with something.

'I can only assume not, daughter, or else we would surely still be living that way now? Did Moses not set up the twelve tribes of Israel? And were there not clans within the tribes? This, surely, tells you that God wished so see us divided into manageable units.'

'That's true.' Salome looked relieved. 'Thank you, Mother.'

Herodias smiled at her.

'It is all in the Scripture, dear child, if you just know where to look.'

'Or which priest to ask?'

'Exactly! Thank the Lord for priests, or none of the rest of us would ever get anything done. Talking of which, we have a feast to prepare.'

'For my birthing day?'

Herodias swallowed guiltily. She had forgotten the girl turned sixteen shortly.

'For that, yes,' she said hastily, 'and also to mark fifteen years since your stepfather acceded to the tetrarchy of Galilee and Perea.'

'It is still a tetrarchy then?'

'Yes,' Herodias snapped, then felt bad. She reached for Salome's hand. 'I told you, we could not see the emperor. All we were permitted was a visit with his lieutenant and that only after a great deal of work on our behalf by my sister-in-law.'

She thought fondly of Kypros. The dear woman had hounded Sejanus to accept a dinner invitation until, with great and most ungracious reluctance, he had done so and Herodias had had a chance to try and work her charms on him. The man had, however, proved dry and dull. An ex-soldier, he was obsessed with the military and wanted nothing more than to talk swords and shields with Antipas. Her husband had risen to the occasion with his usual charm, engaging the man on every topic he chose until they could finally slip in a few hints about the governance of Judea but it had been swiftly dismissed.

'Pilate is a good man. He served under me, you know, on the Danube. A fine soldier.'

'He must miss military service,' Antipas had said slyly.

'Do you think?'

'How could he not? Sitting around in a provincial palace with little to do but mediate between bickering locals must be so much less rewarding than standing in line with your fellows and fighting for the Empire.'

'True, true. I miss the field myself, but Pilate and I both grow old. A man must know when his prime fighting days are over and turn to his mind as a finer weapon than his arm.'

Herodias had almost choked on Kypros' delicious lamb. There was *nothing* fine about Pontius Pilate's mind.

'It is hard for him, I think,' she'd said, 'governing the Jews.'

'It would be hard for anyone. They're an unruly lot.'

If the oaf had realised he was talking to a Hasmonean princess, he had made no sign of it. Herodias had bitten back several keen retorts and summoned all her patience.

'Their laws are old and complex, but very effective if astutely applied. The High Priests have great control if backed by the right leader.'

He'd swivelled suddenly in his chair and fixed her with beady eyes.

'You do not think Pilate is that leader?'

'I think Rome might be better served by a Jewish ruler. It would have to be one who understands Rome, of course, one who was, perhaps, raised here, but who can also appeal to the local population in a more ... intimate way than a foreign governor.'

Sejanus had given her a sly smile.

'You have someone in mind, I assume? Someone, perhaps, sitting at this table?'

She'd let her eyes slide to Antipas. In truth, if they could only secure the throne, she would be the one who truly understood the Jews, who could truly control them, but this rough-edged soldier had no way of understanding that and it had not been worth making him try.

'My husband was a great friend of the emperor's, you know,' she'd said. 'They were educated together. They write still.'

'I know. I read all his correspondence.'

'Of course. I'm sure he's very appreciative of your assistance. Even so, he might enjoy seeing his old friend again now that he has made such progress in his studies, do you not think?'

For a moment, a brief, glorious moment, she had thought Sejanus was going to say yes but then a server had leaned over to take his plate and he'd given a little shake of his head and said, 'That won't be possible I'm afraid. The emperor does not take visitors any more.'

If Herodias had been alone, she would have screamed and thrown things but polite society, even in Rome, frowned on such behaviour, so she'd had to grit her teeth and mutter something inane like, 'what a shame'.

'I will, however, pass on your concerns about Judea. There might be room for some ... adjustments.'

It had been the best she was going to get and she'd had to sit back with a stiff smile and try not to die of boredom as the conversation had swung back to swords. She knew far more than she cared to about blade design as a result and had only made it to the end of the evening by internally plotting which of Sejanus' organs she could most effectively dig out with which weapon given half a chance.

'Put it this way,' she said to Salome now. 'I have decided that it will be more effective to mount a campaign here, in the Holy Land, than to try and appeal to a recluse of an emperor, or his upstart of an advisor. That is why this feast must be the finest one seen in the area for many years. I have invited all the most influential people from Trachonitis in the North to Perea here in the South, and we will make sure they leave impressed with our style, wealth and ability to govern. Understood?'

'Understood, Mother.'

◈

Two weeks later and all Herodias felt she understood any more was the need to crawl into bed and sleep and sleep. The fortress at Machaerus was impressive but it was miles from any decent market and getting goods up the steep hill was hell. She'd spent a fortune on beautiful silks to hang from the dour walls in both the women's and the men's dining rooms and finally tracked down enough candles to make a decent display all evening long. The musicians and acrobats were ordered to keep people entertained and the menu was decided and in progress. Every bedchamber was cleaned and prepared, the servants' quarters had been cleared out to make way for the many personal staff that would be coming with their masters, and Herodias' own gown had been completed just this morning. It was a little loose – all this running around had sent the flesh dropping from her bones – but better that than too tight.

She suppressed a twinge at the thought of the one reason why her gown might not have done up around the middle. She had still not bled since her marriage a year ago, but her belly remained resolutely flat and she could only assume her womb was, as she'd feared, closed for business. Antipas had not mentioned it once but the other day, after a particularly stirring evening in their bedchamber, she had felt the need to apologise. It did not come naturally so she'd been indignant when he'd laughed.

'Oh Herodias, I did not marry you to reproduce. God knows, another of you would be glorious indeed, but the one I have is enough for me.'

She could have cried. In fact, once the candle had been out and Antipas had slipped into easy oblivion, she *had* cried. Stupid really. Just tiredness. She'd be better once this wretched feast was out of the way. She glanced out the slit of a window for the sun. It was starting to tip down from its highpoint and people would surely start arriving once a little of the heat left the earth. Taking a last approving look at her gown, she headed back down to the hall to supervise the final preparations.

It looked magnificent, if she said so herself. The silks were bright, the vines and flowers lush, and the candles all ready for lighting. The musicians were here and setting up on the little stage in the far corner of the men's hall, and a small army of serving girls were sweeping the floors and chasing cobwebs from the ceilings.

'Perfect,' she said, clapping her hands.

'It is, my lady,' Chuza agreed, coming in through the rear door behind the top table. 'You have done a magnificent job.'

'With your help, Chuza. I know no one else who could have found so many candles.'

'I have built up a few contacts in my years, it is true.' He looked proud but uneasy too. Was he missing his child? He seemed to talk about the baby and his pretty little wife all the time. It was most peculiar. Herodias was used to having to ignore women's baby-babble, but to have it from a man was too much.

'All well, Chuza?' she asked reluctantly.

'Yes, my lady. There is just one small thing . . .'

'Which is?'

'The acrobats.'

Not his baby then, at least, though perhaps that would have been preferable.

'What about the acrobats?'

He swallowed visibly, his Adam's apple vibrating in his throat.

'They have sent a messenger to say that, sadly, they cannot make it.'

'What?! We found them ages ago. A contract was drawn up, terms agreed.'

'It was, my lady, and they have returned the deposit that we paid them with apologies.'

'What's wrong? Are they sick?'

'Not sick, my lady.' Chuza looked rather nauseous himself. 'Their leader asked me to tell you that two of their troupe have er . . . have converted.'

'Converted? To what? Monkeys? I'd have thought that would be helpful.'

Chuza attempted a laugh but it came out strangled.

'To the New Way, my lady.'

'The what?'

'New Way.'

'What new way?'

'It is a term coined, I believe, by, by . . .'

'John the bloody Baptiser?' He nodded miserably. 'Fantastic! And this "New Way" means you are not allowed to turn somersaults, does it?'

'It is not that, my lady. More that they are, are . . .'

'Spit it out.'

'They are boycotting the feast because you are holding—'

'John the bloody Baptiser.'

'Correct.'

'And they converted this morning, did they? They couldn't tell me any sooner because, what, the "New Way" doesn't allow for politeness or consideration?'

'It would appear not, my lady.'

Herodias sunk her head in her hands. They had the musicians at least, but the acrobats had come highly recommended by several local notables and she had been so pleased to secure them. The period after food could drag otherwise and with nothing to watch people drank too much and argued. This was a nightmare.

'How are they converting if John is locked up in here?'

Chuza looked even more miserable.

'It seems his cousin, the Galilean, is gathering quite a following. It seems he has stopped his carpentry and taken to the road, and everywhere he goes, people drop their tools and flock to hear him. He speaks well and is gathering a reputation as a healer. John has been hailing him as the . . . the Lamb of God.'

'The Lamb of God? A carpenter from Galilee? And how has he been "hailing" him, Chuza, from a cell below Machaerus?'

'Messengers have been travelling between them.' He put up his hands to ward off her anger. 'That's to say, they *were* doing. We have put a stop to it, Princess Salome and I.'

'Salome?'

'She visited him, ordered him locked away and his followers despatched.'

Herodias was impressed, but it still didn't solve the problem of this Jesus man romping around Galilee, stopping everyone working, or of her acrobats.

'Antipas!' He was here somewhere, she knew he was. He'd been out this morning, checking the meat from the hunt so he must be close. 'Antipas!'

The doors flung open and he came rushing in.

'Are you well, my love?'

'Am I well? I'm not sure. I am in full health, thank you very much, but am I well? That depends on whether having your prisoner sending out a full-scale mission of conversion to the "New Way" – a way, incidentally, that involves sitting around talking about love instead of doing any work – from our very own fortress in Perea, into our very own tetrarchy in Galilee.'

'What? How?'

'How indeed. Truly, Antipas, if you had just listened to me and had the man executed before we went to Rome things could not have escalated in this way. Now I find out that even acrobats are refusing to come because he is imprisoned here. We have no entertainment for our feast and, worse, we have a focus for sedition in our own fortress. People love a victim, Antipas, but their memories are short. A prisoner can be freed, a dead man can only be forgotten.' Antipas paled. Good. Perhaps now he would see what harm his indulgent tolerance was bringing to his own lands. 'We have to stop this, husband. We have to execute John.'

'On what charges? There are laws, Herodias, and he has broken none of them.'

'Incitement to riot.'

'He did not order those men to attack Salome.'

'Blasphemy. He is calling the carpenter the Lamb of God.'

'But not God himself? No? It is not, then, blasphemy.'

'Revolution.'

'A worry, for sure, but not actually a crime under Jewish law. Indeed, there have been times when we have actively encouraged it. Your own Hasmoneans led a revolution, did they not?'

'Against the enemy.'

'The enemy as defined by them. Any revolutionary would say the same.'

Herodias stamped her foot.

'Are you on his side?'

Antipas threw up his hands.

'Of course not. I find him every bit as irritating as you.'

'I doubt that.'

'But I must be seen to be a just and fair ruler, you know that. Are you not always telling me not to shirk reality?'

Herodias rolled her eyes.

'Fine. We'll just have to trap him. Bring him out to the feast.'

'What?!'

'Bring him out, after dinner. Chained, of course, but semi-free. He won't be able to resist the audience, I'm sure, and we'll soon get him saying something damning.'

'And if we don't? If he is so eloquent that he converts half our guests.'

Herodias shivered. Antipas had a point. It was a high-risk strategy but she was fed up with this. They had to wrest back control of the Holy Land from this band of peasants and tonight was as good a time as any.

'It's worth a try.'

Chuza cleared his throat.

'The man is raving, my lady. It may achieve your aim, but I'm not sure it will be as entertaining for your esteemed guests as the acrobats.'

'Yes, well, we don't have the acrobats, do we? They're too busy tumbling to their self-indulgent consciences. Where am I to get another act at this late notice?'

Chuza looked despondent but Antipas' eyes had lit up.

'Have you seen your daughter this morning, Herodias?'

'Salome? No.' There was another irritation. 'The damned girl has been carefully missing since we broke our fast, avoiding the preparations no doubt.'

'Perhaps, but I think she has just been lost in her own world.'

'Doing what?'

Antipas smiled.

'Dancing.' He came forward, sliding an arm around her waist. 'She is really very good, wife – professional almost.'

Herodias looked at Antipas as comprehension dawned. It wasn't ideal, a princess performing like a common dancing girl, but she had done it in Joppa before, to great acclaim. This was a closed party with only the finest guests and, really, what other option did she have?

'Very clever, husband,' she said. 'Very clever indeed. Almost you are forgiven for keeping this stupid Essene alive.'

'Almost?'

'Almost. Now, excuse me, I must find my daughter. We have musicians to talk to and a dance to plan.'

She clapped her hands. A royal dancer! If she played this right, it could work out even better than the acrobats. Bring on the feast.

Chapter Thirteen

Salome

Salome felt a small, possibly fond, shove in the small of her back and had to focus on keeping her balance as she was propelled into the centre of the men's dining room. It would hardly do for the professional dancer to fall flat on her face.

I'm not a professional dancer, she reminded herself and felt the panic that had been threatening to overwhelm her all day rise up through her entire body. How on earth would she make her limbs do what she wanted flooded with fear like this? How would her feet trace pretty steps, or her arms make graceful movements when all her poor limbs wanted to do was flee.

'Salome!'

The gasp of her name came from the top table and she looked over to see Philip sat at Antipas' right side. It was not he who had spoken, however, as he was looking at her with curiosity rather than surprise. No, the exclamation had come from several seats further down where she saw Ari, eyes wide and hand to his mouth as he stared at her standing before the men in her dancing costume. It was a modest dress, with flowing skirts, loose-fitting bodice and layers of scarves, but she felt she might as well have been naked for the way he seemed to drink in the sight of her. His admiration calmed her a little and she was able to move forward into the central spot from which she would start her dance.

It had seemed easy earlier in the day when Herodias had come rushing to her with the idea and hurried her into the hall to rehearse. She had been surprised her mother was prepared to let her dance in public, but excited by the honour. The floor was wide and the boards flat, the notes from the musicians' instruments had bounced pleasingly off the painted ceiling and her mother had been gratifyingly rapt in her praise. She knew now, of course, that she'd had no alternative, but at the time it had lifted her steps and she had enjoyed the dance. She could not see how that was possible now, with fifty men leering at her and all her mother's hopes for promotion resting on her slim shoulders.

The head musician coughed and she was forced to look his way. She held up a finger, begging for a moment to compose herself, though Lord knew it would take longer than that.

'What shall I dance?' she'd asked Herodias when she'd first set her in here.

'Oh, something that will please the men. Do you have one about war?'

'No, Mother!'

'Shame. No matter, they will just like seeing you move. Could you make it ... attractive?'

'Seductive you mean? I am a princess, Mother, not a cheap whore. It would surely dishonour you were I to parade myself ... ?'

'Not parade, Salome—'

'And give fuel to rumours about your own morals ...'

'True, true. Well, what do you have?'

In reply, Salome had thrown herself into a piece she'd been working on in the privacy of her own rooms ever since her stormy encounter with the Baptiser. It had little story, yet, for she did not know where it was going, but it had helped her give expression to some of the worries and fears in her head. In there, they pounded like a blacksmith's hammer on hot iron, but if she let them out through her arms and legs, they untangled slightly. She found no answers, but she did find a little peace.

'Perfect,' Herodias had said, clapping enthusiastically. 'No idea what it's about, but perfect. Lots of nice, er, movements.'

Salome had supressed a smile and signalled to the musicians to go through it again, pleased that her battle for expression had been a victory of sorts. Now though . . .

She looked again around the men. They were all leaning expectantly forward, mugs of beer and glasses of fine wine sloshing as they picked at the shreds of meat stuck in their teeth. The room was hot and smelled of male – a curious mixture of leather, sweat and something sharp and musky that Salome could only pinpoint as danger. Antipas tapped impatiently on the table. Philip placed a hand over his half-brother's and said something quiet in his ear, but the head musician was coughing again, more urgently now, and she could not just stand here like a fool.

She glanced back for Herodias, hidden in the shadows of the doorway, and saw her desperately nodding her into action. Squeezing her toes, she pushed herself up onto the balls of her feet and drew her hands slowly round into position before her. Her eyes strayed again to Ari and it was his smile and sudden, unexpected wink, that released her at last. She swept her leg round in the first motion of the dance and heard the flute trill out in response. The lyre joined and then the tambour and she half closed her eyes and let the music carry her. The men faded into mere shapes around the edges of the floor and, as she threw herself into the dance, she ceased to be a sixteen-year-old princess, forced to entertain her stepfather's guests, and just became herself, curving and swooping with the emotions driving upwards from within.

She was the River Jordan, swelling with pilgrims keen for baptism. She was a fishing boat on Lake Galilee, carried on a tide of words spoken by a man with kind eyes and a low, imperative voice. She was an old man, healed of his limp and a young woman no longer bleeding. She was love and she was compassion, but she was also power and control. She danced out the confusion these wild preachers had sent tearing through her mind. She danced out the questions they had set itching through her blood: Was it better to care for an individual's soul or the prosperity of the group? Was it better to break a law for love or to obey it for duty? Was Moses more a prophet or a leader? Was wealth a sign of favour, or an obstacle to salvation? Was there a life after the one trodden out on this earth and, if so, was the key to be found in deeds, or words or thoughts, or none of these?

Salome danced on, making shapes with her scarves, trailing the blue one like water, the brown one like earth, and the red one like blood. Somewhere outside her, she caught murmurs and claps but this dance was not for them now, but for herself. The musicians' notes rose, blending and building to the crescendo they had rehearsed this morning and she let her body go with them, but already she was dreading the end. In her dance she was safe, as if some magician had drawn a circle around her; once she stopped, she must step out of its charms and face the real world once more.

But the tune was sinking to its conclusion and she must conclude with it. She took her final turn, swept her scarves in a last curve through the smoky air of the hall, and sunk, head dipped, to the floor. For a moment there was silence and then, as if thunder was rolling up over the Judean hills, applause rang out. Salome kept her head down, drawing it in and blinking back the tears that sprung inexplicably to her eyes, and it was not until footsteps rapped across the wood and a hand reached for hers, that she dared to look up.

'Salome! Daughter! That was magnificent.'

Antipas was before her, drawing her up to standing and parading her around the hall like a prize fighter. His hand was large and sweaty around her own and his voice like a shofar horn as he boomed out his praise. And now Herodias was coming forward, beaming and taking her other hand, and Salome had no idea what to do with herself. Her body was still flooded with the rush of the dance and she wanted nothing more than to escape to her own rooms to let it calm.

She gave a quick curtsey and tried to make for the door but Antipas was having none of it.

'What a princess!' he was calling, a slur in his words. 'Beautiful, elegant and talented. You are a lucky man, indeed, Philip, that she will soon be your bride.'

'How soon?' Philip demanded. 'She is sixteen now after all.'

Salome darted a glance to Ari and he sent a pained one back. Was this marriage of hers a disappointment to him too?

'Soon, Philip,' Antipas said. 'Very soon. But for tonight I think the lady deserves a reward all of her own, do you not? Come, Salome, name your prize.'

Salome blinked at him.

'My prize, Sir?'

'Anything you desire – up to half the value of my kingdom!'

Salome saw Herodias' eyes gleam as she gave her an urgent nod but her thoughts were still in the dance.

'I have my father's lands, thank you, sir. They are enough for me.'

There was an intake of breath around the hall and she felt a sharp dig in the ribs from her mother.

'A woman can never have too much land,' Antipas said tightly.

'Nor a man either, hey, Antipas,' someone called.

'Especially if that land was Judea,' another put in and a throaty growl went around the room: 'Bloody Romans.'

'Come, Salome,' Antipas said loudly and with strained urgency. 'Choose your prize. A jewel perhaps.'

Salome snatched at this. A jewel could, surely, offend no one.

'That would be most kind, Stepfather.'

'Excellent, excellent. You!' He ushered a serving boy forward and gestured him to hold out the silver platter he was carrying. Morsels of meat clung to it but as Antipas began pulling rings off his fat fingers, the boy hastily wiped them away with the towel he carried over his shoulder. The rings clinked onto the platter.

'Choose, girl,' Antipas ordered. 'Choose!'

Salome reached out and picked up a large, amber ring. She did not much care for it but she was desperate to escape the heat and noise of the hall and the ring seemed an easy way out.

'One of your old rings, Antipas?' Aristobulus called. 'Surely such a beauty deserves something finer than that?'

Salome groaned.

'Truly, I am most pleased.'

Antipas gave a forced laugh.

'Your handsome cousin is correct. Here, daughter, take them all.'

'No, I . . .'

'Take them all!'

He thrust the silver platter at her and she had little choice but to grasp it before the rings clattered to the floor and embarrassed them all.

'You're too kind,' she stuttered and, with a curtsey, started to turn away.

She could see the doorway and the blissfully empty hall beyond. She took two steps toward it, the rings chinking against the platter, and then froze. There, tied up in chains in the alcove to its left, was John the Baptiser.

'Pretty baubles, Princess,' he called out, his voice hoarse but with a lilt of contempt that carried it easily around the dining room. 'And so needed, is it not, for someone with so little wealth like yourself?'

'Silence!' Antipas roared.

'How will they fit you, Princess? Oh, I know – your fingers will swell with the greed of your kind and that will hold them nice and tight.' Salome's flesh crawled. She put her head up high and took two more steps to the door. She could feel Herodias at her back and was glad of her strength. 'Just one of those rings could feed a community of pilgrims for a year,' John called.

'As could getting off their contemplative arses and growing some corn,' Herodias shot back.

The men around the table cheered, delighted by this new amusement. Salome stared longingly at the doorway but it seemed so far away.

'Mother, come on,' she hissed.

She would have tugged on Herodias' arm, save that both her hands were caught up in holding the platter.

'You would have given her greater riches, Antipas,' John jeered, 'if you had stripped her jewels from her, not laden her soul with more.'

'He would have given her greater riches if he had cut off your damned head and put it on her platter,' Herodias shot back.

'Mother!'

But the men nearest cheered the suggestion in raucous delight. Antipas, halfway back to his seat, shifted and glanced back. Salome felt caught between him and Herodias, like a sacrificial lamb on a leash. Urgent looks were passing between them and the charge burned her.

'You would like that, Salome?' Antipas asked.

'She would,' Herodias said firmly.

'Salome?'

'No, Sir. I am well content with—'

'With nature's rich jewels, dug out of her earth by slaves and worn by their cruel masters. I tell you now, it will be harder for a rich man to get through the eye of the needle than to reach heaven!'

The murmurings of the men grew in volume. No one was sure of this heaven of which the madman spoke but the implication was clear enough.

'Give the girl the head,' someone called.

'No, I . . .'

'If this man is so keen to reach the afterlife, it will be doing him a favour,' another shouted.

'Really, I do not want . . .'

But Salome's small, thin voice was lost in the bays of the men, flushed with wine and clattering their eating knives against their platters as if they were readying for a hunt. As, indeed, they were. Salome looked in a panic to her mother, but Herodias was staring at John and her eyes were alight with dark victory.

'Do it,' she told the guard.

'Salome?' Antipas cried.

She could hear panic in his voice and knew he did not like this. He could not condemn the man to death on a point of law, but he could bestow it as a gift. She looked to John and he seemed to lean so far out in his chains that she could almost taste his prison-foul breath.

'Do it,' he hissed at her. 'Why not? Your soul is already damned by your wealth and your ignorance and your frivolousness. Does God want your dancing? Why on earth would he?'

Her heart flared.

'How dare you?' she flashed at him. 'How dare you stand here in my home and condemn my simple pleasures? You are the ignorant one, you are the damned.'

'Well said,' Herodias cried. 'Kill him.'

'Kill him,' the men chanted. 'Kill him, kill him, kill him!'

'Salome?!'

Salome felt the room spin around her. The fury of the many important guests filled her ears but not loud enough to drown out John, spitting fury at her and her family.

'Kill him,' she burst out.

Two words. Two tiny words. Barely had they left her mouth than the guard at John's side lifted his sword and, with a swipe faster than a scarf passing from one hand to another, cut straight through the Baptiser's neck. His body slumped, limp and useless, in the chains that still bound it and the head fell, bumping across the wood, spurting blood. The guard snatched it up and, as the hall swam before Salome, he placed it onto the platter she still held in both hands. It sank onto the rings, squashing them into bloody oblivion and all Salome was left with were two empty, staring eyes.

'No!' she gasped.

Her hands went to her face and the platter fell but she did not wait to see the head bounce once more across the floor of the feast, scattering jewels. Picking up her dancing skirts in her bloodied hands, she turned and fled.

Part Two

Chapter Fourteen

Herodias

Herodias paced the long gallery at the front of the palace in Tiberias, keeping a nervous eye on the road leading to its gates. Philip could arrive at any point in the next day or two and she hadn't actually spoken to Salome yet. It wasn't that she was afraid of her daughter – of course not – just that she'd been so damned moody since the night of the feast that even exchanging a sentence or two with her was a chore. Still, her groom was on the way and it was only fair that Salome had a little warning. Herodias gave herself a stern nod and, gathering up her skirts, went to find her daughter.

She was in her chamber, where she was so often these days, head down over one of the dusty parchments she'd had shipped over from her father's estates. She had threatened to go and live there again after the unpleasant events at Machaerus, but Herodias had done nothing to help arrange it and the girl hadn't mustered the will to sort it out herself. The parchments had been a compromise. They were dry things as far as Herodias could see – dusty old historians and philosophers pontificating about events long past and ideas with little relevance to the modern day – but at least they'd occupied Salome and stopped her storming around the palace with a black cloud over her head.

Herodias had tried to be understanding. It had all grown a little out of hand, even she could see that. The result was excellent but the means of execution could have been subtler. Poor Salome had danced so beautifully and looked so touchingly stunned at the applause that had greeted her. Herodias had felt very proud, especially with Philip beaming and Aristobulus gazing adoringly at her. She would do all in her power to keep that young man unmarried – a few commissions in foreign lands should sort it – so that if, bless him, Philip did not last that long in his new bride's bed, Salome would have a lovely second husband to turn to. In the meantime, however . . .

'Salome? May I come in?'

She didn't really see why she should ask, as it was her palace, but it didn't hurt to start politely. Salome, apparently, didn't feel the same way as she just grunted. Herodias strode firmly inside.

'How are you, daughter?'

'How do you think?'

'You look well.'

'My body is well, mainly in that it is still attached to my head, unlike some.'

Herodias prayed for patience.

'It is a month since the feast, sweet one. Do you not think it's time to put it behind you?'

'Put murdering a man behind me?'

'You did not murder him.'

'I ordered his murder.'

'His *execution*, Salome. It is a vital difference. The man was a criminal.'

'The man was a philosopher. He had ideas, that is all, and they were never going to hurt anyone, were they?'

'I disagree.' Herodias slid onto a seat next to Salome. 'Ideas are precisely what can drive people to violence and rebellion. Was not Socrates executed for defiling the Greek religion and corrupting the Athenian youth?' Salome blinked. 'What's wrong? Did you not think your old mother had any education.'

'No, I . . . That is, of course I know you are an intelligent woman.'

'And an intelligent leader. I'm sorry about the manner of the Baptiser's death. It was rather overdramatic.'

'Overdramatic?! Mother, it—'

'Cutting his head off right there and then was brutal.'

'There was blood everywhere.'

'There was. Men lack subtlety I'm afraid. But at least it is done and the guests all took the story abroad that he was violent and disruptive and insulting to Jewish leadership and his execution was justified.'

'Because they are ashamed of their part in it. It was barbaric, Mother.'

'It wasn't a very dignified means of execution, I agree, and there was no need to put it on the platter. The guard got carried away.'

'It was awful! His head was just there, staring at me. I see those eyes all the time, when I'm awake, when I'm asleep, and filling the bit in between, which is where I seem to spend most of my time these days.'

Herodias swallowed. The girl was more affected than she'd realised.

'It *was* awful, Salome, and I'm sorry you were caught up in it. But the man was vile to you.'

'So? A princess should surely be able to rise above such things. I should have asked for his release as my gift, not his death.'

'And let him out in the world again? John was a madman and a dangerous one. He wanted everyone to hand over their goods to him and live in some sort of holy poverty – a scam if ever I heard one.'

'He lived in poverty too.'

'For now. I hear the Essenes have huge reserves of gold buried in their precious rocks up in Qumran – far more than you'll see honestly displayed here in the palace.'

'Really?'

'I swear it. John's death was unpleasant but necessary. He was preaching anarchy. We have a system of tithes precisely to ensure that people give to the Temple according to their means, and that money is spent building synagogues all over the Holy Land and training priests to help the people understand God's teaching. The royals, too, spend much of their wealth on public buildings and safe, clean new cities like this one. It's not like the leaders all just sit around on their gold.'

Salome looked at her. It was far from approval but perhaps interest – progress indeed. She had to tread very carefully now. The Baptiser was gone and the Holy Land did not seem to have collapsed into mourning or rioting as a result. Pesach had passed in Jerusalem with no more petty violence than usual and there had been no sign of the other one, the cousin. Someone said he had gone into the desert to spend forty days in mourning and he could stay there as far as she was concerned. Rumours about him had been spreading like wildfire – lame men walking, blind men seeing again, even a ridiculous one about him raising a girl from the dead. Pure hysteria! She couldn't believe Antipas had allowed the bloody Baptiser to communicate with him from Machaerus whilst they'd been away, but they were back now and it was stopped.

Some big man called Andrew had come to Machaerus the next day asking for his body and Herodias had ordered it released from its chains and let him take it away. The head, however, she had refused him, not wanting it paraded. Instead, she had thrown it into the fortress dung-heap where the worms could eat it away even further than it had already been addled. She had stuck a guard by the compost night and day to prevent anyone stealing it before it became too rancid to be of any use to petty revolutionaries.

The flesh would be long gone now and it was time the shadows of its severing were as well. Salome was the worst of it but Antipas had been pathetically subdued ever since and Chuza even more so. The damned man sloped around the palace with his son strapped to his chest like a woman, doing – as far as she could see – no damned work at all. If it wasn't for his chirpy little wife, things would be collapsing around them and that was no good for anyone.

'What we need, sweet one, is a little joy to cheer everyone up.'

'Joy?'

Salome squinted at her as if she had suggested some aberrant practice.

'Joy,' Herodias confirmed with her best smile. 'For the people, for the palace and above all, for you.'

'Joy? For me?'

Herodias peered at her daughter. Those dusty parchments were doing her no good at all. Surely they were meant to sharpen her brain, not turn her into a dullard?

'Why not, Salome?'

'But – what joy?'

'Your wedding of course.' Herodias clapped her hands loudly, though not quite loudly enough to cover Salome's gasp of horror. 'Think about it,' she rushed on. 'It will give Chuza something lovely to organise and, Lord knows, he needs it to give him back his usual verve. Johanna will be a great help to you, I am sure, and the people will love the occasion. We can have a day of holiday with carriages through the streets and wine in the fountains and everyone will have something pleasing to focus on, instead of all this doom and gloom about poverty and the end of the world.'

'But I will have to ... to marry.'

'Well yes, that's how it usually works.'

'Marry Philip?'

'He is your betrothed, sweet one.'

'And move to Trachonitis?'

Herodias tried to keep her face positive, though she had to admit that she could understand the girl's reluctance to move into the hills, miles from anything.

'I hear Philip's new city of Caesarea Philippi is very fine. Lots of people are moving there. Teachers and artists and philosophers.'

'Philosophers?'

There was the faintest spark in Salome's clouded eyes and Herodias crossed her fingers firmly behind her back and nodded. There were bound to be some philosophers, surely? They went everywhere.

'Philip is keen to encourage learning.'

'That is good.'

'Yes, and I'm sure you will be a great support to him in his endeavours.'

Salome drew in a shaky breath.

'I will try. I suppose. When do you propose to hold the wedding?'

Herodias shifted on her seat.

'I think soon.'

'How soon?' Salome looked panicked. 'Next year?'

'*This* year. In fact, I thought this month.' Salome sprang furiously to her feet but there was no way to back out of this now. 'Philip is on his way here and eager to make you his bride.'

'Mother . . .'

'You are sixteen now, after all.'

'As marked by my wonderful birthing day feast and the luscious present of a severed—'

'And you were promised to him at sixteen.'

'I was promised to him? What of me, Mother? What of what I want?'

'You swore the betrothal oath, daughter.'

'Because you made me.'

'As is my duty as a loving parent.'

'No!' Salome pointed a sharp finger at her. 'No, I'm not having that. There is no love in this wedding. It is all about power.'

'Not all, daughter, I promise you. There *is* love—'

'There is not. There is no need for love when you have land, remember?'

Herodias ground her teeth, as she seemed to do increasingly often these days. She would have to get the girl married and away before she had none left.

144

'You are misquoting me, daughter. I said merely that respect and mutual ambition were more important in a marriage than some spurious notion of emotional compatibility.'

'So you do not love my stepfather then?'

Herodias flinched back at the question and almost fell off her stool.

'Antipas and I have an excellent partnership.'

'Do you love him?'

She jumped up.

'This is about *your* marriage, Salome, not mine.'

'My marriage that you are going to force me into? The same way you forced me to ask for the death of an innocent man.'

'John the Baptiser was not innocent. He was criticising me openly, Antipas too. That sort of thing is very dangerous.'

'For you?'

'For the whole region. Honestly, Salome, can you not see that we have enough problems trying to keep the damned Romans at bay without criticising each other? There are plenty of people in this world lining up to attack the Jewish nation. We must stand firm against them, not turn on each other.' Salome looked down, twisting her fingers round and round and looking, suddenly, more six than sixteen. Herodias placed gentle hands on her slim shoulders. 'It will be good to move on, Salome, to look to the future and a new part of your life. You will make a wonderful wife and ruler.' Salome looked up, her eyes swimming with tears and Herodias bent to kiss her. 'Joy, Salome, truly you need some joy. A happy day, a celebration for all.' Salome gave a tiny nod and Herodias pressed her advantage. 'You can, perhaps, do a new dance for your husband – something you have crafted your—'

'No!'

Salome leapt back so violently that she sent Herodias staggering into her dressing table, jarring her elbow. The pain shot through her like an arrow.

'No?'

'I will not dance for Philip, or for you, or for anyone ever again. My dancing cost a man his life.'

Herodias pulled herself up tall, battling to ignore the stabbing sensations in her arm.

'Your dancing – your *beautiful* dancing – gave you the power to choose a man's death, daughter. There are too many people working to rob women of any power, so you must seize every ounce that you can get with both hands.'

Salome, however, simply stood there shaking her head so violently that Herodias feared she might shake it off.

'That is not the sort of power I want.'

'Then you are a fool. Think, Salome. Listen to yourself. You did not like the outcome – fine. Learn from that and next time, make a different choice. But make sure that there *is* a next time.'

Salome let out a curious noise, half hiss, half scream and Herodias backed away from her. The girl was raving. The sooner she was married and out of her rapidly greying hair, the better.

'Prepare yourself, Salome,' she said. 'Philip will be here within the next day or two. You will receive him, you will smile at him, and you will marry him.'

Her only answer was another hiss and Herodias hurried hastily away. It was done, the girl was told and not a moment too soon. Now it was up to her to get herself ready.

Chapter Fifteen

Salome

Salome wasn't sure where the fluid was coming from for so many tears but they just kept pouring out of her. She was going to be the only bride going to the Chuppah in a boat.

'Don't cry, sweet one,' Johanna said, dabbing at her eyes with a linen kerchief. 'I want to put a little kohl on your lashes to accentuate them but like this it will run down your cheeks in dark rivers.'

'Let it,' Salome said, but without much feeling.

Philip didn't deserve a fright of a bride, nor a reluctant one. He was a good, kind man who had been very gracious to her since he'd arrived at the palace in Tiberias a week ago. Salome had done her best to be polite to him, not for her mother, definitely not, but because he had gone out of his way to make her feel at ease. He had brought her thoughtful presents, had sat and told her all about his aims for just rule of Trachonitis, and asked her opinion in a way few had ever done before. He was old, sadly. His sparse hair was grey, his skin was wrinkled around the edges of his face, as if his ears might slide right down it, and his knees leaned towards each other as he walked. Salome could not begin to imagine him beside her in bed, let alone on top of her, but that was not his fault she supposed, and she could do far worse.

147

Far better too, she thought, another stream of tears leaking out as she pictured Ari, strong and lean, with a twinkle in his eye and a ready laugh.

'Salome!' Johanna sat back, the kohl brush quivering in her hand. 'It really won't be that bad, I promise you.'

Salome shook her head, cross with herself.

'I know. Truly I know, Johanna. This is no shame on Philip, only on myself.'

Johanna put down the brush, took Salome's face in both hands, and kissed her on one cheek after the other.

'It is no shame on you, either. You have been through a hard time.'

'But ought to be able to put it behind me.'

'It's not always that easy. Believe me, Chuza is still struggling too. He's talking about resigning as steward, it's so bad. Sometimes he sits up in the night, sweating and crying out about heads and platters and blood. It takes me ages to bring him out of the darkness and he is a man who has seen much of the world. It must be far worse for you.'

Salome gave Johanna a hug.

'Thank you.'

'For what?'

'For understanding. Mother thinks I'm being weak and deliberately churlish. She thinks I should throw my "petty emotions" in the dung heap where she flung poor John's head.'

The tears were back. Salome wiped furiously at them. Downstairs she could hear the guests arriving and she was still sitting here in her chamber robe, her eyes red and her guts churning. It wasn't fair on Philip.

'Right,' she said, as firmly as she could. 'There will be no more tears. Paint me up, Johanna, and make me beautiful for my groom.'

Johanna kissed her again.

'You are beautiful already, sweet one. He is a lucky man and I can only pray that having such a stunning young bride in his bed will not send his old heart over the edge.'

'Johanna!' A giggle escaped Salome's mouth and she welcomed it. 'Bless you, you are a good friend. I will miss you.'

'And I you. Truly.'

Salome grabbed at Johanna's hand.

'Come with me.'

'What?'

'Come with me, all of you. You said Chuza was thinking of giving up the stewardship here in Tiberias, so why not work for me – us – in Caesarea Philippi? Philip has asked me several times for suggestions on how to improve his arrangements there and this is the best possible suggestion I could make. Chuza would do a wonderful job with his estates and you could still work with me and keep my stupid eyes from leaking.'

'You mean it?'

Salome grabbed her friend's hands.

'Truly I do. I would have to ask Philip, of course, but a bride is usually granted a boon so this could be mine.'

'You would take us as your bride-gift?'

'I can think of nothing better. Last time I was offered a prize, I made a terrible choice. I have learned my lesson. Would you come?'

Johanna looked awkwardly down, running her fingers across the kohl brush over and over.

'I'd have to ask Chuza,' she said eventually.

'But . . .?'

'But, we have talked of another plan.'

'Really? What is it?'

'You will think us mad.'

'Never!'

'Oh, you will.'

She leaned in towards Salome but at that moment Herodias strode into the chamber.

'Are you ready, daughter? Oh! Oh, no. What on earth are you playing at, Johanna? I told you to have the girl ready for midday and look at her!'

Johanna's face fell and she grovelled before Herodias.

'I am sorry. I, I—'

'She was held up by me, Mother.'

'That I do not doubt. You cannot stop this now, Salome.'

'Neither am I trying to do so, but it is hard to make up your eyes when they are running tears.'

Herodias tossed her head, making the beaded tassels on her headdress clatter irritably together.

'You are going to have to toughen up, Salome. It's a hard, cold world and if you wish to make your way in it, you must find the sharpest steel within yourself to cut through. Now, how long will you be?'

'We were just about to do Salome's kohl, my lady,' Johanna assured her. 'And then I can dress her.'

'I can dress myself,' Salome muttered and then hated herself for it, because had she not just been begging Johanna to go with her to Caesarea Philippi? What would John the Baptiser make of that?

Think not of it, she instructed herself crossly. John the Baptiser was gone, his body somewhere on the Mount of Olives, his head in the dung heap at Machaerus, and if, all too often, she found herself wondering what he would be doing now if she had asked for his release instead of his death, it was a pointless self-torture. No one could rise from the dead.

'Hurry then,' Herodias said.

'We will go faster if you leave us alone, Mother.'

Herodias looked at her and, for a moment, Salome saw hurt in her rich eyes. Well, so what? She was forcing her under the Chuppah for 'joy', so she could damn well get on with being joyous. She gave her a honeyed smile. Herodias' eyes narrowed and then, with a muttered 'you'd better do,' she swept out.

'Quickly.'

Johanna, looking panicked now, dabbed the kerchief over Salome's face and, finding it dry, picked up the kohl brush but Salome reached out and grabbed her hand.

'Tell me of your plan, Johanna.'

'There's no time.'

'There is. I will sit very still, I promise, and not cry one single tear and you can paint me and talk to me at the same time.'

'Salome . . .'

'If you do *not* talk, I will squirm and cry and kohl will run down my cheeks and onto my dress and—'

'All right, all right, I will tell you. But you must be still as a statue.'

'Of course.' Salome composed herself, shoulders back, face rigid. Johnna lifted the brush. 'Talk.'

'Give me a chance.' Salome felt the kiss of the brush against her lashes as Johanna drew in a deep breath and began to speak. 'Chuza and I both feel that, perhaps, if we think about it further and are both agreed and—'

'I feel an itch . . .'

'No! I'm telling you. It's simply that . . . we would both like to . . . to follow Jesus of Nazareth.'

'What?!'

Salome startled and Johanna tutted.

'Now look!'

She pointed Salome to the mirror where she could see a line of kohl running from her top lashes across her forehead and up into her hair. Despite herself, she giggled.

'It will wipe off. What do you mean, follow him?'

'I mean give up our work here in the palace, take our goods to the community, and live with them.'

'The community?'

'There are a large number of people following Jesus. When he came back from the desert two weeks ago, he nominated twelve men to stand at his side and help him organise the massing followers. In a little time, they are going to take to the road, travelling around Galilee to spread word of the New Way.'

Salome gaped at Johanna and she seized the chance to daub her lips with ochre.

'You would go on the road with all those men?' Salome gasped, when her lips were free again.

'It's not just men. Perpetua will travel with Peter, Jesus' mother Mariam, and sister Elisabeth go with him, plus a young woman called Mary from Magdala and many others besides. Jesus welcomes the women and listens to them, especially Mary who is a clever woman with a fierce understanding. She is often quickest to interpret Jesus' parables.'

'Parables?'

'The stories he tells to help people understand God's word.'

Johanna tugged Salome up to remove her robe, then rushed to take the red and scarlet bridal gown from its hanger. Salome stepped into it, still trying to process what her friend was telling her.

'Is this Jesus a priest?'

'No, but he is a man of great wisdom. They say that when he was twelve, his parents lost him in Jerusalem and finally found him in the Court of the Gentiles, discoursing with the elders. He has no sanctioned training but, truly, he speaks far more clearly than any priest.'

'About love?'

Johanna rushed around to Salome's back to tie the bodice into place.

'About love, yes, amongst other things. He told a parable the other day about a man who was dying on the street. The Jews who came along passed him by on the other side, because it was the Sabbath and, as you know, you are not meant to work on the Sabbath. You are not meant to tend or heal a goat let alone a man. So they passed on, as scripture tells them, but then a Samaritan came along and he tended the man – and was blessed by God.'

'For breaking the Sabbath?' Salome asked, confused.

'For showing compassion, for valuing his neighbour higher than himself.'

Salome frowned.

'This Jesus wants us all to act like Samaritans – pagan scum with few rules and no morals?'

Johanna came back round to the front and shrugged.

'And yet who saved the dying man?'

Salome's mind was spinning.

'Mother said the carpenter had gone to ground.'

'She was wrong. He went into the desert in mourning for ... That is, in order to have time for contemplation, and now he has thrown himself into his mission with full vigour and is asking all to follow. He is a new Moses, come to lead us out of the slavery of too many rules and hypocrisies and into the freedom of the New Way as John foretold.'

'Is he, then, baptising them?'

She shook her head.

'His followers do that. They work in pairs, one man and one woman to guide people into the water and wash away their sins. Then Jesus baptises them in the Holy Spirit.'

'The what? Surely this is all hokum?'

Johanna adjusted the seams on her gown.

'The words may sound alien but the ideas are plain common sense. The holy spirit is simply the spark of God within us all. We can choose to hide it away or we can use it to light a fire within ourselves and spread light across the world.'

'It sounds . . .' What did it sound? Salome considered. It sounded wild and anarchic. It sounded as if it ran counter to all the principles of obedience and exactitude that governed the Jewish faith as she'd been brought up to know it. It sounded like a scam, or a hoax. It sounded

'Salome!' Herodias's voice called. 'The congregation is gathered below. You better be ... Ah. Good.' She stood in the doorway and looked her up and down. 'Very nice.'

Salome did not look her way, neither did she turn to see her own reflection in the long bronze mirror against the wall. Her eyes were fixed on Johanna and the way she shone as she spoke of this man, this Jesus, the carpenter turned preacher from Nazareth.

'It sounds wonderful.'

She glanced down at her gown, the richest of scarlets, run through with gold thread and embroidered all around the hem with beautiful stitching. Suddenly it felt as much a prison as the cell in which John the Baptiser had been incarcerated – the cell she had ordered sealed. Her stomach roiled and she was seized with a mad longing to grab Johanna's hand and beg her to take her with them to join the simple men and women following the Nazarene, to give up the palaces and riches of her life as a princess and see if, without them, she could find this spark inside herself.

'Are you ready, Salome?'

Herodias' voice seemed to come from somewhere outside the room, outside the very ether. She heard the clatter of the important guests below and pictured Philip standing beneath the Chuppah, waiting to suck her into rule and all its tasks and responsibilities. The neckline of her gown felt too tight and she put up a hand to tear it away and flee.

Then she remembered.

She was the woman who had condemned John the Baptiser to death. *She* was the one who had danced for his head, who had held it on a silver platter and bathed herself in his blood. *She* had killed Jesus' cousin, the man who had been sent to wake the world up to his teachings, and she had no place at his side. Not now and not ever.

Land not love, that was her destiny, and she had sealed it with her own bloodied hand.

'I am ready, Mother,' she agreed and, hardening her heart, she lifted her rich skirts in her soft hands and went, dry-eyed, to her groom.

Chapter Sixteen

Herodias

'Herodias? My love? Is all well?'

Herodias blinked out of her reverie and bestowed a beaming smile on her husband.

'Of course, of course. All is excellent. I was simply, you know, thinking.'

'I see.' He put his arms around her waist. 'And what were you thinking about, wife?'

He was looking at her teasingly, knowingly even. She tried to squirm away but he was holding tight.

'Many things. You know us women, always something to organise.'

'You are marvels. But you are, perhaps, thinking that it is a shame you are the only woman around here now?'

'No!'

'You are perhaps reflecting that life is less slick without Johanna and Chuza to grease the wheels of palace life?'

'Definitely not. They were fools to resign lucrative royal posts and there are many who will fill the stewardship once we get round to interviewing.'

'I'm sure you're right.' He reached out and took her chin gently in his big hand, tipping it up towards him. 'You are perhaps, then, missing your daughter?'

'No! Don't be ridiculous, Antipas. She is securely wed and off to rule her own lands. Why would I be sorry about that?'

He smiled.

'I did not say you were sorry about it, simply that you missed her.'

'Yes, well, I don't.'

'Why not?'

She blinked at him, surprised.

'Because . . . because the correct order is in place and all is well.'

He bent and kissed her, slow and deep. She resisted him at first but his lips were soft against hers and his arms strong around her and, oh, it felt good. Reaching up her arms around his neck she lost herself in his embrace, revelling in the soft care of it. Then she remembered herself.

'Are we to bed, husband?'

He shook his head.

'That was not a kiss of lust, my gorgeous wife, but of love.'

'Love?'

She gave a nervous laugh and he looked curiously at her.

'Yes, love. I love you.' She gasped. 'You know that surely? Come, Herodias, I travelled to Rome to secure a divorce to marry you. I risked the wrath of King Aretas for casting his daughter aside. I stood up to the condemnation of my peers and the ravings of prophets.' Herodias shivered at the reminder. 'I would hardly do that if I did not love you.'

'I thought you did it because I was Hasmonean.'

'It is not your finest feature, my beauty.'

'And because I had more ambition than Phasaelis, because you wated Judea and needed a strong woman to aid you in that quest.'

'I did want Judea – *do* want it – but I wanted you more.' She gaped at him. 'Did I not tell you that? Did I not make it clear?'

She thought back to the early days of their marriage. He had, she supposed, showered her in praise and endearments but she had thought it the natural outpouring of their political match-up. And, perhaps, a certain animal urge.

'You have been most complimentary throughout our marriage,' she said stiffly.

'Complimentary?' Antipas threw back his head and laughed. 'They are not compliments, wife, not pretty phrases designed to soothe or coerce. They are expressions of the depths of my feelings for you.'

'Right.'

Herodias had no idea what to do with this. Honestly, she'd been feeling weak enough already without Antipas piling this onto her. She was, in truth, missing Salome and it was very disorientating. The girl had been by turns sulky and wild for most of the last two years, and they had done little but argue in that time. Herodias had found her daughter largely irritating – too like her father, thoughtful and questioning and soft. She didn't want to lose her, of course. The memory of seeing her covered in blood on the ground outside the law courts still haunted the darkest of her nightmares, but that did not mean that she should *miss* her.

She was only a girl, after all. She wasn't the son Herodias had craved and at times, she knew, she had resented Salome for making it out of her womb whole when not one of her three boys had been able to do so. Her daughter was certainly stubborn, tenacious even. When she got hold of an idea, she didn't let it go, so no wonder she'd clung onto life inside her. And Herodias was glad she had. One child was better than none, even if it was a girl with no right to inherit titles and no ability to fight and not even, it seemed, the will to stand up and make the most of what little power she did have as a woman.

'Do you love me?' Antipas asked softly.

Herodias cringed.

'I don't hold with all this talk of love, husband. I respect you greatly. I enjoy your company. I am proud to have you as my partner, in bed, at board, in government. I am glad I married you, despite the trouble it has caused. Is that not enough?'

He smiled, but it was less open this time and Herodias thought she saw hurt at the back of his eyes and hated it. Why did he have to force this? She thought she'd got the emotional one out of her household and didn't need him starting.

'It is not enough,' he said quietly.

'Well, it should be.' She yanked back out of his arms. 'Love is for those who have no land.'

He looked at her curiously.

'Who told you that?'

'Who? I'm not sure. It's just ready wisdom, is it not?'

He shook his head and she thought about it again. God, her head was hurting with all this nonsense. And then a memory came to her of her grandmother, the Lady Salome. In the ten years in which she had lived in her household, the old lady had taken many opportunities to lecture her on how a woman might make her way in the world, but on her twelfth birthday she'd sat Herodias down and talked to her with the utmost sternness.

'Land, Herodias, that is what you must seek. Land is a woman's security and a woman's weapon. It is what will give you independence and power. Do not listen to those who try and lull you with talk of love. They have conditioned us, Herodias, conditioned us to believe that love is all we need. It is how they keep us meek, how they keep us tied to them. Clever is it not? And so easy to believe. Who doesn't like to be cuddled? Who doesn't like to be told they are pretty, or sweet, or fun? Who doesn't like to be given gifts and told they make someone's world go around? But it is an act, Herodias, a lie.

'They make their *own* world go round and need you only to make it spin more easily. When a man gives you a gift it is because it makes him feel good about his own generosity. And it is because it binds you to his side where he can keep control of you. Do not shirk reality, Herodias – land, that is what you need. Love is for those who cannot have it, so do not let yourself be short-changed.'

'My grandmother told me,' she said quietly to Antipas.

'The Lady Salome, who divorced her second husband?'

'As I divorced Boethus. As you divorced Phasaelis.'

'To marry each other. She did it simply to be free.'

'She did it because he was plotting against her brother and she had no wish to be dragged into his treason simply by being his wife. Was that not fair?'

He considered.

'She certainly did well out of it.'

'God rewarding her for a wise decision.'

Antipas gave a small nod and wandered away, reaching into the tree for one of the still hard pomegranates as if it held secrets he wanted to probe.

'You lived with the Lady Salome for how long?'

'Ten years – from four to fourteen. when she died and I was married to Boethus, who, note you, was at the time nominated as Herod's sole heir.'

'I remember. As was I at one point. As were we all. The man played with his heirs like a cat with mice.'

'Well, Salome made sure she was not scratched.'

'And taught you well, it seems. She told you that you were not allowed to love?'

'No! She told me I would be fobbed off with love and not to let that happen. She told me land was far more valuable and she was right, was she not, for land cannot be dropped or forgotten or moved to someone else. Land is solid and secure.'

He came back to her suddenly.

'As is love, if it is bestowed by the right person.' She frowned and he kissed her nose. 'You can, you know, have both land and love . . .'

'But—'

'But nothing. It is simply something for you to think about, my sweet.' He kissed her again, long and gentle, until she was giddy with his heat and with the swirls of his words. She leaned in, pushing herself against him and heard his breath quicken. 'Perhaps,

159

after all, bed might be a good idea,' he murmured. 'It is very hot, is it not, and a siesta might be the only sensible course of action.'

'Sensible,' Herodias echoed helplessly against him but as he turned her, arm tight around her waist, towards the palace, they saw a messenger coming running across the lawns and groaned.

'What is it?' Antipas demanded, unusually snappy.

Herodias grinned and squeezed his bum, making him squirm entertainingly. The messenger's reply, however, cut through all her amusement.

'Visitors, my lord, due within the hour.'

'What visitors?'

'The Lord Agrippa, my lady's brother, and his family.'

'Agrippa?!' Herodias cried and looked to Antipas in dismay, as all erotic charge drained from the afternoon like oil from the crusher.

❖

'We just tired of Rome, really, didn't we, Kypros? It's very shallow, you know. Well, you do know, don't you, Antipas? You grew up there.'

'I did,' Antipas agreed tightly.

They had been at dinner for nigh-on an hour and Agrippa had barely stopped talking, all in much the same vein.

'And you visited recently, sister.'

'I did,' Herodias agreed. 'And found you much occupied by the city's charms.'

Agrippa's eyes narrowed.

'I like to throw myself into things. It's so rude to a host not to enjoy yourself as best you can – as I am doing now with this delicious food.'

'So, what made you leave Rome, if you were enjoying yourself as best you could?'

Agrippa leaned forward, spitting out a wing from his third fried locust.

'History, sister, culture. It was you, really – you inspired me, made me ashamed even. I am from the Holy Land, am I not? I am of Hasbedean descent.'

'Hasmonean,' Herodias corrected him loudly.

'That's what I said.'

'It's not.'

'It's what I meant. Relax, sister. I'm telling you that I'm maturing. I have a family and I wanted them to see their heritage.'

He gestured expansively to Kypros at his side and their two eldest children sat, bleary-eyed, at the bottom of the table. Agrippa-the-younger was six and buoyed by the pastries, but his sister, Berenice, was just four and all-but asleep where she sat. Their three younger siblings, including the new baby, Drusilla, were tucked up in the nursery, and this pair really needed to join them but Agrippa would not stop talking long enough for Kypros to seize the chance to summon the nursery maids. She looked weary too, Herodias noticed with little surprise. Drusilla was but three months old and the journey from Rome must have taken a toll on her poor mother.

She stood up.

'That is very good to hear, brother, and you are most welcome but I think perhaps your family have seen enough of any land for one day. Kypros, shall we see the children upstairs and let the men enjoy a pipe?'

Kypros rose gratefully and went to Berenice, who wrapped little arms around her mother's neck. Young Agrippa was less enthusiastic.

'Can I enjoy a pipe?' he demanded.

Agrippa roared with laughter.

'That's my boy! Not quite yet, lad, not quite yet. But if you get plenty of sleep you will grow big and strong and can join the other men.'

'I *am* big and strong,' Agrippa protested mulishly, flexing a tiny bicep.

Again Agrippa laughed but it was thinner this time and, with impressive speed, Kypros whipped her son, still protesting, out of the room.

'You don't have to come,' she told Herodias, as she made for the stairs with a now tantrum-ing six-year-old. 'Look, the maids are here.'

Sure enough, two young women were running down the stairs to take the children.

'Their help will be most welcome, I'm sure,' Herodias said smoothly, 'but I will come all the same. It is your first night in my house and I would like to see you settled.'

Kypros looked at her astutely.

'And hear the true story of our departure from Rome?'

Herodias chuckled.

'Perhaps.'

'It is a sorry tale.'

'Then the sooner you tell it the better.'

It all came out as the nursery maids calmed Agrippa and got both children into sleepwear and tucked up for their mother's kiss.

'Rome is sick of Agrippa, Herodias. Or, at least, sick of his debts. So many people have bailed him out that there is no one left to turn to and we are destitute. I had to sell some of my jewels to pay for our passage here and more of them to hire the horses Agrippa deemed worthy for a grand arrival in Tiberias. He is all show, Herodias, and I confess I am weary of it.'

Herodias looked at the dark shadows under the poor woman's eyes and the sag to her slender shoulders and drew her spontaneously into her arms.

'Fret not, Kypros. You are with me now. I will take care of you and the children. And I will take care of my brother as well.'

'How?'

Herodias smiled.

'Kiss your little ones, then let us go back down and join the men.'

'Herodias . . .'

'Leave it to me, sister.'

'Sister?'

'If you allow?'

'Allow?' Kypros hugged her, hard and fierce. 'I am honoured.'

They went down arm in arm to find the men sat over a bubbling hookah. Agrippa was still talking, droning on about the high esteem in which the emperor held him, and Antipas was drawing far more deeply on the scented smoke than he would normally do. Herodias crossed to him and faced Agrippa.

'So, brother, you are with us for how long?'

'Oh, a little time. It is important for the children to see the Holy Land.'

'You will travel around then? A grand idea. There are many lovely hostelries around Galilee, down the Jordan and, of course, in Judea, and I'm sure they will be delighted to house rich guests in style. They get much business at the pilgrim festivals but less in the rest of the year so they will fall over themselves to help you spend your coin.'

Agrippa gave her a tight smile.

'I'm sure but I, er, I think my wife has done enough travelling. She is newly out of her childbed you know.'

'I know. I saw your gorgeous baby daughter in the nursery, sleeping soundly. It seems a shame you had to drag mother and baby from Rome so soon after the birthing.'

'Yes, well, it is easier sailing in the summer months.'

'With the heat beating down?'

'Well now . . .'

But Herodias had had enough of his self-delusional nonsense.

'Oh, come on, Agrippa,' she snapped. 'We all know why you're here. You have run out of creditors in Rome and are looking for charity from your family.'

'I wouldn't put it quite like that.'

'Which is half the problem.'

Agrippa looked sulky and Kypros fidgeted nervously at his side. Herodias sent her a reassuring smile.

'Don't worry, brother, we will be happy to have you in Tiberias to get you back on your feet.'

'You will?'

'We will?!' Antipas looked up at her, alarmed.

'Of course. I am sure, are you not, husband, that we can find my brother a job. Has our dear steward, Chuza, not just departed to . . . to . . .' She stumbled a moment at the thought of that competent, capable man leaving decent employment to drag his wife and child round after some rabble-rouser, but pulled herself back together instantly. If he wanted to be an idiot, that was up to him. 'To follow other interests? And does that not leave a vacancy for the job?'

'A job?' Agrippa gasped, as if they were offering him a dose of the plague.

'A job,' Antipas agreed, looking slyly up at Herodias. 'A fine plan, wife.'

'But . . . how on earth would I know how to do a job?'

'Come, brother, you are a talented man with a gift for getting on with others. You will have a full staff, so will only need to supervise. You will not have to get your hands dirty, simply be sure that others are doing so effectively.'

'A job?' Agrippa said again, clutching at his heart as if it might expire at the mere idea.

Kypros, however, had had enough. She strode over and faced him down.

'It is a fine offer, husband. You should be grateful.'

'Grateful? For work?'

'Yes, for work – for gainful employment to support your family whom you love.'

Herodias flinched but her brother took no issue with that part of the statement.

'I am royal, Kypros, I do not work. It would be beneath my dignity.'

'So, husband, is grubbing around spending other people's money and I am sick of it. You will take this job that Antipas has so kindly offered you, or I will.'

'You?'

'Yes. I see no shame in honest work.'

Agrippa's eyes lit up.

'I'm sure you'd be very good at it, wife. You are so organised and smart and . . .'

'Oh, no, Agrippa! If I take the job, then you will go on your way.'

'But the children—'

'Will stay with me.'

She glanced to Herodias, who went to her side and gave a firm nod.

'The royal nursery would love to be full and it will be my honour to help raise my nephews and nieces and give them a good, Jewish education.'

'So why can't I—'

'What? Party whilst your wife earns the money? Come, Agrippa, surely even you would be shamed by such an arrangement?'

Agrippa looked from Herodias, to Kypros, to Antipas. All stared sternly back at him and, in the end, he threw his hands in the air.

'Fine! You win. I'm sure you all think it a fine joke making me sweat and toil.'

'Not at all,' Antipas said quietly. 'I will be at work alongside you. I have two tetrarchies to command and they require constant attention.'

Agrippa looked at him as if this had never crossed his mind before, then drew deeply on the hookah.

'A job!' he said for a third time. 'What is the world coming to?'

Herodias looked to Kypros, who blew her a grateful kiss, and felt her spirits lift for the first time since the wedding. She had not wanted these guests but it seemed that, perhaps, they would fill the palace with a little of the joy that had been sadly missing since Salome had left.

Chapter Seventeen

Salome

'The evening went well, I think,' Philip said, sinking into a chair with a sigh of pleasure. 'Do you agree?'

Salome smiled at her husband.

'Very well. The ambassador from Osroene seemed especially happy and has invited us for a return visit in the spring.'

'He liked you, Salome.'

'He liked *us*. He said that you rule Trachonitis with judgement and wisdom.'

'Sssh, wife, you will make my head swell. Goodness, I'm tired.' Philip stretched out his thin arms above his head and yawned. 'I fear I may not be very attentive to you.'

'It's fine. Let's get some sleep.'

Salome helped Philip out of his robe and watched as he eased himself gratefully under the covers. She took off her own gown, laying it over the rail for her maid to deal with in the morning. It had been a late dinner and Philip had insisted on their personal staff being allowed to go off duty. It was the sort of considerate thing he did all the time and Salome blessed him for it.

Married life was not that bad at all, she thought, as she clambered in at her husband's side. Trachonitis was a little remote and hilly but it was far from wild and Philip's city at Caesarea Philippi was a marvel. Salome had initially been scared to ride to its location at the foot of Mount Hermon, the legendary mountain where the rebellious angels had descended to mate with the daughters of man and create the giants who'd first walked the earth. She'd been worried about going to live in the city established by Alexander the Great for the worship of Pan, which featured just outside its walls the legendary 'Gates of Hell' – a gaping yaw of a bottomless cave. And she had been wary of the predominantly pagan population of the area with their idols and their false gods.

In reality, she had found a prosperous, clean, Greek city built outside the walls of a set of pagan temples that were impressive but already considered relics of an ancient past. People visited them as curiosities rather than for active worship and in Caesarea Philippi there was a substantial Jewish population who had made her very welcome. Salome had set out from Tiberias a week after her wedding expecting to be on the road to purgatory – and feeling sure she deserved it. What she had found, instead, was a calm and happy tetrarchy that had readily welcomed her as its first lady.

Philip put an arm round her, pulling her in against his skinny frame and dropping a sleepy kiss on her neck. The marital bed had been a quiet place, not surprising perhaps in a man into his fifty-fifth year. Philip had initiated her into the way of men and women in a simple and relatively speedy manner and seemed to take at least a week to get up the energy for another go. There was no sign of an heir, which would not please her mother, but maybe the poor man's seed was no longer ripe and the act itself wasn't so bad. Salome had found it a little squashy and hot but otherwise bearable and Philip was always very lovely to her the next morning, so on the whole it seemed a reasonable price to pay for a comfortable life.

Even the pagans had been kind to her and Salome had been astonished to find them simple human beings like herself, and not the warped creatures she had been luridly warned against as a child. She'd had ample opportunity to meet them, for it was

Philip's practice to travel his entire realm twice a year, carrying his judgement chair with him in a cart so that he could set up a court in every town and hear the people's grievances. They had just returned from a tour in which Salome had listened to him making patient, intelligent judgements on all manner of complaints and been impressed and proud.

She had also seen more places and met more new people than ever in her life before. Until this, she had not really thought about the fact that almost her entire social circle was related to her. There were many different Herodian lines, of course but even so, they all traced their roots to the prolific Herod the Great and it had been a curious joy to meet people with very different pasts.

It was also interesting to be so far from Jerusalem and the insidious pull of the Temple. The Jews here had their synagogue and their teachers, they observed the Sabbath and the festivals, but their lives did not seem to revolve around their faith in quite the way that Salome was used to further south. They were on the border of the Holy Land, shadowed by the great mountains that divided Moses' Promised Land from the glittering eastern mass of Syria, and life was lived in a rather more eclectic way.

Sometimes Salome remembered what Johanna had told her about Jesus teaching that a Samaritan could behave as well as a Jew by following the basic laws of humanity and could understand what he meant. Herodias was gloriously fierce in her Hasmonean heritage and a strong defender of Jewish rights and privileges, and Salome appreciated that in her, but out here in Trachonitis it was possible to see the shadows between the glaring sun of the strictest strains of their faith and she had to admit that she liked them. There was, somehow, so much more room to breathe.

Salome lay back in her husband's arms and closed her eyes. She was still haunted by the staring eyes of John the Baptiser in the darkest reaches of the night but some nights now, with Philip's gentle care and his people's kind welcome, sleep was carrying her over the chasm of the nightmare. She still wished all the time that that terrible night had gone differently but she was starting to accept that she could not go back, and she could feel her bruised soul – whatever that really was – knitting together. She wasn't sure if she deserved such peace but it was a relief all the same and she floated gladly into sleep.

❖

The next day, worn out from her travels and the late dinner, Salome slept long past sunrise and woke, confused and disorientated, to find her maid shaking tentatively at her shoulder. The girl leapt back as soon as Salome opened her eyes, tugging on her forelock.

'Beg pardon, my lady. I hated to disturb you but she said I must.'

Salome rubbed sticky sleep from her eyes.

'Who?' She looked around for Philip but he was already up and gone. Ashamed of herself, she sat hastily upright. 'Who said that?'

'Your visitor, my lady.'

'I did not know I had a visitor today.'

'She was not expected, but she says you will want to see her.'

Salome groaned.

'Is it my mother?'

'The Lady Herodias?' The maid's eyes widened. 'No. No, I'm sorry it is not—'

'Don't be sorry.'

Salome breathed again but if it was not Herodias demanding her immediate appearance, then who?

'She said to tell you that Johanna was here and that—'

The maid got no further, for Salome was up and grabbing at the nearest robe.

'Johanna? Johanna is here? In Trachonitis?'

'Waiting right outside the door, my lady,' the astonished maid said. 'Shall I show her in?'

'Yes. Oh, yes please.'

She'd barely slipped the gown over her head when the door

169

opened and Johanna came tumbling inside. Salome ran to her, hugging her tight.

'Slug-a-bed,' Johanna teased, stroking her hair, which had, as usual, sprouted in all directions out of the plaits meant to hold it tight.

'I have been very busy,' Salome apologised.

'And I, but here you see me – up with the lark.'

Salome held her old friend out at arm's length to see her better. Her clothes were a little rougher than when she'd been a palace servant but they were clean and bright. Her face was sun-browned and her hair caught up in a simple headscarf, but she radiated all her usual energy – and something else too. A calm, perhaps, that had been absent before.

'You look very well, Johanna. Life on the road suits you.'

Johanna blushed.

'It is not quite how you make it sound, Salome. We do not sleep in bushes or gutters. We are supported by people everywhere we go, often the Essene communities but also others who have heard Jesus speak and are inspired by his message. We sleep in haylofts and halls, in courtyards and byres and synagogues.'

'Synagogues?'

'Some priests are sympathetic to the New Way, especially in the more remote communities. They are sick of the tangle of laws and prohibitions imposed upon them by the Sadducees and the Pharisees and want to get back to a simpler faith with humanity, justice and fairness at its heart.'

'And that is what your Jesus preaches?'

'He is not *my* Jesus, Salome. He is here for everyone.'

'Gentiles too?'

'If they will listen with a good heart, yes.'

'I have met many gentiles here in Trachonitis and they are good people but, Johanna, they are not God's people.'

'You have been listening to your mother for too long, Salome. Do you not understand? Jesus is not just a preacher. He is not just a carpenter with some good ideas. Jesus is *it*, Salome – the Messiah, the Christos. He has been sent by God to herald the coming of the final days. We are here, Salome, at the very crux of existence. Is that not the best news you have ever heard?'

Johanna's eyes were burning with blue fire and Salome staggered before her passion. This was the same lively, energetic woman she had known before but now her energy had found a channel and it was formidable.

'It does sound exciting,' she allowed cautiously.

'Exciting! It is vital, critical, urgent. This winter Jesus has chosen seventy people to go out and spread the New Way as widely as possible. Chuza and I have been chosen, Salome. We will preach.'

'That's amazing. Are you not scared?'

'Terrified, but God will guide us.'

'You will be fantastic, I am sure. And little Chuza-Amos?'

'Will come with us. He has been welcomed as part of the apostolic family and blessed by Jesus himself.'

Her eyes shone and Salome felt a rush of envy. She had been congratulating herself on finding some peace here in the hill country of Trachonitis, but Johanna, meanwhile, had found something so much more. Salome was not convinced, yet, that her friend was right, but it was good to see her so sparky.

'Is that why you are here, Johanna? To preach? I am sure Philip will grant you a platform; he is very open to new ideas.'

Johanna laughed.

'That is very kind, Salome, but it is not I who will be needing a platform here, but Jesus.'

'Jesus?' Salome stared at her. 'Jesus is here? In Caesarea Philippi?'

'He is.'

Salome's heart contracted with such violence that she had to hunch over to keep it beating. Her lungs shrunk with it so that every breath felt only half there and she staggered backwards and sunk onto the bed.

'He has come for me.'

Johanna said something in reply but she could not hear it over the rush of furious blood in her head. She could see it all again, John's head bouncing to the floor and being thrust onto the platter in her hands, the blood running off it and down her gown, the blank, staring eyes. She dug her fingers through her skirts and into her legs, clawing at them with her nails.

'He knows it was I who had his cousin murdered and he has come for retribution.'

She bowed her head, forced her hands to still. She had known it would come, had known she deserved it, she just hadn't expected it quite so soon.

The slap she had expected even less.

'No!' Johanna's voice was loud but controlled. Salome put a hand to her smarting cheek and stared up at her friend. 'No, Salome, it is not that. Have you listened to nothing I have told you about Jesus' teachings. He is not about retribution or revenge. He is about love, care, forgiveness.'

Salome shook her head violently.

'I do not deserve forgiveness.'

'Everyone deserves forgiveness, as long as they ask with a clean heart. Come and meet him, Salome. He will explain it so much better than me.'

'No.' Salome's entire body was shaking and she wrapped her hands into the covers of the bed to try and steady herself. 'No, Johanna, I cannot. I am too weak, too sinful, too evil.'

Johanna gave a soft little laugh.

'Listen, sweet one, please, listen. No one is evil and all who repent can be saved.'

'Saved?' Salome looked up, caught on this small but infinitely enticing word.

'Saved, yes. Please, Salome, come and meet him. Come and meet Jesus.'

What could she say to such an entreaty but yes? Even so, as she let Johanna unpeel her fingers from the covers and lead her out of the safety of her marital chamber and down to meet the man who had shaken the whole Holy Land into a new state of watchfulness, she felt shudders still rattle her body. Whatever Johanna said, and however good and kind this man might be, she was sure that he would want vengeance for his cousin. It would be her head on a platter before the day was done. Would they send it to her mother? It seemed only fair, but the thought of it tore at Salome's heart and it was only Johanna's hand in her own that kept her moving forward to her fate.

Chapter Eighteen

Salome

'Jesus, this is Princess Salome, Lady of Trachonitis.'

Johanna bowed out and Salome was alone with Jesus of Nazareth in Philip's antechamber. The crowds were calling for their teacher outside but he had spared time to see her – time to condemn her.

'I'm sorry.' Salome flung herself onto her knees, not even daring to look into his eyes. They had been kind the last time she'd met them from afar but they would not be now and she did not want to see it. 'I'm so sorry. I was a fool. No, not a fool. Far, far worse. I was mean and cruel and . . . and evil.'

'Not evil, Salome.' The voice was calm. He spoke quietly, but the words seemed to hum through her as if shouted from the hilltops. She dared a quick look up but still could not meet his eyes. What was he going to say? Was there worse than evil? 'Few men and women are naturally evil, child. We make mistakes, we get carried away, act in spite or anger or fear, but not out of evil.'

'Is it not evil, to turn on a man in chains, who has done nothing more than tell you that your way of life is wrong, and order his head to be cut off? It is not your average sin, teacher. It is not like stealing a loaf or pulling someone's hair or even setting fire to their house. I took a man's life – an important man's life – and I deserve whatever punishment you decree.'

Jesus put a hand on her head.

'Do you repent, Salome?' Surprised, she looked up and suddenly there were those eyes – blue and clear and kind, still kind. She started to shake again and might have collapsed fully to the floor had he not bent down to clasp her shoulders. 'Are you sorry?'

'Yes! Of course, yes. Every morning I wake wishing it had been different. Every day, I wish I had stood up and said no – stopped the chanting and told everyone in that damned hall that John had done nothing but speak his mind and should be let go. I was offered a gift by my stepfather – *any* gift. I could have chosen John's release and he would have granted it, I know he would. He didn't like having him imprisoned either. But my mother ...'

She ground to a halt. She could almost feel Herodias at her side again, spitting fury at John's insolence, seemingly defending her child, but in truth working cunningly towards her own ends. Herodias had been so assertive, so sure. Salome had merely ... But no, she would not use anyone else as an excuse for her terrible behaviour.

'What is my punishment?' she demanded.

'Oh, Salome.' Suddenly Jesus was on his knees too, so that his face was almost level with hers and his eyes penetrating her with their infinite care. 'You are punishing yourself far more cruelly than anything I could sentence and God sees that. He does not want vengeance.'

'Of course He does. And He should. I cut down his messenger.'

'You were a part – a small part – of a group that cut down His messenger, that is true.'

'It was my gift!'

'Offered under duress, but, Salome, that is not the point. I tell you again, that God does not want vengeance. He is not a god of fire or fury, but of love.'

'Love?' Salome whispered, hearing it in her mother's clipped, dismissive tone.

'Love, Salome. If you turn to Him, confess your sins and repent, He will forgive you.'

'Forgive?' Salome could not take this in. 'Why would He do that?'

Jesus gave a low laugh.

'Does a parent not want the best for their child?'

Salome's brow furrowed.

'I'm not sure,' she said, hearing her voice sulky and petulant. Then she reminded herself of the way Herodias had clasped her when the stone had hit her brow. *Do not die, Salome. Please, do not die.* 'Perhaps.'

'What is best is perhaps where the arguments lie,' he said perceptively, 'but they do want the best. They do want their child to do well and to be happy, otherwise what would be the point in bringing them into the world?'

'To inherit their land?' Salome suggested, unable to shake off her darkness.

Jesus gave a small sigh.

'It is harder, I think, when you have much to give up, but true riches are in the people around you, Salome – in your loved ones, your friends, members of your community. True riches are in how you feel about the world and about God.'

She stared at him. He was far less wild than John had been. His speech was gracious and calm, but did that make him any less mad?

'How I *feel* about God?' she asked. 'God is not there to feel anything about. He is there to be worshipped and feared. He is there to be appeased with sacrifice and tithes, to be glorified with worship and to be hailed for his mercies.'

'Ah, Salome, you are a clever girl, I think. Where is God?'

'Where?' This man was definitely not sane. Why on earth were so many people following him around when he did not grasp even the very basics of their faith? 'He is in the Temple, of course, in the Holy of Holies.'

'No.' Jesus gave her shoulders a little shake. 'No, Salome, that is wrong. God is not hidden away in the Temple, accessible only by those with titles and fancy robes; God is in your heart.'

'No! He—'

'He is in your heart and you can feel him. You can talk to Him, you can pray to Him and you can feel Him.'

'No. A priest—'

'Is not needed.'

She gasped.

'You cannot say that!'

'I can, because it is the truth.'

'But it is ... is ... dangerous. It is an attack on the whole syna-gogue. They will not like it.'

He shook his head sadly.

'They *do not* like it, Salome. And, yes, that makes it dangerous, but it does not make it any less true.'

Salome felt her eyes widen. No wonder people followed this man. The thought of talking directly to God was desperately enticing, but what he spoke was surely blasphemy. And impossible besides.

'How would *I* ever feel God?'

Jesus smiled at her.

'You dance, do you not, Salome?'

She shuddered.

'Not any more.'

'Ah. A shame.' He paused as if he might say more but did not. 'Very well, when you used to dance, how did it feel?'

That one was easy.

'As if my emotions, my feelings, my thoughts and my confusions were finding shape in my limbs and making sense that way.'

'Good. That is what prayer can be too.' His grip on her shoul-ders tightened and he lifted her gently to her feet. 'You do not need me for the forgiveness you seek, Salome. It is God's to give and I tell you now that if you speak to Him from your heart, He will grant it. You will be cleansed of your sin and can move for-ward in the New Way.'

It was an enticing idea. Salome felt her head swim with the possi-bility of letting go of the darkness that had been swamping her since Machaerus and stepping into the light. Could it be that simple?

'Try it,' he whispered. The crowd noise was growing frantic out-side and half of Salome could hear people trying to keep order, but the other half – the louder half – could only hear Jesus' promises. If she spoke to God, He would forgive her? Could it be? 'I must go.'

She shook herself out of her reverie.

'No! I mean, please, stay and dine here in the palace. You and all your followers.'

'All?' He tipped an ear to the noise beyond the door, an amused smile on his handsome face.

'All,' Salome said firmly.

'That would be very kind. Thank you.'

He was at the door now and she saw him draw in a breath and ready himself to step out to the masses once more and wondered what toll so many demands took on a man.

'No, Jesus,' she said firmly, 'thank *you*.'

❖

They dined, in the end, in the gracious gardens at the back of the palace, for there was not enough room in even Philip's large hall to accommodate Jesus, his closest disciples, and the crowds who had flocked up to Caesarea Philippi after him. Philip had barely batted an eyelid when she'd asked his permission to feed several hundred people and had set the kitchens grinding corn and baking bread, and ordered two barrels of salted fish to be broached, plus several more of his finest beer. Salome had loved him then and told him so. He'd looked surprised.

'That gladdens my heart to hear, Salome. I consider myself already fortunate to have such a kind, wise, beautiful wife but one who cares for me also is a blessing indeed.' He'd kissed her, then whispered, 'This Jesus has offered you the forgiveness you sought?'

She'd looked at him in surprise.

'How did you know I sought forgiveness?'

'Ah Salome, it was a terrible night. We all need forgiveness for it but most of us, used to battle and the darker corners of justice, have seen worse in our lives and could perhaps bear the burden of the harsh deed a little more easily than you. I would feed this man a thousand times over if he has helped you find a little peace.'

'He says God will forgive me, if I ask Him.'

'*You* ask Him?'

'That's what he says.'

'Interesting. Well, he seems a wise man, so perhaps he is right. Now, come, we have food to prepare.'

They all sat at long trestle tables, laid out beneath the setting sun and piled with bread, salted fish, and fruits, both fresh and dried, from the palace gardens and stores. The tables were set in groups and singles, wherever there was room between the flower and herb beds, rather than in strict lines of precedence and it made for a happy, easy atmosphere. Sitting watching everyone eat their simple fare and chat happily amongst each other, Salome thought it was perhaps the finest feast she had ever been to.

She looked to Johanna, sat with Chuza, their baby asleep in a basket at their feet, the picture of contentment. She remembered Chuza, so low and dark-browed after the night of the death-feast in Machaerus, and marvelled at the happy, easy man talking to his peers. It was not just the setting sun that was lighting up his face, but a quiet radiance that seemed to come from within. Johanna, too, looked relaxed. She was still restless, ever leaping up to help others to food or drink, but without the slightly manic edge Salome remembered.

They were sat with the girl from Magdala, Mary. She was a small creature with a sharp nose and even sharper eyes and Salome prickled as she saw Johanna chatting intently with her. Clearly her one-time friend was not missing the palace, or herself, at all.

'It is very kind of you to house us,' a soft voice said at Salome's side and she pulled herself away from her jealous study to pay attention to her immediate guests.

'It is the least I could do,' she told the man, a tall, sharp-eyed fellow she had seen marshalling the crowd earlier.

'Because of John?' he asked. She sucked in a sharp breath and he looked intently at her. This lot all seemed to do that; it was most discomforting. 'God will forgive you.'

'So Jesus says,' she managed stiffly.

'He is right. But it is not easy. It is not just a matter of saying sorry and moving on – you must also change your attitude, your way of life.'

Salome swallowed. Something about this man reminded her of the hard drive of the Baptiser.

'You mean I should give you all my wealth?'

He threw up his hands.

'Not me. I have all I need here, with my company. If you see need, you should of course respond to it according to your means but no, we do not come with a begging bowl. This is a far, far bigger mission.'

His eyes shone and it softened him a little.

'I'm sorry, I didn't catch your name?'

'Peter. Simon Peter. Lately fisherman of Capernaum with my brother Andrew.' He indicated a younger man on his far side.

'And now?'

'And now disciple to Jesus, and apostle besides.'

'Apostle?'

'Emissary – one who will carry his message.'

'Ah. You are one of the seventy who will go out to preach this winter?'

'I am, with my wife, Perpetua.' He gestured to a woman at the next table. She was chatting away with an older lady Salome thought might be Jesus' mother, Mariam, but she glanced across and gave Salome a small nod.

'You are lucky you are able to travel together.'

'It is not luck but good judgement.'

'Do you have children with you?'

Peter tensed.

'We have not been so blessed.'

'I'm sorry, I—'

He put up a hand.

'We were sorry too, for a long time, but now God's purpose is revealed to us and we can only be glad that we are free to preach his message of redemption.'

'That's very good.'

'It is. Now, if you'll excuse me, I think Jesus needs me.'

Salome glanced over to Jesus. He seemed to be deep in conversation with Philip but she was not sorry to see stiff-backed Peter leave his seat. His brother, Andrew, looked ruefully at her.

'Forgive him, my lady. Peter never sits still for long. He is ever-impatient to spread the word.'

'A fine quality, I'm sure.'

'But not a restful one.'

Andrew smiled. He had the same features as Peter but his jaw was softer, his cheeks rounder, his hair curlier, so that he seemed a little more yielding than his brother. Salome refilled his beer glass and he raised it to her with another smile.

'You have followed Jesus for how long, Andrew?'

'About nine months, since he came to live in my brother's house in Capernaum, but I was a follower of John before that.'

Salome looked at him aghast.

'I'm so sorry. That night was so awful.'

He put up a hand.

'You have spoken to Jesus of this, I think?'

'Of course. I asked his forgiveness.'

'And he gave it.'

It was not a question, but a statement.

'He did, but—'

'Then it is done.' He smiled at her. 'Truly, Princess, it is done. We must look forward to the New Way not back to the old one.'

'You make that sound so easy.'

'It can be, if you give yourself to God. And is it not better to be cleansed and move forward with a good heart, than to dwell in endless darkness?'

'Of course, if you can.'

'I can. Can you?' She bit her lip, unsure that she could, but Andrew just reached for another chunk of bread, looking amiably around. 'I thought Trachonitis would be wilder than this,' he observed.

'Me too,' she agreed, following his lead out of the darker subject matter.

'You are newly arrived?'

'Brought here by my husband four months ago.'

He looked at her curiously.

'It must be strange to be a woman, lifted from one life and deposited into another just like that.'

Salome laughed, the sound surprising her.

'I suppose it is, though I have been brought up to expect it and Philip is very kind to me.'

'That's good. It is a vital characteristic in a spouse.'

'You think so? My mother chose him for his title, wealth and connections.'

'And which do you appreciate more, those or his kindness?'

'The latter,' she said instantly, then considered. 'Though, to be fair, I have them all so it is hard for me to truly say.'

He nodded thoughtfully.

'You speak well, Princess.'

'Salome, please,' she corrected him, feeling awkward with a title amongst this band of equals.

Andrew opened his mouth to reply but at that moment Peter clinked his eating knife against a glass and everyone looked up.

'Our gracious host has just asked Jesus a vital question, one I think we should all consider.'

Philip glanced to Salome, who gave him an awkward shrug. This Peter was abrasive but hard to ignore.

'What question?' someone called.

'He wishes to know who Jesus is.' A ripple ran around the many diners. Again, Philip looked to Salome, clearly puzzled at the attention such a simple question was attracting but it seemed to matter a great deal to Peter who was staring intently at the Nazarene. 'Who are you, Jesus?'

Jesus stood, looked around them all and then asked, 'Who do people say I am?'

'You are Moses,' someone cried, 'returned to restore the Holy Land to us from the wicked Romans.'

Jesus put up a hand. 'I am not here to fight.'

'Not yet,' a thin-faced man called from a nearby table.

'Not ever, Judas Iscariot,' Jesus said sternly. 'My only weapons are words.'

Judas looked contrite and sunk into his seat as someone at his side called, 'You are Elijah.'

'Jeremiah,' another supplied and suddenly there was a clamour of voices.

Salome looked around them all, intrigued. Philip's question had not been so simple after all and these people were happily following this man without truly knowing why.

'You are John the Baptiser, risen again,' someone else shouted out and Salome felt a stab of pain and had to clutch at the table to stay upright.

'Nonsense,' Andrew cried, leaning protectively towards her. 'I knew John well and he and Jesus worked together. Did not John baptise Jesus before he was imprisoned? How, then, can they be the same man?'

There was a murmur of agreement and Salome looked gratefully to Andrew. She did not, she knew, deserve help from him or any of this earnest company of good people, many of whom must have, like Andrew, followed John before Antipas – well, Herodias – had ordered him put away. They had every right to turn upon her but, instead, they had accepted her with open hearts. It was humbling, and Salome was torn between a longing to stay with them to learn more, and to escape and think this all over in quiet. Her mind tumbled and her legs itched to dance but she pressed her hands firmly down upon them and tried to focus.

Jesus was waiting for the noise to die down which, before his commanding presence, it swiftly did.

'And you, Peter,' he asked, 'who do you say I am?'

Peter straightened his back and looked straight at his teacher.

'I say, Lord, that you are the Messiah, the son of the living God.'

The people exploded at this, cheering and clapping rapturously. Salome watched Jesus, who stood quietly, hands pressed together, watching the joy around him. Eventually it settled once more.

'It seems, Peter,' he said, 'that God has spoken to you and through you. You are the rock upon which my church will be built.'

'Church?' Peter queried. 'What is a church?'

Salome was as puzzled as he. The Aramaic word, *lodoth*, was not one usually used as a noun, but a verb, a calling to gather for the purpose of testifying or bearing witness.

'You will know,' Jesus told him. 'When the time comes, you will know, Peter, and you – all of you – will make it happen.'

There were more cheers, especially from the tables a little further back who had perhaps not caught the strange word and were simply enjoying the tone of purpose from their leader. Peter, however, was standing, deeply puzzled, at Jesus' side.

'But Lord, how will I know? And what will I do about it? Speak to me, instruct me, tell me what to do.'

Jesus shook his head.

'I will no more tell you what to do than God does. It is in your heart, Peter, as it is in the hearts of all believers. Now, eat, drink, be merry, for there are hard times ahead.'

Peter did not look happy but retreated as ordered and picked at a crust of bread. Salome saw his wife go to him, stroking his back and murmuring in his ear, and wondered how they bore the strange charge that seemed to have been laid upon them.

'Where will you preach?' she heard Philip ask Jesus.

'Everywhere I can reach, for as long as I can.'

'They will be after you, you know that?'

'I know that.'

'Caiaphas and the Sadducees will not stand for ideas that undermine their position and authority.'

'Of course not.'

'You are in great danger if you continue to speak so openly.'

'But in even greater danger if I do not.' Jesus put a hand on Philip's arm. 'We are but a short time in this life, Tetrarch, and a long, long time in the one to come. Do not store up riches on earth, but in heaven.'

'I understand your philosophy,' Philip said evenly, 'but even if you can look to happiness in death, it is surely madness to court it, especially if you have a mission?'

Jesus looked troubled.

'I pray regularly for guidance on that. These are violent times and our message may need violent means.'

Philip looked shocked.

'You said you were not here to fight.'

Jesus just smiled at him.

'And I did not say that the violence would be mine. But, come, we have preyed on your hospitality long enough and must depart.'

'Sleep here, please. There are pallet beds enough for all and guards to keep you safe.'

'You are most kind and I will be glad to accept for it grows late. But it is God, not men, who will keep us safe, until such time as it no longer suits His purpose.'

❖

Those words echoed through Salome all night long and she tossed restlessly, very aware of the Nazarene and his followers sleeping beneath the stars in the gardens below her chamber. This man expected trouble, maybe even welcomed it. He knew he was courting the condemnation of the Temple and the powers that ran it, but that did not seem to deter him. And she? She knew that those powers included her stepfather and, even more vitally, her mother. Herodias was ferocious in her guardianship of Judaism in its most traditional form and would not take kindly to the momentum that was gathering behind the carpenter with the tongue of gold.

Talk to God, Salome, and He will forgive you.

She tried. All through the night she tried, but God, she feared, was not listening and in truth she could not blame Him. She was grateful when the first rays of the sun spared her from her torment and slipped out of bed, leaving Philip sleeping, to go and order more bread and fresh cheese from the kitchens for their guests to break their fast.

It was all over too quickly. Suddenly the group were gathering their packs and bags and preparing to move on. Jesus was going up into the hills to pray with Peter and a handful of others and the rest were heading into the villages of Trachonitis to spread his word. They were buzzing with purpose and Salome stood between them feeling static and dull.

'Come with us, Salome,' Johanna said, throwing her arms around her waist.

'You know I cannot.'

'Why?'

'I am a married woman, Johanna.'

'As am I.'

She indicated Chuza standing nearby, their son strapped to his chest.

'But your husband does not rule a tetrarchy.'

'Neither does yours – the Romans rule and he is merely their instrument.'

Salome felt anger rise.

'That is not true. The Romans may control the region but we, Philip and I, can stand between them and the people and ensure that a just and fair rule is in place to improve their lives.'

Johanna bit her lip.

'That is true and you do it well. I'm sorry, Salome. I spoke out of place. It is simply that Chuza and I have found such happiness, such freedom, in following the Messiah, and I would love that for you too.'

Salome noted the word 'Messiah' and shivered. Was it true? Was it possible that she was living her little life at the very crux of history? And, if it *was* possible, what should she do? She admired Johanna's courage in taking to the road with Jesus and, she had to admit, she was jealous of it, but she could not just pick up her pack and leave Philip. She had sworn an oath to him. She owed him loyalty, partnership, commitment.

'It has been wonderful to have you all here, Johanna, and I wish you well.'

Johanna sighed but gave her another hug.

'And we you. Perhaps we will see you in Jerusalem? We travel there for Sukkot before we disperse to preach.'

'Jerusalem? Is that not dangerous?'

Johanna shrugged.

'Perhaps, but God is with us so all will be well.'

Then, with a quick kiss on Salome's forehead, she was gone, off to take Chuza's arm and fall in with Mary, Mariam, Elisabeth, Perpetua and all the other chattering followers to head out of the palace and into the hills, poor but together. Salome stood and watched them go until they were but a speck of dust on the horizon and she was alone again in the empty palace.

Chapter Nineteen

Herodias

'And this,' Herodias flung an expansive hand around the glorious building before them, 'is the Temple.'

'It's beautiful,' Kypros gasped. 'So magnificently vast and imposing, is it not, children?'

Little Agrippa and Berenice nodded, gazing around the colonnaded Court of the Gentiles and up to the magnificent Gate of Susa that led into the grand buildings of the Inner Temple. Herodias beamed at them.

'All built by our family, for the glory of God.'

'For the glory of themselves more like,' came a rough reply and Herodias spun round to glare at her brother.

'You do not like it, Agrippa?'

'I do not think it is here to be "liked". It is here to radiate power and wealth.'

'Yes, of the Jewish nation.'

He shrugged.

'If you wish to believe that, sister, but I think we all know better. Our dear grandfather was far more interested in his own power and wealth than in his people's.'

'Land not love,' someone said behind him and Salome stepped out and smiled a sickly smile at Herodias.

Herodias shook her head. She had been glad to see her daughter when she'd arrived at the Hasmonean palace yesterday but it had taken only about five minutes for the damned girl to start needling her. Honestly! She'd thought that marriage might have brought Salome to adulthood but, no, she had delighted in riling Herodias from the moment she arrived, going on about the carpenter from Nazareth and muttering peculiar things about talking to God. Herodias was beginning to fear that the girl was touched, which would be most embarrassing.

'How many do you think died building the Temple?' Salome asked now.

'I have no idea,' Herodias snapped. 'And it is not important.'

'The lives of men are not important?' Agrippa asked.

'You know that is not what I meant.' A small crowd was gathering and Herodias glared at her brother and daughter. They were a most unlikely double-act, the dissolute semi-Roman and the uptight adolescent, but here they were, facing her down together. 'Every life is precious but the safety of the workforce is down to the constructors, not the designers.'

'It is, I am sure, down to the budget,' Salome said. 'One less golden rooftop would mean more workers and more breaks for those workers and then less of them would die.'

'But, of course,' Agrippa chimed in, 'that would not look as pretty for the pilgrims, right, sister?'

'Do not meddle in things you do not understand, brother. All you have ever constructed is trouble. Now, Kypros, come through and see the Temple itself.' She grabbed her sister-in-law's arm and hurried her across the Court of the Gentiles, past the many stalls changing Roman coins into Temple shekels and selling animals for sacrifice, and towards the steps up to the Inner Temple. 'Caiaphas, the High Priest, is waiting to meet us and show us round. He can be a little priggish – Antipas doesn't like him much – but he's a great friend to the family. He understands how much the Holy City means to us as the heart of the Jewish nation and is keen to help us preserve it from outsiders.'

'Romans, you mean,' Agrippa said, leaning on one of the many notices warning the uncircumcised not to enter the Inner Temple on pain of death. 'I don't know why everyone around here is so hung up on them. They're not so bad.'

A few people looked around and even Salome took a step away from her unlikely ally. Herodias rushed to his side.

'Hush, Agrippa – that is near treason around here. You will rouse the mob.'

'Will I indeed?'

Agrippa looked around as if this might please him greatly and Herodias cursed herself for ever thinking it a good idea to bring him to Jerusalem for Sukkot. She had hoped that seeing the Temple in all its grandeur might impress upon him something of the heritage he seemed to care so little for, but maybe her loose-living brother was beyond redemption.

He had made but a cursory pass at his job as steward, rarely turning up for duties until midday and often leaving again barely an hour later, citing important people to see. These, from what she could gather from her spies in the city, were mainly drinking buddies in the darker taverns, and tension was starting to mount between him and Antipas. Her husband had stayed in Tiberias and Herodias had hoped that bringing her brother away would give him some relief but it looked as if it would bring *her* trouble, especially with Salome in her usual dark mood.

'Caiaphas!'

She looked round in relief as the High Priest, resplendent in his second-best robes, came striding down the steps to receive them. His ceremonial garb for the high festivals was encrusted with gold and jewels and kept under lock and key until the great Sabbaths, sadly by the Romans, who had chosen to take custody of them as if they were state property and not the symbol of the great mystery of God. It was one of Herodias' aims to regain possession of those vital garments, but at least Caiaphas had plenty of 'ordinary' ones that more than dazzled the common man.

Caiaphas was followed by the key men of the Sanhedrin – Sadducees of the ancient priestly caste, also finely robbed – and, as they bowed low before Herodias, the crowds in the Temple forecourt gathered eagerly to see who had deserved such a welcome. She looked proudly around.

'I thank you, your Holinesses, for your kind greeting.'

'And you for gracing us with your presence, Lady Herodias. You have come at a needful time.'

'I have?'

Caiaphas was looking intently at her and she felt her stomach contract.

'Shall we head inside?' she suggested, 'My guests are keen to see the beautiful Court of the Women and—'

But Caiaphas cut her off, clearly set on a public scene.

'It is the aqueduct, my lady.'

'Which aqueduct?'

Caiaphas flung his arms dramatically wide and the golden thread in his elaborate hems flashed in the stark sunlight.

'King Herod's aqueduct. Pontius Pilate has ordered a long extension far beyond Solomon's pools to increase the water supply to the city.'

'That sounds worthy,' Kypros said. Caiaphas glared at her and she looked nervously to Herodias. 'Does it not?'

'Is there a problem with the project, Caiaphas?'

'Only, my lady, that he has appropriated Temple monies to fund it – our sacred tithes, given by our hard-working Jewish people for the administration of our own affairs.'

'How dare he?' Herodias gasped.

'I think you'll find,' Agrippa said casually, 'that it is entirely legal. After all, the project is benefiting our hard-working Jewish people, is it not?'

Herodias stared at him.

'What do you know of this, Agrippa?'

He gave her a sly smile.

'I did not only party in Rome, sister. We were force-fed Jewish law by some very dull priests over the years and this I remember. Correct, Caucasus?'

'Caiaphas,' the High Priest corrected him through clenched teeth. 'And yes, by the absolute letter of the law Pilate is within his rights, but by the *spirit* of the law it is deplorable. The Roman governor taxes our people at terrible rates and can surely fund an aqueduct – a Roman construction—'

'And an excellent one,' Agrippa said.

'Out of those funds,' Caiaphas finished, his voice gaining in pitch with every word.

'The funds gained from the terrible rates of taxation?' Agrippa pushed.

'Yes.'

'Remind me, Cairabras.'

'Caiaphas!'

'What rate is that? Seven per cent is it not?'

'It is around that, yes.'

'As opposed to the ten per cent the Temple charges them?'

'As dictated by the laws brought down from Moses himself.'

'And set out before there were Roman governors to take an additional toll. Some might say that the fair thing for the Temple to do would be to take only the three per cent that makes up the extra now that the, erm, economic circumstances have changed.'

Caiaphas went purple in the face and Herodias stared at her brother in astonishment. She had thought him a dullard as well as a profligate but it seemed that his loose living had not harmed his wits, if he chose to employ them. Now she was truly regretting bringing him along. The damned man was bound to stand on the side of the Romans, he was all but one of them. She looked nervously at the crowd, growing by the minute.

'Caiaphas,' she said urgently, 'I really think we should take this discussion somewhere private.'

Caiaphas looked as if he was starting to agree, but before they could withdraw from the public glare, trumpets sounded out at the Gate of the Prophet in the South-west corner and an overdressed palfrey trotted into the courtyard with the last man Herodias wanted to see perched atop.

'Pilate,' she groaned.

'Lady Herodias, what a pleasure.' He leapt down from the horse with surprising agility and offered her the briefest of bows. 'Lady Salome. And my Lord Agrippa!' His eyes lit up. 'How good to see you again.'

Herodias groaned more deeply. Of course her damned brother would know the governor personally. 'And the Lady Kypros and your lovely children.'

He bowed to them all – far lower, Herodias could swear, than he had done to her or Salome. Berenice had retreated into her mother's skirts with the press of the crowd, but little Agrippa was standing, legs akimbo, clearly enjoying the attention.

'Welcome to Jerusalem,' Pilate went on. 'Is it your first visit?'

'Since I was a child,' Agrippa agreed. 'It is very enlightening. We have already been party to some most intriguing debate.'

'Agrippa,' Herodias warned.

'On repairs to an aqueduct.'

'Ah yes.' Pilate rubbed his hands like the fool he was. 'My designers have proposed an excellent extension to the existing structure to bring water from the Spring of Arroub into the Pools of Solomon that, as you know, struggle to provide enough water for all in the city, especially in the summer months. It is a fine piece of engineering.'

'And is costing a fortune,' Caiaphas said, 'from Temple funds.'

The crowd hissed and Pilate looked nervously around. Really, had the man no idea where he was?

'As is sanctioned under Jewish law. It really will make a big difference to the poorer folk in the Western quarter and I am sure, Caiaphas, that you welcome that.'

'Of course I welcome it but not at the expense of God's holy mysteries.'

'They seem most well served to me,' Pilate said, gesturing around the Temple.

'That,' Herodias said, drawing herself up tall, 'is because you do not understand God's holy mysteries. And that is why you should not be in charge of this most sacred of cities.' The crowd roared approval and Herodias felt it rush through her, as heady as wine. 'This is the one God, Pilate – the sacred, unseen Jehovah. He is not to be appeased with a bowl of wine, like your paltry Roman deities.'

More cheers from the crowd.

'My lady, the Temple has funds to spare and—'

'They are not "to spare". They are for the good of the Jewish nation.'

'Who live in this city.'

'And all over the known world. You think your Empire fine, Roman, but there are Jews in every city around the Mediterranean and beyond. We have been spread far and wide by the persecution of others, but we have stayed strong, we have stayed united.'

'Strong!' the crowd echoed. 'United!'

'And we have stayed loyal to the beating heart of our sadly disparate peoples – the Temple. Now you are tapping into it as if it is your personal bank and not the repository of the hopes, the dreams and the resources of an entire nation.'

Pilate looked stunned and Herodias seized the chance to shut down this over-heated confrontation.

'We will discuss this, Pilate, when the blessed festival of Sukkot has been celebrated with due reverence. But remember, Tiberius himself charged you with respecting the Jewish people and I expect to see that charge obeyed. Good day.'

She swept her guests determinedly past the notices banning the uncircumcised and up the Temple steps, Caiaphas and the Sadducees forming a golden guard around them as the people cheered wildly and Pilate and his men slunk away. Herodias paused a moment at the door to wave and drink in the roar of approval.

These were truly her people, this was truly her city. Let the Romans mess with that at their peril.

Even so, she was glad to get into the safety of the Inner Temple and to be ushered to a quiet room in the Chamber of Oils at one corner of the Court of Women where they could all sink onto couches. Caiaphas called for mint tea and sweetcakes and sent a serving boy to fan Herodias' hot face. She leaned thankfully back.

'Magnificent, my lady,' Caiaphas crooned. 'Truly magnificent.'

Kypros sat down next to her and patted her leg.

'It was, indeed, very well said.'

Herodias looked at her gratefully and even Agrippa edged her way.

'That was pretty impressive actually. You should act, Herodias.'

'She does,' snapped another voice. Salome.

Hurt stabbed through Herodias but she fought it away and took a sip of her tea. It was fresh and scented but, oh, it lacked the zing of a glass of wine. She felt a sudden rush of longing to have Antipas here with her but shook it away. She could stand on her own two feet; had she not just proved as much?

'That, my dear daughter, was not an act. That was my truly felt and honestly held belief.'

'That we should not spend the Temple monies on things to improve the people's lives?'

'That we should not spend the Temple monies on things decided upon by foreigners.'

'Even if they are good things?'

Agrippa gave a delighted little ooh and Herodias felt herself shrivel. She was prepared to stand up and fight the wretched governor, but did she really have to go through this with her own family?

'It is the principle of the matter, Salome. If we let them dip into our purse for this, then what's to stop them doing it again and again?'

'Does it matter, if the purse is full.'

'It will soon empty. Would you let someone else take from your own purse?'

'If their need was greater than mine, yes.'

Herodias shook her head at her.

'Ninety-nine per cent of the population of the Holy Land has a need greater than yours, Princess, but I do not see you handing out coins.'

Salome winced.

'You are right, Mother.'

'I am? I mean, yes, good.'

'I am a hypocrite indeed. We all are. We would rather the Temple had jewelled chalices and marble altars—'

'And golden roofs,' Agrippa put in unhelpfully.

'Exactly! And golden roofs, than we would some poor folk had fresh water every day. It is exactly as John said – it is harder for a rich man to get into the kingdom of heaven than a camel to pass through the eye of the needle.'

'What?' Herodias stared at her. 'Are you quite well, daughter?'

'Better than ever before. I had a guest in Caesarea Philippi last autumn you know, a fascinating guest. He came with Johanna and Chuza.'

'The carpenter?' Herodias groaned.

'The Messiah.'

'Salome! How dare you? Here of all places!'

'How dare I proclaim the Messiah predicted in Scriptures here, where they are kept?'

'How dare you proclaim some Nazarene peasant as the fulfil-ment of God's promise!'

'Have you met him, Mother?'

'I have not. Neither do I wish to. I am told he is preaching to Jews and Gentiles alike.'

'If they wish to listen, yes. Is that so wrong?'

'Is it so wrong?! Have you listened to none of the history you have been taught? Do you remember nothing of what your own

Hasmonean ancestors went through to stop Gentiles taking everything from us? People stand ready to persecute Jews at every point, daughter. They hate us because we follow the one true God and are not prepared to accept their phoney ones. They are always looking for ways to drive us from our lands, from our goods, even from our very beliefs.' She stood up furiously, knocking her mint tea aside. 'No wonder these Romans are preying on us if one of our own is working to split us in two.'

'That is not Jesus' intention.'

'He has told you his plans, has he? He has taken you into his confidence and explained the fulfilment of his mission?'

'No. But he speaks well and true. And he heals people everywhere he goes.'

'You have seen this?'

'Johanna has. Chuza too. Listen, Mother.' Salome stood too, grabbing Herodias' hands in a grip so fierce it turned her fingers white. Herodias tried to pull away but the girl was inflamed. 'What if it *is* true? What if Jesus *is* the Messiah? Think on it, please. This could be it, Mother – this could be God's final coming. Would you miss it?'

Herodias looked into Salome's wild eyes and felt guilt flare. Her daughter had been like this since the execution of the Baptiser. It was her fault. She should have had him quietly hanged in his cell and the whole matter would have faded away.

'If this man is the Messiah, then, no, Salome, I would not miss it. But if he is just a charlatan disrupting the peace and turning Jew against Jew, creating a chasm wide enough for a sword-wielding Roman to step gleefully into, then, yes, I would rather anything than that.'

'He is not a charlatan. He is a good, kind, clever man.'

'That does not make him the Messiah, child.'

'We will see, won't we?'

'We will see,' Herodias agreed. 'And I just pray that by the time we do, we have not lost everything we have worked so hard to build.'

'And to gild,' Salome threw at her and, with a dark look to Caiaphas, she stormed from the room, her footsteps tapping angrily away across the courtyard.

'Well, that was fun,' Agrippa said gleefully. 'I like Jerusalem more than I'd thought I would.'

'Shut up, Agrippa,' Kypros snapped but Herodias was already turning away.

This man, this Jesus, was dangerous. If he could rend the royal family asunder, what could he do to the Jewish nation? It did not bear thinking about and if she was to be a good ruler, she had to stand up and somehow sort it out. Sukkot was ruined and right now, looking around the grandeur of the Temple she normally loved so much, she wished with all her heart that she could be snuggled away in a simple tent with Antipas as she had been two seemingly endless years ago. It felt like a long, hard winter ahead.

Chapter Twenty

Salome

Salome shivered, wishing she'd kept her winter boots on instead of optimistically switching to sandals this morning. The sun was spring-bright but the air was as chill as it had been when she'd been here, in the Holy City, for the tempestuous Sukkot last year. The cold, at least, matched her mood as she looked out of her carriage window at the mass of pilgrims filling the road to Jerusalem. It had been a long trip from Caesarea Philippi, but the roads had grown more and more crowded the closer they'd got to the Holy City and now, within sight of the walls, the noise of eager chatter filled the air.

There was an excitement to Pesach this year, especially on the road from the north. The Galileans had been full of talk of Jesus who had, it seemed, been preaching all around the lake over the winter months. Simple men and women had been exchanging his "stories" as they might previously have exchanged gossip about their neighbours, and discussing what they thought he meant.

She had heard of him feeding five thousand people on just a handful of loaves and fishes, of him healing lepers and cripples, even of him walking on the waters of the lake and calming a storm. She had no idea what to make of these tales but the people shared them like fine cakes, revelling in their unlikely hero, and Salome guiltily listened in to every morsel she could catch. From what she could gather, Jesus and his disciples had headed towards the Holy City some weeks ago, preaching their way down the Jordan valley, and she found herself hoping she might see him again, talk to him even.

A little boy ran past in pursuit of another, giggling merrily, and Salome's eyes followed them enviously. Even as a child, she had spent this annual trip looking out of the window of the royal carriage at all the others laughing and running free, glad to be away from teaching and out at play. She had watched them laughing and skipping, falling and crying, being picked up, brushed down and sent off laughing and skipping once more, whilst she'd sat in her carriage. She'd seen little ones begging for the sweet pastries from the many sellers along the way whilst she'd turned her nose up at the fine foods brought in a basket for her princessly enjoyment. She felt bad about that now.

This trip, she had noticed the creak in the back of parents trying to carry a squirming child, the wince at a tunic ripped, or a pair of sandals worn down, the elevated price of the precious pastries and the worry in the adults' faces as they counted out their few coins and balanced saving enough for the equally elevated cost of a lamb for the sacrifice, against feeding their children. She had climbed out of her carriage and walked with the large group travelling all the way from Trachonitis and had ordered her men to pay for pastries for all each morning. People had been grovellingly grateful and that had felt bad too.

Yesterday, a poor mother's simple gown had been torn in a brawl and Salome, seeing her looking in despair at the ruined garment had grabbed one of her own from the chest in her carriage.

'Here, take this,' she had offered, but the mother had fallen to her knees.

'No, Princess, I couldn't. I mustn't. It wouldn't be right.'

'Of course it would. What is not right is you having nothing decent to wear.' The woman had shaken her head over and over. 'Why should I have more than you?'

'Because you're royal. Wearing your dress would be like putting on God's own clothing.'

Salome had not seen it that way but her persistence had been distressing the woman more than helping her so she'd had to give up and get back into her fine carriage with her fine foods and her fine gowns and watch them all struggle. The one bit of light in their faces had been when she'd gone past and they'd nudged each other and bowed and gone rushing to tell others. If all were equal, they would not have that, she supposed, but still it did not seem fair and she'd only agreed to ride into the city today because Philip's guards had been so anxious for her safety and she'd not wanted to put them under more duress by walking.

'Salome?'

She jumped at the deep voice at the window, bracing herself for her stepfather and, presumably, her mother, but it was not Antipas sat astride a fine horse alongside the carriage.

'Ari!'

He had filled out since she'd seen him last year, his lean body growing broader across the shoulders and his chin sprouting a fine beard that made him look at least five years older. He bowed his head and reached into the carriage to kiss her hand with extravagant style.

'You look wonderful, Lola.'

Her heart skipped ridiculously at the nickname. No one had called her that since her father had died.

'I look dusty and bedraggled from the road.'

'Then I cannot begin to imagine how you will shine once you have had a chance to bathe.'

She giggled.

'Don't be ridiculous, Ari. You look well too. Very . . . large.'

'Large?' He laughed. 'I was hoping more for handsome, or muscular, or, or . . .'

'Big-headed?'

He rolled his eyes.

'You're too sharp for me, Lola.' He looked around, suddenly serious. 'May I join you in your carriage?'

'Of course.'

She sat, feeling self-conscious, as he called the driver to halt the carriage, tied his mount to the side and clambered in with her. He looked larger still, up close. Her body tingled, uncomfortably pleasant at his sudden proximity and she fought to look composed as they set off again for the final crawl into the city.

'What do you make of Jerusalem, Lola?' he asked, his voice low.

'Make of it?'

He glanced out of the window as they approached the gates.

'It seems restless to me.'

'It always is.'

'Yes, but more so than usual. Have you heard about this Nazarene? Joseph, is it?'

'Jesus. And yes, I've met him.'

'Met him?! What's he like?'

'Inspirational. Clever and eloquent, with an incredibly calm manner and one of those voices that seem to carry over a crowd.'

'Right. Sounds impressive. What does he look like?'

She smiled.

'Handsome.'

'Lola!'

'Sorry, Ari. He is though. Handsome and commanding, with these incredibly blue eyes.'

'Am I to get jealous?'

Her breath caught.

'Jealous?'

'Come, Lola, you must know I had ... hopes. I thought perhaps you did too?'

'I'm a married woman, Ari.'

'For now. How is Philip?'

She swallowed, the carriage growing warm and stuffy.

'He is not very well. He caught an ague over the winter and has struggled to throw it off. I told him not to travel so he had time to recuperate. He was not happy to miss Pesach but his health is more important.'

She thought back to the conversation. In truth, Philip had been too weak to protest. The ague had clawed its way into his lungs and breathing was a struggle. She had worried about leaving him but someone from the family had to offer sacrifice and, if she was honest, she had been keen to see Johanna and the others around Jesus, and had seized on his insistence that she should go.

'Rest,' she had instructed sternly. 'Please, Philip, you must rest. I do not want to hear that you have been up dragging your justice chair around the tetrarchy. People can wait a little longer to have their suits heard once you are fully well.'

'Yes, wife,' he'd agreed, a promising spark in his eye.

'I mean it, Philip. I do not want to lose you.'

He'd reached up an arm then, pulling her down for a kiss and she had given it gladly. Philip would never be the sort of husband a girl dreamed of – the sort of husband Ari might have been – but he had been so very good to her and she was happy in Trachonitis. It suited her to be on the edge of the Holy Land, the edge of the Herodian game-playing, especially the edge of her mother's restless power struggles.

At that thought, she shifted on her padded bench. Herodias would surely be at the palace and she wasn't sure she could face her just yet. She would search her for signs of a budding Herodian heir and her disappointment at his lack would be clear.

'Shall we go into the Temple, Ari?' she suggested, nodding to the great building looming up ahead of them. 'Perhaps Jesus will be there and I can introduce you.'

'To your handsome prophet? Why would I want—'

'Oh, Ari, hush. I only said that to tease and only meant, besides, that he is handsome in a way that draws crowds. He has assurance, calm, presence. When he speaks, everyone listens.'

'Which is perhaps why the authorities are so worried. Look – there's a double guard on the walls and the Sadducees are out in force, the Pharisees too.' He pointed to the Temple steps, crowded with members of the group, as if they were guarding the public building. Every second man seemed to be wearing the long tassles of the 'pious', with a phylactery strapped ostentatiously to his forehead.

'What do they think they're doing wearing those outside of prayers?' Ari scoffed. 'They look stupid, like they want everyone to know how big their other appendages are.'

'Ari!'

He looked sheepish.

'I apologise, cousin. I am a rough soldier these days. But I tell you now, it can only build resentment. The Pharisees "live amongst the people" as if this is some sort of honour, but who wants someone parading around being openly better than them?'

'That's what Jesus says. Well, something like that. I wouldn't presume to quote him direct but perhaps you can ask him yourself. I bet he's in the Court of the Gentiles.'

She leaned out, looking eagerly around, although Aristobulus was right about the mood in Jerusalem. As they made it into the city proper, she could sense it in every street. The happy ease of the road from Galilee seemed to disperse as the houses crowded in on them and she watched with renewed envy as the common people peeled gratefully off towards the open spaces of the Mount of Olives.

Even in the roads leading to the Temple, women and children were keeping to the shadows, avoiding the groups of men muttering on every corner, and Jerusalem felt even closer to anarchy than usual. The sensible thing to do would be to stay away but Salome wasn't feeling sensible. Besides, her mother would almost certainly be waiting for her in the palace and she'd take a muttering crowd over that any day.

'Come on,' she said, grabbing Ari's arm and banging on the roof of the carriage to order a halt. 'Let's go.'

◆

They slipped through the crowds, arm in arm. Salome was glad she was still in her travel gown and so, once away from her shining carriage, did not stand out too sharply from the mass of peasant pilgrims. She was gladder still of Ari's protective bulk at her side. It was only the first day of Holy Week and already the city was rammed. It smelled of sweat and urine, of food and animals. Many had brought their own lamb, keen to avoid the hiked-up prices of the local beasts, and the poor things were trailed on leads, looking bewildered and afraid.

'Let's get into the Temple,' Ari said, making straight for the steps. 'At least that way if there's any trouble, we can find Caiaphas to shelter you.'

She was touched by his concern and alarmingly aware of his closeness as they made their way through the thronged gates into the Court of the Gentiles. She knew, these days, what the marriage bed involved and could already imagine how it might be something so much more with a man like Ari than with wizened Philip. She frowned at herself and dismissed the treacherous thought instantly, but Ari was still at her side and her body was more reluctant to give up the imagining than her mind. She was delighted, therefore, when she spotted Jesus in one corner of the vast courtyard, and could distract it.

The teacher was hard to miss as he had by far the largest crowd around him. Indeed, almost everyone there was jostling to get close, leaving the other teachers preaching furiously to thin air.

'There!' she said, dragging Ari across.

It was packed tight around him and Salome peered despairingly into the heads of the back listeners.

'We'll never get close.'

Ari laughed.

'Of course we will.' He lifted one arm, revealing the fine sword at his belt, and called authoritatively, 'Make way for Princess Salome. Make way please.'

People turned, grumbling, but spotted her and instantly parted, many tugging forelocks as they went. Salome felt horribly self-conscious but was glad of the passage all the same and hastened forward, offering grateful smiles to all who let her through. The people at the front had noticed now and, as they reached them, Johanna came rushing forward.

'Salome! Welcome.'

Salome embraced her friend. She looked as well as she had before, save that her belly was swollen tight against her dress.

'You're pregnant?'

'God has chosen to bless us again, yes.'

'I'm so pleased. But ... where will you give birth?'

'He will provide.'

She was so calm, so serene. This was not the frantic Johanna Salome had known before.

'You could come to us at Trachonitis? We would be delighted to have you.'

'Praise God!' Johanna threw her arms up. 'Thank you.'

'My pleasure,' Salome said, uncertain if this was an acceptance or not.

But now Jesus had finished his teaching and was walking towards the Inner Temple, or trying to. So many clamoured to touch him that it was almost impossible for him to make any progress across the vast courtyard. The burly disciples were doing their best to clear the way but the crowd were so frantic to reach the healer that they paid little attention. Ari stepped forward.

'Allow me.'

He drew his sword but instantly Jesus stepped up and placed a restraining hand on his arm.

'No weapons, please. All God's children must be allowed to come to me.' Ari stared at him, confused, then slowly re-sheathed his sword. 'Thank you.'

'You are Jesus of Nazareth?' Ari asked, amusingly tongue-tied.

'I am he. And you are?'

'Prince Aristobulus. I am honoured to meet you.'

'And I you, as I am honoured to meet any of the Lord's flock.'

'Right. Yes. I see. You attract many people.'

'God attracts them. I am merely his mouthpiece.'

'Salome says you speak very well.'

'She is too kind.'

Jesus threw Salome a quick smile and she felt herself flush with the brief attention, but now an old woman flung herself at Jesus' feet and they all had to stop whilst he bent to speak to her. A crowd of Pharisees were heading their way, Salome noticed. Jesus paid them not a moment's attention but the crowd fell back, nervous at their determined gait and radiant piety. Salome saw the disciples bristle and step into an instinctive guard around Jesus and the woman he was tending, and she swallowed.

'Are you sure Jerusalem is safe for Jesus?' she asked Andrew, nearest to her.

'Not sure at all,' he said, his eyes on the approaching Pharisees. 'But he was determined to come. The Temple is the heart of our faith, but it is also the seat of its greatest corruption.'

'True,' Salome agreed grimly, planting her feet more firmly on the dusty cobbles as the people jostled around them. 'There was a dispute last autumn about payment for an extension to King Herod's aqueduct. Pilate wanted to use Temple funds for it but the Sadducees were furious.'

'I bet they were. They want that money for their robes and jewels.'

Salome nodded grimly but then remembered the words of the woman on the road.

'Though do the people not need something to look up to? Some ceremony? Some mystery?'

'You think we need gold to be inspired?'

Salome looked at her feet, rightly chastised.

'I think the people think that they do.'

'Which is what we have to change.'

'And change now,' someone said on her other side and she turned to see a thin-faced man she vaguely remembered from Jesus' time in Caesarea Philippi. Andrew stiffened.

'This is not the time, Judas,' he hissed.

'Why not? If not now, when? The people are behind us and we can strike – strike against the Romans holding us prisoner in our own country and the priests greasing their way for their own luxurious comfort. We may not have weapons but we have numbers and we have God on our side. This could be our chance to turn over the old order and usher in the New Way.'

'Not with fighting, Judas, you know that, Jesus has told us so many times.'

'What if Jesus is wrong?' Andrew sucked in his breath. 'Oh, come, Andrew, he is a wonderful, inspirational man as we all know, but he cannot do it all. Is it not our job, as his followers to lead the movement that will propel him to greatness?'

'No,' Andrew said shortly. 'It is our job as his followers to follow.'

Judas glared at him and Salome shifted awkwardly, scared by this dissension amongst the disciples and even more scared by what it might mean in a city ripe for revolution. Jesus had lifted the old woman to her feet and she was dancing in a small space before him, making everyone cheer. Jesus smiled but he had obviously caught the tension in their corner of the crowd and came over to them.

'What's wrong, Andrew?'

'Nothing,' he said but the simmering look he sent Judas belied the word.

'Just a little debate about the aqueduct,' Salome said hastily.

'What about it?'

'The Romans are taking Temple funds to extend the aqueduct and the High Priest is objecting,' she explained.

Jesus looked at her, his eyes darkening, and then suddenly he shook his fist in uncharacteristic anger and stamped away. The crowd, sensing his mood, fell back and for a moment Jesus stood alone at the foot of the steps, spinning slowly as he took in the bustling commerce all around this central section of the outer courtyard.

'Enough!' he shouted suddenly.

All eyes turned. Even the Pharisees stopped in their mincing tracks.

Jesus spread his arms wide and turned slowly.

'Have you not all had enough? Are you not all fed up of paying your hard-earned money to these crooks?' Silence. Everyone in the Court of the Gentiles, it seemed, was holding their breath. 'Well, you should,' Jesus shouted, his voice louder than Salome had ever heard it before.

Someone grabbed at her arm and she turned to see Johanna pressed up tight against her. Jesus' blue eyes were afire and he strode across to the nearest trestle table, where a moneychanger was counting out Temple shekels for a fretting pilgrim.

'You should be ashamed of yourself!'

In one, fluid motion, Jesus grabbed the edge of the table, and upturned it. Coins went spinning everywhere, chinking their merry escape across the cobbles, though it lasted mere moments before people were diving gleefully for them.

'What's he doing?' Johanna gasped in Salome's ear.

'I don't know.'

Peter and Andrew were looking nervously at each other. Judas clapped delightedly and James and John hurried forward, but Jesus was moving on to the next table, and the next and the next. In swift progression they were all upturned and more coins flew across the yard until the ground was filled with people fighting to retrieve them. The moneylenders shouted furiously, waving their fists, torn between attacking Jesus and fighting to claw back their profits. Up on the walls, the Roman soldiers watched, apparently content to let the Jews scrap between themselves.

Now Jesus was moving on to the many men selling lambs and doves for sacrifice, leaping from one to the other with ferocious energy, unfastening cages and severing leads to release them. The birds flapped free, filling the air above the gasping crowd with the beat of their wings, and the lambs charged wildly between the people, pop-eyed and desperate as they sought escape. Salome looked around, terrified, but Jesus had reached the steps and bounded up them to turn on the terrace and face the cheering crowd.

'The Temple – *your* Temple – has become a den of thieves and it must stop. These men change your money into Temple coins at criminal rates, they sell their animals at prices twice their usual value, and they grow fat and flaccid on your hard work.'

The crowd roared its agreement and Jesus turned to the merchants, pointing an accusatory finger as they scrabbled to retrieve their ill-gotten goods.

'You are crooks, every one of you, and you—' He turned his finger on the group of priests who had come rushing out at the disturbance, 'you are as bad, you hypocrites. You could stop this immediately. You could impose caps, you could control this profiteering so that Pesach could be what God intended it to be – a celebration of the saving of all Israelites, not just those with money to spend.'

The crowd – those who were not scrabbling for coins or chasing animals – were leaping up and down, shouting their agreement. Judas was striding between them, encouraging them, but up on the balustrades around the outside of the courtyard, the Roman guards were finally snapping to attention. They would be down the steps in a moment, breaking up the crowd in their usual rough way, and it would be the weak amongst them who suffered.

'Jesus,' Salome cried in warning.

He was too caught up in his righteous fury to hear her.

'Take these rotten goods away,' he shouted at the merchants. 'And do not make our father's house a house of trade ever again.'

With that, to Salome's huge relief, he turned his back on the masses and strode through the Gate of Susa, his disciples hurrying after, closing ranks around their leader to block the crowd who were straining to follow. The guards were streaming down from the four guard posts at the corners of the Court of the Gentiles, rods lifted for any who chose to defy them, and the people swiftly dispersed.

'This way,' Ari urged Salome, guiding her after Jesus into the Court of the Women.

A soldier stormed up to them but stopped dead as he caught Ari's fine clothes and the sword in his hand, then backed off and went after easier prey. Chuza was sweeping Johanna to safety and Salome was glad to follow, but her whole body was buzzing with what had just happened and, as the mood settled, she crept back to the Gate of Susa to peer out across the Court of Gentiles below.

'Who is he?' she heard people asking each other everywhere.

'They say he's the Messiah,' came the reply, time and again.

'He's of the line of King David, you know.'

'I heard tell that a star hung over his birthplace to mark it. It is in the Magi's holy records.'

'Are you sure? Can you prove it?'

'Only *he* can prove it,' one man stated clearly above the rest. 'Isiah tells us that the Messiah will ride into Jerusalem on an unbroken colt. If he does that, we will know. We will know that we stand at the end of days and that our saviour is come.'

Those remaining in the court thrilled to his words and even the battering of the Romans did not still their chatter. Salome turned back to the Court of Women and looked across to Jesus, seated in a shady corner whilst Perpetua ran to fetch him water. Judas was striding excitedly up and down, taunting the Sadducees, and James bundled him away as everyone else formed a guard around Jesus. This morning all order and respect had been stripped from their Temple and now there would be trouble indeed.

Chapter Twenty-one

Herodias

'A colt? He's riding in on a colt?'

Herodias stared in disbelief at the messenger grovelling before her.

'Right down the middle of the main avenue, my lady, with people crying Hallelujah and laying palm leaves in the streets before him.'

Herodias rubbed her hands and looked to Antipas.

'Send for Caiaphas.'

'Must we involve that bore?'

'You know we must. He's the High Priest, and the fine point of Jewish law. Surely his men will be able to pin the damned man down now?'

The carpenter had gone too far. There had been that crazy show with the moneychangers yesterday when she'd just arrived and the wretches had been demanding compensation from Caiaphas ever since. Luckily, they rented their pitches at their own risk, so no claim would ever stand up, but it had been a nuisance all the same. Jerusalem rang with Jesus' name and it could only end in riot. You couldn't go around shouting at Temple officials and accusing them of corruption without giving people ideas.

'Is it illegal to ride into Jerusalem on a donkey, Mother?'

Herodias glared at Salome. She'd left Agrippa behind in Galilee to avoid precisely this sort of pointless nit-picking, but she'd forgotten about her dear daughter. The carpenter had clearly crept under her skin and the girl was in serious danger of becoming one of the rabble if she wasn't careful. Apparently she'd been out in the crowds whilst the man had thrown tables around like a petty revolutionary. Honestly! Where was her dignity, her royal pride, her simple common sense? Had she not learned her lesson that time she'd been hit by a stone in Tiberias?

Herodias shivered at the memory of her daughter's blood flowing down her face, but then gave herself a stern talking to. Salome was a vulnerable child no more, but an adult – and a troublesome one.

'It is not, as you well know, Salome, a mere donkey. The man has chosen an unbroken colt – acknowledged symbol of the Messiah.'

'But still not illegal.'

Herodias tutted furiously. The girl was right of course but this man was clearly getting cocky and it had to be possible to catch him out some time soon.

'It is grounds enough to call him for questioning. The Sadducees have their finest minds on the case and will catch him out in some blasphemy any day now.'

'The Sadducees are riled because Jesus called them hypocrites.'

'In which he is entirely correct,' Ari put in.

The boy had been glued to Salome's side since he arrived. It was disrespectful to poor, ill Philip and, frankly, a little bit pathetic, and Herodias was only putting up with it because he was some protection for her wilful daughter. Mind you, he had a point here. The Sadducees *were* an insufferable lot, with jumped-up ideas of their own importance and delusions about their piety. Antipas was always saying as much and, whilst Caiaphas was her friend, that didn't mean she couldn't see him for the grasping, power-seeking creature he was.

Takes one to know one, she could almost hear Salome telling her. Well, fine – Herodias did want power, not for its own sake, but because she understood this land. She knew its history, its culture, its wants and ways. She understood what its people needed and she had been brought up to care for them. You needed power to do that and she wasn't going to have navel-gazing goodie-goodies criticising her for it.

'The Sadducees can be a little pompous,' she said carefully, getting a spluttered laugh from both Salome and Ari. 'Really,' she snapped, 'are you two going to behave like children all day long? This is a serious matter.'

'Very serious,' Salome agreed. 'Jesus has some amazing ideas for reform, both practically and spiritually. The authorities should be inviting him in to discuss them, not trying to "catch him out".'

'Discuss them? Is this man trained? Is he a priest? Is he even a teacher?'

'He has much to teach,' Salome asserted stubbornly, 'so that makes him a teacher. And besides, what's wrong with opening up intellectual debate to those not already indoctrinated in the ways of the Temple?'

'Indoctrinated?'

'Yes. Set in their ways, closed to change and highly protective of their own interests and opinions. Much like royalty.'

Herodias turned to Antipas.

'Do you hear this? What's going on? Why are the younger generation turning on us?'

'We're not.' Salome leapt up, surprising Herodias by grabbing at her hands. 'Mother, listen, this is important. We are at—'

'A crux in history, so you say. Or we could just be at a point where some troublemaker is trying to stir us all up.'

'Jesus is not a troublemaker.'

'You think riding into Jerusalem as the very incarnation of Isiah's prophecy is not trouble making?'

'I think he has had enough of not being listened to and I don't blame him. Stop a moment, Mother, please. You are an intelligent woman so apply your intelligence to what's going on. Either Jesus is the Messiah, in which case you have so much to gain in supporting him, both here on earth and in the afterlife.'

'The after . . . ?'

'Or he is not.'

'Very much the more likely scenario.'

'But even so, he is a good man with sound ideas. You said yourself that the Sadducees are pompous. You know it is more than that. You know the Temple is full of corruption. You could be the ruler who weeds that out. You could be the ruler who sets the Jews back on the path to redemption. Jesus has the ear of the people – why not use that?'

Herodias stared at her daughter. Was this madness or a curious sort of sense?

'I will think on it,' she agreed.

Salome blinked, then smiled. Her arms twitched as if she might hug her in the way she had as a child, but then she thought better of it and stepped back.

'Very wise.'

❖

For the next three days Herodias paced the palace. The problem of the carpenter nagged at her and the man was certainly doing nothing to make it go away. Every day he was in the Temple preaching and every day the crowd around him grew. Herodias had asked Caiaphas to have him questioned – not with wicked intent but in an earnest way to give him the chance to expound on his teachings. He had sent all his sharpest priests but the damned man was very evasive.

Yesterday they had asked him whether he thought that Jews should pay taxes to their Roman overlords. The crowd had apparently been very excited by this question and pressed close. Jesus had first asked them to produce a Roman coin suitable for paying such a tax and a Pharisee had dug in his deep pockets and produced a denarius. The crowd had held its breath, desperate to be liberated from the crippling payments and the priests had held their breath too. If Jesus had told the people not to pay, they would have had him instantly on incitement to riot.

'Whose head is inscribed upon that coin?' he had asked.

The crowd had hissed, knowing full well that it bore the graven image of the emperor, and this the Pharisee had confirmed.

'It is Caesar's.'

'Well then,' Jesus had said, 'Render unto Caesar the things which are Caesar's, and unto God the things that are God's.'

It was clever, Herodias had to admit that much. This carpenter was remarkably learned and quick wit besides.

'Perhaps we should have him here, to the palace?' Antipas suggested in bed that night when she woke him tossing and turning in the undertones of the pilgrims camped up the Mount of Olives. Antipas had been drinking in all the tales and was in danger of becoming as fixated upon the man as Salome.

'As our guest? Would that not be seen as condoning his teachings?'

'It would be seen as showing an interest.'

'Too many are showing an interest. It is all anyone is talking about. God's own holy mysteries are being forgotten in the midst of the hysteria.'

'Which is why we might be best talking to him ourselves. I'm sure Salome could arrange it.'

That hit Herodias in the guts.

'*I* could arrange it, if I so chose.'

'Of course you could, my dear, but a personal invitation might be easier than an official summons. And less noticeable.'

Herodias saw his point but hesitated still. She could just imagine Salome's smug face if she asked her to bring her peasant friend to the palace.

'The last time we brought one of this lot into our custody it did not end well,' she said darkly.

'It ended the way I thought you wanted it to.'

She grimaced at her husband in the half-light of the restless city.

'It did end the way I wanted it to, but it has not had the desired effect. It turns out the Baptiser was the least of our problems.'

Antipas pulled her close, burying his head in her hair and saying into it, 'Some say this Jesus is John reincarnated.'

That made her jump. Clearly that dark night in Machaerus haunted her poor husband too and she pulled back and grabbed his face in both her hands.

'Some will say anything to scandalise. How could he be? He already existed before we cut John's head off.'

He winced. It was harsh to put it so bluntly, she knew, but there was no point in hiding from your mistakes. You had to own up to them and move on. Dwelling was of no use to anyone, and neither was listening to foolish gossip.

The next morning however, new news came in.

'The Nazarene has raised a man from the dead.'

'What?'

'Truly, Lazarus out at Bethany was dead and gone four days but when Jesus went into the house and kissed him, he was raised again.'

'I see.' Herodias eyeballed the eager messenger who quailed satisfyingly. 'And why was he still in the house four days after death? Every good Jew knows that you should bury the dead before nightfall.'

'I, I'm not sure. Perhaps he was in his tomb. Yes, now I remember, they said that he was in his tomb and Jesus ordered it opened. Mary and Martha, his daughters, did not want him to do that for fear of polluting his holy nose with the smell of rotting flesh but Jesus commanded it so they rolled back the stone and there he was – alive. There has been great rejoicing.'

'I am sure. If the poor man was trapped in a tomb for three nights he'd be delighted to be let out.'

'He was dead. All swear it. It is a miracle, my lady, a true miracle.'

Salome came rushing in then, full of it.

'You have to believe now, Mother.'

'I don't have to do anything.'

Salome growled at her – actually growled.

'I've just seen Johanna, she was there. She saw it with her own eyes. Jesus told the crowd he is the resurrection and the life. He told them that those that believe in him will live even when they are dead. Is that not amazing?'

Her rampant enthusiasm was irritating.

'I suppose it depends if you think living forever is a good thing. To me it sounds rather exhausting.'

'Mother! What will it take to make you believe?'

It was a good question but now Aristobulus was arriving, asking for details, and even Antipas was quizzing the girl and she was swelling like a toad in a flood and it was unbearable.

What if they're right, Herodias forced herself to think. She would look the fool indeed if Jesus was the saviour of the Jewish race. But on the other hand, if *this* was the saviour – this blue-eyed carpenter from out-of-the-way Galilee, riding on a colt and preaching love to all – then what sort of salvation would it be? Not the sort Herodias was looking for! This Jesus was more likely to embarrass Pontius Pilate than send him packing.

'They say he is the son God,' Antipas was saying. 'Is that possible?'

'I heard his mother was a virgin when he was born,' Ari said. 'And that Magi followed his birthing by a star and that Herod the Great knew of it and ordered all babes in Bethlehem slain.'

Herodias snapped out of her thoughts.

'Well, that's not true. This Jesus is, what, thirty?'

'Thirty-three.'

'So he was born in one of the last years of Herod's reign. The man was ordering many executions at that time, of men and boys alike, but only those in his own family that he feared might steal the inheritance he did not want to give.' She gave a wry chuckle. 'Now there's a man who would have loved eternal life.'

'Mother!' Salome cried. 'This is not a joking matter. God will smite you down for talking this way.' She opened her arms to the skies. Nothing happened and Herodias could not stop herself snickering. 'Not immediately,' Salome snapped. 'You're so childish.'

Herodias groaned. This was getting farcial. There were three days to go to the Sabbath and right now all she wanted was to reach it, make her sacrifice, and escape back to Tiberias with her husband. If, that is, he stopped going on about the carpenter. Let the man preach. Let the people follow him and imagine great things of him if they wanted. If he was the Messiah, it would become clear in time, but Jerusalem was not the place to explore the matter, especially not at Pesach when tempers were always up. But now Ari leaned forward, eyes gleaming.

'They are hailing him as the new King of the Jews.'

'What?' Herodias leapt up.

'How dare they?' Antipas was at her side immediately, his eyes clear at last.

'He is of the line of David, you know,' Ari said.

'And that,' Salome piped up, 'is a more ancient lineage than our own.'

That did it. Herodias glared at her stupid, ignorant, foolish daughter.

'You would let it all go, just like that? You would let some peasant take our crown?'

'It is surely God's crown, Mother, and if He has chosen to bestow it on others—'

'God has not chosen this, Salome – the mob have chosen this. They have taken this man and trumped him up into something they are desperate for him to be and I understand that. Times are hard, taxes are high, land ownership is tenuous. But that is all the fault of the Romans. It is Pilate we need to get rid of, not us, not the Herods who have only ever worked for Jewish good.'

'Jesus will, perhaps, be a different type of king.'

'No,' Antipas said, and Herodias thought she had never seen him so magnificent. '*We* will be King and Queen of the Jews and no other. Come, my dear, we must call Caiaphas. There is work to do.'

'Yes husband,' she agreed delightedly and hurried after him, leaving the youngsters gaping like the sheep they were.

Caiaphas welcomed them with open arms.

'It is sedition, my lord, my lady. Revolution even. I am always open to new ideas ...' Herodias and Antipas exchanged looks but said nothing, 'but this man is simply attacking the Temple and all it stands for and that way anarchy lies. I find—'

But Herodias did not want to hear the High Priest's views.

'We have to stop him,' she said.

'Right. Yes. But how that is the question. The man is followed by so many people in the daytime that it would be impossible to seize him without a massive riot. And at night he retreats to Bethany.'

'And raises people from the dead?'

'Apparently so, though the supposed man, note you, is a friend of his. Convenient, is it not?'

'Very. But, Caiaphas, there must be a way. Could someone not just, you know ... fire an arrow at him?'

'I have tried suggesting as much to Pilate, who has many fine bowmen, but he is reluctant to get involved. He is claiming this is a point of Jewish law and will not weigh in until the Sanhedrin have tried the man and proclaimed judgement on him.'

'Coward.'

'It is a nuisance, for sure. What we need is a way into the Nazarene's close circle.'

Instantly Herodias thought of Salome but then dismissed it. There was no way the girl would betray her friend. Not that he was her friend, just someone she had given food to once, but no doubt she didn't see it like that.

Then she remembered something Salome had said the other day about one of Jesus' twelve disciples. Twelve disciples – honestly! That was a deliberately provocative number, designed to evoke the twelve tribes, and still they said the man wasn't political! But that was beside the point right now, for had she not mentioned that one of them wasn't happy with him, that he wanted a full uprising against the authorities, both Roman and Jewish. What had been his name?

'Judas!' she said, pleased. Her brain wasn't creaking too much yet. 'Judas Iscariot. Find him, Caiaphas, and have him sent to me. I think it's time this poor, discontented man and I had a little chat.'

Chapter Twenty-two

Salome

'Salome. Salome, wake up.'

Salome prised open her eyes, sleep-fugged and confused, to see Johanna standing over her in the near-dark, shaking her with increasing violence.

'I'm awake. Stop it.' Johanna pulled her hands away but still loomed close over her. 'What's wrong? What are you doing here?'

'The guards still know me from before. They didn't need much persuasion to let me in. And it's chaos down there anyway.'

Salome sat up in bed, realising that she could hear raised voices below.

'What's going on?'

'That's what I've been trying to tell you. It's Jesus, Salome. They've arrested Jesus.'

'Who have?'

'Well, the High Priest first off. He had him hauled to his own house for questioning, with all the Sanhedrin there too, but not officially because they're not allowed to meet at night.' She spat. 'Hypocrites. They were there, ready, and at the first tendrils of light, bang – it's official and they pronounce him guilty of blasphemy and cart him off to Pontius Pilate to order the death sentence.'

Salome fought to take this in. If there were 'tendrils' of light in the sky, they were thin indeed and she was struggling to wake up and accept this was real. Her maid was up now, woken from the pallet at the end of her bed, and skittering around nervously.

Salome waved her to open the heavy curtains at the window and stared out at Jerusalem, rose-pink in the first rays of the sun creeping over the myriad tents on the Mount of Olives. It was quiet in the city, only the bakers and a handful of over-eager sellers up to prepare for the busy day ahead. Tomorrow was the Sabbath and Jerusalem would be at peak capacity for the next few days, the streets noisy, smelly and ready for violence. At the moment, though, it slept.

In the palace, however, all was action.

'Who's here?' she asked Johanna.

Her friend grabbed her arms.

'*He* is, Salome – Jesus is. Pilate questioned and questioned him but says he can find no fault in him.'

'Praise God.'

'Yes, but now he has sent him to Herod Antipas, as ruler of Galilee, because Jesus is from Nazareth. He's down below, Salome, being questioned by your stepfather. Will you come?'

Salome was already grabbing a robe from her bewildered maid and making for the stairs. The sight she saw in the open hall below made her blood curdle. Jesus stood in the centre, before Herod Antipas on his throne. Caiaphas and a handful of his top men were behind Antipas and his private soldiers were ranged around the edge, swords drawn as if the prisoner might present a danger to the royals. A ridiculous notion. Jesus had his back to her, his hands and feet bound with rope, his simple tunic torn almost to nothing, and great welts and bruises across his back.

'What have they done to him?' she gasped.

'What the Romans always do,' Johanna said. 'They're animals. They think that beating a prisoner – innocent or guilty – is an acceptable way of softening them up, of making them "amenable to questioning". They have experts, Salome, men with whips who pride themselves on being able to rip so much of a man's flesh off him that his inner organs show to the crowd.'

'That's just barbarism.'

'Not in their eyes. The skill, you see, is to do it in such a way as to keep the man alive. Far more "sport" for the crowd.'

Salome swallowed bile and, picking up her skirts, hastened down the stairs. Antipas was questioning Jesus but not getting far and no wonder. The poor man could barely stand, let alone focus on the bumbling interrogation. Salome heard her stepfather suggest Jesus performed a miracle to prove he was who he said he was and groaned at the crass approach. Jesus wasn't a street magician, to pull tricks on demand.

She reached the bottom of the stairs and looked around, unsure what to do for the best, and that's when she spotted Herodias, standing in the shadow of the staircase, watching the proceedings like a wolf. She marched over to her.

'What have you done, Mother?'

'Me?'

Herodias pressed innocent hands to her heart but Salome wasn't fooled.

'Yes, you. Antipas hasn't the will to arrest Jesus. This is all your doing.'

'This is not, Salome, "all my doing". One of Jesus' own disciples raised questions about him with the High Priest, who had him arrested for questioning.'

'One of his own?'

'Indeed. You are too quick, Salome, to blame me for everything. The carpenter was duly quizzed by the Sanhedrin and they, it seems, have found him guilty of blasphemy in due process of the law.'

'Due process? There is questioning, Mother, and then there is interrogation. Torture!'

Herodias tutted.

'Do not be hysterical, please, daughter.'

'Hysterical? Have you seen him?'

'He is a prisoner, Salome, proven guilty in Jewish law. He is claiming to be the son of God – that is blasphemy. It is arrogance and ignorance and an insult to God above.'

'Unless it's true.'

Herodias tossed her head.

'I told you not to be hysterical. I thought I had brought you up to consider facts, to bring some intelligence to situations, not to fall prey to populist emotions.'

'It seems, Mother, that you brought me up to manipulate any situation for my own personal gain, at the expense of the feelings of others, at the expense of the lives of others, at the expense of the very truth.'

Herodias ground her teeth, a noise so familiar from Salome's childhood that it was as if her mother was biting on her own flesh.

'Am I questioning the Nazarene?' Herodias demanded. 'No. Your father is.'

'*Step*father,' Salome hissed. 'Antipas is my stepfather. You killed my real father by divorcing him and dancing off after a better option. Well, well done, Mother – you must be very proud.'

'I did not kill your father, Salome. He died of an ague.'

'Alone and unloved, before I could even go and see him.'

Herodias shifted.

'I am sorry about that.' She shook herself. 'But, really, girl, I did not "kill" him.'

Salome glared at her.

'It's an irony, isn't it – if you'd only waited a few more months, you could have married Antipas anyway and without any of the fuss of the divorce. Then John wouldn't have criticised you for it and you wouldn't have had him arrested and his poor head cut off.'

Herodias raised a finger.

'Oh no you don't, Salome – *you* had his head cut off.'

'I know! And not a moment has gone past since that I have not regretted it. It cannot happen again, Mother. You cannot do this again. These men have important things to say and you cannot silence them just because it makes you feel uncomfortable.'

She looked back to Jesus as he staggered, his feet tangling in the ropes. It was only one of his guards yanking him roughly back upright that stopped him crumpling to the ground.

'Leave him alone!' Salome shouted.

The whole hall turned to look and her face burned but this was no time to shirk the public gaze. She strode forward, putting herself between the prisoner and her stepfather. Jesus turned as she passed and as his blue eyes met hers, she was taken back to that first time in Tiberias, when she'd been dancing and he'd waved at her from the shores of Lake Galilee. It felt like a ridiculously long, innocent time ago but it was less than two years. How had it come to this so swiftly?

Jesus' eyes were clouded with pain and red with lack of sleep but there was still kindness in them when he looked upon her. She had to repay that somehow and she faced down Antipas.

'I am told that Pontius Pilate has found no fault with this man.'

'Pontius Pilate couldn't find fault with a mosquito in a swamp,' Caiaphas growled.

'Perhaps,' Salome snapped, 'because the mosquito is doing nothing wrong.'

'Bar biting poison into men.'

'Who should not be in his swamp in the first place. What is the charge against Jesus?'

'Antipas,' Caiaphas said urgently, 'will you let this scrap of a girl interrupt the court?'

'Scrap of a *Princess*,' Antipas corrected him. 'This is her home, Caiaphas. Why should she not speak?'

'She's a . . . a female.'

Antipas grunted.

'Come, man, you have a wife. You must know that females have much to say.'

'But little of worth.'

Salome glared at him.

'Perhaps, High Priest, you could judge that once you have heard my words and not before they are spoken?'

Antipas gave a soft chuckle. He did not like Caiaphas and Salome had to use that now.

'Father . . .' The word stuck in her throat but now was no time for personal sensibility. 'Have you found any fault in this man?'

'None,' Antipas said easily.

'He claims to be the son of God,' Caiaphas thundered.

'Does he?' Salome asked. 'Or do others claim that of him?'

'You are splitting hairs. The man rode into Jerusalem on a colt.'

'As do many every year. It is a popular form of transport in these parts if you do not have a fine carriage.'

Caiaphas' eyes narrowed.

'He has criticised us, the Sadducees, honoured for centuries as the keepers of God's word.'

'And therefore, surely, above the criticisms of a mere peasant from Galilee.'

'He has defiled Jewish law. He healed people on the Sabbath.'

'A crime indeed. Imagine having the humanity to help someone else at the peril of your own purity.'

'He has eaten with lepers and prostitutes.'

'Something that it might benefit you to do, for how can you cure them locked far away in your precious Temple?'

Caiaphas stepped forward, jabbing a furious finger at her.

'The Temple!' he raged. 'He has defiled the Temple. He turned over tables and let animals loose.'

'That, surely, is a crime against the business-owners, not against the Sanhedrin. I would have thought that the priests would like to see prices lower so that the pilgrims could show their devotion to God without their families having to suffer poverty. God, I believe, would rather children ate than his altar ran with blood.'

'Which is precisely why ignorant, untrained fools should not be allowed to pronounce on points of Jewish law.'

Antipas put up a hand.

'Enough, Caiaphas. You are in my palace now, in my court.' He came to Salome and put a hand on her shoulder. 'You feel passionately about this man, daughter?'

The soldiers jeered and Salome dug her fingers into her skirts, praying for patience.

'I feel passionately that he should be allowed to teach without persecution. I feel passionately that the Temple should be a place where all men can share ideas and not just those in charge. That is, surely, why we have the court of the Gentiles? Why anyone can step up and preach? What makes this man different from the others?'

Herodias came striding forward.

'Because he says he is the King of the Jews, fool.'

She spoke low, aiming only for her and Antipas. It was clear she was not comfortable speaking in front of Caiaphas or the guards and Salome hated her for that. She was prepared to pour her poison into Antipas' ear in the privacy of their bedchamber but not to stand up for it here, where it truly counted.

'He does not say he is King of the Jews, Mother,' she said, loud and clear, 'any more than he says he is the son of God. It is others who proclaim him as such.'

'Well, they are wrong. And they are dangerous besides.'

Herodias looked around the Hasmonean palace, her eyes flickering over the representatives of the Sanhedrin, the Jewish guards, the members of their household, clutching each other and watching the proceedings open-mouthed.

'Look at us, Salome – we are the rulers here, or we should be. The Romans have taken that from us and we have to battle every day to hold onto any morsel of control. They take our monies, they police our Temple, they even hold our ceremonial robes under their petty lock and key. They have taken Judea, the heart of our nation, and with just one tiny mistake from us, they will take Galilee, Perea and Trachonitis as well. If that happens, then within months we will no longer be a Jewish state, we will no longer be the Holy Land – we will be Rome. Just Rome. Do you want that, Salome?'

'No,' she conceded. 'I do not want that, Mother. You are right – they are a danger to us. You are even right, perhaps, that it would only take one mistake to let them dig further into us than they do already, but the mistake here,' she gestured to Jesus, 'would be to kill this man. Can't you see, it's what Pontius Pilate wants. Why has he sent him here, to Antipas? He wants *us* to condemn him. He wants us to turn on our own because that way he's won. That way Rome has taken not just our taxes but our hearts.'

She stared at Herodias, willing her to understand. Her mother was afraid, she understood that. Her mother was a proud defender of the Jewish faith and for that she had to admire her, but her lust for power corrupted her thinking and corrupted Antipas' in turn.

'Please, Mother. Look at him – he's no danger to you. He's no king and, if you and my stepfather wish to stand as such, then free him. Step up as Jewish rulers and don't let the Romans take one of our own.'

She could feel the air in the palace crackle, as if a storm were coming. Everyone was silent, waiting. Jesus stood in the centre, head bowed, and for a moment Salome wished he would speak, would defend himself with the eloquence with which he had won over so many, but then she chided herself for putting this on him. This was not Jesus' fight. This was a royal battle. They had to choose whether to side with Caiaphas and the protectionist Sanhedrin, or with the people. Glancing to the High Priest, tall and bold in his fine robes and then to Jesus, beaten and bloody in his ropes, she feared the battle was lost already. Had, indeed, been lost a long time ago.

'No,' Herodias said. 'You are young, Salome, emotional. You see only the poor man before you and I commend you for your compassion, but he is inciting riot in the city and we cannot have that.'

'He's done nothing wrong.'

'And yet so much is wrong around him. Bless you for your tender heart, child, but he is just one peasant, he matters little.'

'I don't think—'

'Enough, Salome. It is not your place to think and certainly not your place to speak. This is your father's court.'

'Stepfather's.'

'And you should respect it. Stand back.'

Salome put her hands on her hips.

'No.'

'No? You would defy me, your mother?'

'If I must. If you send Jesus to his death, you are no mother of mine.'

Herodias eyes narrowed.

'You would deny me?'

'Yes.'

'You would, then, deny your royalty?'

Salome swallowed but this was important.

'Yes. I did not stand up for John and I was wrong not to. I will not be wrong again. I tell you, this man is special and we should protect him. We should stand up as Jewish leaders and give him our blessing. You should do that, Mother, and you will be hailed throughout history as the saviour of our saviour.'

'Enough!' Herodias all but screamed. She gestured to the guards. 'Take her away.'

Two men stepped nervously forward, reaching out to restrain Salome but unsure how to approach a princess. Salome put up hands to ward them off.

'You need not, for I am leaving.'

'Good,' Herodias snapped. 'You and the prisoner both. Antipas?'

Antipas went back to his chair and sat heavily upon it.

'Send him back to Pilate,' he said. 'Tell him I find no fault with him in Jewish law.'

'Antipas?!' Herodias shrieked.

'But if he has broken Roman law then I will not stand against him.'

Herodias looked furious, Caiaphas also, but the guards, fed up perhaps of the delays or uncomfortable before the warring royals, seized Jesus' arms and marched him, limp and bleeding, from the palace.

Salome grabbed Johanna and marched after them.

'Salome!' Herodias called but she did not look back. She had chosen her side and, whatever pain it might cause, she would not turn from it now.

Chapter Twenty-three

Herodias

Herodias stood in the hall as it slowly emptied out. Caiaphas swept his Sanhedrin friends after the prisoner with the martyred air of one who has to get the job done himself, the household members faded hastily away, and the guards, at a nod from Antipas, retreated to their guardroom. Within minutes it was just the two of them.

'Not a good night,' Antipas said nervously.

Herodias groaned.

'It could have been. If you'd just agreed with Caiaphas the moment the damned man was dragged in here, he'd be on a cross by now and halfway to being forgotten forever.'

'Surely, wife, I have a duty to actually listen to a complainant?'

He did, of course, but this felt dangerously close to spiralling out of control. Already it had sent Salome storming from the palace. Honestly, the girl had no decorum, no dignity. It was the dancer in her, all emotion and freedom of expression. Not that she danced any more.

For a moment Herodias remembered the guard cutting John the Baptiser's head from his shoulders, remembered the arc of blood and the bounce of the head across the floorboards. They should not have put it on the platter Salome was holding, should not have burdened the girl with that gruesome prize, but sometimes rulers had to take a bit of gore. It was just part of the deal.

The Jesus man had got under her tender daughter's skin, that was the problem. She was soft, like her father had been, and the man had clearly worked his charms on her. He was handsome of course – or he had been – and he had those piercing eyes that made you feel he could see right into you. It was disconcerting, Herodias could see that, especially if you were weak. Had the wretched man trekked all the way up to Caesarea Philippi just to get Salome on side? Had it been Johanna and Chuza's idea? She'd seen the woman in the palace just now. It must have been her who'd woken Salome up and started the whole stupid showdown.

Herodias' skin burned with the humiliation of it. Imagine Caiaphas seeing her own daughter defying her in that way, denying her even? The guards too. There would be gossip all over the city and people would stare at her in the Sabbath procession and whisper things. Still, it wouldn't last long, it never did. Everyone would leave the melting pot of Jerusalem and go back to their towns and villages and forget. The grain harvest would be in soon and that would occupy their little minds far more than some pathetic royal argument. Especially if the troublemaker was dead.

'Will Pilate condemn him?' she asked Antipas.

'I'm not sure. He's not a man to choose a side if he can avoid it.'

'Much like someone else,' Herodias fired at him.

'I spoke the truth, wife.'

'You shirked the responsibility.'

He took a step forward.

'I trod a careful path.' He reached out to put his arms around her but she resisted. 'Listen, please. This man is, as you rightly say, dangerous. Not in himself – in truth I think him a gentle intellectual with some interesting ideas – but in those he is attracting. That man you had here to the palace . . .'

'Judas Iscariot?'

'That's the one. He's the dangerous type and it doesn't take men like him long to latch onto figures like Jesus and make them the focus of rebellion.'

'Luckily, this one ran out of patience with him.'

Antipas inclined his head.

'A rat of a man.'

'But *our* rat.'

Herodias, remembering the interview with the supposed disciple, felt suddenly weak-kneed and wished Antipas would try again to hold her, but he stayed back. Judas had crept into the palace under cover of darkness two nights ago. He'd been spitting bile about his supposed 'master', complaining that he did nothing but talk and that he associated with lily-livered do-gooders, pushing away men like himself who wanted real action.

Herodias had assured him that she admired men of action, that the palace needed them. She had suggested to him that turning in the Nazarene would be very good for his career and he had lapped it up. He'd snatched at the silver they'd offered him as a 'down payment' and promised to return to talk about his future employment once the deed was done. Clearly, he had led Caiaphas to Jesus somehow but he had not turned up at the palace yet and she prayed he never did. Rats like him were the last thing she needed and she already had the guards primed to seize him. There would be no trial for Judas Iscariot, no drawn-out farce of questioning, just swift justice. It's not like anyone would miss him anyway. In fact, if she was lucky, his fellows would do him in first. They ought to; the man was a traitor to them.

Herodias glanced to the palace doors. The city was starting to wake up. The noise level was rising and the tang of cooking was filling the air as the pilgrims bolstered themselves for the day ahead. They needed to get Jesus out of the way fast. He had to be dead and buried way before sundown so he did not defile the Sabbath.

'If you'd just pronounced him guilty,' she hissed at Antipas, 'we could have had him stoned for breaking the Sabbath and been done with it. The Romans will want to bloody crucify him and that could take ages. And draw a crowd.'

'Perhaps Pilate will hold him until next week? At least then everyone will be gone.'

'There's only one way to find out.'

'You're not going out there?' Antipas asked, looking to the door as if there were ravening beasts beyond.

'I have to see. I have to know what happens.'

'I'll send messengers. They'll bring back a full report. It's violent, Herodias. You won't be safe.'

Now he did reach out for her and she stepped gratefully into his arms.

'I have to know, Antipas.'

He sighed.

'Then I'm going with you.'

◆

They went in their plainest clothing, cloaks pulled up over their heads despite the warmth of the new day. It was not far to the Herodian palace and, to her relief, there were not yet many in the streets. Most people were taking advantage of the holiday to get a little extra time in bed and even the camp up on the Mount of Olives was only just stirring. She could make out a hundred plumes of smoke heading for the still pink skies as the people kicked their fires into life but no one, thankfully, was in a rush to get into the city. Clearly the news was not yet out. Either that, or the people did not care as much about this Jesus as he thought.

Pilate was set up in a grand chair on the steps of the palace. No Jew would enter the Roman dwelling in this holy week as it would break their ritual purity, so the governor had set up judgement outside. That, at least, showed some sensibility she supposed, though right now she rather wished he'd defied the Sanhedrin and just done the damn thing in private. The last thing they needed was to give the carpenter another platform.

Pilate, mind you, looked as uncomfortable as Antipas had and Herodias cursed them both for their ridiculous indecisiveness. It was just one bloody peasant. Why couldn't they get on with it? She clutched at Antipas' arm as they slid into the back of the crowd and looked around. Herodias' heart lurched as she spotted Salome, standing right at the front with Johanna and a clutch of other women. The Nazarene's male disciples, she noticed, were nowhere to be seen. Typical! The men ran away and only the women stood fast. For a moment she admired the little band, then she shook herself and focused on Pilate.

The Roman governor was deep in debate with his advisors whilst Jesus stood, bleeding pathetically onto the smart steps before him. To one side Caiaphas and his gang were radiating fury and now the High Priest stepped forward and addressed Pilate.

'This man,' he said carefully and clearly, 'is hailed as King of the Jews.'

Pilate looked down his nose at Jesus.

'A poor king. Can you do no better than that, Caiaphas? No wonder you do not rule your own land if this is the best you can offer.'

Herodias, furious, went to step forward, but Antipas wrapped his arms around her, holding her back.

'This is not your fight, Herodias.'

It was never her fight, she reflected furiously. That's why they were in this mess. She was the only one of Herod the Great's descendants with the care and the will to hold the Jewish people together but, simply because she was a woman, she was prevented from doing it. Consigned to the back of the crowd as if she did not matter. She looked to Salome, standing defiantly at the front with her new friends, and again felt admiration for her bold daughter, but again suppressed it. This was Salome's fault. If she hadn't stepped in and given Antipas her spiel about freedom, they wouldn't be in this sticky situation at all. Jesus would be dead and they'd all be back in their beds, resting for God's holy Sabbath, as they should be.

'You speak true, Pontius Pilate,' Caiaphas said, all obsequious, and Herodias forced herself to listen. The man clearly had a plan. 'But is this not a Roman state?'

'It is.'

'And is not Caesar the only king?'

'Caesar is Emperor,' Pilate allowed uncertainly.

'And would he not consider it unlawful, therefore, for someone else to set themselves up as a ruler, unacknowledged and unsanctioned by his sacred authority?'

Pilate swallowed.

'Tiberius instructed me to respect Jewish customs and law,' he said. 'As did you, Caiaphas. Remember the graven images?'

'Of course, Governor, and you have been most respectful ever since. We greatly appreciate it, as must the emperor, but not, surely, at the expense of his own authority?'

The words dripped with scorn and Pilate winced visibly.

'No,' he agreed. 'Not that. The man is clearly guilty.' His shoulders slumped and he waved the guards over. 'Crucify him.'

Herodias sucked in her breath. At last! But now the women at the front, her own damned daughter included, were setting up a weeping and wailing, and the Roman governor hesitated again. The eldest of them, perhaps Jesus' mother, threw herself at his feet, clasping his legs and pleading with him. He tried to extricate himself but the woman, for all her age, looked strong. She was speaking urgently and suddenly he bent to listen then stood up again, a smirk on his weaselly face.

'What a fuss over one man,' he said, looking Jesus up and down curiously. 'But still, out of respect for Jewish customs etcetera, etcetera ... Guards!'

He called two men over and, with a brief word, sent them chinking up the road towards the Antonian tower, the fortress where the Roman garrison was quartered and where the prison was held. Slowly he held his hands aloft to the small crowd.

'It is custom, I am told, for myself, as governor of Judea, to offer a pardon to some condemned criminal to mark the festival of Pesach.'

Herodias looked to Antipas in horror. That bloody woman!

It was, indeed, an ancient custom but one rarely followed these days. Pilate was looking for a way out and the peasant had given him it. The crowd murmured uncertainly and Pilate grinned and stood watching, clearly pleased with his public show of benevolence. Salome and her new friends were clutching each other and leaping up and down and, as the guards returned, Herodias could see why.

They pushed before them a burly, unkempt man, heavily chained. His name whispered around the crowd like a curse: Barabbas. This was a criminal of the worst kind – a thug, a thief and a bandit, who came down from the Judean hills every year to prey on pilgrims travelling for the festivals. He'd been arrested just a few days before for beating up a lone woman and child for a single loaf of bread, and had been thrown into the prison where he spent most of his festivals until he'd served his time and was released to start the cycle again. This time, however, the poor woman had died of her injuries and he had been sentenced to death.

Now Pilate set Barabbas on one side of his chair and Jesus on the other and looked down on the small crowd. The two men made a striking contrast. Barabbas was wrestling in his chains, trying to shake his fists and spit defiance at his gaolers; Jesus just stood there, looking out with those blue eyes of his. Herodias wasn't sure if he was too weak from his beatings to do anything else, or if this was a deliberate and frankly irritating ploy to look innocent. If so, it was working. Pilate was offering the crowd the choice between saving the miserable creep of a bandit on his right or the handsomely quiet sufferer on his left. They'd got so far and now this.

Herodias looked guiltily to Caiaphas. She had promised the man she would help bring Jesus to justice and she had done that but now, in this mess of a trial, her own damned family had clouded the process so much that they were stuck here, at the mercy of the very swell of popular opinion that had created all the trouble in the first place.

She looked to Jesus and, seeing the peculiar calm on his swollen

238

face, wondered for a moment if perhaps he *was* something special. Was God looking down on this peasant? Was He going to save him? Herodias' throat constricted and she looked again to Caiaphas. To her surprise, however, she saw no panic in the high priest's face. He was glancing around the crowd, nodding to people, and as Herodias followed the line of his eyes, she realised why he was calm. The crowd at this early hour was filled mainly with the members of the Sanhedrin who'd been dragged out of their beds to pass their dawn judgement. A few women had gathered but they had the well-dressed look of the men's wives and their friends, alerted to the excitement happening at the heart of the still sleepy city. The peasant women at the front had not looked around, not noticed that they were almost alone in supporting the Nazarene – and neither had Salome.

Not so clever now, daughter.

Herodias leaned against Antipas and watched as Pilate looked across the clutch of people around the steps of his stolen palace, almost amused as he offered them the choice of a 'murderer' or their 'King of the Jews'. She saw Salome lead the women in screaming for Jesus but their voices were small and weak and the roar of the criminal's name from the loaded crowd behind them, drowned them with ease. Herodias saw her daughter's new friends look around in amazement and growing horror. Too late they realised that they were, for once, surrounded not with their hand-picked bunch of believers but with the force of Jewish law. They turned, tried to run into the streets for help, but found their way blocked. They shouted louder but there were tears streaming down all their faces now and it clogged their already drowning words.

A shame really.

Pilate tossed his head in arrogant disbelief at the Jewish choice, then nodded at the guards to untie Barabbas' ropes and toss him to his saviours. The thug couldn't believe his luck and paraded around the stage, hands held aloft like a prize fighter as the crowd shifted nervously. Pilate, meanwhile, called for a bowl and ostentatiously washed his hands in it before ushering Jesus into the bowels of the palace with a bored, 'Crucify him.'

'And be sure,' Caiaphas added darkly, 'that he's dead before dusk.'

'No!' The cry, high and wrenched through with agony, was Salome's, Herodias was sure of it, but the girl had made her choice and must stand by it.

'Let's go,' she said to Antipas and he gladly hastened her away.

Already the streets were filling. People must have heard the shouts for Barabbas and were pouring out of houses and down from the Mount of Olives. Cries of distress and horror bounded off the narrow walls of the packed city and Herodias had rarely been gladder to reach the palace. She ordered the gates locked and just made it into the hall before her knees buckled.

'My poor wife,' Antipas said, cradling her. 'My poor dear wife, this has been too much for you. Come, let me put you to bed. You must rest, recuperate. Tomorrow is the Sabbath, the celebration of the glorious salvation of the Israelites.'

'It is,' she murmured.

She felt weak, stupid, but her head was spinning and her blood pounding and she wanted nothing more than to crawl under the covers and forget about this horrible mess. She let Antipas undress her like a child and slide her into their bed himself. She drank the juice he offered, tasting the bitter edge of poppyseed and being grateful for the release she knew it would offer. But even so, as she slid into sleep, she heard Salome's voice: 'I deny you as my mother,' and wondered if true rest would ever be possible again.

Chapter Twenty-four

Salome

They stood at the back gate, a bedraggled huddle of females waiting for a sight none of them wanted to see. Mariam was weeping, clutched in the arms of her white-faced daughter, Elisabeth, whilst Johanna and Perpetua muttered together, low-voiced. Salome looked across to the scrubby mound where already three tall supports, permanently erected for the Romans' favoured method of execution, stood waiting. It was known as Golgotha, the place of the skull, and, as Salome stared at it, she couldn't shake off the thought of John the Baptiser's own skull rotting in the dung heap in Machaerus.

If she craned sideways, she could see the fortress past the Salt Sea on the eastern horizon, a dark crag against the morning skyline. Were John's empty eye sockets watching this second terrible death from the vegetable peelings of palace life? Would Jesus look up there from his own execution and bemoan his one-time friend and cousin? And why was she, yet again, at the centre of this tragedy?

'There has to be something we can do,' she said. 'There has to be a way to stop this.'

'We've tried,' Johanna said bitterly. 'They tricked us.'

Salome nodded. It was her fault. She should have looked around the crowd. She should have spotted that it was packed with Sanhedrin. She was the one who knew them, the one with the connections and the political experience to work it out. But no, she'd been too caught up in Jesus' suffering and had not taken the time to consider the situation. Her mother would have been ashamed of her.

She let out a low growl at the thought of Herodias. This was all her fault. She was the one who'd wanted Jesus disposed of, just as she'd been the one who'd wanted John dead. She excused herself on the grounds of the Jewish nation, but who was she to dictate what they needed? And who was she to cast men's lives onto the pyre of her own ambitions?

'Mother no longer,' she muttered furiously, but there was no point dwelling on that now.

She had been guilty of not thinking enough; she had to focus.

'Where are the men?' she asked, grabbing at Perpetua's arm. 'Where is Peter? Where are Andrew and James and John? Why have they forsaken him?'

'They're in hiding,' Perpetua said. 'They were threatened with arrest and had to scatter. It's only us women that the authorities are happy to leave at large as they think us useless.'

'Well, we're not,' Salome said, though, Lord help her, they – she in particular – had been useless so far. 'But we need help. We need people to listen, to stand with us. Surely now, with Jesus condemned, Peter and the others can come back.'

'For what?'

'To speak up for him, to incite the crowd – to save him.'

'Jesus did not come here to fight,' Mary said piously. It infuriated Salome.

'Maybe not, but *we* can fight for him. We *should* fight for him, or what is the point of us being here at all?'

'To bear witness.'

'To what? To a tragedy? To a miscarriage of justice? To a man's unfair death? How does that help?'

Mary shrugged.

'I'm not sure,' she admitted, 'but it is what we have. Jesus knew this was coming, Salome. He knew last night, I am sure of it. He told us, when we were all eating together, that one of us would betray him and he was right – Judas brought the High Priest's guards to him in Gethsemane. We thought we were safe there. We thought we could pray in peace but no – one of our own brought death into our sanctuary.'

'So surely it behoves the rest to make that good?'

'He sat there,' Mary said, almost trance-like. 'Jesus sat there at the table and he broke bread and he told us that next time we did that, we were to think of him. He knew, Salome. He knew they would take him and he was preparing us.'

'So you would be ready to help.'

'I don't know but the day is not yet done. God will not let his son die, I'm sure of it.'

Her eyes were misted, manic even, and Salome suspected she was holding onto her strange calm with the very tips of her fingers and excused her for it. But they surely could not all just stand here and let this happen?

'Where's Peter?' she demanded of Perpetua again.

'Hiding, I told you. He's a marked man. He was there when they first dragged Jesus before Pilate, he and John both. He wanted to bear witness, to stand up and defend him, but the guards recognised him, set upon him. He had to deny who he was and flee so as not to be set in chains too. Jesus would not want that. He told Peter to be his rock.'

'Rocks don't hide.'

Perpetua flinched but Salome didn't care. They were letting this happen and she couldn't bear it.

'Truly, Salome,' Johanna said, tugging her away from Peter's indignant wife. 'They are better hiding. Chuza is safe with our son and ready to rise up again when ... if ...'

Salome stared her down.

'There will be no when, or if, unless we do something. And fast.'

She looked around, wracking her brain for solutions. What was the point of being royal if she could not bring some sort of influence to bear? But it was all happening so fast and she could think of nothing.

'Mariam?' A man came up to them – tall and well-groomed, in the smart robes of the Sanhedrin. Mariam looked up from her weeping, confused.

'I am she.'

'Joseph of Arimathea at your service, madam. I am so, so sorry for this. It has been poorly done.'

'By the Sanhedrin,' Salome said, stepping forward.

He looked to her curiously.

'Princess Salome?'

Salome drew herself up tall.

'No. Just Salome.'

He gave her a little bow.

'I see. You stand with these women?'

'I do, though, as you see, precious few do.'

'They are afraid, and right to be so. The guards, our own and the Romans', will be on high alert for riots. They will stamp on any sign of trouble with the full force of the law.'

'See,' Perpetua said.

Salome drew in a deep breath.

'I see. But there must be something we can do or Jesus will die.'

Mariam let out a sob.

'My baby boy. He will die alone and in pain.'

'Not alone,' Mary said stoutly. 'We will be here.'

'But we won't be able to hold him. We won't be able to mop his brow or ease his pain. And we won't even be able to bury him. They will cast him into common land with the vagrants and crim- inals and he will never rest easy.'

'No,' Joseph said. 'That, at least I can help you with. I have a tomb nearby – a simple one but secure in the rocks just beyond Golgotha. I offer you it, Madam, as some small recompense for the actions of my fellows.'

Mariam looked up at him.

'Truly? Thank you, Sir. Oh, thank you.'

'Thank you, indeed,' Mary said stiffly, 'but we will not need it. Jesus will not die.'

Joseph looked at her pityingly and went to say more, but at that moment the gates in the wall behind the fortress swung open and, at the crack of a whip, a man – or what was left of man – crept out, a huge wooden beam across his shoulder.

'Jesus?' Johanna gasped but it was not him and neither was the next man.

The third however . . .

Mariam burst forward, pushing past the guards to clutch at her son. They were swift to react, flinging her bodily aside, but not before she had kissed his brow. Her hand went to her own head, confused, and Salome saw to her horror that she was scratched and bleeding. What had the guards done to her with such speed?

But looking again to Jesus she saw the reason why. Someone within the prison had fashioned a rough diadem of twisted vines studded with long thorns that dug into his already lacerated flesh, and across the heavy beam he carried was nailed a hastily painted sign reading 'Jesus, King of the Jews'. Those driving him along were taunting him, telling him to command this to stop, to order his release, to save himself. Jesus, eyes fixed on the ground, ignored them but as they jostled him, his broken limbs gave way and he collapsed to the ground, the wood landing on him with a dull thud.

'Get up!' the guard barked. 'Get up and bear your burden like a man.'

'Like a beast more like,' Mary cried, 'which is what you are, every one of you, hounding an innocent to the cross.'

'You want to go in his place?' one of the guards taunted.

'Yes,' Mary said, rod-backed. 'Yes, I do. I will.'

The guard looked taken aback and his fellow tugged on his arm.

'Don't waste time with them. We've got to get him killed before the sun goes down.'

'Why?'

'Some Jewish thing. Not worth messing with. You know what they're like.'

The first guard shrugged and yanked Jesus to his feet but he was limp in their arms, his eyes stormy and dark with pain.

'He can't carry it,' Salome cried.

'He can and he—'

'I will bear it for him.'

It was Joseph, stepping up in his robes of office and taking the cross beam from the stunned guards. 'That is allowed, is it not?'

'If you are willing, sir.'

'It is the very least we can do.'

'Right. Fine.' The guards looked nervously at each other but the front prisoners were being driven on to Golgotha and they could not afford to halt the procession. 'Prisoner fall in.'

Joseph shouldered the beam, purple in the face, but determined. The splinters on the rough wood dug into his fine tunic and his smooth-fleshed hands bled almost immediately but he uttered no complaint. Jesus, pushed along at his side reached out and touched his shoulder and Joseph looked close to tears.

'I'm so sorry.'

'God's will be done.'

Mary clutched at Salome.

'That's what he said last night, when they took him. He must know something, Salome. He must have a plan. All will be well, it must be.'

She was not so calm now and Salome took her hand and clutched her close. She thought back to Jesus riding into Jerusalem on a colt just five short days ago and felt sorrow wring her heart. How the people had acclaimed him then. How they had strewn palm leaves before him and cried Hallelujah! Now they lined the rough track out to Golgotha, open-mouthed and staring. Why did they not rise up and defend their saviour?

'He is the Lamb of God,' Johanna said. 'Did he not tell us that? He is the Lamb of God, and what happens to lambs?'

'They get sacrificed,' Perpetua said dully.

She gestured back into the city where the bleat of many sheep could be heard. It had not taken long for the furious sellers to round them up after Jesus had let them loose at the start of the week and the poor creatures were back in pens, waiting to be sold to the highest bidder in order to have their throat cut on the altar tomorrow. The high priests, having sent Jesus to his death before breakfast, would be getting ready for tomorrow's day of murder. Not for the first time, Salome questioned the God who was thirsty for so much blood. This had to be the point at which He showed that it was time for a new way, for Jesus' way. This had to be the point the killing stopped.

She looked to the sky for the miracle that must come, but stark blue looked blankly back and now they were reaching Golgotha and the guards were taking the beam from Joseph and flinging it to the ground. Past it, the two thieves were being nailed to their own, their cries of agony piercing the air, and Salome thrust herself forward as Jesus' guards grabbed at his left arm, forcing it against the dark wood and lifting an iron nail above his hand.

'You are killing the Messiah.'

'Rubbish,' the soldier scoffed. 'If he's the Messiah, he can stop this any time. Come on Messiah – got a thunderbolt for me? No? Didn't think so. Well, I've got one for you.'

And with a wicked glint, he pushed the tip of the nail into the centre of Jesus' palm and brought the hammer down on it, hard and true. Jesus cried out and his body bucked against the pain. The guard climbed carelessly over him to repeat the process with his right arm, cracking it mercilessly as he forced it into position against wood already stained with the blood of too many victims.

'My boy,' Mariam wept. 'My poor boy.'

She tried again to reach him but there were more guards stationed around the crosses and they formed a barrier to keep back the crowd as Jesus was hoisted up onto the central post. His face, once so soft and gentle, was contorted with pain, but he forced his eyes open to look down on them.

'Take care of my mother,' he managed.

'We will,' Perpetua assured him.

'As we always do,' Mary said. 'But you will be able to look after her too.'

Jesus gave her a strange, half-smile but then the sadistic guard yanked his feet together against the upright and drove another, even longer nail through his poor flesh and he screamed again. Salome thrust her hands over her ears, hating the sound and then hating herself for not even being able to endure that tiny amount of pain.

'How long will it take?' she gasped out.

'Hours,' Johanna moaned.

'We must do something, get him something.'

'Like what?'

Salome thought of the poppyseed Herodias took in her tea if she was "overwrought". God, her mother didn't know what suffering was.

'I'll be back,' she said to Johanna.

'But . . .'

'I promise, I'll be back.'

She turned, darting towards the city, ducking through the crowd that was growing around the three dark crosses. She heard them chatting with each other and hated them for their casual approach.

'Guess he wasn't so special after all,' she heard one man say dispassionately to another and she stamped not-so-accidentally upon his foot as she pushed past. She heard him cry out and was glad of it.

An apothecary was easy to find, but harder to persuade to dig out the poppyseed potion.

'It's not safe,' he told her, his eyes darting to the door in case he was caught dealing in such substances.

'It is in this case,' Salome told him.

'It's not safe for *me*,' he retorted stubbornly, but the sight of the ring she pulled from her finger had a remarkable effect on his scruples. 'Not too much,' he said, scrabbling a little bottle from deep under the counter and thrusting it at her. 'Or it could kill.'

'Good,' she said and turned from his horrified look to head back up the hill.

Nothing had changed, save perhaps that the crowd, bored now, had thinned, preferring to head back to their campfires, and to find new teachers in the court of the Gentiles, ones who were not dying in front of them. Salome hated every one.

The group of women around Mariam had, at least, grown as word had passed to Jesus' followers, lodged out in the villages around Jerusalem. Jesus was twisted on the cross, his breathing laboured in his stretched chest and blood congealing around the nails in his poor hands and feet.

'Poppyseed,' Salome said to Mariam. 'It will ease his pain.'

She pointed to the bowl of vinegary wine that the guards were charging relatives a fortune to offer up on a sponge to the victims. Both the thieves had taken a draught and if they could only drop the poppy oil onto it, it might ease Jesus' passing.

'Or it could kill,' the apothecary's voice said in her head and she had sudden misgivings. What if Mary was right? What if a miracle was coming? What if Jesus was to be saved and she ruined it all by poisoning him?

Perpetua was producing a purse and beckoning the guard over. She waved at Salome to hand her the bottle and Salome passed it reluctantly over.

'Only a little,' she said.

'Or what?' Perpetua asked darkly.

'Or we may interfere with God's purpose,' Mary told her.

Up on the cross, Jesus' eyes flickered open and he looked down on them. They found Salome's and she fought to meet his gaze, seeing endless pain in his eyes and trying to fill her own with the kindness he had always radiated and that he now so bitterly needed. The sponge was lifted high and he sucked thirstily on it, battling to swallow where his poor throat hung forward. For a little time nothing seemed to happen and then he gave a quiet sigh and seemed to breathe easier.

'Is that a blessing?' Salome whispered to Johanna.

'For now,' her friend whispered back, 'and that is all we can offer.'

The day ground on. The sun rose high above the dying men, their shadows shortening to mere puddles at their feet before starting to draw out again on the other side, but for the women standing in their shifting shade, nothing seemed to change. Salome began to feel that she would hover for ever here, on the cusp of death and then, in a flurry of activity one of the thieves gave up the ghost and his family crowded round, clamouring for his body as it was lifted from the wood. Jesus, roused, glanced over and his face creased with something like envy.

'We should pray,' Mary cried.

'Here?' Salome asked.

'Of course here.' She dropped to her knees at the foot of the cross and the others followed suit. Salome looked self-consciously around. 'Oh I'm sorry, Princess, is your public image more important than Jesus' fate?'

'No!'

Stung, Salome joined the others. She wasn't sure she liked Mary much. The girl was as sharp-tongued as she was sharp-eyed and ridiculously confident for a ... She stopped herself. Mary's birthplace and status were not important and at least she was prepared to stand up and be counted, unlike the hiding men and the rapidly dwindling crowd.

'I'm sorry, Mary. I'm just not used to praying direct.'

Mary threw her a wide smile, dazzling in its intensity.

'Well get used to it. God listens to those who come to Him with—'

'An open heart,' Salome finished.

'Exactly.' Mary looked to the others. 'Let us pray, now, as Jesus taught us to pray: Our Father in heaven, hallowed be thy name. They kingdom come, Thy will be done, on earth as it is in heaven.'

Salome glanced around the restless crowd, the bored guards and the two remaining sufferers suspended brutally above them. There was, surely, no way God's will was being done here?

'Give us this day our daily bread and forgive us our sins as we forgive those who sin against us.'

Salome glanced at Mary in surprise. Did they forgive? Did she? Did she forgive Caiaphas for seizing an innocent man? Did she forgive Pilate for growing bored of defending the prisoner and letting him die so he could get to his breakfast? Did she forgive Antipas for being too weak to stand up and save one of his own people? Or Herodias for, well, anything?

She did not.

But if they came to her with an open heart, would she? Could she? She had killed Jesus' cousin and friend. She had ordered his head on a platter as a dance trophy and yet Jesus had forgiven her. He'd asked no penance save her repentance, had demanded no restitution or retribution.

'And lead us not into temptation, but deliver us from evil.'

Salome glared at the guards as Mary spoke this line. They glared impassively back.

'For Thine is the kingdom, the power and the glory, for ever and ever. Amen.'

'Funny looking glory,' one of the guards said and they all laughed uproariously.

'Show some respect,' Joseph snapped, but that just made them laugh harder.

'For you lot? Hardly. You think you're so much better than us, don't you with your "one god". Well, as far as I can see he's no bloody use to you.'

'Washed his hands of them, I reckon,' his mate said, 'and who can blame him? Funny lot – encouraging all these teachers and then turning on them when they don't like what they teach.'

It was a good point and Salome buried her head in shame, but then Jesus let out a groan and they scrambled up from their knees, staring at him.

He looked down and tried to speak but the words rasped unintelligibly.

'Oh God,' Mary cried, flinging her arms wide, 'have mercy on this your son. Save him and let all who see bear witness to your greatness.'

All eyes turned to the sky but nothing more than a wisp of cloud appeared across the sun. Jesus groaned again.

'Please,' Mary begged.

She looked desperately to Jesus. He had been on the cross for six hours now – six long, painful hours in which nothing had happened bar his poor, broken flesh getting weaker and weaker. Salome couldn't bear it. Trapped in there was a great mind, a great soul. It should not be tortured in this too-human flesh.

She reached for the poppyseed bottle, still three-quarters full. Perpetua saw her and gave a small nod but at that moment Jesus threw back his head. The crowd gasped and pushed forward. Salome felt their heat at her back and stared upwards, willing something to happen, willing God to step in and save Jesus, to prove to everyone here that he was the Christos, the Messiah, the Saviour.

And to prove it to Herodias, hiding back in the palace.

Jesus let out a loud roar and the guards jumped, shocked out of their complacency. Mary clutched at Salome's hand and she, in turn, grabbed for Johanna as the others huddled in and they focused on their leader.

'My God,' Jesus cried, his voice seeming to bounce off the back walls of Jerusalem, just fifty paces away. 'My God . . .' The crowd held its breath. 'My God, why have you forsaken me?'

His head lolled forward, his blue eyes closed, and Salome heard the creak of old wood as his heart gave up the battle and his full weight fell forward. His left hand ripped, the flesh tearing open to let the arm swing ghoulishly forward and then . . . nothing.

They all stood, frozen.

'Nooo.'

Mary fell to her knees, keening despairingly. Mariam fell too, clutching at her and weeping, 'my boy, my boy, my boy,' over and over. Perpetua buried her head in her hands and Johanna looked to Salome, utter bewilderment on her pretty face.

'He's gone,' she stuttered.

Salome could only nod and stare up at the husk of the man who had set the Holy Land alight these last two years. He looked hollow, empty, devoid of anything but the ugly lines of wasted flesh. The tangle of a crown fell from his slumped head and landed at her feet and she bent and picked it up, feeling the cruel bite of the thorns and welcoming it.

She backed away, watching as a soldier stabbed his spear into Jesus' side to check he was truly dead, as a messenger scampered happily towards the Temple to tell Caiaphas and his scavengers the good news of a tidy pre-Sabbath death, as Joseph saw the body brought down and pulled out coins for a cart from opportunists hovering nearby. She watched him point across the scrubland behind the terrible hill of death, towards a run of tombs carved into the rock and saw Jesus' poor remains scooped onto the cart and bumped away as the guards summoned slaves to carry the crossbeam back to the fortress for its next victim. Wood was valuable; life, it seemed, not so. The left nail was still embedded in the crossbeam, a piece of Jesus' flesh dangling limply, and Salome turned as it passed her and threw up into a shrub.

'Messy business, crucifixion,' someone said, patting her on the back. 'Not everyone's got the stomach for it.'

Salome swung furious round to see a plump older lady smiling kindly at her.

'He died,' she sputtered out.

'They do, dear,' the lady said with a grimace. 'They always do.'

Not this one, Salome wanted to wail but she'd made enough of a fool of herself already. Mariam was following the cart, leaning on Joseph's arm with the others clucking after her, just like any old peasant's death.

'Coming?' Johanna asked but Salome shook her head.

What was the point? She'd been a fool; they'd all been fools. They'd stood here waiting for a miracle, a story to fit with the glorious ones about the stars at Jesus' birth and the Magi prophets, about healings and raisings and a Messiah come to save them all. It had been wishful thinking, no more.

What had her mother called her? Over-emotional? It was true. She had stood up against Herodias in her own palace, called her names, denied her as a mother and renounced her royalty as if she'd been the heroine in some Greek tragedy, not a nobody of a minor royal and for what – a broken body and too many broken hearts.

Turning her back on Golgotha, Salome traced her way through the streets of Jerusalem in a daze, heading instinctively towards the Hasmonaean Palace. The crowds were out, eating and drinking, fighting and making up, buying overpriced lambs and doves, and counting down the hours to the ancient festival of Pesach as if nothing had changed. And, really, nothing had – which was the true tragedy.

She slunk into the palace, head low.

'Salome? You're back then?'

'I'm back, Mother.'

'You don't fancy life as an ordinary mortal after all?'

'I don't fancy life as an ignorant, emotional fool. You were right, Mother. You were right and I was wrong. He was no Messiah, just a Galilean peasant with pretty eyes and a clever tongue. The New Way was no way and I made an idiot of myself. I hope you're satisfied.'

'Oh, Salome!'

Herodias took a step towards her, but she put up a hand; she couldn't bear to be patronised.

'I would like to go to my room, if you will permit it?'

'Of course I will, Salome. You're my daughter and I . . .' Salome looked up. 'I will always be here for you.'

Salome gave a dark laugh.

'Thank you, Mother. You know, for a moment there I thought

you were going to say you loved me. There are new depths to my foolishness yet, it seems. I forgot, you see. I forgot, amidst all the tears and the hurt and a day spent watching a man twist his way agonisingly into death, that love is for those without land. Right?'

'Salome, I didn't mean—'

'Well, you know what, maybe Jesus *was* just a Galilean peasant but the New Way was a good one all the same. Love *is* the best way and the only thing foolish about that, was me expecting you to understand. Good night, Mother.'

'Salome, listen!'

But Salome did not want to listen. She wanted only to weep and weep in the desperate hope that some of her misery would drain from her with the tears. Gripping her skirts, she blocked her ears to her mother and ran for her chamber, flinging herself onto her bed and crying for a good man lost and an even better dream destroyed.

PART THREE

Part Three

Chapter Twenty-five

Herodias

Herodias stood, head bowed in outward respect, fuming. She'd understood when Salome hadn't come out to see her on her arrival in Trachonitis. The girl must have known how hard her journey into this backwater hill-city had been but even so Herodias had understood – Salome had been in attendance on her dying husband. That had to take priority. She could, mind you, have taken a moment to send servants, to order baths drawn and fine food cooked but, even so, Herodias had understood. Death was a very consuming business, or so she'd been told. She'd been lucky enough to miss Boethus' passing and Antipas was still very much alive and well. Even so, there was no excuse not to include her mother in the funeral ceremony, especially with so many people here. She looked a fool tucked in with the other women whilst Salome stood alone at the entrance to the tomb. Grief did not have to blind her to the rules of precedence.

The priest began the mourning prayer and with a jolt, Herodias remembered her grandmother, the first Salome's, death. She'd been woken by a strange sound, like an animal in distress, and run to find the source. Her grandmother – never one to do anything quietly – had been flailing around in her bed, maids crowded around her and a doctor biting his lip uselessly to one side.

'Get out!' she'd shouted. 'All of you, get out and leave her alone.'

She'd shooed them away, knowing the formidable old lady would not have wanted anyone to see her distress, then she'd gone to the bed, grabbed her arms and held them firmly down at her sides.

'Calm, Grandmother. You must be calm.'

Salome's clouded, grey eyes had opened and she'd looked at Herodias in shock.

'I'm always calm,' she'd said, as clear as a bell and then her eyes had filled with sadness and she'd said, 'I'm dying, Herodias.'

'Perhaps.'

'Definitely. Never shirk from reality, my girl. It does no one any good. Now, this is really quite painful, so pass me the wine, please. More than that. Thank you.'

She'd gulped it down, her whole face, it had seemed to a fourteen-year-old Herodias, creased up in pain. Then she'd gripped Herodias' hand and lain there, tensed against the rigours of her own body for what had felt like forever before, finally, without another word, her hand had gone limp and Herodias had known she'd departed and been able to relax too. Even so, she hadn't cried. Not then, not through the dress-tearing ceremony, not when they'd processed the body through the streets of Jericho, and not in the grand funeral at the city synagogue. She hadn't cried at all until, some months later, Sukkot had come round and she'd slept alone in the tent in the garden. She'd wept all that night, curled up on herself, then she'd got up, washed her face in the dew, and determined never to do it again. Salome had gone and that had been that. Never shirk from reality.

Two months later, she'd been married.

To her surprise, Herodias felt tears prick now, not for dear Philip, though of course his passing was sad, but for the grandmother who had raised her with such ferocity and after whom she'd named the daughter now standing, ice-like, at the front of this funeral. It was not as grand as the Lady Salome's had been but Herodias had to be impressed by the number of people who'd travelled to Philip's

260

city – really rather a lovely one, if on the edge of civilisation – to honour him. She'd heard the horns sound out his death at dawn, the mournful note echoing off the hills again and again, as if the very earth was moaning. She suspected the sound might even have travelled down the valley to Galilee, so piercing had it been, but thankfully they'd been tipped off a few days ago that Philip was failing and had been here already. Some of these other people must have got on their donkeys within minutes of hearing it to make it to the ceremony. He had clearly been very well liked; she had done the right thing marrying her daughter to him.

Herodias glanced up at Salome. The girl was pale against her traditionally rent mourning gown, her eyes shadowed and her cheeks hollow. Kypros had commented that she looked very like Herodias now and Herodias supposed that grief had lent her a certain beauty. A dignity too. She was no longer a girl, but a woman – and an angry one.

Herodias looked indignantly around her once more. She should not be here, amongst the mass of mourners, but at the front. The man had been her son-in-law for heaven's sake and she was entitled to be seen mourning him with her daughter and the other important figures. What must Kypros think? She glanced awkwardly to her sister-in-law, stood at her side, but her head was bowed as the priest chanted the prayers. A look across the synagogue to her brother, however, found Agrippa smirking at her. He'd been insufferable since they'd come back from that damned Pesach, going on and on about how 'marvellous it was to see the Jewish justice system so smooth and elegantly applied'. He was right, of course, the whole Jesus business had been a mess, but it was over and done with now. If only she could get Salome to see that.

She'd thought that they would be able to get back to normal once the man was exposed for the charlatan he'd been. 'You were right, Mother,' Salome had said to her, for possibly the first time in her uppity little life, and Herodias had done her best to be gracious about it. It seemed, however, that Salome hated her more for being right than she would have done for being wrong and, after a horribly uncomfortable Sabbath, she'd left for Caesarea Philippi.

It had been for the best. She'd been most embarrassing, running up to poor Caiaphas in the middle of their royal sacrifice, and sticking her hands into the poor lamb's death-wound, drawing out the blood, still warm, and smearing it down her dress like a woman possessed. They'd had to hustle her into a back room until she'd calmed down and a new robe could be brought, or who knows what rumours would have shot around Jerusalem. They'd never snatch the rule of Judea from Pontius bloody Pilate if people thought there was madness in their veins.

If she was honest, Herodias had been glad to see the back of her daughter. She'd thought that a few quiet months up in the hills would calm her down and, sure enough, she looked calm, but in a worryingly glassy way. Her limbs were limp, her body rigid, and her eyes almost frighteningly empty. She clearly needed her mother but she'd refused to let Herodias come close. Even when Philip had died, she'd not let her into the private chambers. She'd denied her entry to the garment-rending ceremony and Herodias had been forced to stand outside the door, listening to her daughter's cries of grief through the heavy wood. It had been most uncomfortable. And the servants had stared terribly.

Salome was upset, of course. It had taken poor Philip a long time to die by all accounts. Herodias had paid one of her daughter's maids to send reports and it had sounded terribly overdramatic – a lot of rallying and then failing again. Typical man; had to make a fuss about it. Poor Salome had clearly not received the rest that she'd needed after all the hysteria around the fake Messiah. Herodias thought again of the elder Salome. It had felt like her death had taken forever and it must have been barely an hour, so the weeks and days that Philip had persistently drawn breath must have been very wearing. Salome would come round once he was buried.

The prayers were reaching their apogee now, the priest's

voice rising in a wail of a chant, and with it, Salome cracked. Her face crumpled, tears falling from her eyes, and her knees seemed to fold under her. Herodias leapt forward but Salome caught the movement and sent her such a glare that she dared not mount the steps. Her arms physically ached and for a moment she considered throwing all decorum to the winds, to clasp her daughter to her bosom, but she did not want to be pushed away. Besides, now the men were coming forward for the procession and she had to stand there as Antipas and Agrippa – Philip's half-brothers – stepped up at the front of his coffin to bear it to the vault. Antipas looked handsomely sad, Agrippa cockily smug and she hated her brother for his place in the ceremony whilst she was left with the crowd.

This had to change. She had to talk to Salome. Luckily, as Philip's widow, the girl would sit in Shiva for the next seven days and in that holy state she was bound to accept the visits of all friends and family. That Herodias, her own mother, had to wait in line with the rest, was an insulting indignity, but the damned girl had always been stubborn and there was nothing else for it. Herodias had to tell her that she understood how upset she was. She had to offer to take Salome home, to pretty Tiberias, where she could heal in comfort. She also had to explain to her how important it was that they worked together to secure Trachonitis for the family.

The tetrarchy was vacant now and there was a danger that the emperor, from his stupid seclusion on his stupid island, would take it into the Roman Empire. That could not be allowed to happen. Far better if it came to Antipas, to strengthen his hold on the Holy Land and make Judea the natural next step. That Jesus fellow had not turned out to be King of the Jews and the sooner Salome let go of the crazy idea and embraced her own royalty – and that of her loving stepfather – the better.

Herodias thought again of her grandmother's funeral and of the shock of her passing hitting her, alone in the Sukkot a few months later. It was her marriage to Boethus that had drawn her out of the

263

past and into the future. That had turned out to be something of a disappointment, of course, but at the start it had seemed so full of promise and if only her groom had been less of a sap, it could have been glorious.

The coffin was passing them now and Herodias' eyes fell on the fine young figure holding the back corner: Aristobulus. She smiled.

◈

'Daughter?'

'Mother.'

Salome's face was fixed but Herodias decided not to let it bother her. She'd been like this as a toddler too, after all, and it was best not to indulge her.

'I'm so very sorry for your loss. Philip was a good man.'

'He was. A fair and just ruler and a kind husband.'

Not a word of thanks for choosing him for her, Herodias noted. But still . . .

'And his loss must be hard for you after . . .' How to say it? Whatever way, it would be wrong so she might as well just leap in, 'after the sadness of Pesach.'

'Of Jesus' death you mean?' Salome shot at her, her voice at least raising in pitch.

'I do mean that, yes.'

'Then say so. Pesach wasn't sad, was it? Pesach was just business as usual, everyone queuing up to have their poor overpriced lambs slaughtered to feed the Temple's lust for blood.'

Herodias blinked.

'Salome, that is nigh-on blasphemy.'

'That is truth, Mother. Come, you've brought me up to face things head on, to speak out for what I believe. What's so different now? Jesus was slaughtered, just as those lambs are slaughtered and both, it seems to me, were unnecessary.'

Herodias closed her eyes a moment, urging herself to stay focused on the right elements of this little outburst.

'Jesus' death was very poorly dealt with. I'm sorry.'

The word did not come easily for her, but Salome's look of shock made it worthwhile.

'You're sorry?' she stuttered.

'I am. It should not have happened that way. Pilate was weak and your stepfather, bless him, was weak also. Had I been in charge, it would all have been handled with far more finesse.'

Salome was staring at her very strangely.

'More finesse, Mother.'

'More efficiency if you prefer.'

'I do not prefer. God help us!' She threw up her hands, rather overdramatically. 'I thought you were sorry that an innocent man had gone to the cross, but no, you are simply sorry that he was not killed more "efficiently".'

Herodias groaned; the girl was a lot trickier than she'd been as a toddler. She'd underestimated her.

'I am sorry that he had to die at all. I am sorry that he overstepped the mark in such a flagrant way. He was clearly a good man and an inspired teacher. If he could just have been content with that, we might all have learned much and in a far more civilised way.'

Salome gave a funny little grunt that might, just might, have been something close to agreement.

'He had such good ideas,' she said, more quietly now.

'There are boundaries, Salome.'

'Boundaries can be moved.'

'True. That's so very true. And talking of that, Trachonitis is in danger of—'

'You are here to talk to me of land, Mother?'

Herodias bit her lip.

'Of course not,' she said hastily. 'We are talking of ideas, are we not? Of philosophy and law?'

Salome looked at her sideways but, caught up in the carpenter still, let it go.

'Jesus focused, not on the fancy trappings of priests and Temples and rituals, but on Moses' commandments. He taught a simpler, cleaner faith with God at its heart. What was so wrong with that?'

Herodias thought carefully.

'Nothing was wrong with that, Salome. It does us all good, sometimes, to get to the essence of our beautiful religion and perhaps, for intelligent people like yourself and the band that you met around Jesus, the commandments are enough.'

'How do you mean?'

At last, Salome's eyes sparked with something that was closer to interest than grief or anger, and Herodias willed herself to tread carefully.

'I mean that you have the wit and care to follow those commandments with grace in a way that, perhaps, men and women of lesser intelligence might struggle.'

'Mother!'

'Listen, Salome. *You* may realise that when Jesus told you to love your neighbour as yourself, it meant to treat him with respect and care. Others, less scrupulous, might think it means you can take a share of his goods.'

'Don't be ridiculous.'

'I am not. How much you value others depends, perhaps, on how much you value yourself.'

Salome stared at her, then gave a slow nod.

'I see that,' she conceded. 'But what's your point?'

'My point is that that's why we have to have priests, learned men who read the scripture and offer everyday ways of living to honour God's will and ensure a just and fair society for everyone.'

Salome was frowning now, fighting to think this through. That, at least, was progress.

'But surely hassling people over the right way to take their mitzvah or eat their food or pay their taxes, is going too far? Surely that is not what God meant when he delivered the commandments to Moses?'

'Perhaps not and, Salome, you can be a part of effecting change.'

'Me?'

'Of course. As I told you once before, Moses was a prophet but he was also a leader. He made tough decisions for his people to lead them to safety in the Promised Land. He did not just offer them a philosophy to live by, but also the everyday means to do so. That is what rulers are for. You, Salome, are a ruler and if you see corruption, then it is within your power to step in and change it. You do not have to follow a preacher in the street, you can effect change from deep within the corridors of power.'

'*I* can?'

'Of course! Wake up, Salome. Put that enquiring mind of yours to proper use. You are a royal. You have influence that many dream of. Influence that this Jesus dreamed of—'

'Mother, you mustn't—'

'Are you hearing me, Salome? If you're so passionate about change, then step up and do something about it.'

Salome gasped.

'I'm in Shiva, Mother.'

'For now. But that's only seven days. After that, you are free.'

'Free. That's no way to talk of the loss of a husband.'

'Oh, why not. It's the truth, daughter, and the sooner you face it the better. Philip was a good man, a good husband. We chose well.'

'You are looking for praise?'

'I am considering the facts. Stop being over-emotional. Philip was a good husband and I am sorry he died but he did. He is gone and you are a widow and you have choices ahead of you.'

Salome folded her hands primly over each other in her lap.

'I intend to retire to my father's estate near Joppa.'

'Retire? Goodness, daughter, you are seventeen years old – you cannot retire. I thought you wanted to make a difference?'

'I do, but—'

'I thought you wanted to see a better world.'

'Yes, but—'

'I thought you respected this Jesus' ideas. I thought you believed in them, that you thought them worth pursuing.'

'I did, but it all went wrong. I was a fool and I have learned my lesson.'

'But is it the right one? You were a fool, perhaps, to believe him the Messiah – though you were far from alone in that – but you were not a fool to listen to provocative ideas and think about how you might apply them. If you "retire" now, you are turning your back on the world you claim to want to help and what use is that?'

Salome's lip wobbled.

'I hadn't thought about it like that. But, Mother, what power do I have? I am a mere widow.'

Herodias smiled.

'For now. But we can change that.'

'How?'

'Come, daughter, you know how.' She reached for Salome's hand and was encouraged when she let her take it. 'I truly wish that you could step up and speak out for what you believe in, that you could call meetings and tour round meeting people and effect change in the way that I know – I truly know – you are capable of. But you cannot. Not because you are weak, or delicate or have sensibilities that must be protected, but because of that myth, created by men to keep us where they like us – beneath them.'

'Mother!'

'It is the truth, Salome. Women are denied the right to stand up and be what they can be. Society keeps them squashed down, hidden away in the shadows and that, my girl, is a tragedy as great as the death of one man. There are thousands of women out there who could do great things and they are not allowed to because men are afraid we would be better at it than them. It is an annoyance, a tragedy even, but there are ways around it. There are ways, daughter, to rule from the shadows. You just have to be clever. And you have to find the right shadow to stand in.'

Salome frowned.

'You are talking in riddles, Mother.'

Herodias smiled.

'You need a husband, Salome.'

'I do not, I—'

'You need him as a tool to wield upon the world.'

Salome stared at her, wide-eyed.

'A, a tool . . . ?' She almost laughed.

'A tool,' Herodias agreed. 'An axe, or a hammer, or a—'

'Needle,' Salome suggested.

Herodias frowned. It wouldn't be her tool of choice, but at least Salome was getting the point.

'If you wish. So, you will consider it then?'

'Perhaps. In time.'

Damn. Herodias looked to the ceiling.

'In time, of course. You want to grieve, to recover.'

'Exactly.'

'I understand that.'

'Thank you.'

'I just hope that he doesn't find anyone else.'

Salome jumped.

'Who? Who doesn't find anyone else, Mother?'

'Oh, it doesn't matter. Time, you're right. Time is important. And I'm sure a woman of your standing and beauty will always be able to find a husband when you're ready.'

Salome shifted on her chair.

'But who are you talking about?'

'Oh, just someone who came to me yesterday, who pressed his suit for you in a most pretty way.'

'Yesterday? Someone at the funeral then?'

Herodias battled to keep her smile hidden.

'Someone who was very keen, who assured me he'd treat you with the utmost kindness and respect. And someone, besides, with a very pleasing shape.'

'Mother!'

'It's important. There are men who can far better fill the space in a woman's bed than others, and this one ...'

'Mother, please, this is hardly the place.'

'Of course, I'm sorry. You are right. I'll go now.'

She rose and, to her delight, Salome rose too. She put out a hand to her arm.

'Thank you for coming. It was nice of you.'

'I'm your mother, Salome. I will always have your best interests at heart.'

'Yes. Yes, I know that. And you think this, er ... ?'

'This suitor?' She was teasing now, Herodias knew she was, but oh it was entertaining.

'Yes. You think he would be in my best interests?'

'I do. A man you could wield well, not a hammer or an axe but a veritable sword.'

'I see. And he is ... ?'

She was tempted to keep it going for longer but a good player knows when to close out.

'He is your cousin, Aristobulus.'

Salome's instant blush was all the answer she needed. She had played the game to perfection and it seemed they had a new wedding to plan.

Chapter Twenty-six

Salome

Salome stepped under the Chuppah, blinking as if the sacred canopy was shrouded in mist. It had been like this for weeks, all of life seeming hazy, with just pinpricks of light coming through, as if death had blinded her to life and she was having to fight to focus on it again. It was no way for a bride to feel and she smiled anxiously at Ari as he stepped up at her side, not wanting to offend him. None of this was his fault.

He smiled back, easy and confident, and she steadied. He looked very handsome in his fine white kittel and she felt a shiver of delight run through her at the thought he was to be her husband, quashed it out of guilt, and then felt guilty in turn for the quashing. This was ridiculous.

'Don't turn from joy, sweet one,' Herodias had said to her just before they'd left the palace for the synagogue.

It had been a rare moment of care from her stern mother; a rare moment of wisdom too. What was the point in wallowing? Philip's passing had, in the end, been a mercy on his poor suffering body, and she had nursed him to the best of her ability. If she had been fogged from the events of the terrible death that had preceded his, then he had not noticed – or at least not commented – and she

271

hoped she had made her kind husband's last days as comfortable as possible.

Nursing him, if she was honest, had been a blessed escape. Whilst she had sat at his sick bed, she had not been obliged to face the world. She had not had to entertain guests or ambassadors, had not had to sit in judgement, or travel around the tetrarchy. The good men and women in Philip's service had taken care of the day to day running of Trachonitis, leaving the first lady free to tend its leader – and her own, horribly bruised soul.

Soul, she scoffed at herself, hearing the word in her mother's supercilious voice. A 'soul' was part of the New Way, and the New Way had hit a dead end. She had thrown herself into believing that she was present at a crux in history, at a moment of truth for Jews everywhere, and she had been wrong. That she had been in good company was no excuse. They had all carried each other along on a wave of hysteria – again, the word in her mother's voice – and had crashed onto the shore of reality.

Or, at least, she had.

Strange rumours were coming from Jerusalem. The traders carried them to Tiberias and they had crept into the palace with the rich fabric for her wedding gown, the barrels of wine for the feast, and the musicians for the dancing.

Have you heard? They're saying Jesus rose again.

Yes, on the third day after his burial.

Mary from Magdala saw him, Peter and Andrew and the other disciples too.

Judas, the traitor, hung himself with shame when he saw him.

Jesus walked the earth for forty days and then he was taken up to be with God.

His father.

Salome had tried to block her ears to the crazy whispers but they had crept around the sides of her fingers and buried deep into her brain. Could it be true, she'd wonder, in the darker reaches of the night and then, with dawn, she'd scold herself and run down to the lake to try and soak some sense into her fevered brain. She could not let this happen again.

Jesus was dead. She had seen it herself. She'd seen him suffer the agony of the cross, she'd seen him shout out in despair, she'd seen his breath leave his body, his arm ripped from the nail and his head collapsed onto his empty lungs. She'd seen the soldier spear his side open and his mangled corpse dragged down from the cruel wood. He had been no Messiah, just a man with piercing eyes and even more piercing ideas and she had to forget him.

'Salome?'

Aristobulus' voice was soft but concerned and she blinked back to the present. The priest was looking at her to circle her groom and she was standing here like a fool, ruminating on vicious, desperate rumours spread by a group of men and women who refused to let go of their foolish dream.

'Ari.'

She smiled at him and he smiled back. Her body gave another little shiver and she let it, delighted in it. This good, strong, handsome man was offering her a new life and she must reach out and grab it. A little of the mist lifted and she trod the three circles around him with a firm tread. Stepping back in at his side for the seven blessings, his fingers found hers, warm and strong, and shot her a look that went straight to her core.

Already, to her shame, she was looking forward to the night.

◆

The feast was long and noisy. Antipas and Herodias had invited everyone of import to celebrate the happy day and they were all, it seemed, as eager to cast off the clouds of this dark year as Salome. Galilee had been subdued since Pesach. Tiberias, filled with eager new citizens, had been too busy trading to worry but reports had come in from Capernaum, Bethsaida and Magdala that people were lost and confused. When she'd first arrived back in her stepfather's capital city, Salome had been soothed by the idea of others suffering as she was, and tempted to ride out and join them, but why bother? What was done was done and certainly tonight, as people whirled themselves into the dancing with heady abandon, it seemed that the area was starting to heal.

Salome stood at the side, nursing a cup of spiced wine and watching the reels turn. Her limbs ached to join in, to fling themselves into the swings and turns that had always helped her make sense of the world, but she gritted her teeth and forced them still.

'Wife.'

The voice at her ear was low and sweet and she glanced coyly back.

'Husband.'

She felt a hand at her waist and leaned into it.

'I wish all these people would go home and I could take you to bed.' Salome's pulse pounded in her throat, thudding out her desire, and she put a self-conscious hand up to hide it. His lips brushed across her fingers, doing nothing to help the blush spreading across her face. 'I will make you happy, Salome, I promise.'

She turned into him.

'I know it. And I hope I will make you happy too.'

'Oh, you will.'

He bent down and kissed her lips, pulling her closer against him. She gave into him, ignoring the fond titters nearby – though hoping her mother wasn't watching as she would be unbearably smug.

'We have many glorious years ahead,' Ari assured her, 'but for now, shall we dance?'

Salome's heart thudded and not, this time, with desire. She pulled away.

'I cannot.'

'*Cannot?* Why?'

'I made a vow.'

'A vow not to dance? Why on earth would you do that?'

'Because ...' Suddenly the room felt too hot, the crowds too close. 'Because I chose to,' she said stiffly.

'But why?'

'Does it matter?'

'It does, yes. I am your husband and I want to dance with you on this, our wedding night. It does not seem so unreasonable.'

'To you perhaps.'

His hand was still at her waist and she twisted to avoid it. He looked hurt but that could not be helped. If he did not respect her wishes that was his problem.

'Salome, please. I surely, at least, deserve an explanation?'

She supposed he did, though speaking the words aloud felt like ripping a bandage off an open wound.

'I made a vow the night that John . . . that the Baptiser was killed.'

'Oh. Oh, I see. Yes, that was a bad time.'

'Thank you.'

He stepped closer again.

'But it is over now, behind us.'

She stared at him, horrified.

'It is not behind *me*, Ari.'

Turning her back on her new husband, she picked up her skirts and moved as swiftly as she could, without attracting too much attention, towards the door and the cooler air beyond. The guards leapt to attention but she strode past them, making for the cover of the lush gardens. The mist was back in her head but this time it was swirling red around her and she welcomed it.

'Salome.'

He was coming after her. She broke into a run, making for a nook in one of the tamarind bushes just down the path.

'Salome!'

He was too fast. She heard the heavy tread of his boots and flinched in anticipation of his hand on her arm, but he just ran past her and stopped, blocking her way but not attempting to touch her.

'Yes?' she snapped.

He stood there, looking at her with a curiosity that made her feel horribly exposed.

'You are not what I was expecting,' he said eventually.

'You were expecting some meek, biddable mouse of a wife?'

He smiled.

'Not a mouse, no, but maybe a chinchilla – rare and beautiful but still . . .'

'Biddable?'

'Yes.'

'I'm sorry.'

He tipped his head on one side.

'It's not such a bad thing. Chinchillas, I'm sure, are very boring after a while. A mountain lioness is much more of a challenge.'

She blinked at him in the thin starlight, unsure what to make of the comparison. Her mother would certainly be a lioness, but she was nowhere near as fierce as Herodias.

'I don't dance, Ari. If that offends you, I'm sorry, but I don't dance.'

He put up his hands.

'I won't ask again.'

His compliance surprised her and she felt compelled to explain.

'It's just that, last time I danced someone died.'

'That wasn't your fault, Lola.'

The pet name shivered through her like a kiss.

'Thank you, Ari, but it was. John's death was my gift, my prize.'

'John's death was called for by every man in that room.'

'But ordered by me.'

He shook his head, looking genuinely surprised.

'That's not how I remember it.'

'It's how it was.'

'It's how it was for you, I see that. And I won't ask you to dance again, though I will welcome it if ever you change your mind.'

'Ari . . .'

'Come, Lola – you can state your position, surely I can state mine as well? If this is going to be a marriage of equals, rather than of . . .'

'Man and chinchilla?'

276

'Exactly. Then we must be equal in both directions.'

She drew in a breath.

'Fair enough.'

Again, he tipped his head on one side.

'This is going to be interesting,' he said, stepping a little closer.

'Taming your lioness?'

'I'm not sure I want her tame.' He reached tentative hands to her waist and she felt the touch of him run like heat down her hips and pool between her legs. 'May I kiss you, lioness?'

'Not if you call me that.'

He grinned.

'Very well. May I kiss you, Lola, my Lola?'

It was too much to resist. Pushing herself onto her tiptoes, she pressed her lips to his. His response was immediate, his kiss deep and searching. He pulled her to him, so that their bodies were pressed together and she felt her whole self flare.

'I want you, wife.'

'Here?'

'Here.'

He pushed her gently into the nook in the bush, his lips running down her throat and across her collar bone, his hand scrabbling for the laces of her dress. She pushed him away and undid them herself. It had never been like this with Philip. She had never felt this urgent need to feel him close to her, inside her. She let her dress drop away, heard him suck in his breath, and felt beautiful for the first time in far too long. She might not dance with this man but there were other ways to move together.

'I want you too.'

The words fell from her lips and he kissed hungrily at them. His hands roamed all over her body, stroking, nipping, teasing until her skin felt as if it might be his skin. She let her own hands trace the lines of him, hard and muscular and pulsing with energy. She thought again of Philip and his quiet, unassuming way of making her his wife, but then Ari's fingers delved lower and too many sensations flooded across her body to make any sort of rational thought possible.

'Now,' she gasped, no longer a princess, no longer a bride, just a woman in urgent need. 'Take me now.'

And as he lifted her up and entered her, she let herself go on the glorious wave of her new marriage. *Don't deny yourself joy, sweet one,* her mother had told her this morning and, God help her, she had been right again!

Chapter Twenty-seven

Salome

JOPPA

KISLEV (NOVEMBER), 31 AD

'Did you order this for dinner tonight?'

Ari held up the little sack of the Persian delicacy known as rice, as if it were a dead rat. Salome abandoned the roses she'd been pruning and went across to him.

'I did. There's a girl from Babylon working in the kitchens and she was telling me of a wonderful recipe her mother used to make with it, so I ordered some from the market. I thought it would be good to try.'

Ari pulled open the top of the bag and dug a hand inside.

'Have you seen it? It's just grains.'

'Apparently it's very nice when cooked well.'

'Seems unlikely.'

'Well, we'll find out, won't we.'

He grimaced but returned the white grains to the sack.

'I suppose we will, I just don't see what's wrong with bread.'

Salome shook her head and kissed him.

'Times change, husband.'

'I know,' he agreed on a groan, 'wives, it seems, no longer do what they are told.'

'Nonsense. You told me to order something tasty for dinner and I have done.'

'I meant meat.'

She grinned up at him.

'Then you should have said so.'

'Meat tomorrow?'

'If you're good.'

'I'm always good,' he protested. 'You're the one that misbehaves.'

'At least I'm not boring.'

'No,' he agreed ruefully. 'You're certainly not that.' He looked across the roses, her trug, kneeler and clippers laid next to them. 'Are you sure you should be doing that?'

'Cutting flowers? Why on earth not?'

'Well, you know, in your condition.'

Salome put a hand to her stomach, feeling the familiar thrill at the thought of the new life beneath her skin. The doctors had confirmed her pregnancy just last week and, although there was only the tiniest tightening of her belly to show for it so far, Ari was very excited.

'God has blessed us, Salome,' he kept saying – at least when he wasn't complaining about dinner.

She kissed him.

'My mother was riding a horse the day before she gave birth to me, Ari.'

'Your mother is a woman apart.'

Salome considered this.

'I suppose she is.'

Ari laughed.

'Suppose?! She used to terrify me when we all went to Jerusalem for festivals. I'd hide if I heard her voice in the courtyard. I tell you now, I've never been more scared than when she summoned me to her rooms after Philip's funeral.'

'She summoned you?'

'Yes. To suggest that I marry you.'

'That was Mother's idea?'

He shifted awkwardly.

'Did you not know that?'

'She told me you had sought my hand.'

'Well, I did. I mean, I would have, if I hadn't been too scared of Herodias. Don't look at me like that, Salome. Does it matter? Here we are, married and with a baby on the way.'

'Here we are,' she agreed and she supposed it didn't matter, save that it meant her mother had been in control as usual.

Still, she wasn't in control any more. Salome was living on her own coastal estate, bequeathed to her by her father. Ari was working with Antipas, helping him to govern Galilee and Perea, in return for a promise of Trachonitis once they secured it from Rome. Tiberius had, to Herodias' fury, subsumed it into the Governorship of Syria. The emperor's soldier-deputy, Sejanus, had apparently been outed as a cheat by the Lady Antonia, grandmother to Caligula, one of the little Imperial heirs, and Tiberius was at least nominally back in charge.

Herodias had excitedly hoped this would mean he'd listen to Antipas again but, although the pair of them had persuaded him to let the area administer its own taxes, it was no more theirs than Judea. Antipas was confident that when 'the waters settled' they'd get it back and, although Salome couldn't see from whence his confidence came, the promise kept Ari happy for now.

As for her, she was content to be back in the place she truly thought of as home and honoured to hold it in her own right. The estate was, to be fair, a little quiet. The port of Joppa was busy enough but Boethus' estates were a fair ride away and she could sometimes, these days, see why her mother had railed against the remote location and been so excited to get to Jerusalem for the festivals. It was very beautiful and they had all they could wish for – including delicacies like rice – but there were rarely guests or passing traders and it could, just occasionally, get a little dull. She was glad Ari was travelling with her stepfather or he would certainly be bored and she had to admit that securing Trachonitis and going back to Caesarea Philippi was not a prospect that she dreaded. Not that she'd ever say so of course, especially not to Herodias.

'I'm off to look at a new horse,' Ari told her. 'I'll take this rice stuff back to the kitchens, shall I?'

'Please,' she agreed, smiling as he crossed to the palace with the bag held out before him as if it might bite, then turning back to her roses.

She tried to focus on pruning them at just the right place to encourage growth next year, but it was hard not to let her eyes wander to the lawns where she had once danced to her father's music. It felt so long ago but she could almost, if she squinted into the low winter sun, see Boethus playing his lyre and perhaps herself too, dancing with the freedom of someone who had not yet known any troubles in the world.

Someone, she reminded herself sternly, who had not yet had a man killed.

She snipped viciously at a rose, watching with grim satisfaction as its head fell to the soil below. At least out here on the coast, they didn't get too many of the rumours flowing out of Jerusalem, though the wildest ones seemed to make it somehow. The other day she'd heard that some of Jesus' disciples had been sprung from prison by an angel of the Lord. Herodias had been visiting, or, 'checking up on us,' as Ari put it. Certainly, the visit had seemed to come just days after she'd called in the doctor to confirm her pregnancy, suggesting she had contacts – 'spies,' Ari said – in their household.

Either way, Herodias had been there to hear the story and had said she suspected it was an angel with some nice gold in his pocket now. Salome had shushed her but she'd woken in the night, wondering about it, not so much because of the angel as because the disciples had been arrested. What were they up to, to attract the censure of the authorities, and where would it lead? She'd thought the Jesus story done, but it seemed they just weren't letting it go. Poor fools.

The roses were all headless now and, gathering up the scattered petals, Salome transferred them to the compost heap, trying not to think of John's head, still, as far as she knew, in the one up at Machaerus. Her back was stiff and, stretching it out in the last of the sunshine, she headed for the house, only to see a maid come running towards her.

'What is it, Ruth?' she demanded. 'Is someone hurt?'

Ruth shook her head but had run so fast with her message that she was out of breath to pass it on. Salome prayed for patience and at last the silly girl could speak.

'You have visitors, my lady. A man and his wife, a little boy and a baby.'

Salome squinted at her, trying to think who this could be.

'Are you sure they're for me?'

'Oh yes, my lady. The woman was most excitable. Said to tell you that Johanna was here.'

Salome gasped in pleasure and hurried inside. Always Johanna surprised her! Crossing the hall to the big main doors, she saw she and Chuza seated in the reception area, a babe asleep in Johanna's arms and little Chuza-Amos running up and down the hallway, his arms aloft like a bird. Seeing her, he swerved, swooping convincingly as he passed and crying, 'I'm an eagle!'

'So you are,' Salome agreed, tears springing to her eyes as Johanna rose and came towards her.

They hugged carefully so as not to wake the little one and Salome stroked the downy head, trying to imagine herself holding such a precious bundle in six months' time. It was almost impossible and, yet, surely if scatty Johanna could manage to keep not one, but two babies alive, she could do so too.

'Girl or boy?' she asked.

'A little girl. Esther, after my mother.'

'That's lovely. She's so sweet.' Salome was struck with sudden guilt. She'd promised her friend a safe birthing place in Caesarea Philippi and then Jesus had been killed and Philip had been so ill and she'd forgotten all about it. 'Where did you have her, Johanna?'

'In Jerusalem.'

'No! Was it safe?'

'Oh, yes. We were staying with Mariam, Jesus' mother. She has been very good to us and it meant we were still a part of things in the city.'

'Things? What things? Oh, but you must be tired. Come in, come in.' She went to greet Chuza and ushered them both through into the best withdrawing room and onto couches, calling for drinks and food as she went. 'Ari! Ari, where are you?' Ari came out of his office and looked in surprise at the new arrivals. 'We have guests, husband.'

'So I see. What a pleasant surprise. Not many pass here.'

'We are on our way up the coast to Caesarea Maritima.'

'Then we are glad you diverted this way. You'll stay? There's plenty of room.'

'That would be very kind, but only for one night. We are on urgent business.'

'You are?' Salome asked.

Johanna beamed at her.

'We are. We are charged with setting up a church there.'

'A church?!'

Salome remembered the strange word from Jesus' visit to Caesarea Philippi last year. He had called Peter the rock upon which it would be built and no one had understood. Salome still did not, but it seemed that Johanna was very certain.

'A church, yes – an assembly of the called.'

'Like a synagogue?' Ari asked.

'In a way, but more than just a building. The church is the people who come together and commit to the New Way.'

'The New Way?' Ari asked.

284

Salome shifted nervously.

'It is what Jesus preached,' she told him.

'But Jesus is dead.'

'No, he isn't!' Johanna cried. 'That's how it looked, that's even how it felt, but he wasn't dead, not in the true sense. His flesh was done but his spirit was alive and well and dwells with us still.'

Salome squinted at her old friend.

'Have you been in the sun too long, Johanna?'

Johanna shook her head at her, in a strange, slightly patronising way, as if she were a child too young to understand. Salome glanced to Ari, who gave her a subtle eye-roll, not that Johanna would have noticed for she was far too caught up in her own words.

'You left too soon, Salome,' she said, her eyes alight. 'Did she not, Chuza? Did she not leave too soon?'

'Not *too* soon, wife. That's to say, how was the princess to know? *We* didn't know. We were simply too struck down with sadness to gather ourselves and leave.'

'And thank God!'

'Thank God.'

They beamed at each other and Salome felt, yet again, like a child trying to work out her parents' conversation.

'What happened?' Ari demanded.

Johanna jumped up and down so much that little Esther woke and gave a startled wail. Johanna dropped a kiss on her forehead and handed her to Chuza who rocked her expertly until, with a contented snuffle, she dropped off again.

'Isn't she good,' Salome commented but Johanna was not to be deflected.

'It was amazing, truly. We were so cast down after the crucifixion. The men were in hiding and the women so saddened that we had no desire to leave the house until we must do so to embalm Jesus' body on the third day. I went to the tomb with Mariam and Mary at daybreak, so as not to draw attention to ourselves. The Romans had been guarding it, wary of trouble, but they'd given up by the third day and there was no one there. Mary went ahead. She's so brave. Truly, she has the courage of a man.'

'Women can have courage too,' Salome protested.

'Perhaps but it's not usual, is it?'

'My mother is very courageous.'

Johanna gave a dark laugh and Salome saw Chuza catch his wife's eye with a warning and began to wish she hadn't asked them to stay. She'd had no idea they were going to be lectured.

'I'm sorry,' Johanna said hastily. 'Maybe many women are brave. I am not, so I hung back. In truth, I didn't want to see that poor broken body again and was rather hoping I could just stay at the door and hold the oils but in the event we neither needed the oils nor saw the body.'

'Why not?' Ari asked.

'It was gone. The stone was rolled back and it was gone.'

'Who took it?'

'No one. That's what I'm telling you. No one "took it". Jesus was risen from the dead.'

Ari glanced at Salome. 'Risen from the dead?' he repeated incredulously.

'How do you know?' Salome asked.

'Because Mary saw him. I panicked, Mariam too. We thought there was trouble afoot and we took the embalming jars and ran from Golgotha but Mary stayed. I told you, she's—'

'So brave,' Salome agreed, 'we know.'

'You don't believe me?' Johanna asked, looking hurt.

Salome felt mean.

'It's not that I don't believe you, Johanna, simply that there could be other explanations.'

'No, there—'

Chuza stood up and put an arm on Johanna's shoulder to silence her.

'You are right, of course. I was sceptical also but Jesus has since appeared to too many to doubt it. Mary saw him in the garden by the tombs and then Peter and the others in a room in Jerusalem. Thomas would not believe it and Jesus had him thrust his hand into his sword wound and he swears it was true flesh and blood. Ask him yourself.'

'How would we do that?'

Johanna jumped up again. Salome had forgotten how restless she'd always been and now it was combined with a fierce passion that made her very hard to resist.

'Join us in Jerusalem for the next festival. It will be Hannukah soon – a time of new beginnings. What could be more appropriate?'

Salome looked at her friend, eyes shining with renewed belief, and envied her. For a moment she wanted to throw all her carefully built caution to the winds and jump up with her, but she had responsibilities now. She put her hand to her belly.

'I cannot, Johanna. I am with child.'

'You are? Wonderful!'

'Is it not?' Ari agreed, putting a protective arm around her.

'God blesses you indeed, and He will care for you and for the little one if you put your trust in Him.'

'We already do.'

'Wonderful. So come to Jerusalem.'

'No,' Ari said.

'No?'

'I do not want my wife in danger.'

Salome glanced at him, feeling at the same time a warmth at his care and a prickle of annoyance at him speaking out for her.

'It is more,' she said, 'that I do not like Jerusalem now.'

She shuddered at the memory of the terrible Pesach but Johanna simply threw up her arms and laughed.

'You will, I promise you. You will when you see how it is changed, how *we* are changed. Peter started it at Pentecost. He went right up onto the balustrade around the Court of the Gentiles, stood there between the bemused Roman soldiers and told everyone down below that Jesus was risen. There was jeering at first, of course, but he called upon the Holy Spirit and there, in the sky, was a dove, flying above us all as a sign, and one by one the people in the court threw up their arms and sang their praises to God. Peter spoke to them so eloquently. He was truly inspired and soon everyone was praying in a hundred different tongues. He called them to baptism in the New Way and I tell you now, fully three thousand people followed him to the Pools of Bethsaida and gave themselves to God.'

'Three thousand?' Salome stuttered, looking to Ari whose arm had tightened uncomfortably around her.

'At least,' Chuza agreed. 'Andrew tried to take names down but there were so many he ran out of parchment. It was a miracle. You should have seen it.'

Salome looked from husband to wife, marvelling at the energy radiating from them.

'I wish I had.' That, at least, she meant sincerely, for how was she to believe this without seeing it with her own eyes? How was she to know it was not just another delusion, a way of perpetuating a story to which so many had dedicated their lives? 'And now you are setting up a . . . a . . . ?'

'Church, yes. Well, a thousand churches, all linked together in one great church across the world.'

'The world?' Salome gaped at them.

'You are ambitious then,' Ari said drily.

'We must be,' Johanna told them earnestly. 'Jesus did not just come to save the Holy Land, but all people on God's earth. The New Way is still there to follow. It's not about land, or political power; it's about love and reaching out to other people. And you can be a part of it.'

'Our baby . . .'

'Can come too. Look at us.'

Johanna reached for Chuza's hand where it held their baby girl and gestured with the other to Chuza-Amos, still flapping his imaginary wings. They all looked so healthy, so happy, so free.

'We are rulers, Johanna,' Ari said stiffly.

'Of which province?'

Ari sucked in his breath and Salome winced.

'None, yet, but Antipas assures us Ari will have Trachonitis very soon and then . . .'

'And then you will be stuck in the hills, influencing no one.'

Salome could feel Ari's anger bristling down his arm, heavy on her shoulders, and did not blame him. There was no need for this.

'And then,' she said with dignity, 'we will travel our tetrarchy ensuring justice for all people and building up our influence to help effect change.'

'What change?'

'Johanna,' Chuza warned but there was no stopping her.

'Tell me, please, what change?'

'I want to put a stop to the corruption in the Temple,' Salome told her stiffly. 'I want to simplify the laws and make the faith more accessible to ordinary people.'

'Do you?' Ari asked, looking sideways at her.

'That would be wonderful,' Chuza said.

'That would be impossible,' Johanna sniped.

Salome had had enough. She stamped her foot, stepping away from her husband and towards her one-time friend.

'And yet, Johanna, it is what you are trying to do too. You do not find me criticising your choices, so what gives you the right to criticise mine?'

Johanna gaped at her and Chuza pulled her away.

'The princess is right, wife. You go in too strong.'

'But Chuza,' she turned to him, placing her hands at his waist and gazing up into his eyes, 'he is risen. We have seen it. We have seen the joy it brings, the changes it can make to the world. It is so important.'

'Important enough to take our time over, my love,' he told her. 'You must tread softly with those who have not had their eyes opened as we have.'

Salome stood there, watching them awkwardly and seeing, in that intimate moment between the two, far more to convince her something was truly shifting in the world, than in any of Johanna's hot-headed diatribe. She glanced back to Ari, standing rigidly at her side, glaring at the pair. What was going on here? And what did it mean for her?

Chapter Twenty-eight

Herodias

A boy! At last, a boy for the family, a male Hasmonean to carry on her line.

Herodias looked fondly down at the creature who had been brought out to her, then winced as he let out a wail. Aristobulus-the-younger might be a boy but he was still a baby – funny, mewling, unpredictable things. Still, he would grow and, in the meantime, that's what nursemaids were for.

'You!'

She gestured one of them forward and handed over her grandson with relief. The girl cooed away to him, babbling the sort of fond nonsense that made Herodias want to scream, but at least it stopped the noise and she could think clearly again. There was much to be done. Poor Salome had been in labour for what felt like forever. She'd always been inclined to make a meal of things, but even Herodias had begun to worry when they'd headed into a second day without any sign of progress. The midwife had asked her to be with her daughter so she'd dutifully gone into the birthing chamber but, oh, it had been depressing, all dark and sweaty, and Salome had mainly just been lying there moaning so she'd excused herself as soon as she reasonably could. She'd stayed close, of course – what mother wouldn't – but there'd been no need to have them both suffering, so she'd kept to the nice airy parlour next door.

Ari, to her surprise, had been in there too, pacing up and down, sighing an increasingly irritating amount and barely eating at all. She'd thought him stronger than that.

'Sit down and have some pie, man,' she'd insisted, when his performance threatened to take away her own appetite.

He'd sat down opposite her, taking the slice she'd offered but doing a very poor job of anything more than spreading it around the plate.

'She'll be fine,' Herodias had told him, attempting to be understanding. 'This is what women do.'

'The waiting is agony.'

'Try being stuck at home waiting for your husband to come home from battle – that can be months, not just a day or two.'

'It's not the same.'

'I think you'll find it's virtually identical – having to wait for the outcome of a battle that could result in a great prize, but also comes fraught with danger of injury or death.'

He'd gone a little white then; she'd perhaps gone a bit too far. Still, he had to understand.

'Salome will do it. She's slight, I grant you, which isn't ideal but – hush moaning, boy – she's a fighter. Stubborn, determined and never lets anything get in the way of her ambitions.'

'That's true,' he'd admitted. 'She's been, er, stronger willed than I'd expected.'

Oh, Herodias' heart had swelled with pride at that point.

'Has she indeed? I'm delighted to hear it. In what particular way?'

He'd shifted, spraying more crumbs around.

'She doesn't, you know, do what she's asked very often.' That had made Herodias laugh out loud. He'd looked at her indignantly. 'Surely a wife should do what she's asked?'

'That depends if what you are asking is sensible.' She'd reached over and taken his hand. It wasn't her usual style but she'd had to stop him breaking the pie up somehow. 'Believe me, you will learn the value of a strong woman at your side, Ari. You don't want some milksop with no opinions of her own.'

'Sometimes I wouldn't mind that.'

'It might soothe your masculine pride, but you are better than that, are you not? You can see, can you not, that Salome is a bright, intelligent woman.'

'Of course.'

'So use that. Share things with her, consult her, listen to her.'

'Yes,' he'd agreed, tugging to escape her grip. 'Yes, I will. Because I do love her, Herodias, truly I do.'

She'd let him go at that and he'd gone back to his pacing. She'd waved a server to take away his ruined pie and tried to concentrate on finishing her own, but it had been too late, her appetite had truly gone. What was the world coming too, she'd wondered, with men so pathetic. Thank heavens, he was finding Salome strong; it looked like he was going to need it.

Still, he seemed to be bouncing around now. He was inside with Salome which was odd, when the real interest was out here, but at least it meant she got his namesake to herself. It was a shame he was to be Aristobulus but it was to be expected really and at least Salome hadn't insisted on Boethus. That would have been very tricky, especially with her own dear Antipas. Talking of whom . . .

'Herodias! Good news I hear. Where's the little one?'

She gestured to the nursemaid and watched in surprise as he gathered the child up into his big arms, stroking its downy head and gazing down on it with distinctly soppy devotion.

'Isn't he gorgeous?'

'He's all red and wrinkled, Antipas.'

'That will drop out. He's so perfect. Look at his little limbs and his bright eyes and his tiny, tiny fingers.'

Herodias moved obligingly closer. She supposed it was rather perfect – a tiny human being to come out of another. An everyday miracle. She felt a dangerous lump in her throat and gulped desperately to stop it turning into tears. Antipas looked so happy holding his step-grandson, so natural. She threaded an arm into his, feeling the warmth of the baby against her fingers.

'I'm sorry I didn't give you a baby.'

'I'm sorry *I* didn't give you one, my love, but fret not – we have Aristobulus now.'

She looked at him in amazement. It was all so simple in his world.

'You do see the best in situations, my . . .'

She dried up. This was all getting a bit too emotional for her liking. Antipas smiled teasingly at her.

'My . . . ?'

'Husband,' she said, pulling her hand out of his arm. Then, not liking the whisper of hurt in his eyes, added, 'My dear husband.'

He shook his head but leaned over to kiss her, making the baby squeak.

'I think, do you not, that it's time we presented this little chap to the people.'

Now he was talking!

They took him out of the inner rooms, across the courtyard and up the steps that led to the balustrade looking out across the paved grounds that led down to the main road and the lake beyond. News had leached out and many people had gathered, eager for news. Herodias paused on the steps, forcing Antipas, behind her to stop too. She drunk in the excited murmur of the crowd and looked down on her husband and new grandson.

'They love us.'

'Of course they do. Look what we've given them.'

He gestured as best he could with the child hampering him, presumably trying to indicate all of Tiberias, and she nodded. She was so glad that Salome had agreed to come here for the birthing. If she was honest, she'd been surprised at how readily her daughter had taken her up on the suggestion, but thank the Lord she had, for there would be nothing but a handful of peasants to greet the new Herod out on Boethus' old estates.

'May I?'

She held out her arms for the baby and Antipas relinquished him immediately. Baby Aristo – so-called to avoid confusion with his father – shifted and for a moment his features creased.

'Don't cry,' she begged him, feeling uncharacteristically helpless in the face of this tiny, wilful creature, but Aristo just opened his eyes and stared straight up at her, bright and curious. 'Hello,' she said softly, and then, feeling horribly self-conscious, turned and headed up the steps onto the balustrade.

The roar was immediate. The crowd below saw her and the babe in her arms and began cheering and shouting acclamations. Many had brought flowers and threw them in the air so that for a moment the blue of the skies and the lake beyond were streaked with colour.

'Behold!' Herodias cried out to them, 'Aristobulus Herod – your new prince.'

The roars, if anything grew louder. Herodias felt a momentary twinge of guilt that it was not Salome and Ari standing here for their approval, but the girl was exhausted after all that labouring and Ari had chosen to be in the dark birthing room with her, so, really, there had been nothing for it but to step in and pass on the good news.

'A feast,' she said to Antipas over the shouts. 'We should order a feast in the palace, with wine and treats for the people.'

This was a day of happiness, and they must make the most of it.

❖

In the end, although the people got their treats immediately, the royals waited eight days for the feast to give Salome time to recover and be purified, and to celebrate Aristo's circumcision, carried out with great pomp in the synagogue in Tiberias. Herodias would have loved to take him to the Temple for a ceremony befitting a true Hasmonean but Antipas had put his foot down.

'We can have him blessed when we are next there,' he'd said, 'but travelling would be dangerous for both mother and child.'

He'd been enticingly firm about it, so Herodias had given in, reflecting that at least this way they got to celebrate twice. The delay also gave her more time to prepare. She was determined to have the grandest feast ever seen in the new city – a feast for the royals, a feast for Salome and a feast for herself, an accumulation of the three she should have had for the sons that had died in her own stupid womb.

'You have done better than me,' she told Salome when the girl was recovered enough to see her, two whole days after the birth.

'Nonsense, Mother,' she'd said crisply, 'for you had me.'

It had made Herodias laugh and laugh, until she'd been in danger of becoming almost hysterical and had had to give herself a stern talking to. It had been relief, perhaps, that Salome was perfectly well and relief, too, that her daughter was right. The chain of blood had come good and that kept them all bound safely together.

'Have a daughter next time,' she'd suggested and laughed again when Salome had gaped at her in astonishment. 'They're a lot of trouble,' she'd added with a wink, 'but really rather good fun.' And then she'd left, before things got too soppy and Salome thought she'd lost her sanity.

Now, she looked out over the assembled guests and felt pride fill her so full that she was in danger of bursting. Life had not been easy. She had, at times, been tortured more than she would like to admit over divorcing Boethus, especially when the damned man had gone and died just a few months later. As Salome had once said, waiting for that would have saved a lot of trouble, not the least with that damned Baptiser. It had been a bad night, that feast, but this one was going very well indeed.

The men and women had dined apart, as was decreed, but Antipas had suggested that God would surely not be offended if they met together afterwards and, apart from a few older folk, who had left with amusingly shocked looks on their faces, everyone seemed very happy with the arrangement. As Kypros had said approvingly to her at dinner, royals had to show they could move with the times and, with the musicians ordered to play only the slowest tunes, it was all very decorous. Baby Aristo was asleep in his royal cot to one side, attended by several doting nursemaids, and Salome looked as if she would willingly join him. She was feeding her son herself, as tradition dictated, but the boy was big and was draining her, poor girl.

'You can slip away if you wish, daughter,' Herodias said, going across to her.

'I am rather tired.'

'And you can, you know, add a little goat's milk into Aristo's diet, especially in the middle of the night. I'm sure one of this lot would willingly administer it.'

'Mother!' Salome looked guiltily around but no one was listening. 'Is that not against the Talmud?'

Herodias waved this away.

'The Talmud was written by men, who know nothing of the pain of a cracked nipple or the weariness of a midnight feed. I did it for you and it worked a treat.'

'Really?'

Herodias shook her head at her.

'You would leave your family for a street-preacher, but not slip a little extra milk into your son's diet?'

Salome frowned at her.

'That's mean, Mother.'

'But fair.'

'And he wasn't just a street-preacher, he was an inspirational man. Maybe more.'

Herodias narrowed her eyes.

'What do you mean, more?'

'Johanna visited me. They believe that Jesus was risen from the dead.'

'Risen? By whom?'

'By God.'

Herodias rolled her eyes.

'Will they never stop? They were brave, those friends of yours around the carpenter, I'll give them that. They stood up for what they believed in and that has to be respected, but there's a time to stand up and a time to *give* up.'

'But . . .'

Herodias put up a hand.

'Now is not the place, Salome. Go. Get some sleep. And order yourself a goat – it will make all the difference.'

Herodias kissed her and waved Salome away, relieved to see her go. Hopefully, with some rest, she would not be subject to these damned people and their insane persistence. A New Way was not needed, simply a few repairs to the old one, and who were better placed to affect those than the Herods?

Turning back into the room, Herodias went over to Antipas, taking his arm to look around the room. The guests were thinning out as it grew late and, in truth, she felt a little weary herself.

'I would gladly be abed,' she confessed to her husband, who laughed.

'It's been a busy time, wife. The feast was magnificent.'

'Galilee needed something positive.'

He nodded, sombre suddenly.

'Have you heard the rumours that . . . ?'

She hushed him.

'Not now. Please.'

'Very well.'

She looked gratefully to him but then there was a scuffle in the corner of the room and she spotted her wretched brother manhandling one of the musicians. She strode over, Antipas tight on her heels.

'Agrippa, what do you think you're doing?'

Agrippa turned to her and she saw his eyes blurred with drink and groaned inwardly.

'What am I doing? I'm trying to get this damned minstrel to play something with a bit of life, that's what I'm doing.'

'Then please don't. We specifically requested quiet tunes.'

'Why?'

'Because this is a respectful gathering to celebrate a royal circumcision, not a wanton party.'

'Hah,' he spluttered. 'You lot over here in the so-called "Holy Land" wouldn't know a wanton party if it leapt up and bit you.'

'And are all the better for that,' Herodias said firmly.

People were starting to look and she took Agrippa's arm, trying to steer him outside to cool down but he was having none of it. Kypros hurried across, brows drawn and, to Herodias' mortification, people turned to watch.

Agrippa gave a nasty laugh.

'You think so? You think your petty little city is a fine place? I tell you now, it's a backwater, a puerile, insular, unclean little backwater in the middle of—'

'Enough!' Antipas stepped forward, pushing Herodias manfully behind him as he squared up to his brother-in-law. 'You chose to come here, Agrippa. You arrived destitute from too many years of dissolute living and we took you in. We gave you a job.'

'A job!' Agrippa threw his hands in the air and cast his eyes around the now agog crowd. 'Have you ever heard the likes of it? A man of my stature with a "job". That was no kindness, Antipas, that was no charity – that was simply you rubbing my nose in my temporary misfortune, making a show of power as petty as your stupid little "city".'

'How dare you? I put the very bread on your table – and that of your family.'

'He does,' Kypros agreed, trying to grab Agrippa's arm. 'Please, husband, hush. Antipas and Herodias have been most gracious to us and we must be thankful.'

'For their smug, patronising, stupid damned job? For their poorly ground bloody bread? I don't think so. I've had enough of this. I'm going somewhere where they will value me.'

'And where's that?' Antipas demanded. 'The depths of the lake with all the other bottom-crawlers?'

Herodias bit back a laugh and reminded herself that this was not funny. Agrippa, spoiled brat that he had ever been, was ruining the end of her magnificent feast. People were staring. There would be talk.

'I will go to Syria,' Agrippa said, pulling himself up as straight as he could manage, though it took the support of the wall to achieve it. 'To Antioch. I know the governor there from my time in Rome. Rome – a proper city, built on proper history.'

'Seven hundred paltry years of it. Jerusalem is—'

'Newly built by our shared ancestor, Herod the Great, barely thirty years ago.'

'Newly *re*-built,' Antipas corrected him with commendable dignity, but Herodias had had enough.

'Fine, brother – go. See how the Roman governor likes having you as his guest, for you are not worthy of a place in the Holy Land.'

A few of the guests gave a cheer and Herodias felt her insides settle a little. But then she saw Kypros' face crease with distress, and her momentary triumph dissolved. And as Agrippa grabbed her friend's arm and marched her from the room, she felt sadness descend, and with it fear.

❖

We should never have done that,' she told Antipas, striding up and down their bedchamber when, finally, everyone was gone and they could theoretically rest. 'We should never have thrown my wretched brother out.'

'What choice did we have, my love? He was being despicable about all that we have set up here. Despicable and wrong.'

Antipas tried to take her in his arms, but she was too agitated for comfort.

'I know that, husband, but now he's on the loose and that's dangerous.'

'For Kypros?'

Herodias shook her head.

'Kypros knows how to look after herself. I am very sorry to lose her company, for I have greatly enjoyed it this last year, but I do not fear for her security. She is a resourceful woman. It is we who need to worry.'

Antipas laughed.

'What can Agrippa do to us? He is a destitute, friendless wastrel. You worry too much, my love.'

Again, he tried to hold her and again she ducked his arms.

'He is destitute, for now, and he is most certainly a wastrel, but Agrippa is never friendless. He will worm his way into someone's good books and then he will look for revenge. We would have been better to keep him close.'

'Save that we might both have gone insane?' Antipas suggested and, with a bitter laugh, she gave up and fell gratefully into his open arms.

This was not, she was certain, the last they would hear of her spoiled brother, but for now she was weary. If only she'd gone to bed before Agrippa's spat with the minstrel, none of this might have happened but, as she had learned too many times in her life, you could not change the past, simply tread into the future with as much confidence as you could muster. She had Antipas, she had Salome and she had baby Aristobulus. Together, surely, they could outflank a destitute prince?

Chapter Twenty-nine

Salome

Salome felt horror pulse through her veins as the carriage drew close to Jerusalem, the city that she feared would never again feel holy to her. The familiar buildings loomed ahead, forever now streaked with blood in her eyes, and she shrunk from them. Herodias had been desperate to bring little Ari to the Temple for a full blessing and, of course, they were bound by law to travel for Pesach. She had been let off last year, heavy with child, but there had been no such excuse this time, so here she was. She hated it.

For Salome, the Temple was now where Jesus had thrown the moneylenders tables around and as good as drawn a mark on his own back for Caiaphas and his vultures. The palace was where he had been brought in the middle of the dark night, bruised and broken, to stand trial for no greater offence than shaking up the established order. And Golgotha, previously just a lump in the ground, seemed to loom over the whole city like a giant, blood-streaked shadow.

'Are you well, wife?'

Ari leaned solicitously across and she turned gratefully back into the carriage.

'I do not like this place any more.'

'Jerusalem?' He looked shocked but composed himself. 'It is a busy, violent city for sure but God dwells here and we are lucky to visit.'

Jesus' words back in Caesarea Philippi flashed into Salome's struggling mind: *God is not hidden away in the Temple, accessible only by those with titles and fancy robes; God is in your heart.*

It was a seductive idea, for if God was in her heart, then there was no need to battle their way into Jerusalem ever again. They could spend five days in quiet contemplation instead of on the dusty roads. They could give the money they threw at the Temple directly to the poor and the lambs could be allowed to live in the fields instead of being turned into rivulets of blood in the crowded streets.

'Salome?'

Ari was looking at her in concern and she shook herself away from her potentially treacherous thoughts and forced herself to smile.

'When is Aristo's blessing?'

'Tomorrow, before it all gets crowded for Pesach. Caiaphas has put in a request to Pilate to get his ceremonial robes early to honour our son.'

He looked so pleased with this that Salome bit back her initial reaction that it was God who would honour Aristo, not Caiaphas' fine jewels. The mention of the wretched Roman governor who had, ultimately, sent Jesus to his death grated on her, but was also a reminder that there were more issues at stake than Temple corruption. As Herodias had often told her, the Jews had enough enemies without turning on each other. She forced another smile.

'I'm not sure Aristo will enjoy it much.'

They both looked to their son, finally lulled into sleep by the rocking carriage after long hours of restless energy earlier today. He would turn one year old in a month and, although not yet walking, he crawled at some pace and had a particular fondness for throwing himself off any surface if not watched at all times. Too often on this journey, he had tumbled gleefully from the seat into the footwell and it was a miracle he had not yet incurred more than minor bumps.

'Caiaphas will certainly have his hands full keeping him still long enough for the blessing.'

Ari gave her a wicked smile and Salome relaxed a little. All would be well. With her husband at her side, all would surely be well.

Her son awoke as they bumped over the cobbles into the Hasmonean palace and Herodias' face appeared through the window, making them all jump.

'Welcome, Aristobulus – welcome to your ancestors' fine palace.'

'Thank you,' Ari said drily but Herodias ignored him and reached in to lift his namesake up and through the window.

'Mother!' Salome said in alarm. 'That's very high and—'

'And the boy is fine. See.'

Aristo was, indeed, squirming happily in his grandmother's arms. He was devoted to her, crawling eagerly across any room the moment she entered and she, in turn, was unusually soft with him. The other day Salome had even caught her babbling to him in the way she purported to despise in the nursery maids.

'Having a nice chat, Mother?' she'd been unable to resist asking.

'Yes, thank you,' she'd said, all dignity, though there'd been a tell-tale blush across her throat. 'I've just been telling Aristo the history of the Hasmonean revolt.'

'You have? It sounded like nonsense-speak to me.'

'Well, then, you can't have been listening carefully enough. You should know by now that I don't do nonsense-speak. What on earth would be the point?'

'Nothing at all, Mother,' Salome had agreed. 'Shall you be testing him later?'

'I shall be testing him throughout his life,' she'd said sternly and Salome, sure that on this point at least Herodias spoke true, had left it at that.

Now, though, as she watched her mother showing her son the palace, a little of her new hatred of the city settled and she looked around the beautiful building, trying to see it through his young eyes. She peered at the carved columns, the mosaiced floor, and the curled balustrade and tried to focus on the ancient history threaded through the walls and not the recent blood across the tiles. Jesus was dead, whatever Johanna would have her believe, and they must move forward.

At that thought, she glanced to Kypros, standing quietly to one side. The poor woman had come back to Tiberias a few weeks ago, her children in tow but no sign of Agrippa.

'The Governor of Syria threw us out after just a few weeks in Antioch, fed up of the bills Agrippa was running up. It's a beautiful place, you know, and rich in resources, but Agrippa can spend fast and no one had any inclination to mine more gems to fund his loose living. We went to Egypt. I think he was under some sort of illusion that the Alexandrians might be 'his sort of people' and indeed they were, but whilst they throw a good party, they had no intention of paying for him to attend. I secured him a loan through a man I did a few favours for years ago, took a share of it to get the children and I here, and sent him back to Rome.'

'Good on you,' Herodias had said crisply. 'Let's hope the man drinks himself into an early grave.'

'Mother!' Salome had protested.

'What? Never shirk reality, Salome. Agrippa was a useless brother and an even more useless husband. I am glad you came to us, Kypros.'

'I can work.'

'I know it.'

And she had, stepping into the role of steward with far more nous than Agrippa had ever shown and the profits on the estate were up already. Salome had watched her aunt gaining in confidence every day and been glad of it, though she saw her sometimes watching Herodias and Antipas chattering away together, or reaching out to touch each other – both things they still did all the time – and saw sadness in her eyes. It was not easy to be a woman alone and she admired her courage.

It was in this spirit that she headed out with Ari later, leaving their son having his afternoon nap, worn out from the attentions of the doting palace staff. Herodias and Antipas, sadly, had chosen to come along and were swift to encourage the attentions of the crowds. Salome watched her mother gliding between the doting people as if their adulation was her due and envied her confidence. The people, she could see, loved her more for it and a tiny bit of her despised them for that, then felt bad for laying her own preconceptions on others.

It took ages to get to the Temple and longer yet to make their way through the Court of the Gentiles to where Caiaphas was waiting, all smiles and sycophantic bows, to talk them through tomorrow's ceremony. Salome did her best to sit and listen to the seemingly endless details and was hugely relieved when the business was finally done and Caiaphas and Herodias fell to chatting.

Excusing herself for the latrine, she escaped into the Court of the Women and sank gratefully onto a newly vacated bench in the shade for a little peace. Looking around the pretty court, her eyes were inevitably drawn to the Gate of Nicanor, leading into the Court of the Israelites and, beyond that, the Court of the Priests and the Holy of Holies. For the first time, she felt a rush of resentment that she was not permitted inside when pompous Caiaphas, with nothing more to recommend him than a rich family and some spurious training, could jig around in there to his heart's content.

God is not hidden away in the Temple, accessible only by those with titles and fancy robes; God is in your heart. Could it be true? And if it was true, what was to stop her just standing up and walking through that gate.

The notices warning of the death penalty for breaking the ages-old boundaries for a start.

Boundaries can be moved. Is that not what she'd told her mother when Herodias had come creeping to Salome after Philip's funeral, full of news of Ari's request to marry her – a request that turned out to have come not from Ari, but from Herodias herself.

Salome pushed herself to standing and faced the gate. Did she dare? Of course she did not and what, really, would it achieve, save bringing the wrath of the Temple down on her head – and, in turn, the far more formidable wrath of her mother. She sighed.

'Salome? Salome, is that you?' She turned, startled, to see Johanna stood right behind her, flanked by Mary and Mariam. 'It's so good to see you. God's blessings upon you.'

She seemed to have forgotten their dispute back on her father's estates and hugged her enthusiastically. Mariam offered her a warm smile and Salome was pleased to see that, although the older woman was greyer and thinner than she had been last time she'd seen her at the foot of her poor son's cross, her eyes were shining and her hands, when she clasped Salome's, were firm.

'You are well, Mariam.'

'Very well. Working hard.'

'Working?'

'Building the church,' Mary replied for her. 'It is most exciting.' Salome felt herself tense instantly.

'You are still doing that?'

'Of course,' Mary shot back. 'Why would we not be?'

'I'm sure it is, erm, hard.'

'The authorities do not like it for sure. They arrest us regularly but—'

'Arrest you?'

'Of course. They are scared – scared because they know we are right. It only offers us encouragement.'

'Being in danger?'

'Yes. Do you think us so fickle that we would give up on our Lord Jesus Christ already?'

'Jesus *Christ*?'

'It is the Greek for Messiah,' Johanna supplied. 'More people speak Greek than Aramaic so we have adopted it for universality.'

Salome could only stare at her.

'Universality?'

'As word of the New Way spreads, it is important that we can share terms as well as ideas.' It was Mary again, her voice irritatingly prim to Salome's ears.

Johanna, perhaps sensing it, leapt in.

'It is the same with the new offices, Salome. We are growing so fast that we needed a system to help keep order, so Peter has appointed seven deacons to manage our affairs. They are very good.'

'Though all men,' Mary put in darkly.

'Women run most of the churches,' Johanna said, turning to her.

'With no titles.'

'But with every respect.'

'Bar the outward show of it.'

Salome looked from one to the other, intrigued.

'Women run churches?'

Mariam stepped between the two younger women, putting a hand on the back of each to calm them.

'They do and with great success. Many houses in Jerusalem and further abroad are now acknowledged meeting places, where the faithful of the New Way can come together, share ideas and find mutual support.'

She put quiet emphasis on the last two words and looked pointedly at her two companions, who hung their heads, though not for long.

'You should come along,' Johanna told Salome. 'We are meeting in Mariam's house tomorrow evening and you would be most welcome, would she not, Mariam?'

'You would indeed.'

'That's very kind, but my son is being blessed in the Temple tomorrow and Mother has a feast planned.'

'Ah well, if you have a feast planned . . .' Mary sneered.

Salome glared at her.

'In celebration of my son's consecration into the Jewish race.'

'Coming out of your womb brought your son into the Jewish race; you do not need some man in fancy robes to "consecrate" him.'

Salome stared. The words were so very close to her own thoughts just a little time ago that she stared at the sharp-faced young woman who'd uttered them.

'Do you really believe that?'

'Of course,' Mary said simply. 'It is what Jesus taught us.'

'Is it?'

'In part. The New Way is a way unencumbered by petty rules and regulations. Jesus taught us to break bread together and to think of it as his body. He taught us to share wine and remember his blood, given for us. Other than that, our only laws are to love each other as we love ourselves.'

'And if we do not love ourselves?'

Mary looked at her with her piercing black eyes.

'Then we must try again to cast our sins before God, turn from them, and be baptised in the New Way, free from the encumbrances of our past.'

Oh, it was such a beautiful idea. Salome's heart ached to believe this strange girl who seemed so confident in her ideas, but for herself baptism and sin were so closely entangled that it was hard to comprehend the possibility of such a guilt-free approach.

'Salome? There you are!' She turned guiltily to see Ari crossing the court towards her. 'I wondered where you'd gone.'

'Just talking with friends,' she said.

'Friends who would welcome you to their house,' Mary said with intent. 'Both of you.'

Ari looked at her, confused, and, taking his arm, Salome hurried him away.

'Was that Johanna?' he asked, glancing back.

'It was.'

'And the fierce girl?'

'She's called Mary. She's a little intense.'

'A little?! Why does she want you in her house?'

'Mariam's house. It's a church now apparently – an assembly room for . . . for followers of the New Way.'

'The New . . . ? This again. She's as mad as Jesus.'

'Jesus was *not* mad.'

He jumped at her tone and looked nervously around.

'It matters little, wife, he's dead. Come, your mother is waiting to go home and Aristo will surely be awake by now.'

'Of course,' she agreed, because it was easier, but as she was hustled out of the courtyard, she couldn't help glancing back to the strong trio of women in its centre and wondering if Jesus truly was dead after all.

❖

Salome looked across the altar and saw Herodias' face, lit up in the myriad candles and shining with something far more than mere flame. Her eyes were fixed on Aristo, held in Caiaphas' thin hands as he lifted him to God, and her own hands raised involuntarily as she was caught in the holy moment. Salome felt a rush of tenderness for her spiky, difficult, determined mother and smiled at the far-reaching effects of a simple blessing. Her baby boy meant a great deal to them all and was quietly healing wounds by the straightforward joy in his arrival.

Aristo was handed back to his father with no mishaps, the candles proving helpfully mesmerising for the boy, and Ari put an arm round Salome drawing her close as the priest began the prayers. They were in a private room in the Court of Wood, at one corner of the Court of Women and it felt rich in history and grace. Salome looked around at Herodias and Antipas, at Kypros and her children, at her own husband and son, and felt warm in the bosom of her family, and reassured by the graceful rituals of the Temple. Mary could be as derogatory as she liked about 'men in fancy robes' but it was more than that. It was a sense of mystery, of sacrament, of being bound into a community in a time-honoured way. She shook her head. There was no need to pin everything down all the time. She was just happy and that was enough.

The service drew to an end and, with a blessing from Caiaphas, they left the flickering, incense-rich darkness of the room to head, blinking, into the fierce sunshine pouring down on the Court of the Gentiles. Salome stood on the balcony, looking across the teaming crowds, trying to adjust not just her eyes, but her ears to the sudden mass of noise after the soft chanting within.

Something seemed to be going on at the bottom of the steps directly below them, to the right of all the market stalls, still merrily trading away as if Jesus' outburst had been nothing. Salome leaned on the balustrade and tried to make out what was going on. To one side, she could hear her mother loudly telling Aristo what a good boy he'd been and Antipas booming something about wine, but she tried to zone them out and hear the kerfuffle below.

Spotting Johanna and Chuza standing with Mariam and a handful of others to one side, her interest quickened, and, scanning back to the core argument, she saw Peter was preaching. He looked older than when she'd seen him last but more assured too.

'God is here,' he was crying, banging his fist against his chest. 'God is in your hearts and if you turn to him . . .'

The last of his words were lost in raucous heckling from a group in the ostentatiously pious robes of the Pharisees.

'Shut up!' shouted a man craning to hear Peter.

'We will not shut up,' the Pharisee nearest him said. 'We have years of learning, unlike this peasant fisherman and . . . Ow!'

The other man had swung a punch and the Pharisee staggered back, clutching dramatically at his jaw. His fellows stepped forward angrily and voices rose all around.

'Enough!'

A man stepped into the fray, arm raised for peace, and six others came swiftly in at his back. Salome wondered if these were the deacons of whom Johanna had spoken yesterday and watched curiously. The first man spoke calmly to the brawlers, urging reconciliation. Those who had been trying to hear Peter moved back apologetically but the Pharisees stood their ground.

'Stephen, leave it!' Mary said, tugging on his arm and looking worriedly around.

Salome saw men striding from the other sides of the court and recognised Andrew, James and John. They converged on the scene, ready to give the man called Stephen their back-up, but the Pharisees, cornered, began spitting fury and the situation threatened to get out of hand.

'Let's go back inside, Salome,' Ari said, trying to steer her away.

Behind her, she could sense the others retreating, but she was glued to the balustrade, unable to take her eyes off the scene below.

'Not again!' Caiaphas clicked his fingers for the Temple guards.

They came running out whilst, around the other sides of the balustrade, the Roman soldiers stood to attention. It suddenly felt all too like the last, dark Pesach to Salome.

'Don't fight,' she gasped out, but no one heard her over the shouting below.

'You are traitors to the Jews,' the leader of the Pharisees shouted at Stephen, who was still standing bravely before him. 'You claim to preach consideration and love but that's just a cover for subversion and violence.'

There were a few murmurs of agreement behind him.

'That's not true,' Stephen said, stepping forward. 'Peter, my brother-in-Christ was simply urging compassion.'

'Your "brother" is urging people not to pay their taxes.'

'No, he merely said ...'

'He's urging them to stay away from the Temple. The very Temple!'

He flung his hands up and all eyes seemed to turn to where Salome and her family were standing on the balustrade before the inner courts.

'The young prince!' someone called happily and for a moment

Salome thought that the presence of her baby might calm the mood, but the Pharisees did not want it calm.

'He's urging us to turn against those very royals you see now.'

'I don't think he is,' Salome tried to say but someone picked up a stone and flung it at Stephen, making him yelp in pain.

'Stephen!' Mary called, fighting to get to him, but Johanna and Chuza grabbed her just in time.

More stones were flying now, not from the Pharisees, always careful to get others to do their dirty work, but from ordinary people following their lead. Stephen put his hands up over his head as people scrambled to get away from him and the melee stopped Andrew, James or John from getting through. Stephen's fellow deacons tried to pull him away but more stones fell on them and they cowered back. Salome couldn't bear it. She had had to overcome the strongest revulsion to re-enter Jerusalem and just a few minutes ago she had been thanking God for the blessings of his holy rituals in the heart of the Temple, but out here all was violence once more.

'Stop it!' she shrieked, enraged. 'Stop it all of you!'

A few heads turned. A few people nudged each other.

'Salome,' Ari hissed, 'this is not your place.'

He tugged on her arm but she saw sharp-eyed Mary looking curiously up at her and did not want to step away.

'Violence is not the answer. Neither side condones it so why are you both being sucked in? Put down your stones before God sees you defiling his holy building like pagans.'

The last word rang around the Court of the Gentiles like a bell and more people looked up at her. Salome felt the burn of their eyes but could not stop now. She glanced around for Aristo, hoping the sight of the prince would calm things, but Ari had his son clutched to his chest.

'Salome, stop this.'

'No,' she said, shaking her head violently.

'I order you to come inside.'

'No!'

He was backing away from her, his eyes dark, but no matter. She did not need a man to bolster her and she turned back to the crowd.

'I am Hasmonean. My ancestors reclaimed Jerusalem and the Holy Land for the Jews, and they did not do it so they could tear each other apart, not with words and certainly not with stones. This man, Peter, has a right to preach. You do not need to agree with him, you do not even need to listen to him, but it is not your place to stop him, or any of his friends.'

To her astonishment, the fighting had virtually stopped and all faces were turned her way. She shifted her hands on the balustrade and saw the imprints of her fear marked out in sweat upon the stone. In the pause, she spotted Andrew darting to the crumpled body of Stephen on the ground and prayed they were in time to save him. She had to keep talking.

'Two years ago, I saw terrible violence in this city. I saw a man lose his life in the most agonising of ways because of a lack of tolerance and a fear of new ideas. We cannot let that happen again.'

There was a brief silence then, to Salome's horror, Mary called, 'He wasn't just a man. He was God's own—'

But at that a new roar went up and the violence erupted once more. Salome put her head in her hands and groaned. Andrew had, at least, lifted Stephen into his strong arms to carry him away, but from the horribly limpness of his limbs, Salome feared it was too late for the brave deacon. She turned bitterly to follow her family inside and that's when she saw Ari, their son on one hip and his other hand stretched out, palm up, to ward her off.

'Ari?' she asked, confused.

'How dare you!'

'What?'

'How dare you stand and speak as if you represent us all.'

'I didn't, I—'

'How dare you ignore me when I asked you to come to safety?'

'Ari, please—'

'How dare you put us all at risk? One false word and those

stones could just as easily have been flying in our direction and then what?'

'Then I suppose one of us might have died instead of Stephen. Would that be a greater tragedy?'

'It would for us.'

'But would it for the world?'

'Salome!' He shook his head. 'I have put up with enough from you. It's one thing being independent, it's one thing being my equal, but when you set yourself above me, when you ignore me and put me in danger and, more to the point, put our son in danger, then I have to consider my position.'

'Consider your . . . ?'

'I'm leaving, Salome. I'm going home.'

'Home? To my estates?'

He winced and she cursed her stupidity.

'If you do not *permit* that, I will go to friends. They, at least, will welcome me.'

'Ari, please. I don't want you to go.'

'No? I didn't want you to speak, but you went ahead anyway. Hurts, doesn't it?'

And with that, he hitched Aristo higher into his arms and strode through the Gate of Nicanor into the Court of the Israelites where, as a woman, she could not go.

'Ari!' she wailed after her husband and son but neither re-emerged.

She fell to her knees, the hot, noisy storm of the Temple whirling around her, and the last thing she felt as it sucked her down into darkest misery, was Johanna's hands on her shoulders.

'Don't worry,' she said. 'We've got you. We'll look after you.'

'Ari,' Salome moaned again, but they were gone and the hands of women were, it seemed, all she had left.

Chapter Thirty

Herodias

'Where is she?' Herodias stormed into the little house and glared around the handful of people assembled in the front room. 'Where's my daughter?'

A woman stood up, old, with terrible grey hair, pulled into a loose bun, and clothes that had, frankly, seen better days, though with a certain quiet poise that Herodias had to admire.

'Who is your daughter, please?'

Herodias nearly choked.

'Are you being deliberately obtuse?' The woman just looked steadily at her. 'I'm Herodias, first lady of Galilee and Perea and my daughter is the Princess Salome.'

'Of course. Salome is here, yes. She's resting after her ordeal.'

'Why here?'

'I suppose because we were the only ones there to pick her up.'

Herodias narrowed her eyes at the other woman. She was definitely being deliberately obtuse.

'I was there, just inside the Court of Wood. All you needed to do was call.'

'The situation was ... volatile.'

'It certainly was. Your people stirred the crowd up.'

'Our "people" were simply preaching God's own truth. It was the Pharisees who did the stirring and the Pharisees who killed Stephen.'

'He died?' Herodias was taken aback. 'I'm sorry.' The woman blinked as if surprised. Honestly, did she think Herodias was a monster? 'Who are you?'

The woman crossed her hands over her chest.

'I'm Mariam, mother of Jesus of Nazareth.'

'Aah.'

Now it all made sense.

'And you killed my son.'

Ouch. That she hadn't been expecting. This woman wasn't nearly as mild as she appeared.

'I most certainly did not. And neither did my husband. Antipas sent him back to Pilate cleared of all charges under Jewish and Galilean law. It was the Roman who condemned him.'

'Hmm. I was there, you know.'

'And so was I.'

Mariam looked her up and down.

'Have you lost a son, my lady?'

'Three,' Herodias shot back. That surprised this Mariam and she glanced around, confused. 'Now, please can I see my daughter, my only living child?'

Mariam sighed.

'This way.'

She led Herodias up tight wooden steps to a little room on the top floor. There was barely room for the small bed but lying in it was Salome, with Johanna standing at her side and another dark-eyed young woman sitting cross-legged at her feet, vulture-like. Herodias shivered.

'Johanna.'

Johanna dropped into a curtsey.

'Lady Herodias. What … ? That is … you must be here to see Salome?'

'I am here,' Herodias corrected her, 'to *fetch* Salome.'

'She is asleep.'

'Then I shall wake her.'

'She is very tired.'

'And will rest better in her own bed, in her own house.'

'Palace,' the other girl said.

Herodias looked down at her.

'Palace, yes. Is that a problem?'

'No.'

'Good. Now, if you don't mind.'

She pushed past Johanna, who flattened herself against the rough wall, and bent over Salome. She looked very pale and for a terrible moment Herodias was reminded of the time she'd been hit with a stone in Tiberias back when she was still young. Johanna had been with her then too.

'Salome always seems to get into trouble with you, Johanna.'

Johanna glared at her.

'I think you will find that Salome always seems to get into trouble when she's trying to escape you.'

'How dare you?'

'I dare because you are in my home and your daughter is in my bed, where Mary and I brought her when her family abandoned her to the mob.'

'We did not! We were simply—'

'Inside saving your own skin. At least Salome had the courage to stand up and speak out. You should be proud of her.'

'I *am* proud of her. Why else do you think I would be here, in this funny little house. Salome.' She shook her gently. 'Salome, I am here.'

'Johanna?' Salome murmured, only half awake. Herodias refused to look at either Johanna or the other girl – Mary – but she could feel them smirking all the same.

'It is I, Mother.'

'Mother?' Salome's eyes flew open and she looked round in confusion. 'What are you doing here?'

Herodias tutted. These women were making her poor daughter stupid just by being near her.

'What do you think I'm doing here? I've come to rescue you.'

'Rescue!' Mary squeaked indignantly.

Herodias ignored her.

'We were separated for moments and these women carried you off.'

'Out of care, Mother.'

'Hmmm.' Herodias had her own ideas about the motivations of these clawing women with their 'New Way' and their bloodsucking need for converts, but now was not the time for them. 'They have been very kind and I will see them rewarded.'

'We don't want your money,' Mary said.

'Well . . .' Johanna started.

'We ask only that you beg forgiveness for your sins and turn to God.'

'Mary!'

Herodias favoured the silly girl with her most benign smile.

'Then all is well, for I was brought up in the Jewish faith and have been turned to God all my life.'

'Not in the New Way.'

'No,' she agreed, 'not in the New Way but in the old one, handed down to Moses and the Prophets and not made up by a carpenter and his glory-seeking followers. Now, let me take my sins with my daughter and get out of your hair. Salome.'

For a moment she thought Salome was going to refuse to come but then her daughter clambered from the bed and, with embarrassingly effusive thanks to the two young women, went ahead of her down the stairs. At the bottom, Mariam flung her arms around her and Herodias stood, stiff with horror, as her daughter hugged the scraggy woman with what seemed to be genuine affection.

'Thank you,' Herodias said to her, when the show was over. 'The young woman upstairs said you did not want my money but she seems the sort of naïve zealot who believes the world will keep her, so I shall ignore her. You can expect my man later today with a gift for your . . . your . . .'

'Our church. Thank you.'

Herodias inclined her head and stepped gratefully out of the stuffy little house. She bundled Salome into the waiting carriage and climbed into it after her, nodding to the driver. Once they were safely away from the funny place, she turned to daughter.

'What the hell is a church?'

'That is.'

'That? That little hovel?'

'Mother! It's not a hovel. It's an honest, normal home.'

'And a "church"?'

'Yes. People can meet there to share ideas.'

Honestly, Herodias thought, no wonder there was trouble all the time these days if the ordinary folk were meeting to 'share ideas' but that wasn't the point at the moment.

'How lovely for them,' she said crisply. 'Now, how are you, Salome? Were you hurt? Shall I summon the doctors?'

'No! I'm fine. It was just all a little ... overwhelming.'

'Well, of course it was. Standing up like that and speaking to the masses.'

'You think I was foolish?'

Herodias stared at her daughter.

'Of course not,' she said. 'I think you were magnificent.'

Salome gaped at her.

'You do? But Ari said—'

'I've heard what Ari said and frankly, daughter, *he* is the fool. I told him he would come to value a strong woman at his side, but did he listen? It would seem not.'

'When did you tell him that?'

'Oh, when you were in labour and shouting the place down, as you had the perfect right to do. I'd like to see him trying to give birth. Does it matter?'

Salome seemed to be gulping for breath and Herodias couldn't tell if she was going to laugh or cry.

'I thought you'd be furious with me.'

'For what? For standing up and trying to stop a riot? That's what a good leader does and you, my dear girl, have all the makings of a very good leader. If your husband can't see that, he's an idiot.'

'An idiot who has my son.'

'Oh, we'll get Aristo back. We'll get them both back, don't you worry about that. It's just a show of temper, that's all. Men, in my experience, are happy not to be in charge of you, as long as others think that they are. It is a subtle distinction and a most annoying one, but until the world catches up with what half of its people have to offer, it is one we are stuck with.' She looked at her curiously. 'Did you really think I would be cross?'

'Of course. That's why I went with Johanna.'

'Then, why did you come with me just now?'

'I have no idea, Mother. You're just very hard to say no to.'

Herodias felt a laugh build inside her. She fought to hold it back, not wanting to offend, but it burst out anyway. Salome looked at her, then she smiled and suddenly she was laughing too, leaning forward to clutch at Herodias as they both gave in to a mirth she suspected neither of them quite understood.

'Was it all women in that house?' Herodias asked Salome when they'd both finally calmed down.

'It is Mariam's house but she keeps her doors open to all – mainly women who need shelter.'

'Does that Mary stay there?'

'When she's not out preaching.'

'She preaches?'

'So I'm told. She's fearless.'

'She's bold, for sure.'

'And a little scary?'

Herodias grinned.

'There's nothing wrong with that. If a woman is to make her way in the world alone, she must be a little scary. Ask Kypros.'

Salome grimaced.

'Will she divorce Agrippa, do you think?'

321

'If she has any sense.' Herodias swallowed. There were things to be said here and she could not shirk them any longer. 'I am sorry, Salome, if my divorce caused you pain. That was not my intention.'

'I know.'

'I was … frustrated. Not in, you know, that way – though …' She stopped herself. Some things did not need to be said. 'I simply mean that I am a woman made for public office. I was born to it and brought up to it and living in your father's estates in the back of beyond drove me near mad with boredom.'

Salome gave her a rueful smile.

'They are a little remote.'

Herodias laughed.

'You can say that again. You and Boethus always seemed so content there but for me the inactivity was like a million ants on my skin. I hated it. Would I had been a man to stand up and take command as I saw fit, but I am not and the only way out that I could see was to marry Antipas.'

'You seem happy with him.'

She swallowed.

'I am.'

'You love him?'

Herodias flushed.

'Why must people always ask that? Why the preoccupation with love?'

'Love is for those who don't have land?' Salome suggested.

Herodias looked at her, surprised.

'You think so?'

'No! *You* think so. Or, at least, that's what you told me.'

'Did I? Well, it's a good point. Very astute.'

Salome shook her head.

'I do not think the two are mutually exclusive, Mother.'

'No? That's what your stepfather says too.'

'Is it? He loves you then?'

'So he says, poor fool. But that is not the point, Salome. We are not here to talk of men, for the world does enough of that.'

Salome leaned forward and put a hand on her knee.

'You are, you know, Mother, allowed to love.'

Herodias jumped.

'I know that. Of course I know that.'

'But do you believe it?'

Herodias tried to shift away but her daughter's grip was firm.

'Is this what that Jesus man did to you? The world is a harsh place, you know, Salome, and going on about love doesn't help anyone.'

'I agree.'

'You do?'

'Of course. Going on about love is useless, simply loving, however, that can make the world ten times less harsh.'

Herodias stared at her daughter, feeling a ridiculous lump forming in her throat.

'How did you get so wise?' she choked out.

Salome smiled.

'I had a good teacher.'

The lump grew.

'You had a harsh teacher.'

'Perhaps, but that is you. I will be less harsh a parent, because that is me, but I doubt I will be any more . . .' She broke off suddenly and bit at her lip. 'If, that is, I still get the chance to be a parent.'

'Tsk, Salome, of course you will. He is just making a petty show of power.'

'And if he is not? If he goes? Aristo is his, you know, under Jewish law. I have no rights to him.'

'We will find rights if it comes to it, but it will not.'

Salome looked out of the window. Their carriage was pulling back into the palace yard and any moment now the others would be upon them. Her grip on Herodias' knee tightened.

'What if this is a punishment, Mother? What if God is displeased with me.'

'For what? For speaking out in the Temple?'

'No! For ... for ...' She looked to the carriage roof but then seemed to gather herself and looked back at Herodias, her eyes tear-bright in the gloom within. 'For killing John the Baptiser.'

Herodias stared at her, astonished.

'You think of that still?'

'Yes! Often. It was a terrible sin, Mother.'

'It was a dark necessity, daughter.' Salome looked tortured and Herodias couldn't bear it. 'If it was a sin, the sin was all mine. You were young, barely sixteen. I was the one who ordered him brought into the hall, I was the one who asked for his head.'

'And yet, I was the one who gave the final word.'

'Oh Salome ...' For almost the first time in her life, Herodias felt helpless. 'What can I do?'

Salome gulped.

'I would like, if you could see your way to allowing it, to retrieve John's head and restore it to his body. It is a small recompense but I feel I owe him that last respect.'

Herodias could hardly believe it.

'That would heal you?'

'It would help me to heal.'

She thought of the skull, which must surely have been long since picked clean of all flesh by the many worms in the dung heap. That was all it would take?

'Well then, of course you may.'

'Truly? Oh, thank you. Thank you so much.'

And with that her daughter threw herself into her arms and Herodias held her awkwardly, feeling the pulse of the girl's young heart against her jaded one, and stroked her hair as she wept quietly against her. It was a request Herodias could not really fathom but, then, Salome was a woman she could not really fathom either and she was just glad that she had the capacity to make her happy. Sometimes, it seemed, being a mother wasn't nearly as hard as you might think.

Chapter Thirty-one

Salome

MACHAERUS
NISAN (APRIL), 33 AD

Salome reined in and looked up at the great crag of Machaerus, dread freezing her entire body so that the horse beneath her shifted in alarm. If she'd felt horror at returning to Jerusalem for Pesach, it hadn't been a patch on the fear that was flooding through her now.

'It's a bit scary, isn't it?'

Salome thought she'd never heard more of an understatement but the words released the worst of the ice from her veins and she turned gratefully to Johanna, coming up on her own mount.

'It's a lot scary.'

'And we have to go all the way to the top?'

'We do. I'm sorry. It was mean of me to ask you to come.'

Johanna looked at her with genuine incredulity.

'It was lovely of you to ask me to come. I'm honoured. And, really, it's just a little cliff. I bet the view from the top is marvellous.'

Salome smiled at her friend. She'd never known anyone better disposed to find the positives in life and she leaned over in her saddle to give her a hug.

'What's that for?'

'For being you, for being here. It means a lot to me.'

'It means a lot to everyone, Salome. The others will be waiting for us on the Mount of Olives so come on, let's get this over and done with, shall we?'

Salome nodded, grateful for Johanna's matter-of-fact approach. She'd been amazing when Salome had crept back to the house to talk to her about this little mission. She had been in no doubt about how high-handed Herodias was likely to have been with them and had thought perhaps her friends would have been offended that she'd chosen to leave with her, but they'd been their usual welcoming selves. Even Mary had embraced her and when she'd admitted what she wanted to do, she'd looked at her long and hard and said, 'That's brave.'

Salome had appreciated her admiration, though it had also made her more nervous. Now, as she gave the signal to the guards to start the climb up the forbidding cliff, it was only her horse following his fellows that actually propelled her forward. Already the dread night of the death-feast was coming back to her, so vivid and visceral that she could well believe it was still going on in the dark fortress above, waiting to pull her back into the noise and the heat and the dark red blood.

She shook the images away and her poor horse tossed his head, forcing her to concentrate on the narrow path.

If I died, she thought, glancing down the rocky face to her right, *would Ari be sorry?*

She tutted at herself. Of course he would. More than that, he would feel guilty and guilt was such a terrible emotion that she would not wish it on her worst enemy, still less on the man she loved. Even so, it was easier to focus on her own demise than John's and she let her thoughts wander to her husband and child.

It had been two days since he'd stormed away from her in the Temple and she'd heard nothing from him. In two more days, it would be the Pesach Sabbath and, somehow, she had to find him before then and make amends. Her poor breasts, still feeding Aristo morning and night, were leaking in protest at the separation and her arms ached to hold him. To hold them both. First, though, this grim task had to be done.

Jesus had told her in Caesarea Philippi that if she turned to God, confessed her sins and repented, He would forgive her, but what was the use in confessing your sins if you did not work to put them right? What was the point in repenting if you did not repair the damage you had wrought? John was dead but his poor severed head could be restored to his body so that his soul might rest in peace. And perhaps, then, Salome might too.

'Johanna.' She glanced back to her friend, close behind her on the rugged path. 'What is a soul?'

Johanna gave a little laugh.

'Do not mistake me for someone with wisdom, Salome. You should go to Peter or Andrew or Mary with such profound questions.'

'I think you are wiser than you know. Tell me, at least, your understanding of it.'

'Very well, I will try. As I see it, the soul is the essence of a person, their spirit. It is entirely separate from their body and whilst the body can grow old and infirm, the soul will always be young.'

'That's good to know.'

'Isn't it? I try and remind myself of it when I catch sight of myself in the mirror and see my face sagging. I mean, it's not like having a shiny soul is going to help much there, or with the horrible stretch marks on my poor belly, but Chuza says that he loves me even more for the lines of our shared life across my body. I think he might be talking nonsense but he still seems to, you know, fancy me so . . .' She caught herself. 'Sorry. Not the point here.' Salome supressed a smile as her friend gathered herself. 'Your soul is, perhaps, what shines from your eyes and if you do your best to live a good, loving life, then your soul will be saved.'

'Saved?'

'In the afterlife.'

Another word Salome did not really understand.

'What can be after life?'

Johanna gave an awkward laugh.

327

'It's a funny idea, isn't it? I was always told that the dead would lie dormant until the day of judgement, but Jesus taught that when you die, your soul is taken up to heaven – if it's a good soul – and dwells with God and all the angels until the final days. And now, of course, with Jesus, too, for he has been taken up and sits at God's right hand on high.'

'In heaven?'

'In heaven.'

Salome looked to the skies, blue criss-crossed with wisps of cloud. They were nearly at the top of the crag and the skies felt closer than usual. But then they turned the corner and she caught the dark outline of the fortress hard against the colour and sucked in a breath.

'So do you think, Johanna, that John is in heaven?'

'Of course,' she said instantly. 'God will have taken him up and he will be with Jesus.'

'Even without . . .'

'His head? Oh, yes. I told you—'

'The soul is entirely separate from the body. You did.' They rode into the bleak courtyard and Johanna looked warily around. 'So why then, am I doing this?'

'I think,' Johanna said, swinging herself out of her saddle and looking up at Salome, 'that this is less for John's soul and more for your own.'

Salome jumped down too and flung her arms around her friend.

'As I said, Johanna, you are wiser than you know.'

The conversation had kept her sane on the climb but as she looked around the tight courtyard, she felt iron clench around her heart. John might be in heaven, but she was in Machaerus and her flesh was crawling with the memories of the last time she'd been here. Johanna took her arm.

'Where should we look, sweet one?'

Salome blinked. John's head, she knew, was in the dung heap, for Herodias had told her that clearly, along with a few choice words about it being where it belonged. Imagining the skull with the onion skins, fish bones and egg shells had tortured her ever since but it had not occurred to her until now to ask where it actually was. Thankfully the steward was coming striding out of the fortress to greet them and, although it felt like sand in the wound to have to admit to the officious little man what she was here for, it was only what she deserved.

'The dung heap, Princess?'

'Yes, please.'

He glanced to the guard who gave an awkward shrug.

'Of course, of course. But perhaps, first, some refreshment? If you'd like to come through to the hall ...'

'No!' He sprung back, clearly offended. He was new, only appointed a few months ago, and would have no knowledge of the events that had driven Salome here. 'Sorry,' she said hastily. 'I do not mean to be rude, it is simply that we are, er, in a bit of a hurry. We need to get back down again before sunset, so thank you, but if you could possibly show us the way?'

'To the dung heap?'

'Exactly.'

'Very well.'

There was a small pause as he summoned a boy from the kitchens. Clearly the dung heap was not on his usual rounds either but the boy happily led his illustrious guests round the side of the kitchens, through a remarkably pleasant herb and vegetable garden at the rear, and up to where, against the big retaining wall at the edge of the clifftop, wooden planks held in a mass of kitchen mess. Salome looked at it in dismay. Was she going to have to climb in there and dig down into the depths of the filth to find what she sought?

It's only what you deserve, she thought, and hated herself for quailing. Had she not watched Jesus' bones crack on the cross? Had she not seen nails driven through his flesh, and his very lungs collapse in on themselves with the weight of his own broken body? What was a little muck in comparison?

She looked to the boy who met her eyes with open curiosity.

'What do you seek, Princess?'

She swallowed.

'The skull of a man.'

'Like that one?' He pointed and, swivelling around, Salome saw a bleached white skull sitting on a jutting corner stone just above them. 'We call him bright eyes because, well, it's a joke. A poor one perhaps.' He scuffed his feet on the dirt path. 'But, anyway, someone dug him out of there when we were composting the veg beds last year and he's been keeping lookout for us ever since. That is ... I'm sorry. Was he someone you cared about?'

It was a good question.

'Someone,' she said carefully, 'who mattered.'

'Right. Well, there he is. I'm sure we can release him from duties now. He's not a very good lookout anyway. That is ...' He looked desperately to the steward. 'Can I go now, sir?'

'I think that might be best,' his boss agreed and waved him away.

'Thank you,' Salome called after him, but he had scuttled into the depths of the kitchens.

He would doubtless curse his runaway mouth to his fellows, but Salome blessed him for it. Seeing John's head sat on the shelf, treated with love, however rough, had taken some of the base horror out of the trip and now she steeled herself to reach up to it. The skull was smooth and dry, just an empty shell, hard to equate with the man who had spat righteous fury at her in the dungeons of this remote fortress. Salome ran a hand over it.

'I'm sorry,' she whispered.

There was no reply, of course there was not. No walls cracked, no clouds descended, but the world shifted slightly all the same, at least for Salome, and she turned to Johanna with tears in her eyes.

'Here, sweet one.'

Johanna was holding out the ivory casket that Salome had brought from the palace. She had not asked permission to use this Hasmonean relic and was praying that Herodias would not notice its absence, but she had felt strongly that John deserved a worthy vessel for his last journey. She placed the skull gently inside and then looked out over the dung heap, over the wall and across the Jordan valley to Jerusalem. Somewhere on the Mount of Olives, above the east walls of the city, Mariam and the disciples would be gathering at the spot where Andrew had buried John's body and now she could deliver his head. The journey back down the hill would, she was sure, be an easier one than the journey up.

❖

The spot was at the top of the Mount of Olives, marked only by a simple stone, carved with the single word: John. You could walk past it a hundred times and never even notice it was there but, as the sun began to drop on the far side of the Holy City, Andrew led their little group to it with unerring accuracy.

'This is a walk you have done many times?' Salome asked him, contrite.

'I like to visit,' he agreed. 'John was a difficult man but a brave one.'

'I'm sorry, Andrew.'

'I know you are.' He smiled at her. 'You have done the right thing but, trust me, it was all part of God's plan.'

Salome wasn't sure if that was a comfort.

'You think I had no choice?'

He tipped his head on one side, considering.

'No, I don't think that. You had a choice but if you had made a different one, John would have died some other way.'

'My mother would have ordered it.'

'I imagine she would, and not have tortured herself about it as you have. But look, Salome, your care has brought you to us, so it has all turned out for the best, has it not?'

Salome looked back at the little band following them up the hill. She looked at Peter and Perpetua, arm in arm and deep in discussion. She looked at Mariam, ageing but determined, helped along by her daughter Elisabeth. She looked at James and John and the other disciples behind, plus the women who would preach with them when they went out into the world after Pesach. She looked at Johanna and Chuza, who had given up a luxurious life in the palace to live in relative squalor with this group and she marvelled.

He is risen, Johanna had said to her husband back in Tiberias, her words run through with deep urgency. *We have seen it. We have seen the joy it brings, the changes it can make to the world. It is so important.*

Were they right? Salome wasn't sure yet, but she did know one thing – they were good and kind and they saw the world the way she wanted it to be and for now that was enough.

James dug the hole and Peter took John's skull from the casket and offered it to Salome. She shook her head vehemently and looked to Andrew, who stepped forward, took it gently in his big hands and placed it in the earth.

'God bless you, John,' he said in his deep voice. 'May you rest with Him and our Lord Jesus Christ until the final days.' He stepped back as James filled in the hole, then held out his hands. 'Shall we pray together in the words that Jesus taught us?'

There was a murmur of assent and then their voices rose, as one:

'Our Father who art in heaven . . .'

It was the prayer that Mary had led them in at the foot of the cross and Salome felt the power of the simple words ripple out across the dusk. Below, the common people were hastening to finish cooking their meals before the last of the light leached away and, across the valley, the lines of Jerusalem were stark against the blood-red sky. Nearby, someone started up a tune on a flute. It was sweet and lilting and the notes crept between the final words of the prayer, lighting them up:

'For thine is the kingdom, the power and the glory, for ever and ever. Amen.'

'Amen,' Salome whispered: Truth.

She felt the notes tug at her limbs and creep through her heart. Her body felt lighter now and she yearned to give in to them but she had sworn an oath. She looked to the stone, white against the darkening earth, and dug her feet into it but suddenly Johanna caught her hand.

'Release it, Salome. That is what God wants of you now. Release it and live in joy.'

Joy. The word rippled through her, sweeter and brighter than any flute.

Don't turn from joy, sweet one. It was her mother's voice, incongruous here, perhaps, but strong in her head all the same and so, picking up her feet, earth-bound for far too long, Salome let the notes carry her and danced.

There was no shape to it, no arc, no well-crafted story or sense of meaning to the movements or none, at least, that any observer might see. But for Salome, the music moved her limbs in its own way, delving into her and finding new pathways in the twists and tangles of her thoughts and feelings, in the confusions and delights and sorrows that had shaped her life so far. The meaning was not in the dance, but came from the dance.

Words had ever tangled within her and these last years, with no means of getting out, those tangles had become big, gnarled knots, sitting in her stomach, tightening around her heart and clogging every thought she'd tried to form. Now, she gave herself up to the movement of her limbs, feeling the ropes loosen with every step and abandoned leap.

Others were dancing too and the flute, encouraged, picked up its tune. From somewhere in the camp a lyre joined in and then a tambour and, as the sun dropped behind the Holy City and its dark walls were absorbed into the softness of the night sky, it seemed that all life in Jerusalem was up here, amongst the ordinary folk. The light was from their campfires, the music from their hand-carved instruments and the joy from their simple pleasure in being together. It infused through Salome and she abandoned herself to something greater than her own concerns. Was this the soul? If so, it was – for now at least – at one with the rest of her and she let it lead her where it would.

Finally, spent, she dropped to the grass, panting but content. Slowly the shapes around her, that had been but wisps in the air as she'd danced, solidified once more and she saw a figure standing nearby, another in its arms.

'Salome?'

'Ari?'

She hardly dared believe it.

'May I come close?'

'Of course. Please.'

She patted the earth beside her and he came over and sank down, resting their son in his lap. Aristo was asleep and as the light of a nearby fire flickered across his peaceful young face, Salome felt a fierce, desperate love flood through her.

'Have you come back, Ari?'

'Will you have me?'

She opened her mouth for another eager 'of course' but then stopped, forced herself to think carefully.

'I cannot, I fear, be the woman that you would like me to be, husband.'

He nodded.

'That is true, Salome.' Her heart twisted. 'But what is also true, is that you are the woman I want, the woman I need. I have thought about this a lot over the last two days and it seems to me that I am wrong about the sort of woman I would like. My heart is, perhaps, wiser than my mind.'

'Ari . . .'

'Hush. Listen, please. I am not good at apologising so I must get it out before my stupid, stubborn pride stops me again. You were magnificent at the Temple. You spoke with no thought of safety, no concern for what people thought of you, just a sense of justice – of right. You were like your mother.'

'My mother?!'

'But with more compassion.'

'I see.' Salome shifted uncomfortably on the hard ground. Her body was cooling from the dancing and she was clammy and cold as the heat went swiftly from the day. 'Do I want to be like my mother?'

'Do I want to love a woman who makes me look like a weak, feeble idiot?'

'Ari!' He smiled ruefully at her and she shook her head. 'Don't shirk reality.'

'Sorry?'

'It's what my mother has always said.'

'Then she is right.'

'You are not an idiot, Ari.'

'And you are not your mother.'

'Good.'

She looked at him, cradling their son, his eyes filled with love but still wary. It had been a brave confession and, God help her, but she loved him. She leaned forward. 'May I come close?'

He grinned.

'As close as it is possible to be.'

Then he took her in her arms and kissed her, long and deep. Aristo woke and, with a happy giggle, squirmed his way between them and Salome knew that this – this little family embracing her and this wider circle of care beyond – was happiness indeed.

Chapter Thirty-two

Herodias

'King?!' Herodias paced the gardens of the palace at Tiberias, blind to the beauty of the midsummer blooms all around her. 'How on earth can Agrippa be king? And of Judea? Judea!'

Now she understood what people meant when they talked about their heart breaking. Her very self seemed to be cracking apart at the terrible news that had just arrived from Rome. She felt as if all she'd trusted in had been taken from underneath her and the future was as bleak as the cliff face at Machaerus.

'Who even is this Caligula?' she demanded. 'What sort of a name is that for an emperor?'

'A Roman sort,' Antipas said darkly. 'It means little boots.'

'Little boots?! These people are ruling most of the known world and they have a leader called little boots. It's insane!'

'The troops called him that when he was a boy because he was so obsessed with being a soldier that his grandmother had a mini-uniform made for him. She's been grooming him for the imperial throne ever since and just last year the only other heir, Tiberius-the-Younger, died.'

'Died?' Antipas just raised a cynical eyebrow. 'This Caligula is a ruthless young man, then – and now Agrippa has got his claws into him. I told you we'd be better keeping him close.'

'He'd already stormed out by then.'

'He had. He bloody had. But he was destitute; how did he climb so high?'

Herodias looked to Kypros, hovering unhappily nearby. She gave a helpless shrug.

'That man can charm the birds out of the trees. And he has a good eye for which birds to charm. I hear tell he got in with Caligula from the moment he arrived in Rome. He gave almost the whole loan I secured for him to the greedy little thing as a "gift" and has been deep in his inner circle ever since.'

'Money well spent,' Herodias griped.

She had to admire her brother's audacity but this was awful. She'd been through hell – or at least put poor Salome through hell – to stop that damned carpenter being called the King of the Jews, only to have Agrippa snatch the title from under her very nose. This was mortifying.

'He's been given Trachonitis too,' she moaned. 'He'll surround us in Galilee. It will be unbearable once he rides in here, rubbing our noses in it with his big crown.'

'There is no crown of Judea, Herodias.'

'Oh, there will be. Trust me, if Agrippa is involved there will be an enormous crown.'

'He's had designs for it ready for years,' Kypros agreed gloomily.

'I don't know what *you're* worrying about,' Herodias snapped. 'You'll be queen.'

'Only if I go back to him.'

'Which you will.'

'Herodias,' Antipas said, looking at her in a most unflattering way.

'Well she will, won't you?' Kypros bit her lip. 'Of course you will because what choice do you have? There are your children to consider, your own future. Why would you live as the steward of a poxy little tetrarch of Galilee when you can be Queen of Judea?'

'I'd feel bad.'

'You'd feel worse if you did not. And I'd blame you more.

This is the lot of a woman, pulled by the whims and machinations of men.'

'I wish,' Antipas muttered and Herodias rounded on him.

'Why did you not creep up to this "little boots", idiot?'

'Or you, wife.'

She conceded that with a grunt.

'You're the one with Roman friends,' she said, but it was half-hearted at best. They had neither of them liked Rome and both been glad to get home to the Holy Land, which was what made it so unfair.

'We're the ones who know this sacred place,' she said to her husband. 'We're the ones who care about it. All Agrippa cares about is an easy life. He will be a terrible ruler. He will bleed Judea dry. Lord help us, he's barely even Jewish and understands nothing of the mysteries of the Temple. For him, the festivals are simply an excuse to drink even more wine than usual. Oh, I can't bear it, husband. We have to do something.'

'There's only one thing we can do,' Antipas said, 'and you're not going to like it.'

She stared at him.

'Go to Rome?'

He nodded grimly. Herodias' heart fell but, given that it was breaking here, there was little else to do but agree.

◈

ROME

'So let me get this straight.' The young emperor peered down at them from an overblown throne. He was in his mid-twenties and unsettlingly good looking. Herodias had been expecting a spoiled brat of a child, but this was a man in full command. 'You are here to protest at the return of the province of Judea to the Herodian line?'

He was also annoyingly sharp. This was one way of putting it, but not the one Herodias wanted. Even worse, Caligula now glanced to Agrippa, hovering at his shoulder like a sycophantic whore, and she had the sinking feeling that they were laughing at her. Surely her brother should be on his way to Judea by now, like a good ruler, and not still hanging around in Rome? She glanced around the grand hall, wondering if there was a way to back out of this audience, but she'd been forthright in demanding it since their arrival in Rome a week ago, and had to push on.

'Of course not, Emperor,' she said. 'We are here, merely, to offer ourselves in your service in the Holy Land, which we know well and love dearly.'

'I see. Are you not already, my lady, offering me that service? You rule Galilee and Perea, I believe.'

'We do, as a tetrarchy.'

'I see.'

'Not a kingdom.'

'Ah! You want a crown.'

'We want a title that correctly conveys the grandeur of the area. Galilee in particular is old and rich in history.'

'Not to mention rebels.'

'I beg your pardon?'

'Is that not where he came from, the carpenter? The one that created all the fuss last year? I heard some very strange reports about this self-proclaimed King of the Jews.' Herodias winced and Caligula leaned forward, seeming to hover over her like a falcon. 'You did not like that?'

'Of course not, Emperor.'

'You must be delighted, then, to have a true King of the Jews back and one, besides, of your own family line.'

'Agrippa—'

'*King* Agrippa.'

Again, the handsome emperor looked over at her damned brother. She gritted her teeth.

'King Agrippa is a fine man, but his talents are perhaps wasted on a land so far from Rome.'

Caligula thought about that and for a moment Herodias thought she'd scored a hit. She glanced to Antipas, who'd been worryingly quiet so far. He stepped closer and his hand closed around her own. She gripped at it tightly.

'I am new to running an empire, my lady,' Caligula said eventually, 'but it seems to me that it is the lands furthest from Rome that will need my best men if I am to keep them in order.'

She had no answer for that. Antipas held her hand tighter.

'In that case, Emperor,' he said, 'we hope you will do us the honour of letting us escort our kinsman home to take up his throne.'

Herodias swallowed down so hard on the squeak of protest that sprang unbidden out of her throat that for a moment she could barely breathe.

'Hmm,' Caligula said. 'What do you think, King Agrippa?'

Agrippa moved forward, so close to his pet emperor that he was virtually sitting on his knee and Herodias felt more than ever like prey, exposed and vulnerable before these two hunters. Why had they come? She'd hated Rome last time and she hated it even more now.

'It seems a kind offer but I have to admit, Emperor, that, as King of the Jews, I have my own concerns about these two.'

'Concerns?' Herodias snapped.

'Grave concerns. I am not sure you work in Rome's best interests.'

'That's not true. You cannot prove that.'

'No?' Agrippa gave her a nasty smile. 'So, you did not then, demand that Pontius Pilate, Rome's honoured governor, take down the flags of the Empire?'

Herodias looked to Antipas in horror.

'We did,' he said steadily, though Herodias felt his fingers quiver in hers, 'but that was because the images upon them were an affront to the Jewish religion and Tiberius himself, your honoured predecessor, Emperor, had asked that our traditions be obeyed. Blank flags would have been entirely acceptable.'

'But not a symbol of Roman authority?'

'Still that, I assure you. Others have flown them before. If that is the only charge then you must see that—'

'Oh, it is not the only charge,' Agrippa said with a sly smile. 'Did you not conspire with the High Priest, the scheming Caiaphas, to prevent repairs to the Roman aqueduct?'

'No. We merely disputed the source of the funds.'

'A source that Pilate had tapped entirely within the rights of the law, according to the contract drawn up when Judea became a Roman province?'

'But not within its spirit,' Antipas tried.

'The spirit of the law is not something that is very helpful, is it? How do you pin down a spirit? How do you rule on a spirit?' Agrippa leaned, actually leaned, on Caligula's grand throne. 'But it wasn't just the aqueduct, was it? There was the rebel carpenter, the Galilean. Pilate sent him to you, Antipas, to have his death sentence ratified, in a most respectful manner, and you simply threw the criminal back to him, leaving him to carry the ire of the masses who had been seduced into following him when really this man, this Jew, your own subject, should have been condemned by the might of your ancient law.'

'*Our* ancient law,' Herodias said but she knew already that her brother no longer aligned himself with the nation over whom he had just become king.

They were in a perilous situation and, for once, she could think of nothing to say or do to escape. There seemed only one option left to her.

'It was a very fraught time,' she said, falling to her knees and tugging her husband with her. 'Jerusalem was hot-tempered and divided. But the man was dealt with and his followers dispersed and I am sure the city is ready to welcome you now.'

'Really, Herodias?' Agrippa drawled. 'Because I hear the man's followers are far from dispersed. I hear they are shouting louder than ever, making ridiculous claims about their tinpot saviour being raised from the dead and setting themselves up against the Jewish religion. What are you doing about that?'

'I ...'

'Nothing! It is a good thing, then, that I am heading to the Holy Land to take command and I truly think, Emperor, that it would be better if I had control of the whole area. *Full* control.'

Herodias looked to Antipas but now the Roman eagle struck.

'I agree,' Caligula said, as casually as if he was approving a move in a game. 'You, Agrippa, should be king of Galilee and Perea as well as Judea and Trachonitis.'

'But what about us?' Herodias gasped out.

'You,' he said, with a dark laugh, 'had best go into exile.'

'Exile?'

Caligula leapt up, standing over them.

'Before I see you executed for plotting to undermine the Empire.'

'But ...'

'Herodias.' Antipas' voice was low but firm. She looked to him.

'Exile, Antipas,' she hissed. 'We can't just go into exile.'

If she'd thought her heart would break at the idea of Agrippa as King of the Jews, she feared it might actually melt away if she wasn't even allowed into the Holy Land, her home, the only place she'd ever truly known.

'Better that than death.'

'They won't kill *us*.'

'Herodias! Look around you. I thought you were an intelligent woman?'

'I am!'

'Then use your intelligence and let's get out of here while we still have something left to us.'

'Our lives?'

'Our lives together.'

She swallowed, then looked back up at the two hard-faced men above them. She had, it seemed, played the power game one too many times and finally she'd lost. She nodded, pushed herself to her feet and turned to walk away. She would not bow, not to the mocking Emperor and certainly not to her wastrel of a brother. Antipas rose too and she felt him at her shoulder, strong and sure. Her legs shook and he put a hand to the small of her back, steadying her. She fixed on the doors and the dark hallway beyond, desperate, now, to get away.

'Oh, Herodias.' The emperor's voice was light but she knew better than to ignore it. Five more steps, that's all she'd needed. Feeling sick, she turned slowly back to face him. 'King Agrippa has just pleaded with me for mercy on his sister. Such filial affection, how can I ignore it? Antipas is exiled; you, I am prepared to grant a pardon. You may return to the Holy Land and live privately with my blessing.'

Herodias stared at the handsome youth lolling on his golden throne, his fine robes falling open to display a waxed and oiled chest. She glanced sideways to her brother, smirking at her.

'Family ties are so important, do you not think, sister dear?'

Herodias' whole body pulsed. She was being offered a lifeline, a chance to go home, to see Salome and Aristobulus and her gorgeous grandson, to visit the Temple at Pesach, to be part of the great rituals that had for so long driven her life.

And yet . . .

She looked to her husband.

'You should take that, Herodias,' he said and his smile was so genuine, his eyes so warm that she glanced to God in thanks for sending this man her way.

'Not without you.'

'Don't be ridiculous. You should seize this, go back. Your heart is in the Holy Land and I don't want to take you away if you have a chance to stay.'

She looked at him, so earnest in his hope for her happiness, as he had been from the moment he'd asked her to marry him.

'Not without you,' she said again.

'But Salome . . .'

That hurt. Could she live without seeing her daughter? For so long they had fought, so often they had fallen out, but Salome was a woman now with a husband and child of her own.

'My heart, husband,' she said, loud and clear for all to hear, 'is with you. And I don't want to leave you if I have a chance to stay at your side.' Above them Agrippa gasped. Herodias did not even glance his way; her eyes were all for the man at her side, always at her side. 'I love you, Antipas. *You* are all the home I need – if you'll have me.'

'If I'll . . .Oh, Herodias!'

And with that he pulled her into his arms, pressed a kiss hard upon her lips, and then led her to the door. Five steps, taken together, and they were away from the emperor, away from Agrippa and away from Rome.

They scrambled out of the imperial palace, dashing off before the fickle emperor could change his mind. Hand in hand, they kept going until they reached the Porta Capena and the stupid, gloomy run of tombs along the Appian Way that Rome seemed to consider an appropriate guard for the city. At last, they stopped and Herodias leaned on the nearest tomb. Her knees collapsed and it was only Antipas' arms still around her that kept her upright.

'You are regretting your decision?'

'No! I never regret my decisions, such a waste of time. I'm just, perhaps, feeling the impact of what I said.'

'About Agrippa.'

'About you, you idiot. About . . .' She swallowed, but she'd said it once, so she could say it again. 'About loving you.'

Antipas laughed, so loud that it echoed around the big mausoleums as if fifty people were sharing their mirth.

'Was it so hard?'

'Yes!'

'Then let's hope it gets easier with practice.'

He kissed her again, longer and slower, and she melted against him, but reality was crashing back in on her already and she pulled reluctantly away.

'What will we do now? Where will we go?'

He gave her a cheeky grin.

'I have a few ideas, a few, let's call them, contingency plans.'

'You do?'

She gaped up at him, thinking that he had never looked so handsome.

'I have been putting money away where I can, buying up parcels of land in promising looking places.'

'You have?'

'Come, wife, we are Herods; we know how precarious ruling can be. I barely survived my father's reign with my life intact, so I was never going to rest on what I managed to scramble away from that carnage. I have interests in several cities. You can take your pick, though I think perhaps Antioch looks the most promising. A lovely climate and marvellous food. And there is a strong Jewish community there, I'm told, and a very beautiful synagogue, so we can—'

But Herodias needed to hear no more and covered his lips with her own.

'You, husband,' she told him when she finally surfaced, 'are a marvel.'

'And you love me . . . ?'

'Don't push it. Now come, we have a journey to make and the sooner we get away from this godforsaken city, the better.'

'Yes, wife.'

'Good.'

She grinned at him and, taking his hand, headed down the road towards the nearby port of Ostia and freedom. Today, by all the usual reckoning, she had lost everything but somehow, she felt she had gained the greatest prize and she walked with a new lightness in her step towards a future that was theirs to shape as they wished.

Chapter Thirty-three

Salome

It hit her like a tidal wave, the sickness rising unstoppably up her gullet so that she had no chance to do anything bar dart for the nearest flowerbed and pray none of it got on her hair.

'Again, Salome?'

'Again,' she moaned. 'I don't know why. It was never like this with Aristo.'

She looked around for her son, to find him staring in fascination at the unseemly pile of vomit on the soil.

'Why did you do that, Mama?'

She put a hand on her belly.

'It's your little brother or sister making themselves felt.'

He screwed up his nose.

'They don't seem like they're very nice. Can we send them back?'

Salome laughed, despite the churning in her stomach and the sting in her throat.

'They'll be lovely,' Ari said firmly. 'Perhaps it means it's a girl this time?'

'Because girls are more trouble?'

He put up his hands.

346

'Would I dare say that? I'm sure you and your mother have always got on perfectly.'

Salome stuck her tongue out at her husband, then remembered the horrors of the other day and felt a wave of something more than nausea flood over her.

'I'm sorry,' Ari said, taking her arm in concern. 'I shouldn't have joked about her, not after . . .'

'Don't even say it.'

They'd been summoned up the coast to Caesarea Maritima to greet the new King of the Jews. Not invited, or asked, but summoned.

Agrippa, King of the Jews, demands your presence.

It had not been the imperious tone, that had aroused Salome's ire, however, but the words that had followed:

At his investiture to the titles of King of Judea, Trachonitis, Galilee and Perea and all the lands thereof.

'Galilee and Perea are not his!' she'd shouted. 'They are mother's.'

'And, perhaps, your stepfather's?' Ari had suggested.

'Oh, him too. But mainly they are mother's. She has given so much for them; how have they been taken away?'

They had wrung the story from the reluctant messenger, had heard how Agrippa had turned Caligula on the suppliants who'd sheltered him and his family for over a year when he'd been destitute and how he had rewarded that with making them destitute in their turn.

'How dare he?' Salome had raged, stamping her foot so that the poor young man had cowered before her.

'Calm, Salome,' Ari had urged. 'You are getting as scary as Herodias.'

That had shut her up, but not for long.

'We have to do something.'

'No, wife.'

'No?'

'I do not recommend it. It's exactly what Herodias said and look where that got her. Somehow she has prodded the wasps' nest and we must stay away until it calms down and we might have a chance to effect some repairs.'

'But what's the point?' she'd sighed. 'What's left for us here?'

'Your lovely estates?' he'd suggested, indicating their beautiful home. She'd tossed her head.

'You know you are bored here, Ari, and I confess that, though I would never say this to my dear father were he alive still, I am bored too. We need something to *do*.'

'Well, for now, I'm afraid that something is travelling to Caesarea Maritima.'

He'd been right of course and they'd been forced to take to the road, though Salome had had to dismount from her patient horse at least ten times on the eight-hour ride to vomit into the hedges. It had been no better when they'd arrived, although much of her nausea in the romanised city had been from watching her Uncle Agrippa parading through the streets in a gilded sedan with a ridiculous new crown on his head.

'Doesn't he know that the authority of the throne comes from the history of the line, not the shine of the jewels?' she'd whispered to Ari.

'Of course he doesn't,' he'd whispered back. 'This is a man who would abandon his elegant wife at a party to stick his hand up the skirt of a serving maid.'

His "elegant wife" had looked as sick as Salome had felt, despite her royal gowns and matching new crown.

'I will help your mother,' she'd sworn to Salome when they'd seized a brief moment alone. 'I swear, I will help her.'

'Don't worry, Kypros,' Salome had told her, 'Mother can take care of herself.'

She'd said it with confidence, as she'd known Herodias would wish, but she'd been churning with worry inside and had almost jumped out of her skin when someone had grabbed at her arm in the crowded reception.

'Get off me!' She'd stared, confused, at the young woman standing before her, unable at first to place her amongst the shiny guests. Then the dark eyes had bored into her and she'd realised who it was. 'Mary? What are you doing here?'

'Spying on the new king,' she'd said frankly.

'And what do you make of him?'

'He's a shallow, self-seeking sap.'

Salome couldn't have put it better herself and for the first time had felt a little warmth for the spiky young woman.

'He's had my mother exiled.'

'The good Lord help us all! I did not think that possible.'

'Me either,' Salome agreed with a grimace. 'It is persecution of the worst kind.'

Mary had nodded grimly then and, with a glance around, tugged Salome aside.

'It's not safe in the Holy Land, Princess. Not for your mother, not perhaps for you, and certainly not for us. Caiaphas and his Sadducees grow more vicious every day and if this . . .' she made a derogatory gesture in the direction of the new king, 'is the sort of leadership we are now faced with, then it is only going to get worse.'

'What are you suggesting?'

'We are setting up new churches all the way up the Eastern coast of the Mediterranean. The faithful are many and we can work far more effectively away from Jerusalem. Philip has gone into Samaria, Peter and Perpetua to Galatia, and Andrew to Pontus. Barnabus is in Antioch, Thomas in Edessa and others further away still. James has taken ship to Spain and Matthias headed into Armenia. The word is spreading, Salome. Jesus is not dead but lives, both at God's right hand in heaven and here, on earth, through the Church of the New Way.'

'That's amazing.'

'That's the truth of Jesus' resurrection. Join us, Salome. We need vigorous people, not just to preach but to build the infrastructure of the church. Sell your lands and join us.'

She'd been alight with excitement, on fire with her mission, and it had been very hard to resist. Salome had believed, once, when Jesus had come to Caesarea Philippi in what now felt like another lifetime, that she had been living at the crux of history. The dark horror of his crucifixion had cast that hope into the abyss, but had she been right to believe? Was she, in fact, still right to believe? One thing, at least, she had known – she wanted to learn more.

'Perhaps,' she'd said to Mary. And then, considering the party of fools, circulating like flies around the dead meat of their new king, she'd added, 'We'll think about it.'

❖

Now she plucked a camomile leaf from amongst the herbs and chewed on it in a desperate attempt to take away the taste of her own vomit.

'Should we leave, Ari?'

'Happily, but where would we go?'

'Mary says we can have our pick of places. There are communities everywhere. They are making real change, Ari, and they need vigorous people.'

'Do you feel vigorous, my love?'

She chewed harder on the camomile.

'I feel . . . adrift. I was happy here as a child.' She cast a hand around the pretty lawns on which she had danced to the tune of her father's lyre, giddy with the simple joys of her own little world. 'But much has happened since then. Too much, perhaps. I'm a different person now. I don't like that, but there is no shirking reality. The way I see it, Judea is a mess and if there is a New Way, perhaps we should follow it.'

They looked at each other.

'Dare we?'

Salome wasn't sure. She'd never been the adventurous type, but adventure had found her anyway, so perhaps it was time to seize the initiative. Even so, just to walk out into a new city seemed a frighteningly reckless thing to do.

'A letter, my lady.'

Salome looked up to see one of the staff proffering a silver platter bearing a scroll, scarlet wax stamped across it. For a moment she saw a head, blood red, but she pushed it away. That was done, forgiven, repaired.

'Thank you.'

She took the scroll and, looking down at the seal, gasped.

'Mother!'

Cracking it open, she read eagerly.

My dearest daughter.

Too many times I have believed myself to know everything. Too many times I have assumed I have the solutions and too many times I have revelled in you telling me that I am right. This letter is to tell you that, for once, I was wrong. Antipas and I should not have gone to Rome. We should not have taken on the Emperor in his own lair, and we most certainly should not have baited my self-seeking brother when we were, as it turns out, weaponless before him. We have paid the heavy price of exile.

But this letter is also to tell you that, hard as you will know it is for me to say, you were right. You told me once – in quite a temper if I recall – that love is worth more than land and I have learned the truth of that the hard way. Antipas, I have discovered, is worth more to me than Jerusalem. I married him for the power I thought he could give me, but it is strength that I have found in our union, strength and ease and, it seems, simple happiness. Who'd have guessed it?

Only one sorrow remains – that in exile I cannot see you, or your lovely family. I was always, as I fear I told you far too often, pained

351

to have lost the babies that should have been your brothers. What
would pain me far, far more, would be to lose you, too. You have
turned into a brave, commanding, loving young woman and if I had
to die tomorrow – which pray God I do not – then I would at least go
knowing that I gave you to the world. It is a far, far better place for
your presence.

But enough soppiness. Salome, daughter, we are in Antioch. Antipas
has been clever enough to buy property there and it is a fine place. If
ever you could see your way to a journey, I would welcome you with
arms as open as they should always have been.

With care and, yes, love,
Your mother

Salome read it over and over, unsure whether to laugh or cry, but
drinking in every wonderful, spiky, reluctant word.

'Salome?' Ari asked eventually. 'Is all well?'

She looked up at him.

'All is very well,' she agreed. 'Ari, husband, what do you say to
a trip to Antioch?'

It would pain her to leave the Holy Land, as it must surely have
pained her mother, but it seemed holiness, like friendship and
love and the quiet power they brought, could be found elsewhere.
Besides, the deaths of John the Baptiser and Jesus, whom they were
calling Cristos, had changed her homeland and it might be time to
find a new way for them all.

'Your mother is in Antioch?' Ari asked, with an exaggerated
grimace that made her smile.

'She is.'

'Then I suppose it will, at least, be a lively place.'

'So ... ?'

'So I say, yes!'

He smiled and offered his hand. Rising, Salome took it and, with
Aristo holding the other and her belly swollen proudly before them,
they went inside to pack. It would be a wrench to leave all they

knew but it turned out that home, like God, was not to be found in set temples or houses, but deep in the heart.

The dance of life would go on. The steps would be very different but danced from the heart, would carry them all into a new future together.

Acknowledgements

The book is dedicated to my daughter, Hannah, who I think Herodias would have liked very much for her go-getting approach to life. (Though I hope I'm not quite as fierce in my motherly attentions as she was!) I remember Hannah's first night in this world when, after several hours of crying, I sat her up against my knees, looked at her, and said, 'Right, girl, it's you and me and we're going to have to sort out how to do this together.' I think we did just that and being with her has always (or almost always – 9 was a tricky age, and as for 13 . . .) been a great joy for me. As I said in the dedication, Hannah is smart and very hard-working, and has even taught me to appreciate geography! She is naturally kind and caring, but also thoughtful, provocative and fiercely independent. Herodias would definitely approve of the way she stands up to the patriarchy and so do I. I hope I've taught her a few things but she has taught me many in return and I'm very proud of her. Hannah – the whole world, and in particular my little corner, is a far better place for having you in it.

This book is *not* dedicated to my son, Alec, because until he actually reads one of my books that privilege is withheld . . .!! He is, however, pretty wonderful in all other ways. From a cheeky monkey of a child – the littlest of four and swift to learn the benefit of charm – he has grown into a mature, empathetic, hard-working and great fun young man. The happiest, most loving drunk I know, he is also forging his way in the world with style, skill and intelligence and I am hugely proud of him.

Not only do I have two lovely children, but two lovely step-children too – and an even lovelier (oh, come on – you were all cute when you were babies!!) step-granddaughter. I'm thrilled I now get to be GranJo and look forward to the family growing more in the years to come. I am, all round, a very lucky mother.

It would, of course, have been impossible to produce these lovely children without my husband, Stuart, and it would have been nearly as impossible to produce my novels too. He has always been my number one supporter, propping me up in my many moments (indeed, days . . .) of doubt, encouraging me to carry on, and offering an ever-patient ear to my endless writerly ramblings, even at midnight. (It's possible he's just asleep then, but he's there all the same!) He is a dedicated research assistant with a fine eye for detail and an even finer eye for a handy bar in which to 'consider my notes' . . . Now he's retired, I look forward to many more research trips and promise, Stuart, to write a book set on a tropical beach very soon . . .!

Thanks must go to the creative team around me. Captain of this is Kate Shaw, my excellent agent – a wise editor, astute commercial guide, and good friend. This, I believe, is our twentieth novel together and I look forward to many more. I'm also very grateful to the lovely team at Piatkus, especially my editor, Anna Boatman, with whom I dreamed up the concept of this novel and the two that go with it, but also the lovely Kate Byrne who covered Anna's maternity leave with such panache. It's such a pleasure working with you both. Thank you.

A big shout out to my writing crew. Writing is a lonely business and can be quite a confusing and demoralising one at times, so it's been wonderful over the last few years to find some utterly brilliant writing friends. Our bi-annual retreats are now a highlight of my year, both for the productivity and for the amazing friendship and support – not to mention the fabulous karaoke . . .! So – a huge thank you (in alphabetical order!) to Debbie, Helen, Julie, Sharon and Tracy. You're all stars.

And finally, to my readers. Quite simply, this book is pointless without you, so thank you so much for spending your precious time with my characters.

Historical Note

WHAT WE KNOW OF THE HISTORICAL SALOME

Salome is one of those historical characters that people think they know a bit about – they are almost certainly wrong. Many will mention the dance of the seven veils and believe that she was a seductress, or even a prostitute. Some will know that she asked for the head of John the Baptist on a plate but few how old she was at the time, or the pressure she was under to do so. Not many will know that she was a princess of the great Herod family and almost no one will be able to tell you about her mother, Herodias – probably the one person amongst the disparate and dissolute bunch of Herod the Great's descendants who could, if it weren't for her gender, have carried on his independent rule of the Land of the Jews.

In reality, we know very little historical fact about Salome. Her parentage and place on the Herodian family tree is clear. We know that she married Herod Philip, her great-uncle, and then Aristobulus, son of Herodias' brother, Herod of Chalcis, as shown in the novel. There is evidence that they moved to Antioch some time after the death of Christ and also, intriguingly, that their son, also Aristobulus, is recorded as a very early missionary in Britain!

Salome does not appear by name in the Bible. The story of

Antipas imprisoning him and Herodias telling 'her daughter' to ask for his head in return for dancing before his guests is found in Mark 6 and, more briefly, in Matthew 14, but we must turn to the historian Flavius Josephus for the name of this daughter – Salome. And Josephus does not actually mention the dancing or the head on the plate, but simply says that Herod Antipas chose to have John executed in Machaerus because he feared he would incite the people to riot. The truth, quite clearly, lies somewhere in between and as soon as I read about her, I wanted to know more about this mysterious Salome.

There is a Salome recorded in Mark 15 at the foot of the cross, alongside Mary Magdalene, and Mary the mother of James the younger and of Joseph. Mark states that 'in Galilee these women had followed him and cared for his needs.' Salome, Herodias' daughter, was almost certainly with her mother when she moved to the Galilean town of Tiberias with her controversial second husband, Herod Antipas, so that got me thinking – what if they were the same woman? Wikipedia tells us authoritatively that she is 'not be confused with the Salome who ordered the death of John the Baptist', but in the absence of any positive identification of the other Salome, I thought – why not?! When you add the evidence of her son's role as a missionary – and therefore, perhaps, his parents' influence as early Christians – it seemed a compulsive possibility. That got me thinking about how a young woman, drawn into the drama of the disruptive John the Baptist and his cousin, the charismatic Jesus of Nazareth, might have been affected by those experiences. This novel is a result of those wonderings ...

JOHN THE BAPTIST'S HEAD

The execution of John the Baptist is, inevitably, at the heart of Salome's story but we know very few facts about it. Mark tells us it was Herodias who instructed her daughter – who was possibly younger than twelve (the Hebrew word implies as a pre-pubescent girl), though I had her at sixteen in this novel – to ask for the head of John the Baptist as reward for her dance. It therefore seemed likely to me that Herodias was working harder against the man who was speaking ill about her than her husband (hardly surprising as women suffered more from such moral judgements then – indeed, still do now) and that she plotted to get rid of him. She succeeded!

John the Baptist was undoubtedly imprisoned by Herod Antipas, mostly likely in the stark fortress of Machaerus, for the crime of speaking out against him and his new wife, Herodias, who had both divorced previous spouses to be together. Historical report has John – often seen as a saintly man in Christian tradition – as an abrasive, strident, disruptive speaker who was quite probably thrown out of the Essene community at Qumran for being too radical. Given that the Essenes were messianic preachers, standing up against the over-prescriptive, greedy machinations of the Temple (see below for more), being too radical suggests quite a man! John's core message was that the end of the world was nigh and people must cleanse themselves to be ready – hence his instigation of baptism in water – and he was undoubtedly an important ice-breaker for Jesus' similar, but far gentler message of prioritising love of your neighbour over ritual worship.

John seems, at first, to have been allowed considerable leeway in 'prison' to talk with guests and correspond with Jesus and his followers, but that all came to an end at the fateful feast. Herod Antipas, although undoubtedly one of the stronger of the Herods, was not a man who liked to make an unpopular decision. This can be seen by the way he hedged around condemning Jesus and he seems to have shown the same reticence in his dealings with John. Indeed, there is a suggestion he was intrigued by the man's ideas and might well have been happy to let him stay free – if it wasn't for his wife. Whatever the political machinations behind his execution, the intriguing element for me was what it would do to an impressionable young woman to have a man's head hacked off and placed onto a tray she was holding. However violent the times, it would still have been a terrible shock and I wanted to explore that in my fiction.

As is often the way, the tale of Salome's dance has been twisted over time into something far more sexual than originally reported. This was a royal princess, dancing in a closed gathering for a group of dignitaries. There is no way her mother or stepfather would have compromised her modesty and reputation with a salacious dance and although there may have been scarves involved, as that was a tradition of the time, there would have been no removing of clothes or hint of impropriety. The dance would have been stately and elegant. Salome clearly performed it well to be granted a grand prize but that is to her credit as a dancer, not her sexual attractions, especially if she was only twelve.

It is down to various men (of course) over the ages that Salome has been transformed into a femme fatale. One of the main culprits was the French painter Gustave Moreau, who loved biblical inspirations and wasn't afraid to offer his own vision of them. He painted Salome at least 150 times, most famously in *L'Apparition* of 1876 which depicts her dancing near-naked. This image was picked up by Oscar Wilde in his similarly salacious play *Salome*, in which she tries to seduce John, is repulsed and therefore plots his death (because clearly women are only motivated by their own romantic interests!). This utterly spurious take on the story was further popularised by Richard Strauss' opera of the same name so that by the twentieth century Salome had been well and truly turned into a titillating figure. I hope this novel reclaims her as a real, believable, thoughtful young woman.

HERODIAN RULE

The Herods were a very complicated family and I hope the family tree at the start of this novel goes some way to helping a reader understand the tangles of their dynasty. Herod the Great was the main man. He ruled as 'King of the Jews' from around 37 BC to 4 BC, having clawed his way to favour from a relatively lowly role. A young man of ambition, he used his father Antipater's role governing Judea for Julius Caesar as a chance to gain the governorship of Galilee in 47 BC, aged around twenty-five. In 41 BC, Mark Antony named him a tetrarch and, around 37 BC, he marched on Jerusalem with a Roman army, captured it, and took over rule of Judea– taking the title King of the Jews, which was ratified by the Roman Senate.

Herod was a despotic leader, with a reputation for cruelty – not, sadly, unusual at the time. In his favour, however, he ran huge building projects, most notable amongst them being the vast repairs and expansion of the Temple into the vast structure it was by the time of the novel. He also built the new Herodian palace in Jerusalem (used by the time of the novel, to Herodias's fury, by the Roman governors), a port at Caesarea Maritima, and many fortresses, including Machaerus. The taxation to fund these projects was burdensome on the Jews but the projects provided much more employment, and proclaimed the pride of Jewish nation. Herod was also, when it suited him, capable of welfare projects for his people, for example providing for them in the great famine of 25 BC. He was a hard but effective leader, very good at balancing the demands of Rome with autonomy to live as Jews. This was something that many rulers struggled with – see my novel *Cleopatra and Julius* for a study of how that great queen attempted to do the same.

Herod is probably most known, thanks to many a nativity play, for the 'Massacre of the Innocents' – his supposed order to slaughter all the baby boys in Bethlehem when the Magi told him about the arrival of a Messiah. It is a dramatic story, briefly told in Matthew, but is almost certainly false. Contemporary historians, including Flavius Josephus and Nicolaus of Damascus – who knew Herod – do not speak of it and neither does the Gospel of Luke which otherwise offers the fullest account of the nativity. Even if it were true, Bethlehem was a small town that would have had barely half a dozen baby boys at the time of Jesus' birth, so, however cruel, it would not have been the grand massacre it has become known as.

It's been suggested by historians that the story may have been conflated with Herod ordering the killings of his own sons, which he did ruthlessly as he became increasingly insecure in the grip of a debilitating illness that eventually led to his death. The man had a total of five wives (with some overlap), and seven sons – see the family tree for details. They were variously made his heirs in the years leading up to his death as he vacillated in his favours. In 7 BC, his paranoia was so great that he had his second two sons executed for high treason, condemning his eldest two years later. The succession changed hands several more times in the run up to his death. Briefly – at the time when Herodias married him – Boethus, his third son, stood as sole heir, but then Herod became certain that the only way to stop his heirs from killing him (ignoring the fact he was dying anyway), was to divide his kingdom between his youngest three sons. Boethus, the last victim of his paranoia, was accused of plotting and only saved by agreeing to retire as a private citizen, pushing him (to Herodias' fury) out of the succession.

The division might have worked, save that Archelaus contested the will, fighting for sole rule. All three brothers went to Rome to fight it out but Archelaus had the strongest support and Augustus granted him Judea and Samaria as an ethnarch with the promise he could be king if he proved himself worthy. The other two had to settle for lesser tetrarchies, Antipas of Galilee and Perea, Philip of Trachonitis (and a few other small areas). Archelaus, however, proved an insensitive and selfish ruler and barely clung onto power until 6 AD when Jews and Samaritans made a rare joint move to denounced him to Caesar as terrible ruler.

Their complaint backfired. A furious Caesar summoned Archelaus, confiscated his throne and banished him to the Rhone, then decided to bring the troublesome Jews to heel by imposing direct administration on Judea as a Roman province. The first governor, Coponius, arrived in time for a census of the lands of the Jews to be decreed by Quirinius, the governor of Syria – the census that, according to the Bible, brought Jospeh and Mary to Bethlehem, where Jesus was born. Pontius Pilate was the fifth governor, arriving in time to preside over Jesus' tragic death. Antipas and Philip held onto their tetrarchies and may well have been content in them but the desire to control all the Holy Land – to keep the Jewish lands for the Jews – certainly burned in Herodias' bosom. As the novels shows, she fought for it hard, but with disastrous results.

Herodias and Antipas

From the moment I started reading about Herodias, I loved her. She did many 'wrong' things, not the least ordering the execution of John, but I think she was a woman who suffered huge frustration at not having the power to exert the strong rule that I'm convinced she would have brought to the ever-troubled area around Judea. She seems to have been a woman not afraid to step up and try to change events around her, and I thoroughly enjoyed writing her as a bolshy, hard-headed would-be-leader.

Perhaps the most intriguing details about Herodias however, were two small snippets I found in her history: (1) that she had several miscarriages during her first marriage, and (2) that, despite being offered a reprieve by Caligula, she chose to go into exile with Antipas. This was a woman desperate to have sons but left with only a daughter, who was hampered by the same infuriating restrictions as herself, surely leading to a friction-filled relationship. And this was a woman who, despite leading a life driven by dynastic and power considerations, gave up everything to be with her husband – i.e., a woman in love or, at the very least, putting personal happiness over political clout.

The banishment and her proposed reprieve, as Agrippa's sister, are recorded history from 37 AD. I took a little creative licence in bringing the event forward to 34 AD for the sake of dramatic unity but it still felt like a key moment for Herodias and I used both that and her sad miscarriages to drive the complexity of her character. I hope readers enjoy reading about her as much as I enjoyed writing her.

PHARISEES, SADDUCEES AND ESSENES

These were the three key sects of the Jews at the time of Christ. There are many tangled and complicated differences between them that would take far longer than we have here to discuss, but in essence:

The Sadducees were priestly, aristocratic caste of men who kept themselves aloof within the Inner Temple. They were quite Hellenised and very elitist. They were usually Levites (men from the tribe of Levi – one of the twelve original tribes – who had, way back in the mists of time, been chosen to be the priestly caste), so tended to take the role of High Priest (Caiaphas was a Sadducee) and to dominate the Sanhedrin – the Jewish council who ran the Holy Land, or tried to beneath the infuriating interference of the Romans.

The Pharisees were not a caste but a self-chosen group of men. They tended to be very strict in their religious observations but made it their duty to live and teach amongst the people. Unlike the Sadducees, who stuck only to teachings from the Torah, they interpreted those teachings with the oral tradition of the Jewish people for a theoretically more flexible approach. They were often quite respected, but tended, especially by Jesus' time, to be overly pious and harsh on those they had supposedly appointed themselves to help. And they certainly did not like peasants such as Jesus coming along to do their own interpreting . . .

The Essenes, in stark contrast to the Pharisees and Sadducees, were a monastic group of mainly young men, living in seclusion to study ancient literature. Over time, they developed a far freer, simpler attitude to God than the Temple crowd and this was to be an important basis of Jesus' teachings. They lived in humility, purity and austerity (at least in theory), and, although they resided in communities, they often went out preaching to try and convert people.

Critically, the Essenes were keen on messianism – the expectation of a deliverer – and also, unlike more conventional groups, expected him to be a 'teacher of righteousness' and 'interpreter of the law' rather than a soldierly saviour. Messianic fever was growing under Roman rule and had reached a fever pitch when Jesus chose to start teaching, feeding into the excitement around him – and attracting the attention of authorities keen to avoid rebellion and protect their own privileged positions.

There were many Essene communities but the biggest known one was at Qumran near Jerusalem, made famous by the discovery of the astonishing Dead Sea Scrolls – their 'library' – in the 1940s and 50s. There is clear evidence that John the Baptist was part of this community and quite possibly thrown out of it for being too 'radical', as discussed above. There is also evidence that Jesus may have spent some time there and certainly many of his teachings show clear rooting in Essene ideas.

ZOROASTRIANISM

In addition to the influence of Essene thinking, there can be little denying that of Zoroastrianism on Jesus and, definitely on the developing philosophies of the early Christian churches. This is a fascinating and little-known mystic religion which originated with the prophet Zoroaster, who was probably alive in the second millennium BC. It was the state religion of Iran from around 600 BC to 650 AD.

It's important because, as far as we know, it's the only major pre-Christian religion apart from Judaism to be monotheistic (believe in one God), and many of its features, including belief in free will, messianism, an idea of judgement after death and of heaven and hell, angels and demons, are key to Zoroastrianism. There is a strong suggestion that the easterly Magi were Zoroastrians and their presence in the gospel of Matthew suggests fascinating links between preachers in both religions, who would have been operating in a similar area around and after the time of Jesus. This is something I will be exploring further in my next novel ...

JESUS

This is a novel about Salome. It is *not* a novel about Jesus, or about John the Baptist, but, as their stories critically intersect with hers, they are very important. They are also, of course, far more widely known, with Jesus being at the heart of the vast and historically fascinating religion of Christianity. Despite growing up as a church-goer, I am no longer a believer in Jesus as the son of God. However, what a study of his life and, even more so, of the religion that grew from it, tells me is that if he was *not* the son of God, the phenomenon of Christianity is even more astonishing. He must have been a clever, eloquent and inspirational man to create such a dedicated and brave following who would, in the years after his death, be prepared to die to defend the ideas and way of life that he taught.

I think this also tells us that many people must have been desperate for a change – for a cleaner, stripped-back, more honest and loving form of Judaism, which ultimately, thanks to the inflexibility of the Temple aristocrats, was forced to become a whole new faith. Christ himself never preached a split from Judaism, merely a more humane, direct way of worshipping the one God. He stood up against the proscriptions of the Temple that imposed heavy taxes and duties on the poor. He attempted to free people from the

368

shackles, not of faith, but of the practice of it which had become –
as so often – tied up in rules and charges that had little to do with
true worship and everything to do with protecting those at the top
of the religious tree. He stood up against exclusions and offered,
instead, a religion of community and care – the religion that Moses
stood for, not the one that the rich Temple priests were tying up in
administrative knots.

Jesus was, I believe, a true humanitarian. His key messages were
to love your neighbour as you love yourself and to obey your own
conscience – the voice of God within you. He wanted to bring
happy, open worship to the poor, to lepers, to the 'unclean' and
to women. This latter is especially interesting to me. Christ seems
to have truly listened to and trusted women, especially Mary of
Magdala. There is a fascinating and well-substantiated theory
that Luke's gospel, concerned with the minutiae of domestic life,
could well have been written, at least in part, by a woman. There is
evidence that every one of the twelve disciples had a female coun-
terpart who went out preaching with him and baptised the females
in their crowd. (Common sense alone would dictate this as in society at the time, women getting into the water with a strange man
would not have been allowed.) There is even evidence that women
were at the Last Supper and we know for a fact that many of the
early churches – operating out of houses across the Mediterranean
area – were run by women.

At the heart of this was Mary of Magdala, who was not a prostitute (that misinterpretation has been perpetuated by men for
years, in the same way as Salome's dance has been turned into a
seductress' one), but an intelligent, core follower of Jesus, trusted
and included by him and vital to Christianity in its early years. I
was delighted to give readers a glimpse of her fiery personality in
this novel and invite them to look out for the last book in my series
for much, much more ...

I make no statement in this novel about the veracity of Jesus'
deity – or lack of it. That is for every person to decide for themselves

and I hope we live in a world that is free enough to allow them to do so. I do, however, assert his veracity as a historical figure and a remarkable one. As a semi-historian it has been fascinating to me to look at the intersection of facts, legends and religious beliefs surrounding him. I am grateful to Salome, as a woman very much at the heart of the terrible conflict between Jesus and the Temple authorities, for offering me an intimate lens into a crucial time.

This is the story of Salome and Herodias, a mother and daughter, fighting and loving and fighting again – like mothers and daughters throughout time – but set against momentous events that could not help but change them. I hope it has given readers pause for thought and discussion but, above all else, an immersive and enjoyable read.